Dorothy L. Sayers

The greatest detective novelist of the Golden Age was born in Oxford in 1893. She was one of the first women to be awarded a degree by Oxford University and she was a copywriter in an advertising agency from 1922 to 1929. Her aristocratic detective Lord Peter Wimsey became one of the world's most popular fictional heroes.

Dorothy L. Sayers also became famous for her religious plays, notably *The Man Born to Be King*, which was broadcast controversially during the war years, and her translation of Dante's *Divine Comedy*. She died in 1957.

Hodder & Stoughton is the publisher of all her detective stories and four new Lord Peter Wimsey novels by Jill Paton Walsh. *Thrones, Dominations* and *A Presumption of Death* are based closely on Dorothy L. Sayers' own work. Hodder & Stoughton's Sceptre imprint is the publisher of the revised and updated version of the definitive biography, *Dorothy L. Sayers: Her Life and Soul* by Barbara Reynolds.

DOROTHY L. SAYERS

GAUDY NIGHT

WITH AN INTRODUCTION
BY DAME HARRIET WALTER

HODDER

First published in Great Britain in 1935 by Victor Gollancz Ltd
First published in paperback by New English Library in 1970

This edition published in 2016 by Hodder & Stoughton
An Hachette UK company

9

A CIP catalogue record for this title is available from the British Library

Paperback ISBN 978 1 473 62140 4
Ebook ISBN 978 1 848 94372 8

Typeset by Hewer Text UK Ltd, Edinburgh
Printed and bound by Clays Ltd, Elcograf S.p.A.

Hodder & Stoughton policy is to use papers that are natural, renewable
and recyclable products and made from wood grown in sustainable
forests. The logging and manufacturing processes are expected to
conform to the environmental regulations of the country of origin.

Hodder & Stoughton Ltd
Carmelite House
50 Victoria Embankment
London EC4Y 0DZ

www.hodder.co.uk

The University is a Paradise, Rivers of Knowledge are there, Arts and Sciences flow from thence. Counsell Tables are *Horti conclusi*, (as it is said in the Canticles) *Gardens that are walled in*, and they are *Fontes signati*, *Wells that are sealed up*; bottomless depths of unsearchable Counsels there.

John Donne

Dame Harriet Walter

Since training at LAMDA, Harriet has worked extensively in theatre, television, film and radio. She recently starred in *Death of a Salesman* for the RSC and in Phyllida Lloyd's all-female production of *Henry IV*, following her appearance as Brutus in Lloyd's *Julius Caesar*. Of her many roles with the RSC, where she is an Associate Artist, the more recent have included Cleopatra, Beatrice in *Much Ado About Nothing* and Lady Macbeth. Harriet won the Evening Standard Award for her role as Elizabeth in Schiller's *Mary Stuart* and was nominated for a Tony. She is best known on TV as Harriet Vane in the Lord Peter Wimsey series, and more recently as DI Natalie Chandler in *Law and Order: UK*. She has also appeared in Downton Abbey and London Spy and recent films include *Suite Française*, *Man Up* and the Academy Award-nominated *A Royal Affair*. She will shortly be seen in *The Crown* on television and in the films *Denial* and *The Sense of an Ending*. She has published three books: *Other People's Shoes*; *Macbeth* for the Faber series 'Actors on Shakespeare'; and a photography book *Facing It: reflections on images of older women*. Harriet has been awarded an Honorary Doctorate from Birmingham University, a CBE, and a DBE in the 2011 New Year's Honours List.

By the time Dorothy L. Sayers introduced the character of Harriet Vane into her series of Wimsey murder mysteries, she was sick of writing them. She wanted to be thought of as a serious literary figure and had a love/hate relationship with the success of the Wimsey stories which she considered mere potboilers. At the same time she seems to have been in love with her own creation, Lord Peter. How to part with him and wrap the stories up so she could move on to her more 'serious' works?

While at Oxford, Dorothy Sayers often fell in love with the sort of men who used her as a best friend to whom they could confide about the more beautiful women they were in love with. There was a feeling then (and the smoke lingers still) that brains were not sexy in a woman and that intellectual women were not marriage material. So Sayers used her pen to correct this situation.

In Lord Peter Wimsey she conjured an impossible combination of intellectual brilliance, blue-blood breeding and all-round athleticism, a piano-playing linguist, master of espionage and almost clairvoyant amateur sleuth; the man, we sense, of her dreams. Now in *Gaudy Night* she would test his feminist credentials.

It was time to put an end to Wimsey's lifelong bachelorhood and marry him off, and what better candidate would he find than a female fellow Oxford graduate, a writer of crime novels and a prickly character reminiscent of the author?

So the hero of her dreams, the man she never could find in real life, falls in love with her own alter ego. This alter ego is not a conventional beauty, has a mysterious past and plays very hard to get. She dreads an imbalanced relationship. Wimsey clearly adores her but she suspects her own feelings are less to do with love than indebtedness (to Peter for saving her from the gallows in *Strong Poison*) and this tension between his patience and her evasiveness is all part of the chemistry that keeps us and them hooked through the previous two Harriet Vane novels (*Strong Poison* and *Have His Carcase*). It was time to reward the reader's patience, but how?

In *Gaudy Night* Sayers examines a particular female dilemma close to her own heart: how to develop one's intellectual independence from men, and not miss out on the joys of sex and equality in a harmonious domestic life. A tall order even now, but so much taller in the 1930s.

In 1986, I was offered the role of Harriet Vane in the BBC TV series that would cover all the Harriet Vane novels, excluding *Busman's Honeymoon* which was written by popular request after Sayers had written the play of the same name. The series' working title was *Harriet Vane*. When it aired the following year it was called *The Dorothy L Sayers Mysteries*. Later it was shown in the USA where the title had changed once again to *Lord Peter Wimsey*.

While I understand the reasoning behind these changes, they also reflect the cautious attitude that TV networks had at the time toward hanging a series on a female character. Sayers was far less well known in the

USA than Agatha Christie, hence the second title change which announced the promise of an aristocratic protagonist guaranteed to attract an American audience.

When I first interviewed for the role the series producer, a very old-school BBC type, expressed his concern about *Gaudy Night* in particular as it almost exclusively featured 'a lot of plain middle-aged women'. How to make it palatable? One of the BBC's solutions was to bring Lord Peter into the story as early as possible. This involved a huge change in motivation for my Harriet who as an independent-minded and proud character was determined to put Peter to the back of her mind and solve a mystery on what was very much her own territory of Shrewsbury College, her Oxford alma mater, and was loth to ask any more favours from Peter.

In the novel Peter is constantly referred to either in Harriet's internal monologue or in the rather teasing inquiries that Harriet has to fend off from the salacious dons but doesn't physically turn up until quite late in the plot. We filmed for a month or so in Oxford, and when Edward Petherbridge (aka Lord Peter Wimsey) finally turned up for filming with us he had an instant energising effect on the lot of us women which paralleled that of Lord Peter on the University women. We clustered and clucked around him in an only slightly less embarrassing way than our dramatic counterparts, whose defences collapse under his spell.

That defensiveness is pervasive; the women dons are hyper-sensitive to the prejudices against them from the outside world where people are not only resentful of privilege but also view cloistered academic women as unnatural, unmotherly perverts; Harriet is defensive against some of the more mean-minded dons who resent her worldly success and her racy lovelife; and the mysterious goings-on that Harriet is invited to investigate point to an individual nursing a bitter grudge against the whole lot of them.

The fact that no conventional crime is committed seems to confirm that Sayers had exhausted the whodunnit game and was far more interested in rehearsing these themes. She uses all her narrative skills to lead us on a circuitous gripping journey littered with red herrings and pervaded by the slow-burn of romance between our two protagonists and she manages to weave all these strands into the tapestry of the wider discussion she wants to have with us.

This is Sayers' most personal novel, in which the love story and the crime story are brilliantly intertwined. It is a wonderful novel by any standards and does not need the 'crime' category to justify its existence. Ironically it is with what was ostensibly just another Wimsey mystery that Sayers extricated herself from the potboiler-writer category from which she so longed to escape.

Dame Harriet Walter, 2016

IT would be idle to deny that the City and University of Oxford (*in aeternum floreant*) do actually exist, and contain a number of colleges and other buildings, some of which are mentioned by name in this book. It is therefore the more necessary to affirm emphatically that none of the characters which I have placed upon this public stage has any counterpart in real life. In particular, Shrewsbury College, with its dons, students and scouts, is entirely imaginary; nor are the distressing events described as taking place within its walls founded upon any events that have ever occurred anywhere. Detective-story writers are obliged by their disagreeable profession to invent startling and unpleasant incidents and people, and are (I presume) at liberty to imagine what might happen if such incidents and people were to intrude upon the life of an innocent and well-ordered community; but in so doing they must not be supposed to suggest that any such disturbance ever has occurred or is ever likely to occur in any community in real life.

Certain apologies are, however, due from me: first, to the University of Oxford, for having presented it with a Chancellor and Vice-Chancellor of my own manufacture and with a college of 150 women students, in excess of the limit ordained by statute. Next, and with deep humility, to Balliol College – not only for having saddled it with so wayward an alumnus as Peter Wimsey, but also for my monstrous impertinence in having erected Shrewsbury College upon its spacious and sacred cricket-ground. To New College, also to Christ Church and especially to Queen's, I apologise for the follies of certain young gentlemen, to Brasenose for the facetiousness of a middle-aged one, and to Magdalen for the embarrassing situation in which I have placed an imaginary pro-Proctor. The Corporation Dump, on the other hand, is, or was, a fact, and no apology for it is due from me.

To the Principal and Fellows of my own college of Somerville, I tender my thanks for help generously given in questions of proctorial rules and general college discipline – though they are not to be held responsible for details of discipline in Shrewsbury College, many of which I have invented to suit my own purpose.

Persons curious in chronology may, if they like, work out from what they already know of the Wimsey family that the action of the book takes place in 1935; but if they do, they must not be querulously indignant because the King's Jubilee is not mentioned, or because I have arranged the weather and the moon's changes to suit my own fancy. For, however realistic the background, the novelist's only native country is Cloud-Cuckooland, where they do but jest, poison in jest: no offence in the world.

1

Thou blind man's mark, thou fool's self-chosen snare,
Fond fancy's scum, and dregs of scattered thought,
Band of all evils; cradle of causeless care;
Thou web of will, whose end is never wrought:
Desire! Desire! I have too dearly bought
With price of mangled mind, thy worthless ware.

SIR PHILIP SIDNEY

HARRIET VANE sat at her writing-table and stared out into Mecklenburg Square. The late tulips made a brave show in the Square garden, and a quartet of early tennis-players were energetically calling the score of a rather erratic and unpractised game. But Harriet saw neither tulips nor tennis-players. A letter lay open on the blotting-pad before her, but its image had faded from her mind to make way for another picture. She saw a stone quadrangle, built by a modern architect in a style neither new nor old, but stretching out reconciling hands to past and present. Folded within its walls lay a trim grass plot, with flower-beds splashed at the angles, and surrounded by a wide stone plinth. Behind the level roofs of Cotswold slate rose the brick chimneys of an older and less formal pile of buildings – a quadrangle also of a kind, but still keeping a domestic remembrance of the original Victorian dwelling-houses that had sheltered the first shy students of Shrewsbury College. In front were the trees of Jowett Walk and, beyond them, a jumble of ancient gables and the tower of New College, with its jackdaws wheeling against a windy sky.

Memory peopled the quad with moving figures. Students sauntering in pairs. Students dashing to lectures, their gowns hitched hurriedly over light summer frocks, the wind jerking their flat caps into the absurd likeness of so many jesters' cockscombs. Bicycles stacked in the porter's lodge, their carriers piled with books and gowns twisted about their handlebars. A grizzled woman don crossing the turf with vague eyes, her thoughts riveted upon aspects of sixteenth-century philosophy, her sleeves floating, her shoulders cocked to the academic angle that automatically compensated the backward drag of the pleated poplin. Two male commoners in search of a coach, bareheaded, hands in their trousers-pockets, talking loudly about boats. The Warden – grey and stately – and the Dean – stocky, brisk, bird-like, a Lesser Redpoll – in animated conference under the archway leading to the Old Quadrangle. Tall spikes of delphinium against the grey, quiveringly blue-like flames, if flame were ever so blue. The college cat, preoccupied and remote, stalking with tail erect in the direction of the buttery.

It was all so long ago; so closely encompassed and complete; so cut off as by swords from the bitter years that lay between. Could one face it now? What would those women say to her, to Harriet Vane, who had taken her First in English and gone to London to write mystery fiction, to live with a man who was not married to her, and to be tried for his murder amid a roar of notoriety? That was not the kind of career that Shrewsbury expected of its old students.

She had never gone back; at first, because she had loved the place too well, and a clean break seemed better than a slow wrenching-away; and also because, when her parents had died and left her penniless, the struggle to earn a livelihood had absorbed all her time and thought. And afterwards, the stark shadow of the gallows had fallen between her and that sun-drenched quadrangle of grey and green. But now—?

She picked up the letter again. It was an urgent entreaty that she should attend the Shrewsbury Gaudy – an entreaty of the kind that it is difficult to disregard. A friend whom she had not seen since they went down together; married now and remote from her, but fallen sick, and eager to see Harriet once again before going abroad for a delicate and dangerous operation.

Mary Stokes, so pretty and dainty as Miss Patty in the Second-Year play; so charming and finished in manner; so much the social centre of her year. It had seemed strange that she should take such a fancy to Harriet Vane, rough and gawky and anything but generally popular. Mary had led and Harriet had followed; when they punted up the Cher with strawberries and thermos flasks, when they climbed Magdalen Tower together before sunrise on May Day and felt it swing beneath them with the swing of the reeling bells; when they sat up late at night over the fire with coffee and parkin, it was always Mary who took the lead in all the long discussions about love and art, religion and citizenship. Mary, said all her friends, was marked for a First; only the dim, inscrutable dons had not been surprised when the lists came out with Harriet's name in the First Class and Mary's in the Second. And since then, Mary had married and scarcely been heard of; except that she haunted the College with a sick persistence, never missing an Old Students' Meeting or a Gaudy. But Harriet had broken all her old ties and half the commandments, dragged her reputation in the dust and made money, had the rich and amusing Lord Peter Wimsey at her feet, to marry him if she chose, and was full of energy and bitterness and the uncertain rewards of fame. Prometheus and Epimetheus had changed their parts, it seemed; but for one there was the box of troubles and for the other the bare rock and the vulture; and never, it seemed to Harriet, could they meet on any common ground again.

'But, by God!' said Harriet, 'I won't be a coward. I'll go and be damned to it. Nothing can hurt me worse than I've been hurt already. And what does it matter after all?'

She filled up her invitation form, addressed it, stamped it with a sharp thump and ran quickly down to drop it in the pillar-box before she changed her mind.

She came back slowly across the Square garden, mounted the Adam stone stair to her flat and, after a fruitless rummage in a cupboard, came out and climbed up slowly again to a landing at the top of the house. She dragged out an ancient trunk, unlocked it and flung back the lid. A close, cold odour. Books. Discarded garments. Old shoes. Old manuscripts. A faded tie that had belonged to her dead lover – how horrible that that should still be hanging about! She burrowed to the bottom of the pile and dragged a thick, black bundle out into the dusty sunlight. The gown, worn only once at the taking of her M.A. degree, had suffered nothing from its long seclusion: the stiff folds shook loose with hardly a crease. The crimson silk of the hood gleamed bravely. Only the flat cap showed a little touch of the moth's tooth. As she beat the loose fluff from it, a tortoise-shell butterfly, disturbed from its hibernation beneath the flap of the trunk-lid, fluttered out into the brightness of the window, where it was caught and held by a cobweb.

*　　*　　*

Harriet was glad that in these days she could afford her own little car. Her entry into Oxford would bear no resemblance to those earlier arrivals by train. For a few hours longer she could ignore the whimpering ghost of her dead youth and tell herself that she was a stranger and a sojourner, a well-to-do woman with a position in the world. The hot road spun away behind her; towns rose from the green landscape, crowded close about her with their inn-signs and petrol-pumps, their shops and police and perambulators, then reeled back and were forgotten. June was dying among the roses, the hedges were darkening to a duller green; the blatancy of red brick sprawled along the highway was a reminder that the present builds inexorably over the empty fields of the past. She lunched in High Wycombe, solidly, comfortably, ordering a half-bottle of white wine and tipping the waitress generously. She was eager to distinguish herself as sharply as possible from that former undergraduate who would have had to be content with a packet of sandwiches and a flask of coffee beneath the bough in a by-lane. As one grew older, as one established one's self, one gained a new delight in formality. Her dress for the Garden-party, chosen to combine suitably with full academicals, lay, neatly folded, inside her suit-case. It was long and severe, of plain black georgette, wholly and unimpeachably correct. Beneath it was an evening dress for the Gaudy Dinner, of a rich petunia colour, excellently cut on restrained lines, with no unbecoming display of back or breast; it would not affront the portraits of dead Wardens, gazing down from the slowly mellowing oak of the Hall.

Headington. She was very near now, and in spite of herself a chill qualm cramped her stomach. Headington Hill, up which one had toiled so often, pushing a decrepit bicycle. It seemed less steep now, as one made decorous descent behind four rhythmically pulsating cylinders; but every leaf and stone hailed one with the intrusive familiarity of an old school-fellow. Then the narrow street, with its cramped, untidy shops, like the main street of a village; one or two stretches had been widened and improved, but there was little real change to take refuge in.

Magdalen Bridge. Magdalen Tower. And here, no change at all – only the heartless and indifferent persistence of man's handiwork. Here one must begin to steel one's self in earnest. Long Wall Street. St. Cross Road. The iron hand of the past gripping at one's entrails. The college gates; and now one must go through with it.

There was a new porter at the St. Cross lodge, who heard Harriet's name unmoved and checked it off upon a list. She handed him her bag, took her car round to a garage in Mansfield Lane,* and then, with her gown over her arm, passed through the New Quad into the Old, and so, by way of an ugly brick doorway, into Burleigh Building.

She met nobody of her year in the corridors or on the staircase. Three contemporaries of a far senior generation were greeting one another with effusive and belated girlishness at the door of the Junior Common Room; but she knew none of them, and went by unspeaking and unspoken to, like a ghost. The room allotted to her she recognised, after a little calculation, as one that had been occupied in her day by a woman she particularly disliked, who had married a missionary and gone to China.

* For the purposes of this book, Mansfield Lane is deemed to run from Mansfield Road to St. Cross Road, behind Shrewsbury College and somewhere about the junction between Balliol and Merton Cricket grounds as they stand at present.

The present owner's short gown hung behind the door; judging by the bookshelves, she was reading History; judging by her personal belongings, she was a Fresher with an urge for modernity and very little natural taste. The narrow bed, on which Harriet flung down her belongings, was covered with drapery of a crude green colour and ill-considered Futuristic pattern; a bad picture in the neo-archaic manner hung above it; a chromium-plated lamp of angular and inconvenient design swore acidly at the table and wardrobe provided by the college, which were of a style usually associated with the Tottenham Court Road; while the disharmony was crowned and accentuated by the presence, on the chest of drawers, of a curious statuette or three-dimensional diagram carried out in aluminium, which resembled a gigantic and contorted corkscrew, and was labelled upon its base: ASPIRATION. It was with surprise and relief that Harriet discovered three practicable dress-hangers in the wardrobe. The looking-glass, in conformity with established college use, was about a foot square, and hung in the darkest corner of the room.

She unpacked her bag, took off her coat and skirt, slipped on a dressing-gown and set out in search of a bathroom. She had allowed herself three-quarters of an hour for changing, and Shrewsbury's hot-water system had always been one of its most admirable minor efficiencies. She had forgotten exactly where the bathrooms were on this floor, but surely they were round here to the left. A pantry, two pantries, with notices on the doors: NO WASHING-UP TO BE DONE AFTER 11 p.m.; three lavatories, with notices on the doors: KINDLY EXTINGUISH THE LIGHT WHEN LEAVING; yes, here she was – four bathrooms, with notices on the doors: NO BATHS TO BE TAKEN AFTER 11 p.m., and, underneath, an exasperated addendum to each: IF STUDENTS PERSIST IN TAKING BATHS AFTER 11 p.m. THE BATHROOMS WILL BE LOCKED AT 10.30 p.m. *SOME* CONSIDERATION FOR OTHERS IS NECESSARY IN COMMUNITY LIFE. Signed: L. MARTIN, DEAN. Harriet selected the largest bathroom. It contained a notice: REGULATIONS IN CASE OF FIRE, and a card printed in large capitals: THE SUPPLY OF HOT WATER IS LIMITED. PLEASE AVOID UNDUE WASTE. With a familiar sensation of being under authority, Harriet pushed down the waste-plug and turned on the tap. The water was boiling, though the bath badly needed a new coat of enamel and the cork mat had seen better days.

Once bathed, Harriet felt better. She was lucky again in returning to her room to meet no one whom she knew. She was in no mood for reminiscent gossipings in dressing-gowns. She saw the name 'Mrs. H. Attwood' on the door next but one to hers. The door was shut, and she was grateful. The next door bore no name, but as she went by, someone turned the handle from within, and it began to open slowly. Harriet leapt quickly past it and into shelter. She found her heart beating absurdly fast.

The black frock fitted her like a glove. It was made with a small square yoke and long, close sleeves, softened by a wrist-frill falling nearly to the knuckles. It outlined her figure to the waist and fell full-skirted to the ground, with a suggestion of the mediæval robe. Its dull surface effaced itself, not outshining the dull gleam of the academic poplin. She pulled the gown's heavy folds forward upon her shoulders, so that the straight fronts fell stole-wise, serene. The hood cost her a small struggle, before she remembered the right twist at the throat which turned the bright silk outwards. She pinned it invisibly on her breast, so that it sat poised and balanced – one black shoulder and one crimson. Standing and stooping before the inadequate looking-glass (the present student who owned the room was obviously a very short woman), she adjusted the soft cap to lie flat and straight, peak down in the centre of the forehead. The glass showed her her own face, rather pale, with black brows fronting squarely either side of a strong nose, a little too broad for beauty. Her own eyes looked back at her – rather tired, rather defiant – eyes that had looked upon fear and were still wary. The mouth was the mouth of one who has been generous and repented of generosity; its wide corners were tucked back to give nothing away. With the thick, waving hair folded beneath the black cloth, the face seemed somehow stripped for action. She frowned at herself and moved her hands a little up and down upon the stuff of her gown; then, becoming impatient with the looking-glass, she turned to the window, which looked out into the Inner or Old Quad. This indeed, was less a quad than an oblong garden, with the college buildings grouped about it. At one end, tables and chairs were set out upon the grass beneath the shade of the trees. At the far side, the new Library wing, now almost complete, showed its bare rafters in a forest of scaffolding. A few groups of women crossed the lawn; Harriet observed with irritation that most of them wore their caps badly, and one had had the folly to put on a pale lemon frock with muslin frills, which looked incongruous beneath a gown.

'Though, after all,' she thought, 'the bright colours are mediæval enough. And at any rate, the women are no worse than the men. I once saw old Hammond walk in the Encænia procession in a Mus. Doc. gown, a grey flannel suit, brown boots and a blue spotted tie, and nobody said anything to him.'

She laughed suddenly, and for the first time felt confident.

'They can't take this away, at any rate. Whatever I may have done since, this remains. Scholar; Master of Arts; Domina; Senior Member of this University (*statutum est quod Juniores Senioribus debitam et congruam reverentiam tum in privato tum in publico exhibeant*); a place achieved, inalienable, worthy of reverence.'

She walked firmly from the room and knocked upon the door next but one to her own.

The four women walked down to the garden together – slowly, because Mary was ill and could not move fast. And as they went, Harriet was thinking:

'It's a mistake – it's a great mistake – I shouldn't have come. Mary is a dear, as she always was, and she is pathetically pleased to see me, but we have nothing to say to one another. And I shall always remember her, *now*, as she is to-day, with that haggard face and look of defeat. And she will remember me as I am – hardened. She told me I looked successful. I know what that means.'

She was glad that Betty Armstrong and Dorothy Collins were doing all the talking. One of them was a hardworking dog-breeder; the other ran a bookshop in Manchester. They had evidently kept in touch with one another, for they were discussing things and not people, as those do who have lively interests in common. Mary Stokes (now Mary Attwood) seemed cut off from them, by sickness, by marriage, by – it was no use to blink the truth – by a kind of mental stagnation that had nothing to do with either illness or marriage. 'I suppose,' thought Harriet, 'she had one of those small, summery brains, that flower early and run to seed. Here she is – my intimate friend – talking to me with a painful kind of admiring politeness about my books. And I am talking with a painful kind of admiring politeness about her children. We ought *not* to have met again. It's awful.'

Dorothy Collins broke in upon her thoughts by asking her a question about publishers' contracts, and the reply to this tided them over till they emerged into the quad. A brisk figure came bustling along the path, and stopped with a cry of welcome.

'Why, it's Miss Vane! How nice to see you after all this long time.'

Harriet thankfully allowed herself to be scooped up by the Dean, for whom she had always had a very great affection, and who had written kindly to her in the days when a cheerful kindliness had been the most helpful thing on earth. The other three, mindful of reverence toward authority, passed on; they had paid their repects to the Dean earlier in the afternoon.

'It was splendid that you were able to come.'

'Rather brave of me, don't you think?' said Harriet.

'Oh, nonsense!' said the Dean. She put her head on one side and fixed Harriet with a bright and bird-like eye. 'You mustn't think about all that. Nobody bothers about it at all. We're not nearly such dried-up mummies as you think. After all, it's the work you are doing that really counts, isn't it? By the way, the Warden is longing to see you. She simply loved *The Sands of Crime*. Let's see if we can catch her before the Vice-Chancellor arrives. . . . How did you think Stokes was looking – Attwood, I mean? I never *can* remember all their married names.'

'Pretty rotten, I'm afraid,' said Harriet. 'I came here to see her, really, you know – but I'm afraid it's not going to be much of a success.'

'Ah!' said the Dean. 'She's stopped growing. I expect. She was a friend of yours – but I always thought she had a head like a day-old chick. Very precocious, but no

11

staying power. However, I hope they'll put her right. . . .
Bother this wind – I can't keep my cap down. You
manage yours remarkably well; how do you do it?
And I notice that we are both decently subfusc. *Have*
you seen Trimmer in that frightful frock like a canary
lampshade?'

'That was Trimmer, was it? What's *she* doing?'

'Oh, lord! my dear, she's gone in for mental healing.
Brightness and love and all that. . . . Ah! I thought we
should find the Warden here.'

Shrewsbury College had been fortunate in its wardens.
In the early days, it had been dignified by a woman of
position; in the difficult period when it fought for Women's Degrees it had been guided by a diplomat; and
now that it was received into the University, its behaviour was made acceptable by a personality. Dr. Mar-
garet Baring wore her scarlet and french grey with an air.
She was a magnificent figurehead on all public occasions,
and she could soothe with tact the wounded breasts of
crusty and affronted male dons. She greeted Harriet
graciously, and asked what she thought of the new
Library Wing, which would complete the North side
of the Old Quad. Harriet duly admired what could be
seen of its proportions, said it would be a great improvement, and asked when it would be finished.

'By Easter, we hope. Perhaps we shall see you at the
Opening.'

Harriet said politely that she should look forward to it,
and, seeing the Vice-Chancellor's gown flutter into sight
in the distance, drifted tactfully away to join the main
throng of old students.

Gowns, gowns, gowns. It was difficult sometimes to
recognise people after ten years or more. That in the
blue-and-rabbitskin hood must be Sylvia Drake – she had

taken that B.Litt. at last, then. Miss Drake's B.Litt. had been the joke of the college; it had taken her so long; she was continually rewriting her thesis and despairing over it. She would hardly remember Harriet, who was so much her junior, but Harriet remembered her well – always popping in and out of the J.C.R. during her year of residence, and chattering away about mediæval Courts of Love. Heavens! Here was that awful woman, Muriel Campshott, coming up to claim acquaintance. Campshott had always simpered. She still simpered. And she was dressed in a shocking shade of green. She was going to say, 'How *do* you think of all your plots?' She did say it. Curse the woman. And Vera Mollison. She was asking: 'Are you writing anything now?'

'Yes, certainly,' said Harriet. 'Are you still teaching?'

'Yes – still in the same place.' said Miss Mollison. 'I'm afraid my doings are very small beer compared with yours.'

As there was no possible answer to this but a deprecating laugh, Harriet laughed deprecatingly. A movement took place. People were drifting into the New Quad, where a Presentation Clock was to be unveiled, and taking up their positions upon the stone plinth that ran round behind the flower-beds. An official voice was heard exhorting the guests to leave a path for the procession. Harriet used this excuse to disentangle herself from Vera Mollison and establish herself at the back of a group, all of whose faces were strange to her. On the opposite side of the Quad she could see Mary Attwood and her friends. They were waving. She waved back. She was *not* going to cross the grass and join them. She would remain detached, a unit in an official crowd.

From behind a drapery of bunting the clock, anticipating its official appearance in public, chimed and struck three. Footsteps crunched along the gravel. The procession came into sight, beneath the archway; a small crocodile-walk of elderly people, dressed with the incongruous brilliance of a more sumptuous era, and moving with the slovenly dignity characteristic of university functions in England. They crossed the quad; they mounted the plinth beneath the clock; the male dons removed their Tudor bonnets and mortar-boards in deference to the Vice-Chancellor; the female dons adopted a reverential attitude suggestive of a prayer-meeting. In a thin, delicate voice, the Vice-Chancellor began to speak. He spoke of the history of the college; he made a graceful allusion to achievements which could not be measured by the mere passing of time; he cracked a dry and nutty little jest about relativity and adorned it with a classical tag; he referred to the generosity of the donor and the beloved personality of the deceased Member of Council in whose memory the clock was presented; he expressed himself happy to unveil this handsome clock, which would add so greatly to the beauty of the quadrangle – a quadrangle, he would add, which, although a new-comer in point of time, was fully worthy to take its place among those ancient and noble buildings which were the glory of our University. In the name of the Chancellor and University of Oxford, he now unveiled the clock. His hand went out to the rope; an agitated expression came over the face of the Dean, resolving itself into a wide smile of triumph when the drapery fell away without any unseemly hitch or disaster; the clock was revealed, a few bold spirits started a round of applause; the Warden, in a short neat speech, thanked the Vice-Chancellor for his kindness in coming and his friendly expressions; the golden hand of the clock moved on, and the quarter-chime rang out mellowly. The assembly heaved a sigh of satisfaction; the procession collected itself and made the return journey through the archway, and the ceremony was happily over.

Harriet, following with the throng, discovered to her horror that Vera Mollison had bobbed up again beside her, and was saying she supposed all mystery-writers must feel a strong personal interest in clocks, as so many alibis turned upon clocks and time-signals. There had been a curious incident one day at the school where she taught; it would, she thought, make a splendid plot for a detective-story, for anybody who was clever enough to work such things out. She had been longing to see Harriet and tell her all about it. Planting herself firmly on the lawn of the Old Quad, at a considerable distance from the refreshment-tables, she began to retail the curious incident, which required a good deal of preliminary explanation. A scout advanced, carrying cups of tea. Harriet secured one, and instantly wished she hadn't; it prevented swift movement, and seemed to nail her to Miss Mollison's side to all eternity. Then, with a heart-lifting surge of thankfulness, she saw Phœbe Tucker. Good old Phœbe, looking exactly the same as ever. She excused herself hurriedly to Miss Mollison, begging that she might hear the clock incident at a more leisured moment, made her way through a bunch of gowns and said, 'Hullo!'

'Hullo?' said Phœbe. 'Oh, it's you. Thank God! I was beginning to think there wasn't a soul of our year here, except Trimmer and that ghastly Mollison female. Come and get some sandwiches; they're quite good, strange to say. How are you these days; flourishing?'

'Not too bad.'

'You're doing good stuff, anyhow.'

'So are you. Let's find something to sit upon. I want to hear all about the digging.'

Phœbe Tucker was a History student, who had married an archæologist, and the combination seemed to work remarkably well. They dug up bones and stones and pottery in forgotten corners of the globe, and wrote pamphlets and lectured to learned societies. At odd moments they had produced a trio of cheerful youngsters, whom they dumped casually upon delighted grandparents before hastening back to the bones and stones.

'Well, we've only just got back from Ithaca. Bob is fearfully excited about a new set of burial-places, and has evolved an entirely original and revolutionary theory about funerary rites. He's writing a paper that contradicts all old Lambard's conclusions, and I'm helping by toning down his adjectives and putting in deprecatory footnotes. I mean, Lambard may be a perverse old idiot, but it's more dignified not to say so in so many words. A bland and deadly courtesy is more devastating don't you think?'

'Infinitely.'

Here at any rate was somebody who had not altered by a hair's-breadth, in spite of added years and marriage. Harriet was in a mood to be glad of that. After an exhaustive inquiry into the matter of funerary rites, she asked after the family.

'Oh, they're getting to be rather fun. Richard – that's the eldest – is thrilled by the burial-places. His grandmother was horrified the other day to find him very patiently and correctly excavating the gardener's rubbish-heap and making a collection of bones. Her generation always get so agitated about germs and dirt. I suppose they're quite right, but the offspring doesn't seem any the worse. So his father gave him a cabinet to keep the bones in. Simply encouraging him, Mother said. I think we shall have to take Richard out with us next time, only Mother would be so worried, thinking about no drainage and what he might pick up from the Greeks. All the children seem to be coming out quite intelligent, thank goodness. It would have been such a bore to be the mother of morons, and it's an absolute toss-up, isn't it? If one could only invent them, like characters in books, it would be much more satisfactory to a well-regulated mind.'

From this the conversation naturally passed to biology, Mendelian factors and *Brave New World*. It was cut short by the emergence of Harriet's former tutor from a crowd of old students. Harriet and Phœbe made a concerted rush to greet her. Miss Lydgate's manner was exactly what it had always been. To the innocent and candid eyes of that great scholar, no moral problem seemed ever to present itself. Of a scrupulous personal integrity, she embraced the irregularities of other people in a wide, unquestioning charity, As any student of literature must, she knew all the sins of the world by name, but it was doubtful whether she recognised them when she met them in real life. It was as though a misdemeanour committed by a person she knew was disarmed and disinfected by the contact. So many young people had passed through her hands, and she had found so much good in all of them; it was impossible to think that they could be deliberately wicked, like Richard III or Iago. Unhappy, yes; misguided, yes; exposed to difficult and complicated temptations which Miss Lydgate herself had been mercifully spared, yes. If she heard of a theft, a divorce, even worse things, she would knit puzzled brows and think how utterly wretched the offenders must have been before they could do so dreadful a thing. Only once had Harriet ever heard her speak with un- qualified disapproval of any one she knew, and that was

17

of a former pupil of her own who had written a popular book about Carlyle, 'No research at all,' had been Miss Lydgate's verdict, 'and no effort at critical judgment. She has reproduced all the old gossip without troubling to verify anything. Slipshod, showy, and catchpenny. I am really ashamed of her.' And even then she had added: 'But I believe, poor thing, she is very hard up.'

Miss Lydgate showned no signs of being ashamed of Miss Vane. On the contrary, she greeted her warmly, begged her to come and see her on Sunday morning, spoke appreciatively of her work, and commended her for keeping up a scholarly standard of English, even in mystery fiction.

'You give a lot of pleasure in the S.C.R.,' she added, 'and I believe Miss de Vine is also a fervent admirer of yours.'

'Miss de Vine?'

'Ah, of course, you don't know her. Our new Research Fellow. She's such a nice person, and I know she wants to talk to you about your books. You must come and make her acquaintance. We've got her for three years, you know. That is, she only comes into residence next term, but she's been living in Oxford for the last few weeks, working in Bodley. She's doing a great work on National Finance under the Tudors, and makes it perfectly fascinating, even for people like me, who are stupid about money. We are all so glad that the College decided to offer her the Jane Barraclough Fellowship, because she is a most distinguished scholar, and has had rather a hard time.'.

'I think I've heard of her. Wasn't she Head of one of the big provincial colleges?'

'Yes; she was Provost of Flamborough for three years; but it wasn't really her job; too much administration, though of course she was marvellous on the financial side. But she was doing too much, what with her own work, and examining for doctorates and so on, and coping with students – the University and the College between them wore her out. She's one of those people who always *will* give of her best; but I think she found all the personal contacts uncongenial. She got ill, and had to go abroad for a couple of years. In fact, she has only just got back to England. Of course, having to give up Flamborough made a good deal of difference from the financial point of view; so it's nice to think that for the next three years she'll be able to get on with her book and not worry about that side of things.'

'I remember about it now,' said Harriet 'I saw the election announced somewhere or other, last Christmas or thereabouts.'

'I expect you saw it in the Shrewsbury Year-Book. We are naturally very proud to have her here. She ought really to have a professorship, but I doubt if she could stand the tutorial side of it. The fewer distractions she has, the better, because she's one of the *real* scholars. There she is, over there – and, oh dear! I'm afraid she's been caught by Miss Gubbins. You remember Miss Gubbins?'

'Vaguely,' said Phœbe. 'She was Third Year when we were freshers. An excellent soul, but rather earnest, and an appalling bore at College Meetings.'

'She is a very conscientious person,' said Miss Lydgate, 'but she has rather an unfortunate knack of making any subject sound dull. It's a great pity, because she is exceptionally sound and dependable. However, that doesn't greatly matter in her present appointment; she holds a librarianship somewhere – Miss Hillyard would remember where – and I believe she's researching on the

19

Bacon family. She's such a hard worker. But I'm afraid she's putting poor Miss de Vine through a cross-examination, which doesn't seem quite fair on an occasion like this. Shall we go to the rescue?'

As Harriet followed Miss Lydgate across the lawn, she was visited by an enormous nostalgia. If only one could come back to this quiet place, where only intellectual achievement counted; if one could work here steadily and obscurely at some close-knit piece of reasoning, undistracted and uncorrupted by agents, contracts, publishers, blurb-writers, interviewers, fan-mail, autograph-hunters, notoriety-hunters, and competitors; abolishing personal contacts, personal spites, personal jealousies; getting one's teeth into something dull and durable; maturing into solidity like the Shrewsbury beeches – then, one might be able to forget the wreck and chaos of the past, or see it, at any rate, in a truer proportion. Because, in a sense, it was not important. The fact that one had loved and sinned and suffered and escaped death was of far less ultimate moment than a single footnote in a dim academic journal establishing the priority of a manuscript or restoring a lost iota subscript. It was the hand-to-hand struggle with the insistent personalities of other people, all pushing for a place in the limelight, that made the accidents of one's own personal adventure bulk so large in the scheme of things.

But she doubted whether she were now capable of any such withdrawal. She had long ago taken the step that put the grey-walled paradise of Oxford behind her. No one can bathe in the same river twice, not even in the Isis. She would be impatient of that narrow serenity – or so she told herself.

Pulling her wandering thoughts together, she found herself being introduced to Miss de Vine. And, looking at her, she saw at once that here was a scholar of a kind very unlike Miss Lydgate, for example, and still more grotesquely unlike anything that Harriet Vane could ever become. Here was a fighter, indeed; but one to whom the quadrangle of Shrewsbury was a native and proper arena; a soldier knowing no personal loyalties, whose sole allegiance was to the fact. A Miss Lydgate, standing serenely untouched by the world, could enfold it in a genial warmth of charity; this woman, with infinitely more knowledge of the world, would rate it at a just value and set it out of her path if it incommoded her. The thin, eager face, with its large grey eyes deeply set and luminous behind thick glasses, was sensitive to impressions; but behind that sensitiveness was a mind as hard and immovable as granite. As the Head of a woman's college she must, thought Harriet, have had a distasteful task; for she looked as though the word 'compromise' had been omitted from her vocabulary; and all statesmanship is compromise. She would not be likely to tolerate any waverings of purpose or woolliness of judgment. If anything came between her and the service of truth, she would walk over it without rancour and without pity – even if it were her own reputation. A formidable woman when pursuing the end in view – and the more so, for the deceptive moderation and modesty she would display in dealing with any subject of which she was not master. As they came up, she was saying to Miss Gubbins:

'I entirely agree that a historian ought to be precise in detail; but unless you take all the characters and circumstances concerned into account, you are reckoning without the facts. The proportions and relations of things are just as much facts as the things themselves; and if you get those wrong, you falsify the picture really seriously.'

Here, just as Miss Gubbins, with a mulish look in her eye, was preparing to expostulate, Miss de Vine caught sight of the English tutor and excused herself. Miss Gubbins was obliged to withdraw; Harriet observed with regret that she had untidy hair, an ill-kept skin and a large white safety-pin securing her hood to her dress.

'Dear me!' said Miss de Vine, 'who is that very uninspired young woman? She seems very much annoyed with my review of Mr. Winterlake's book on Essex. She seems to think I ought to have torn the poor man to pieces because of a trifling error of a few months made in dealing, quite incidentally, with the early history of the Bacon family. She attaches no importance to the fact that the book is the most illuminating and scholarly handling to date of the interactions of two most enigmatic characters.'

'Bacon family history is her subject,' said Miss Lydgate, 'so I've no doubt she feels strongly about it.'

'It's a great mistake to see one's own subject out of proportion to its background. The error should be corrected, of course; I did correct it – in a private letter to the author, which is the proper medium for trifling corrections. But the man has, I feel sure, got hold of the master-key to the situation between those two men, and in so doing he has got hold of a fact of genuine importance.'

'Well,' said Miss Lydgate, showing her strong teeth in a genial grin, 'you seem to have taken a strong line with Miss Gubbins. Now I've brought along somebody I know you're anxious to meet. This is Miss Harriet Vane – also an artist in the relating of details.'

'Miss Vane?' The historian bent her brilliant, shortsighted eyes on Harriet, and her face lit up. 'This is delightful. Do let me say how much I enjoyed your last book. I thought it quite the best thing you'd done – though of course I'm not competent to form an opinion from the scientific point of view. I was discussing it with Professor Higgins, who is quite a devotee of yours, and he said it suggested a most interesting possibility, which had not before occurred to him. He wasn't quite sure whether it would work, but he would do his best to find out. Tell me, what did you have to go upon?'

'Well, I got a pretty good opinion,' said Harriet, feeling a hideous qualm of uncertainty, and cursing Professor Higgins from the bottom of her heart. 'But of course—'

At this point Miss Lydgate espied another old pupil in the distance and ran away. Phœbe Tucker had already been lost on the way across the lawn. Harriet was left to her fate. After ten minutes, during which Miss de Vine ruthlessly turned her victim's brain inside out, shook the facts out of it like a vigorous housemaid shaking dust from a carpet, beat it, refreshed it, rubbed up the surface of it, relaid it in a new position and tacked it into place with a firm hand, the Dean mercifully came up and burst into the conversation.

'Thank *goodness*, the Vice-Chancellor's taking himself off. Now we can get rid of this filthy old bombazine and show off our party frocks. *Why* did we ever clamour for degrees and the fun of stewing in full academicals on a hot day? There! he's gone! Give me those anything-but-glad-rags and I'll shove them into the S.C.R. with mine. Has yours got a name on it, Miss Vane? Oh, good girl! I've got three unknown gowns sitting in my office already. Found lying about at the end of term. No clue to owners, of course. The untidy little beasts seem to think it's our job to sort out their miserable belongings. They strew them everywhere, regardless, and then borrow each other's; and if anybody's fined for being out without a gown, it's always because somebody pinched it. And the wretched things are always as dirty as dish-clouts. They use them for dusters and drawing the fire up. When I think how our devoted generation *sweated* to get the right to these garments – and these young things don't care *that* for them! They go about looking all bits and pieces, like illustrations to *Pendennis* – so out of date of them! But their idea of being modern is to imitate what male undergraduates were like half a century ago.'

'Some of us old students aren't much to write home about,' said Harriet. 'Look at Gubbins, for instance.'

'Oh, my dear! That crashing bore. And *all* held together with safety-pins. And I wish she'd wash her neck.'

'I think,' said Miss de Vine, with painstaking readiness to set the facts in a just light, 'that the colour is natural to her skin.'

'Then she should eat carrots and clear her system,' retorted the Dean, snatching Harriet's gown from her. 'No, don't you bother. It won't take me a minute to chuck them through the S.C.R. window. And don't you dare to run away, or I shall *never* find you again.'

'Is my hair tidy?' inquired Miss de Vine, becoming suddenly human and hesitating with the loss of her cap and gown.

'Well,' said Harriet, surveying the thick, iron-grey coils from which a quantity of overworked hair-pins stood out like croquet-hoops, 'it's coming down just a trifle.'

'It always does,' said Miss de Vine, making vague dabs at the pins. 'I think I shall have to cut it short. It must be much less trouble that way.'

'I like it as it is. That big coil suits you. Let me have a go at it, shall I?'

'I wish you would,' said the historian, thankfully submitting to having the pins thrust into place. 'I am very stupid with my fingers. I do possess a hat some-where,' she added, with an irresolute glance round the quad, as though she expected to see the hat growing on a tree, 'but the Dean said we'd better stay here. Oh, thank you. That feels much better – a marvellous sense of security. Ah! here's Miss Martin. Miss Vane has kindly been acting as hair-dresser to the White Queen – but oughtn't I to put on a hat?'

'Not now,' said Miss Martin emphatically. 'I'm going to have some proper tea, and so are you. I'm *ravenous*. I've been tagging after old Professor Boniface who's ninety-seven and practically gaga, and screaming in his deaf ear till I'm almost *dead*. What's the time? Well, I'm like Marjory Fleming's turkey – I do not give a single damn for the Old Students' Meeting; I simply must eat and drink. Let's swoop down upon the table before Miss Shaw and Miss Stevens collar the last ices.'

2

'Tis proper to all melancholy men, saith *Mercurialis,*
what conceit they have once entertained to be most
intent, violent and continually about it. Invitis occurrit,
do what they may, they cannot be rid of it, against their
wills they must think of it a thousand times over,
perpetuo molestantur, nec oblivisci possunt, they are
continually troubled with it, in company, out of company; at meat, at exercise, at all times and places, *non*
desinunt ea, quae minime volunt, cogitare; if it be
offensive especially, they cannot forget it.

ROBERT BURTON

So far, so good, thought Harriet, changing for dinner.
There had been baddish moments, like trying to renew
contact with Mary Stokes. There had also been a brief
encounter with Miss Hillyard, the History tutor, who had
never liked her, and who had said, with wry mouth and
acidulated tongue, 'Well, Miss Vane, you have had some
very *varied* experiences since we saw you last.' But there
had been good moments too, carrying with them the
promise of permanence in a Heracleitean universe. She felt
it might be possible to survive the Gaudy Dinner, though
Mary Stokes had dutifully bagged for her a place next
herself, which was trying. Fortunately, she had contrived to
get Phœbe Tucker on her other side. (In these surroundings,
she thought of them still as Stokes and Tucker.)

The first thing to strike her, when the procession had

slowly filed up to the High Table, and grace had been said, was the appalling noise in Hall. 'Strike' was the right word. It fell upon one like the rush and weight of a shouting waterfall; it beat on the ear like the hammer-clang of some infernal smithy; it savaged the air like the metallic clatter of fifty thousand monotype machines casting type. Two hundred female tongues, released as though by a spring, burst into high, clamorous speech. She had forgotten what it was like, but it came back to her to-night how, at the beginning of every term, she had felt that if the noise were to go on like that for one minute more, she would go quite mad. Within a week, the effect of it had always worn off. Use had made her immune. But now it shattered her unaccustomed nerves with all and more than all its original violence. People screamed in her ear, and she found herself screaming back. She looked rather anxiously at Mary; could any invalid bear it? Mary seemed not to notice; she was more animated than she had been earlier in the day and was screaming quite cheerfully at Dorothy Collins. Harriet turned to Phœbe.

'Gosh! I'd forgotten what this row was like. If I scream I shall be as hoarse as a crow. I'm going to bellow at you in a fog-horn kind of voice. Do you mind?'

'Not a bit. I can hear you quite well. Why on earth did God give women such shrill voices? Though I don't mind frightfully. It reminds me of native workmen quarrelling. They're doing us rather well, don't you think? Much better soup than we ever got.'

'They've made a special effort for Gaudy. Besides, the new Bursar's rather good, I believe; she was something to do with Domestic Economy. Dear old Straddles had a mind above food.'

'Yes; but I liked Straddles. She was awfully decent to me when I got ill just before Schools. Do you remember?'

'What happened to Straddles when she left?'

'Oh, she's Treasurer at Brontë College. Finance was really her line, you know. She had a real genius for figures.'

'And what became of that woman – what's her name? Peabody? Freebody? – you know – the one who always said solemnly that her great ambition in life was to become Bursar of Shrewsbury?'

'Oh, my dear! She went absolutely potty on some new kind of religion and joined an extraordinary sect somewhere or other where they go about in loin-cloths and have agapemones of nuts and grape-fruit. That is, if you mean Brodribb?'

'Brodribb – I knew it was something like Peabody. Fancy her of all people! So intensely practical and sub-fusc.'

'Reaction. I expect. Repressed emotional instincts and all that. She was frightfully sentimental inside, you know.'

'I know. She wormed round rather. Had a sort of a G.P. for Miss Shaw. Perhaps we were all rather inhibited in those days.'

'Well, the present generation doesn't suffer from that, I'm told. No inhibitions of any kind.'

'Oh, come, Phœbe. We had a good bit of liberty. Not like before Women's Degrees. We weren't monastic.'

'No, but we were born long enough before the War to feel a few restrictions. We inherited some sense of responsibility. And Brodribb came from a fearfully rigid sort of household – Positivists, or Unitarians or Presbyterians or something. The present lot are the real war-time generation, you know.'

'So they are. Well, I don't know that I've any right to throw stones at Brodribb.'

'Oh, my dear! That's entirely different. One thing's natural; the others – I don't know, but it seems to me like complete degeneration of the grey matter. She even wrote a book.'

'About agapemones?'

'Yes. And the Higher Wisdom. And Beautiful Thought. That sort of thing. Full of bad syntax.'

'Oh, lord! Yes – that's pretty awful, isn't it? I can't think why fancy religions should have such a ghastly effect on one's grammar.'

'It's a kind of intellectual rot that sets in, I'm afraid. But which of them causes the other, or whether they're both symptoms of something else, I don't know. What with Trimmer's mental healing, and Henderson going nudist—'

'No!'

'Fact. There she is, at the next table. That's why she's so brown.'

'And her frock so badly cut. If you can't be naked, be as ill-dressed as possible, I suppose.'

'I sometimes wonder whether a little normal, hearty wickedness wouldn't be good for a great many of us.'

At this moment, Miss Mollison, from three places away on the same side of the table, leaned across her neighbours and screamed something.

'What?' screamed Phœbe.

Miss Mollison leaned still farther, compressing Dorothy Collins, Betty Armstrong and Mary Stokes almost to suffocation.

'I hope Miss Vane isn't telling you anything *too* blood-curdling!'

'No,' said Harriet loudly. 'Mrs. Bancroft is curdling *my* blood.'

'How?'

'Telling me the life-histories of our year.'

'Oh!' screamed Miss Mollison, disconcerted. The service of a dish of lamb and green peas intervened and broke up the formation, and her neighbours breathed again. But to Harriet's intense horror, the question and reply seemed to have opened up an avenue for a dark, determined woman with large spectacles and rigidly groomed hair, who sat opposite to her, and who now bent over and said, in piercingly American accents:

'I don't suppose you remember me, Miss Vane? I was only in college for one term, but I would know you anywhere. I'm always recommending your books to my friends in America who are keen to study the British detective story, because I think they are just terribly good.'

'Very kind of you,' said Harriet, feebly.

'And we have a very dear mutooal acquaintance,' went on the spectacled lady.

Heavens! thought Harriet. What social nuisance is going to be dragged out of obscurity now? And who is this frightful female?

'Really?' she said, aloud, trying to gain time while she ransacked her memory. 'Who's that Miss—'

'Schuster-Slatt,' prompted Phœbe's voice in her ear.

'Schuster-Slatt.' (Of course. Arrived in Harriet's first summer term. Supposed to read Law. Left after one term because the conditions at Shrewsbury were too restrictive of liberty. Joined the Home Students, and passed mercifully out of one's life.)

'How clever of you to know my name. Yes, well, you'll be surprised when I tell you, but in my work I see so many of your British aristocracy.'

Hell! thought Harriet. Miss Schuster-Slatt's strident tones dominated even the surrounding uproar.

'Your marvellous Lord Peter. He was so kind to me,

30

and terribly interested when I told him I was at college with you. I think he's just a lovely man.'

'He has very nice manners,' said Harriet. But the implication was too subtle. Miss Schuster-Slatt proceeded:

'He was just wonderful to me when I told him all about my work.' (I wonder what it is, thought Harriet.) 'And of course I wanted to hear all about his thrilling detective cases, but he was much too modest to say anything. Do tell me, Miss Vane, does he wear that cute little eyeglass because of his sight, or is it part of an old English tradition?'

'I have never had the impertinence to ask him,' said Harriet.

'Now isn't that just like your British reticence!' exclaimed Miss Schuster-Slatt; when Mary Stokes struck in with:

'Oh, Harriet, do tell us about Lord Peter! He must be perfectly charming, if he's at all like his photographs. Of course you know him very well, don't you?'

'I worked with him over one case.'

'It must have been frightfully exciting. Do tell us what he's like.'

'Seeing,' said Harriet, in angry and desperate tones, 'seeing that he got me out of prison and probably saved me from being hanged, I am naturally bound to find him delightful.'

'Oh!' said Mary Stokes, flushing scarlet, and shrinking from Harriet's furious eyes as if she had received a blow. 'I'm sorry – I didn't think—'

'Well, there,' said Miss Schuster-Slatt, 'I'm afraid I've been very, very tactless. My mother always said to me, "Sadie, you're the most tactless girl I ever had the bad luck to meet." But I am enthusiastic. I get carried away. I don't stop to think. I'm just the same with my work. I

31

don't consider my own feelings; I don't consider other people's feelings. I just wade right in and ask for what I want, and I mostly get it.'

After which, Miss Schuster-Slatt, with more sensitive feeling than one might have credited her with, carried the conversation triumphantly away to the subject of her own work, which turned out to have something to do with the sterilisation of the unfit, and the encouragement of matrimony among the intelligentsia.

Harriet, meanwhile, sat miserably wondering what devil possessed her to display every disagreeable trait in her character at the mere mention of Wimsey's name. He had done her no harm; he had only saved her from a shameful death and offered her an unswerving personal devotion; and for neither benefit had he ever claimed or expected her gratitude. It was not pretty that her only return should be a snarl of resentment. The fact is, thought Harriet, I have got a bad inferiority complex; unfortunately, the fact that I know it doesn't help me to get rid of it. I could have liked him so much if I could have met him on an equal footing. . . .

The Warden rapped upon the table. A welcome silence fell upon the Hall. A speaker was rising to propose the toast of the University.

She spoke gravely, unrolling the great scroll of history, pleading for the Humanities, proclaiming the Pax Academica to a world terrified with unrest. 'Oxford has been called the home of lost causes: if the love of learning for its own sake is a lost cause everywhere else in the world, let us see to it that here, at least, it finds its abiding home.' Magnificent thought Harriet, but it is not war. And then, her imagination weaving in and out of the spoken words, she saw it as a Holy War, and that whole wildly heterogeneous, that even slightly absurd collection of chattering women fused into a corporate unity with one another and with every man and woman to whom integrity of mind meant more than material gain – defenders in the central keep of Man-soul, their personal differences forgotten in face of a common foe. To be true to one's calling, whatever follies one might commit in one's emotional life, that was the way to spiritual peace. How could one feel fettered, being the freeman of so great a city, or humiliated, where all enjoyed equal citizenship? The eminent professor who rose to reply spoke of a diversity of gifts but the same spirit. The note, once struck, vibrated on the lips of every speaker and the ear of every hearer. Nor was the Warden's review of the Academic year out of key with it: appointments, degrees, fellowships – all these were the domestic details of the discipline without which the community could not function. In the glamour of one Gaudy night, one could realise that one was a citizen of no mean city. It might be an old and an old-fashioned city, with inconvenient buildings and narrow streets where the passers-by squabbled foolishly about the right of way; but her foundations were set upon the holy hills and her spires touched heaven.

Leaving the Hall in this rather exalted mood, Harriet found herself invited to take coffee with the Dean.

She accepted, after ascertaining that Mary Stokes was bound for bed by doctor's orders and had therefore no claim upon her company. She therefore made her way along to the New Quad and tapped upon Miss Martin's door. Gathered together in the sitting-room she found Betty Armstrong, Phœbe Tucker, Miss de Vine, Miss Stevens the Bursar, another of the Fellows who answered to the name of Barton, and a couple of old students a few years senior to herself. The Dean, who was dispensing coffee, hailed her arrival cheerfully.

'Come along! Here's coffee that is coffee. Can *nothing* be done about the Hall coffee, Steve?'

'Yes, if you'll start a coffee-fund,' replied the Bursar. 'I don't know if you've ever worked out the finance of really first-class coffee for two hundred people.'

'I know,' said the Dean. 'It's so trying to be grovellingly poor. I think I'd better mention it to Flackett. You remember Flackett, the rich one, who was always rather odd. She was in your year, Miss Fortescue. She has been following me round, trying to present the College with a tankful of tropical fish. Said she thought it would brighten the Science Lecture-Room.'

'If it would brighten some of the lectures,' said Miss Fortescue, 'it might be a good thing. Miss Hillyard's Constitutional Developments were a bit gruesome in our day.'

'Oh, my *dear*! Those Constitutional Developments! Dear me, yes – they still go on. She starts every year with about thirty students and ends up with two or three earnest black men, who take every word down solemnly in note-books. Exactly the same lectures; I don't think even fish would help them. Anyway, I said, "It's very good of you, Miss Flackett, but I really don't think they'd thrive. It would mean putting in a special heating system, wouldn't it? And it would make extra work for the gardeners." She looked so disappointed, poor thing; so I said she'd better consult the Bursar.'

'All right,' said Miss Stevens, 'I'll tackle Flackett, and suggest the endowment of a coffee-fund.'

'*Much* more useful than tropical fish,' agreed the Dean. 'I'm afraid we do turn out some oddities. And yet, you know, I believe Flackett is extremely sound upon the life-history of the liver-fluke. Would anybody like a Benedictine with the coffee? Come along, Miss Vane.

Alcohol loosens the tongue, and we want to hear all about your latest mysteries.'

Harriet obliged with a brief résumé of the plot she was working on.

'Forgive me, Miss Vane, for speaking frankly,' said Miss Barton, leaning earnestly forward, 'but after your own terrible experience, I wonder that you care about writing that kind of book.'

The Dean looked a little shocked.

'Well,' said Harriet, 'for one thing, writers can't pick and choose until they've made money. If you've made your name for one kind of book and then switch over to another, your sales are apt to go down, and that's the brutal fact.' She paused. 'I know what you're thinking – that anybody with proper sensitive feeling would rather scrub floors for a living. But I should scrub floors very badly, and I write detective stories rather well. I don't see why proper feeling should prevent me from doing my proper job.'

'Quite right,' said Miss de Vine.

'But surely,' persisted Miss Barton, 'you must feel that terrible crimes and the sufferings of innocent suspects ought to be taken seriously, and not just made into an intellectual game.'

'I do take them seriously in real life. Everybody must. But should you say that anybody who had tragic experience of sex, for example, should never write an artificial drawing-room comedy?'

'But isn't that different?' said Miss Barton, frowning. 'There is a lighter side to love; whereas there's no lighter side to murder.'

'Perhaps not, in the sense of a comic side. But there is a purely intellectual side to the detection.'

'You did investigate a case in real life, didn't you? How did you feel about that?'

'It was very interesting.'

'And, in the light of what you knew, did you like the idea of sending a man to the dock and the gallows?'

'I don't think it's quite fair to ask Miss Vane that,' said the Dean. 'Miss Barton,' she added, a little apologetically, to Harriet, 'is interested in the sociological aspects of crime, and very eager for the reform of the penal code.'

'I am,' said Miss Barton. 'Our attitude to the whole thing seems to me completely savage and brutal. I have met so many murderers when visiting prisons; and most of them are very harmless, stupid people, poor creatures, when they aren't definitely pathological.'

'You might feel differently about it,' said Harriet, 'if you'd happened to meet the victims. They are often still stupider and more harmless than the murderers. But *they* don't make a public appearance. Even the jury needn't see the body unless they like. But I saw the body in that Wilvercombe case – I *found* it; and it was beastlier than anything you can imagine.'

'I'm quite sure you must be right about that,' said the Dean. 'The description in the papers was more than enough for me.'

'And,' went on Harriet to Miss Barton, 'you don't see the murderers actively engaged in murdering. You see them when they're caught and caged and looking pathetic. But the Wilvercombe man was a cunning, avaricious brute, and quite ready to go on and do it again, if he hadn't been stopped.'

'That's an unanswerable argument for stopping them,' said Phœbe, 'whatever the law does with them afterwards.'

'All the same,' said Miss Stevens, 'isn't it a little cold-blooded to catch murderers as an intellectual exercise? It's all right for the police – it's their duty.'

'In law,' said Harriet, 'it is every citizen's obligation – though most people don't know that.'

'And this man Wimsey,' said Miss Barton, 'who seems to make a hobby of it – does he look upon it as a duty or as an intellectual exercise?'

'I'm not sure,' said Harriet, 'but, you know, it was just as well for me that he did make a hobby of it. The police were wrong in my case – I don't blame them, but they were – so I'm glad it wasn't left to them.'

'I call that a perfectly noble speech,' said the Dean. 'If anyone had accused me of doing something I hadn't done, I should be foaming at the mouth.'

'But it's my job to weigh evidence,' said Harriet, 'and I can't help seeing the strength of the police case. It's a matter of a + b, you know. Only there happened to be an unknown factor.'

'Like that thing that keeps cropping up in the new kind of physics,' said the Dean. 'Planck's constant, or whatever they call it.'

'Surely,' said Miss de Vine, 'whatever comes of it, and whatever anybody feels about it, the important thing is to get at the facts.'

'Yes,' said Harriet; 'that's the point. I mean, the fact is that I *didn't* do the murder, so that my feelings are quite irrelevant. If I had done it, I should probably have thought myself thoroughly justified, and been deeply indignant about the way I was treated. As it is, I still think that to inflict the agonies of poisoning on anybody is unpardonable. The particular trouble I got let in for was as much sheer accident as falling off a roof.'

'I really ought to apologise for having brought the subject up at all,' said Miss Barton. 'It's very good of you to discuss it so frankly.'

'I don't mind – now. It would have been different just

after it happened. But that awful business down at Wilvercombe shed rather a new light on the matter – showed it up from the other side.'

'Tell me,' said the Dean, 'Lord Peter – what is he like?'

'To look at, do you mean? or to work with?'

'Well, one knows more or less what he looks like. Fair and Mayfair. I meant, to talk to.'

'Rather amusing. He does a good deal of the talking himself, if it comes to that.'

'A little merry and bright, when you're feeling off-colour?'

'I met him once at a dog-show,' put in Miss Armstrong unexpectedly. 'He was giving a perfect imitation of the silly-ass-about-town.'

'Then he was either frightfully bored or detecting something,' said Harriet, laughing. 'I know that frivolous mood, and it's mostly camouflage – but one doesn't always know for what.'

'There must be something behind it,' said Miss Barton, 'because he's obviously very intelligent. But is it only intelligence, or is there any genuine feeling?'

'I shouldn't,' said Harriet, gazing thoughtfully into her empty coffee-cup, 'accuse him of any lack of feeling. I've seen him very much upset, for instance, over convicting a sympathetic criminal. But he is really rather reserved, in spite of that deceptive manner.'

'Perhaps he's shy,' suggested Phœbe Tucker, kindly. 'People who talk a lot often are. I think they are very much to be pitied.'

'Shy?' said Harriet. 'Well, hardly. Nervy, perhaps – that blessed word covers a lot. But he doesn't exactly seem to call for pity.'

'Why should he?' said Miss Barton. 'In a very pitiful

world, I don't see much need to pity a young man who has everything he can possibly want.'

'He must be a remarkable person if he has that,' said Miss de Vine, with a gravity that her eyes belied.

'And he's not so young as all that,' said Harriet. 'He's forty-five.' (This was Miss Barton's age.)

'I think it's rather an impertinence to pity people,' said the Dean.

'Hear, hear!' said Harriet. 'Nobody likes being pitied. Most of us enjoy self-pity, but that's another thing.'

'Caustic,' said Miss de Vine, 'but painfully true.'

'But what I should like to know,' pursued Miss Barton, refusing to be diverted, 'is whether this dilettante gentleman does anything, outside his hobbies of detecting crimes and collecting books, and, I believe, playing cricket in his off-time.'

Harriet, who had been congratulating herself upon the way in which she was keeping her temper, was seized with irritation.

'I don't know,' she said. 'Does it matter? Why should he do anything else? Catching murderers isn't a soft job, or a sheltered job. It takes a lot of time and energy, and you may very easily get injured or killed. I dare say he does it for fun, but at any rate, he does do it. Scores of people must have as much reason to thank him as I have. You can't call that nothing.'

'I absolutely agree,' said the Dean. 'I think one ought to be very grateful to people who do dirty jobs for nothing, whatever their reason is.'

Miss Fortescue applauded this. 'The drains in my weekend cottage got stopped up last Sunday, and a most helpful neighbour came and unstopped them. He got quite filthy in the process and I apologised profusely, but he said I owed him no thanks, because he was inquisitive and liked drains. He may not have been telling the truth, but even if he was, I certainly had nothing to grumble about.'

'Talking of drains,' said the Bursar—

The conversation took a less personal and more anecdotal turn (for there is no chance assembly of people who cannot make lively conversation about drains), and after a little time, Miss Barton retired to bed. The Dean breathed a sigh of relief.

'I hope you didn't mind too much,' she said. 'Miss Barton is the most terribly downright person, and she was determined to get all that off her chest. She is a splendid person, but hasn't very much sense of humour. She can't bear anything to be done except from the very loftiest motives.'

Harriet apologised for having spoken so vehemently.

'I thought you took it all wonderfully well. And your Lord Peter sounds a most interesting person. But I don't see why you should be forced to discuss him, poor man.'

'If you ask me,' observed the Bursar, 'we discuss everything a great deal too much in this university. We argue about this and that and why and wherefore, instead of getting the thing done.'

'But oughtn't we to ask what things we want done,' objected the Dean.

Harriet grinned at Betty Armstrong, hearing the familiar academic wrangle begin. Before ten minutes had passed, somebody had introduced the word 'values.' An hour later they were still at it. Finally the Bursar was heard to quote:

'God made the integers; all else is the work of man.'

'Oh, bother!' cried the Dean. 'Do let's keep mathematics out of it. And physics. I cannot cope with them.'

'Who mentioned Planck's constant a little time ago?'

'I did, and I'm sorry for it. I call it a revolting little object.'

The Dean's emphatic tones reduced everybody to laughter, and, midnight striking, the party broke up.

'I am still living out of College,' said Miss de Vine to Harriet. 'May I walk across to your room with you?'

Harriet assented, wondering what Miss de Vine had to say to her. They stepped out together into the New Quad. The moon was up, painting the buildings with cold washes of black and silver whose austerity rebuked the yellow gleam of lighted windows behind which old friends reunited still made merry with talk and laughter.

'It might almost be term-time,' said Harriet.

'Yes.' Miss de Vine smiled oddly. 'If you were to listen at those windows, you would find it was the middle-aged ones who were making the noise. The old have gone to bed, wondering whether they have worn as badly as their contemporaries. They have suffered some shocks, and their feet hurt them. And the younger ones are chattering soberly about life and its responsibilities. But the women of forty are pretending they are undergraduates again, and finding it rather an effort. Miss Vane – I admired you for speaking as you did to-night. Detachment is a rare virtue, and very few people find it lovable, either in themselves or in others. If you ever find a person who likes you in spite of it – still more, because of it – that liking has very great value, because it is perfectly sincere, and because, with that person, you will never need to be anything but sincere yourself.'

'That is probably very true,' said Harriet, 'but what makes you say it?'

'Not any desire to offend you, believe me. But I imagine you come across a number of people who are disconcerted by the difference between what you do feel

41

and what they fancy you ought to feel. It is fatal to pay the smallest attention to them.'

'Yes,' said Harriet, 'but I am one of them. I disconcert myself very much. I never know what I do feel.'

'I don't think that matters, provided one doesn't try to persuade one's self into appropriate feelings.'

They had entered the Old Quad, and the ancient beeches, most venerable of all Shrewsbury institutions, cast over them a dappled and changing shadow-pattern that was more confusing than darkness.

'But one has to make some sort of choice,' said Harriet. 'And between one desire and another, how is one to know which things are really of overmastering importance?'

'We can only know that,' said Miss de Vine, 'when they have overmastered us.'

The chequered shadow dropped off them, like the dropping of linked silver chains. Each after each, from all the towers of Oxford, clocks struck the quarter-chime, in a tumbling cascade of friendly disagreement. Miss de Vine bade Harriet good night at the door of Burleigh Building and vanished, with her long, stooping stride beneath the Hall archway.

An odd woman, thought Harriet, and of a penetrating shrewdness. All Harriet's own tragedy had sprung from 'persuading herself into appropriate feelings' towards a man whose own feelings had not stood up to the test of sincerity either. And, all her subsequent instability of purpose had sprung from the determination that never again would she mistake the will to feel for the feeling itself. 'We can only know what things are of overmastering importance when they have overmastered us.' Was there anything at all that had stood firm in the midst of her indecisions? Well, yes; she had stuck to her work – and that in the face of what might have seemed overwhelming reasons for abandoning it and doing something different. Indeed, though she had shown cause that evening for this particular loyalty, she had never felt it necessary to show cause to herself. She had written what she felt herself called upon to write; and, though she was beginning to feel that she might perhaps do this thing better, she had no doubt that the thing itself was the right thing for her. It had overmastered her without her knowledge or notice, and that was the proof of its mastery.

She paced for some minutes to and fro in the quad, too restless to go in and sleep. As she did so, her eye was caught by a sheet of paper, fluttering untidily across the trim turf. Mechanically she picked it up and, seeing that it was not blank, carried it into Burleigh Building with her for examination. It was a sheet of common scribbling paper, and all it bore was a childish drawing scrawled heavily in pencil. It was not in any way an agreeable drawing – not at all the kind of thing that one would expect to find in a college quadrangle. It was ugly and sadistic. It depicted a naked figure of exaggeratedly feminine outlines, inflicting savage and humiliating outrage upon some person of indeterminate gender clad in a cap and gown. It was neither sane nor healthy; it was, in fact, a nasty, dirty and lunatic scribble.

Harriet stared at it for a little time in disgust, while a number of questions formed themselves in her mind. Then she took it upstairs with her into the nearest lavatory, dropped it in and pulled the plug on it. That was the proper fate for such things, and there was an end of it; but for all that, she wished she had not seen it.

43

3

They do best who, if they cannot but admit love, yet make it keep quarter, and sever it wholly from their serious affairs and actions of life; for if it check once with business it troubleth men's fortunes, and maketh men that they can no ways be true to their own ends.

FRANCIS BACON

SUNDAY, as the S.C.R. always declared, was invariably the best part of a Gaudy. The official dinner and speeches were got out of the way; the old students resident in Oxford, and the immensely busy visitors with only one night to spare had all cleared off. People began to sort themselves out, and one could talk to one's friends at leisure, without being instantly collared and hauled away by a collection of bores.

Harriet paid her visit of state to the Warden, who was holding a small reception with sherry and biscuits, and then went to call upon Miss Lydgate in the New Quad. The English tutor's room was festooned with proofs of her forthcoming work on the prosodic elements in English verse from Beowulf to Bridges. Since Miss Lydgate had perfected, or was in process of perfecting (since no work of scholarship ever attains a static perfection) an entirely new prosodic theory, demanding a novel and complicated system of notation which involved the use of twelve different varieties of type; and since Miss Lydgate's handwriting was difficult to read and her experience

44

in dealing with printers limited, there existed at that moment five successive revises in galley form, at different stages of completion,, together with two sheets in page-proof, and an appendix in typescript, while the important Introduction which afforded the key to the whole argument still remained to be written. It was only when a section had advanced to page-proof condition that Miss Lydgate became fully convinced of the necessity of transferring large paragraphs of argument from one chapter to another, each change of this kind naturally demanding expensive over-running on the page-proof, and the elimination of the corresponding portions in the five sets of revises; so that in the course of the necessary cross-reference, Miss Lydgate would be discovered by her pupils and colleagues wound into a kind of paper cocoon and helplessly searching for her fountain-pen amid the litter.

'I am afraid,' said Miss Lydgate, rubbing her head, in response to Harriet's polite inquiries as to the magnum opus, 'I am dreadfully ignorant about the practical side of bookmaking. I find it very confusing and I'm not at all clever at explaining myself to the printers. It will be a great help having Miss de Vine here. She has such an orderly mind. It's really an education to see her manuscript, and of course her work is far more intricate than mine – all sorts of little items out of Elizabethan pay-rolls and so on, all wonderfully sorted out and arranged in a beautiful clear argument. And she understands setting out footnotes properly, so that they fit in with the text. I always find that so difficult, and though Miss Harper is kindly doing all my typing for me, she really knows more about Anglo-Saxon than about compositors. I expect you remember Miss Harper. She was two years junior to you and took a second in English and lives in the Woodstock Road.'

Harriet said she thought footnotes were always very tiresome, and might she see some of the book.

'Well, if you're really interested,' said Miss Lydgate, 'but I don't want to bore you.' She extracted a couple of paged sheets from a desk stuffed with papers. 'Don't prick your fingers on that bit of manuscript that's pinned on. I'm afraid it's rather full of marginal balloons and interlineations, but you see, I suddenly realised that I could work out a big improvement in my notation, so I've had to alter it all through. I expect,' she added wistfully, 'the printers will be rather angry with me.'

Harriet privately agreed with her, but said comfortingly that the Oxford University Press was no doubt accustomed to deciphering the manuscripts of scholars.

'I sometimes wonder whether I am a scholar at all,' said Miss Lydgate. 'It's all quite clear in my head, you know, but I get muddled when I put it down on paper. How do you manage about your plots? All that timetable work with the alibis and so on must be terribly hard to bear in mind.'

'I'm always getting mixed up myself,' admitted Harriet. 'I've never yet succeeded in producing a plot without at least six major howlers. Fortunately, nine readers out of ten get mixed up too, so it doesn't matter. The tenth writes me a letter, and I promise to make the correction in the second edition, but I never do. After all, my books are only meant for fun; it's not like a work of scholarship.'

'You always had a scholarly mind, though,' said Miss Lydgate, 'and I expect you find your training a help in some ways, don't you? I used to think you might take up an academic career.'

'Are you disappointed that I didn't?'

'No, indeed. I think it's so nice that our students go out

and do such varied and interesting things, provided they do them well. And I must say, most of our students do do exceedingly good work along their own lines.'

'What are the present lot like?'

'Well,' said Miss Lydgate, 'we've got some *very* good people up, and they work surprisingly hard, when you think of all the outside activities they manage to carry on at the same time. Only sometimes I'm afraid they rather overdo it, and don't get enough sleep at night. What with young men and motor-cars and parties, their lives are so much fuller than they were before the War – even more so than in your day, I think. I'm afraid our old Warden would be very greatly disconcerted if she saw the college as it is to-day. I must say that I am occasionally a little startled myself, and even the Dean, who is so broad-minded, thinks a brassière and a pair of drawers rather unsuitable for sun-bathing in the quad. It isn't so much the male undergraduates – they're used to it – but after all, when the Heads of the men's colleges come to call on the Warden, they really ought to be able to get through the grounds without blushing. Miss Martin has really had to insist on bathing dresses – backless if they like, but proper bathing dresses made for the purpose, and not ordinary underwear.'

Harriet agreed that this seemed only reasonable.

'I am so glad you think so,' said Miss Lydgate. 'It is rather difficult for us of the older generation to hold the balance between tradition and progress – if it is progress. Authority as such commands very little respect nowadays, and I expect that is a good thing on the whole, though it makes the work of running any kind of institution more difficult. I am sure you would like a cup of coffee. No, really – I always have one myself about this time. Annie! – I think I hear my scout in the pantry –

Annie! Would you please bring in a second cup for Miss Vane.'

Harriet was fairly well satisfied already with eatables and drinkables, but politely accepted the refreshment brought in by the smartly uniformed maid. She made some remark, when the door was shut again, as to the great improvements made since her own day in the staff and service at Shrewsbury, and again heard the praise awarded to the new Bursar.

'Though I am afraid,' added Miss Lydgate, 'We may have to lose Annie from this staircase. Miss Hillyard finds her too independent; and perhaps she *is* a little absent-minded. But then, poor thing, she is a widow with two children, and really ought not to have to be in service at all. Her husband was in quite a good position, I believe, but he went out of his mind, or something, poor man, and died or shot himself, or something tragic of that kind, leaving her very badly off, so she was glad to take what she could. The little girls are boarded out with Mrs. Jukes – you remember the Jukeses, they were at the St. Cross Lodge in your time. They live down in St. Aldate's now, so Annie is able to go and see them at week-ends. It is nice for her and brings in a trifle extra for Mrs. Jukes.'

'Did Jukes retire? He wasn't very old, was he?'

'Poor Jukes,' said Miss Lydgate, her kind face clouding. 'He got into sad trouble and we were obliged to dismiss him. He turned out to be not quite honest, I am sorry to say. But we found him work as a jobbing gardener,' she went on more cheerfully, 'where he wouldn't be exposed to so much temptation in the matter of parcels and so on. He was a most hardworking man, but he would put money on horse-races, and so, naturally, he found himself in difficulties. It was so unfortunate for his wife.'

'She was a good soul,' agreed Harriet.

'She was terribly upset about it all,' went on Miss Lydgate. 'And so, to do him justice, was Jukes. He quite broke down, and there was a sad scene with the Bursar when she told him he must go.'

'Ye-es,' said Harriet. 'Jukes always had a pretty glib tongue.'

'Oh, but I'm sure he was really very sorry for what he'd done. He explained how he'd slipped into it, and one thing led to another. We were all very much distressed about it. Except, perhaps, the Dean – but then she never did like Jukes very much. However, we made a small loan to his wife, to pay off his debts, and they certainly repaid it most honestly, a few shillings each week. Now that he's *put* straight I feel sure he will *keep* straight. But, of course, it was impossible to keep him on here. One could never feel absolutely easy, and one must have entire confidence in the porter. The present man, Padgett, is most reliable and a very amusing character. You must get the Dean to tell you some of Padgett's quaint sayings.'

'He looks a monument of integrity,' said Harriet. 'He may be less popular, on that account. Jukes took bribes, you know – if one came in late, and that sort of thing.'

'We were afraid he did,' said Miss Lydgate. 'Of course, it's a responsible post for a man who isn't of very strong character. He'll do much better where he is.'

'You've lost Agnes, too, I see.'

'Yes – she was Head-Scout in your time; yes, she has left. She began to find the work too much for her and had to retire. I'm glad to say we were able to squeeze out a tiny pension for her – only a trifle, but as you know, our income has to be stretched very carefully to cover everything. And we arranged a little scheme by which she takes in odd jobs of mending and so on for the students and attends to the College linen. It all helps; and she's especially glad because that crippled sister of hers can do part of the work and contribute something to their small income. Agnes says the poor soul is so much happier now that she need not feel herself a burden.'

Harriet marvelled, not for the first time, at the untiring conscientiousness of administrative women. Nobody's interests ever seemed to be overlooked or forgotten, and an endless goodwill made up for a perennial scarcity of funds.

After a little more talk about the doings of past dons and students, the conversation turned upon the new Library. The books had long outgrown their old home in Tudor Building, and were at last to be adequately housed.

'And when that is finished,' said Miss Lydgate, 'we shall feel that our College Buildings are substantially complete. It does seem rather wonderful to those of us who remember the early days when we only had the one funny old house with ten students, and were chaperoned to lectures in a donkey-carriage. I must say we rather wept to see the dear old place pulled down to make way for the Library. It held so many memories.'

'Yes, indeed,' said Harriet, sympathetically. She supposed that there was no moment of the past upon which this experienced and yet innocent soul could not dwell with unaffected pleasure. The entrance of another old pupil cut short her interview with Miss Lydgate, and she went out, vaguely envious, to encounter the persistent Miss Mollison, primed with every remorseless detail of the clock incident. It gave her pleasure to inform Miss Mollison that Mr. A. E. W. Mason had hit on the same idea earlier. Unquenchable, Miss Mollison proceeded to question her victim eagerly about Lord Peter Wimsey, his manners, customs and appearance; and when Miss Mollison was driven away by Miss Schuster-Slatt, the irritation was little relieved, for Harriet was subjected to a long harangue about the sterilisation of the unfit, to which (it appeared) a campaign to encourage the marriage of the fit was a necessary corollary. Harriet agreed that intellectual women should marry and reproduce their kind; but she pointed out that the English husband had something to say in the matter and that, very often, he did not care for an intellectual wife.

Miss Schuster-Slatt said she thought English husbands were lovely, and that she was preparing a questionnaire to be circulated to the young men of the United Kingdom, with a view to finding out their matrimonial preferences.

'But English people won't fill up questionnaires,' said Harriet.

'Won't fill up questionnaires?' cried Miss Schuster-Slatt taken aback.

'No,' said Harriet, 'they won't. As a nation we are not questionnaire-conscious.'

'Well, that's too bad,' said Miss Schuster-Slatt. 'But I do hope you will join the British Branch of our League for the Encouragement of Matrimonial Fitness. Our President, Mrs. J. Poppelhinken, is a wonderful woman. You would so much like to meet her. She will be coming to Europe next year. In the meantime I am here to do propaganda and study the whole question from the angle of British mentality.'

'I'm afraid you will find it a very difficult job. I wonder,' added Harriet (for she felt she owed Miss Schuster-Slatt a riposte for her unfortunate observations of the night before), 'whether your intentions are as disinterested as you make out. Perhaps you are thinking of investigating the loveliness of English husbands in a personal and practical way.'

'Now you're making fun of me,' said Miss Schuster-Slatt, with perfect good-humour. 'No. I'm just the little worker-bee, gathering honey for the queens to eat.'

'How all occasions do inform against me!' muttered Harriet to herself. One would have thought that Oxford at least would offer a respite from Peter Wimsey and the marriage question. But although she herself was a notoriety, if not precisely a celebrity, it was an annoying fact that Peter was a still more spectacular celebrity, and that, of the two, people would rather know about him than about her. As regards marriage – well, here one certainly had a chance to find out whether it worked or not. Was it worse to be a Mary Attwood (*née* Stokes) or a Miss Schuster-Slatt? Was it better to be a Phœbe Bancroft (*née* Tucker) or a Miss Lydgate? And would all these people have turned out exactly the same, married or single?

She wandered into the J.C.R. which was empty, but for one drab and ill-dressed woman who sat desolately reading an illustrated paper. As Harriet passed, this woman looked up and said, rather tentatively, 'Hullo! it's Miss Vane, isn't it?'

Harriet racked her memory hastily. This was obviously someone very much senior to herself – she looked nearer fifty than forty. Who on earth?

'I don't suppose you remember me,' said the other. 'Catherine Freemantle.'

(Catherine Freemantle, good God! But she had been only two years senior to Harriet. Very brilliant, very smart, very lively and the outstanding scholar of her year. What in Heaven's name had happened to her?)

'Of course I remember you,' said Harriet, 'but I'm always so stupid about names. What have you been doing?'

Catherine Freemantle, it seemed, had married a farmer, and everything had gone wrong. Slumps and sickness and tithe and taxes and the Milk Board and the Marketing Board, and working one's fingers to the bone for a bare living and trying to bring up children – Harriet had read and heard enough about agricultural depression to know that the story was a common one enough. She was ashamed of being and looking so prosperous. She felt she would rather be tried for life over again than walk the daily treadmill of Catherine's life. It was a saga, in its way, but it was preposterous. She broke in rather abruptly upon a complaint against the hard-heartedness of the Ecclesiastical Commissioners.

'But Miss Freemantle – I mean, Mrs. – Mrs. Bendick – it's absurd that you should have to do this kind of thing. I mean, pick your own fruit and get up at all hours to feed poultry and slave like a navvy. Surely to goodness it would have paid far better for you to take on some kind of writing or intellectual job and get someone else to do the manual work.'

'Yes, it would. But at the beginning I didn't see it like that. I came down with a lot of ideas about the dignity of labour. And besides, at that time, my husband wouldn't have liked it much if I'd separated myself from his interests. Of course, we didn't think it would turn out like this.'

What damned waste! was all Harriet could say to herself. All that brilliance, all that trained intelligence, harnessed to a load that any uneducated country girl could have drawn, far better. The thing had its compensations, she supposed. She asked the question bluntly.

Worth it? said Mrs. Bendick. Oh, yes, it was certainly worth it. The job was worth doing. One was serving the land. And that, she managed to convey, was a service harsh and austere indeed, but a finer thing than spinning words on paper.

'I'm quite prepared to admit that,' said Harriet. 'A plough share is a nobler object than a razor. But if your natural talent is for barbering, wouldn't it be better to *be* a barber, and a good barber – and use the profits (if you like) to speed the plough? However grand the job may be, is it *your* job?'

'It's got to be my job now,' said Mrs. Bendick. 'One can't go back to things. One gets out of touch and one's brain gets rusty. If you'd spent your time washing and cooking for a family and digging potatoes and feeding cattle, you'd know that that kind of thing takes the edge off the razor. You needn't think I don't envy you people your easy life; I do. I came to the Gaudy out of sentiment, and I wish I'd stopped away. I'm two years older than you, but I look twenty. None of you cares in the least for my interests, and yours all seem to me to be mere beating the air. You don't seem to have anything too do with real life. You are going about in a dream.' She stopped speaking, and her angry voice softened. 'But it's a beautiful dream in its way. It seems queer to me now to think that once I was a scholar . . . I don't know. You may be right after all. Learning and literature have a way of outlasting the civilisation that made them.'

> 'The word and nought else
> in time endures.
> Not you long after,
> perished and mute
> will last, but the defter
> viol and lute,'

quoted Harriet. She stared vaguely out into the sunshine. 'It's curious – because I have been thinking exactly the same thing – only in a different connection. Look here! I admire you like hell, but I believe you're all wrong. I'm sure one should do one's own job, however trivial, and not persuade one's self into doing somebody else's, however noble.'

As she spoke, she remembered Miss de Vine; here was a new aspect of persuasion.

'That's all very well,' replied Mrs. Bendick. 'But one's rather apt to marry into somebody else's job.'

True; but Harriet was offered the opportunity of marrying into a job as near her own as made no great difference. And into money enough to make any job supererogatory. Again she saw herself unfairly provided with advantages which more deserving people desired in vain.

'I suppose,' she said, 'marriage is the really important job isn't it?'

'Yes, it is,' said Mrs. Bendick. 'My marriage is happy as marriages go. But I often wonder whether my husband wouldn't have been better off with another kind of wife. He never says so, but I wonder. I think he knows I miss – things, and resents it sometimes. I don't know why I should say this to you – I've never said it to anybody and I never knew you very well, did I?'

'No; and I haven't been very sympathetic, either. In fact, I've been disgustingly rude.'

'You have, rather,' said Mrs. Bendick. 'But you have such a beautiful voice to be rude in.'

'Good gracious!' said Harriet.

'Our farm's on the Welsh border, and the people all speak in the most hideous local sing-song. Do you know what makes me feel most home-sick here? The cultured speech. The dear old much-abused Oxford accent. That's funny, isn't it?'

'I thought the noise in Hall was more like a cage full of peacocks.'

'Yes; but out of Hall you can pick out the people who speak the right way. Lots of them don't, of course; but some do. You do; and you have a lovely voice into the bargain. Do you remember the old Bach Choir days?'

'Do I not? Do you manage to get any music on the Welsh border? The Welsh can sing.'

'I haven't much time for music. I try to teach the children.'

Harriet took advantage of this opening to make suitable domestic inquiries. She parted eventually from Mrs. Bendick with a depressed feeling that she had seen a Derby winner making shift with a coal-cart.

Sunday lunch in Hall was a casual affair. Many people did not attend it, having engagements in the town. Those who did, dropped in as and when they liked, fetched their food from the serving-hatches and consumed it in chattering groups wherever they could find seats. Harriet, having seized a plate of cold ham for herself, looked round for a lunch partner, and was thankful to see Phœbe Tucker just come in and being helped by the attendant scout to a portion of cold roast beef. The two joined forces, and sat down at the far end of a long table which ran parallel to the High and at right angles to the other tables. From there they commanded the whole room, including the High Table itself and the row of serving-hatches. As her eye wandered from one briskly occupied luncher to the next, Harriet kept on asking herself, Which? Which of all these normal and cheerful-looking women had dropped that unpleasant paper in the quad the night before? Because you never knew; and the trouble of not knowing was that you dimly suspected everybody. Haunts of ancient peace were all very well, but very odd things could crawl and creep beneath lichen-covered stones. The Warden in her great carved chair was bending her stately head and smiling at some jest of the Dean's. Miss Lydgate was attending, with eager courtesy, to the wants of a very old student indeed, who was almost blind. She had helped her stumbling feet up the three steps of the dais, had fetched her lunch from the hatch and was now putting salad on her plate for her. Miss Stevens, the Bursar, and Miss Shaw, the Modern Language Tutor, had collected about them three other old students of considerable age and attainments; their conversation was animated and apparently amusing. Miss Pyke, the Classical Tutor, was deep in a discussion with a tall, robust woman whom Phœbe Tucker had recognised and pointed out to Harriet as an eminent archæologist, and in a momentary flash of comparative silence, the Tutor's high voice rang out unexpectedly: 'The tumulus at Halos appears to be an isolated instance. The cist-graves of Theotokou . . .' Then the clamour again closed over the argument. Two other dons, whom Harriet did not recognise (they were new since her day) appeared from their gestures to be discussing millinery. Miss Hillyard, whose sarcastic tongue tended to isolate her from her colleagues, was slowly eating her lunch and glancing at a pamphlet she had brought in with her. Miss de Vine, arriving late, sat down beside Miss Hillyard and began to consume ham in a detached way with her eyes fixed on vacancy.

Then the Old Students in the body of the Hall – all types, all ages, all varieties of costume. Was it the curious round-shouldered woman in yellow djibbah and sandals, with her hair coiled in two snail-shells over her ears? Or the sturdy, curly-headed person in tweeds, with a mascu-line-looking waistcoat and the face like the back of a cab? Or the tightly-corseted peroxide of sixty, whose hat would better have suited an eighteen-year-old débutante at Ascot? Or one of the innumerable women with 'school-teacher' stamped on their resolutely cheery coun-tenances? Or the plain person of indeterminate age who sat at the head of her table with the air of a chairman of committee? Or that curious little creature dressed in unbecoming pink, who looked as though she had been carelessly packed away in a drawer all winter and put into circulation again without being ironed? Or that handsome, well-preserved business woman of fifty with the well-manicured hands, who broke into the conversa-tion of total strangers to inform them that she had just opened a new hairdressing establishment 'just off Bond Street'? Or that tall, haggard, tragedy-queen in black silk marocain who looked like Hamlet's aunt, but was ac-tually Aunt Beatrice who ran the Household Column in the *Daily Mercury*? Or the bony woman with the long horse-face who had devoted herself to Settlement work? Or even that unconquerably merry and bright little dumpling of a creature who was the highly-valued se-cretary of a political secretary and had secretaries under her? The faces came and went, as though in a dream, all animated, all inscrutable.

Relegated to a remote table at the lower end of the Hall were half-a-dozen present students, still lingering in Oxford for viva voce examinations. They babbled con-tinually among themselves, rather obviously ignoring the invasion of their college by all these quaint old freaks who were what they themselves would be in ten years' time, or twenty or thirty. They were a badly-turned-out bunch, Harriet thought, with an end-of-term crumpled appearance. There was an odd, shy-faced, sandy girl with pale eyes and restless fingers, and next to her a dark, beautiful one, for whose face men might have sacked cities, if it had had any sort of animation; and there was a gawky and unfinished-looking young person, very badly made up, who had a pathetic air of seeking to win hearts and never succeeding; and, most interesting of the bunch, a girl with a face like eager flame who was dressed with a maddening perversity of wrongness, but who one day would undoubtedly hold the world in her hands for good or evil. The rest were nondescript, as yet undifferentiated – yet nondescripts, thought Harriet, were the most difficult of all human beings to analyse. You scarcely knew they were there, until – bang! Something quite unexpected blew up like a depth charge and left you marvelling, to collect strange floating debris.

So the Hall seethed, and the scouts looked on impassively from the serving-hatches. 'And what they think of us all, God only knows,' mused Harriet.

'Are you plotting an exceptionally intricate murder?' demanded Phœbe's voice in her ear. 'Or working out a difficult alibi? I've asked you three times to pass the cruet.'

'I'm sorry,' said Harriet, doing as she was requested. 'I was meditating on the impenetrability of the human countenance.' She hesitated, on the verge of telling Phœbe about the disagreeable drawing, but her friend went on to ask some other question, and the moment passed by.

But the episode had troubled and unsettled her. Passing through the empty Hall, later in the day, she stopped to stare at the portrait of that Mary, Countess of Shrewsbury, in whose honour the college had been founded. The painting was a well-executed modern copy of the one in St. John's College, Cambridge, and the queer, strong-featured face, with its ill-tempered mouth and sidelong, secretive glance, had always exercised a curious fascination over her – even in her student days, a period when portraits of dead and gone celebrities exposed in public places incur more sarcastic comment than reverential consideration. She did not know, and indeed had never troubled to inquire, how Shrewsbury College had come to adopt so ominous a patroness. Bess of Hardwick's daughter had been a great intellectual, indeed, but something of a holy terror; uncontrollable by her menfolk, undaunted by the Tower, contemptuously silent before the Privy Council, an obstinate recusant, a staunch friend and implacable enemy and a lady with a turn for invective remarkable even in an age when few mouths suffered from mealiness. She seemed, in fact, to be the epitome of every alarming quality which a learned woman is popularly credited with developing. Her husband, the 'great and glorious Earl of Shrewsbury,' had purchased domestic peace at a price; for, said Bacon, there was 'a greater than he, which is my Lady of Shrewsbury.' And that, of course, was a dreadful thing to have said about one. The prospect seemed discouraging for Miss Schuster-Slatt's matrimonial campaign, since the rule seemed to be that a great woman must either die unwed, to Miss Schuster-Slatt's distress, or find a still greater man to marry her. And that limited the great woman's choice considerably, since, though the world of course abounded in great men, it contained a very much larger number of middling and common-place men. The great man, on the other hand, could marry where he liked, not being restricted to great women; indeed, it was often found sweet and commendable in him to choose a woman of no sort of greatness at all.

'Though of course,' Harriet reminded. herself, 'a woman may achieve greatness, or at any rate great renown, by merely being a wonderful wife and mother, like the mother of the Gracchi; whereas the men who have achieved great renown by being devoted husbands and fathers might be counted on the fingers of one hand. Charles I was an unfortunate king, but an admirable family man. Still, you would scarcely class him as one of the world's great fathers, and his children were not an unqualified success. Dear me! Being a great father is either a very difficult or a very sadly unrewarded profession. Wherever you find a great man, you will find a great mother or a great wife standing behind him – or so they used to say. It would be interesting to know how many great women have had great fathers and husbands behind them. An interesting thesis for research. Elizabeth Barrett? Well, she had a great husband, but he was great in his own right, so to speak – and Mr. Barrett was not exactly—The Brontes? Well, hardly. Queen Elizabeth? She had a remarkable father, but devoted helpfulness towards his daughters was scarcely his leading characteristic. And she was so wrong-headed as to have no husband. Queen Victoria? You might make a good deal out of poor Albert, but you couldn't do much with the Duke of Kent.'

Somebody passed through the Hall behind her; it was Miss Hillyard. With a mischievous determination to get some response out of this antagonistic personality, Harriet laid before her the new idea for a historical thesis.

'You have forgotten physical achievements,' said Miss Hillyard. 'I believe many female singers, dancers, Channel swimmers and tennis stars owe everything to their devoted fathers.'

'But the fathers are not famous.'

'No. Self-effacing men are not popular with either sex. I doubt whether even your literary skill would gain recognition for their virtues. Particularly if you select your women for their intellectual qualities. It will be a short thesis in that case.'

'Gravelled for lack of matter?'

'I'm afraid so. Do you know any man who sincerely admires a woman for her brains?'

'Well,' said Harriet, 'certainly not many.'

'You may think you know *one*,' said Miss Hillyard with a bitter emphasis. 'Most of us think at some time or other that we know *one*. But the man usually has some other little axe to grind.'

'Very likely,' said Harriet. 'You don't seem to have a very high opinion of men – of the male character, I mean, as such.'

'No,' said Miss Hillyard, 'not very high. But they have an admirable talent for imposing their point of view on society in general. All women are sensitive to male criticism. Men are not sensitive to female criticism. They despise the critics.'

'Do you, personally, despise male criticism?'

'Heartily,' said Miss Hillyard. 'But it does damage. Look at this University. All the men have been amazingly kind and sympathetic about the Women's Colleges. Certainly. But you won't find them appointing women to big University posts. That would never do. The women might perform their work in a way beyond criticism. But they are quite pleased to see us playing with our little toys.'

'Excellent fathers and family men,' murmured Harriet.

'In that sense – yes,' said Miss Hillyard, and laughed rather unpleasantly.

Something funny here, thought Harriet. A personal

history, probably. How difficult it was not to be embittered by personal experience. She went down to the J.C.R. and examined herself in the mirror. There had been a look in the History Tutor's eyes that she did not wish to discover in her own.

Sunday evening prayers. The College was undenominational, but some form of Christian worship was held to be essential to community life. The chapel, with its stained glass windows, plain oak panelling and unadorned Communion table was a kind of Lowest Common Multiple of all sects and creeds. Harriet, making her way towards it, remembered that she had not seen her gown since the previous afternoon, when the Dean had taken it to the S.C.R. Not liking to penetrate uninvited into that Holy of Holies, she went in search of Miss Martin, who had, it appeared, taken both gowns together to her own room. Harriet wriggled into the gown, one fluttering sleeve of which struck an adjacent table with a loud bang.

'Mercy!' said the Dean, 'what's that?'

'My cigarette-case,' said Harriet. 'I thought I'd lost it. I remember now. I hadn't a pocket yesterday, so I shoved it into the sleeve of my gown. After all, that's what these sleeves are for, aren't they?'

'Oh, my dear! Mine are always a perfect dirty-clothes bag by the end of term. When I have absolutely *no* clean handkerchiefs left in the drawer, my scout turns out my gown sleeves. My best collection worked out at twenty-two – but then I'd had a bad cold one week. Dreadful insanitary garments. Here's your cap. Never mind taking your hood – you can come back here for it. What have you been doing to-day? – I've scarcely seen you.'

Again Harriet felt an impulse to mention the unpleasant drawing, but again she refrained. She felt she was getting rather unbalanced about it. Why think about it at all? She mentioned her conversation with Miss Hillyard.

'Lor'!' said the Dean. 'That's Miss Hillyard's hobby-horse. Rubbidge, as Mrs. Gamp would say. Of *course* men don't like having their poor little noses put out of joint – who does? I think it's perfectly noble of them to let us come trampling over their University at all, bless their hearts. They've been used to being lords and masters for hundreds of years and they want a bit of time to get used to the change. Why, it takes a man months and *months* to reconcile himself to a new hat. And *just* when you're preparing to send it to the jumble sale, he says, "That's rather a nice hat you've got on, where did you get it?" And you say, "My dear Henry, it's the one I had last year and you said made me look like an organ-grinder's monkey." My brother-in-law says that *every* time and it does make my sister so wild.'

They mounted the steps of the chapel.

It had not, after all, been so bad. Definitely not so bad as one had expected. Though it was melancholy to find that one had grown out of Mary Stokes, and a little tiresome, in a way, that Mary Stokes refused to recognise the fact. Harriet had long ago discovered that one could not like people any the better, merely because they were ill, or dead – still less because one had once liked them very much. Some happy souls could go through life without making this discovery, and they were the men and women who were called 'sincere.' Still, there remained old friends whom one was glad to meet again, like the Dean and Phœbe Tucker. And really, everybody had been quite extraordinarily decent. Rather inquisitive and silly about 'the man Wimsey,' some of them, but no doubt with the best intentions. Miss Hillyard might be an exception, but there had always been something a little twisted and uncomfortable about Miss Hillyard.

As the car wound its way over the Chilterns, Harriet grinned to herself, thinking of her parting conversation with the Dean and Bursar.

'Be sure and write us a new book soon. And remember, if ever we get a mystery at Shrewsbury we shall call upon you to come and disentangle it.'

'All right,' said Harriet. 'When you find a mangled corpse in the buttery, send me a wire – and be sure to let Miss Barton view the body, and then she won't so much mind my hauling the murderess off to justice.'

And suppose they actually did find a bloody corpse in the buttery, how surprised they would all be. The glory of a college was that nothing drastic ever happened in it. The most frightful thing that was ever likely to happen was that an undergraduate should 'take the wrong turning.' The purloining of a parcel or two by a porter had been enough to throw the whole Senior Common Room into consternation. Bless their hearts, how refreshing and soothing and *good* they all were, walking beneath their ancient beeches and meditating on ὂν χαὶ μὴ ὂ and the finance of Queen Elizabeth.

'I've broken the ice,' she said aloud, 'and the water wasn't so cold after all. I shall go back, from time to time. I shall go back.'

She picked out a pleasant pub for lunch and ate with a good appetite. Then she remembered that her cigarette-case was still in her gown. She had brought the garment in with her on her arm, and, thrusting her hand down to the bottom of the long sleeve, she extracted the case. A piece of paper came out with it – an ordinary sheet of scribbling paper folded into four. She frowned at a disagreeable memory as she unfolded it.

There was a message pasted across it, made up of letters cut apparently from the headlines of a newspaper.

YOU DIRTY MURDERESS. AREN'T YOU
ASHAMED TO SHOW YOUR FACE?

'Hell!' said Harriet. 'Oxford, thou too?' She sat very still for a few moments. Then she struck a match and set light to the paper. It burned briskly, till she was forced to drop it upon her plate. Even then the letters showed grey upon the crackling blackness, until she pounded their spectral shapes to powder with the back of a spoon.

4

Thou canst not, Love, disgrace me half so ill,
  To set a form upon desirèd change,
As I'll myself disgrace: knowing thy will,
  I will acquaintance strangle and look strange,
Be absent from thy walks, and in my tongue
  Thy sweet beloved name no more shall dwell,
Lest I, too much profane, should do it wrong
  And haply of our old acquaintance tell.

WILLIAM SHAKESPEARE

THERE are incidents in one's life which, through some haphazard coincidence of time and mood, acquire a symbolic value. Harriet's attendance at the Shrewsbury Gaudy was of this kind. In spite of minor incongruities and absurdities, it had shown itself to have one definite significance; it had opened up to her the vision of an old desire, long obscured by a forest of irrelevant fancies, but now standing up unmistakable, like a tower set on a hill. Two phrases rang in her ears: the Dean's, 'It's the work you're doing that really counts'; and that one melancholy lament for eternal loss: 'Once, I was a scholar.'

'Time is,' quoth the Brazen Head; 'time was; time is past.' Philip Boyes was dead; and the nightmares that had haunted the ghastly midnight of his passing were gradually fading away. Clinging on, by blind instinct, to the job that had to be done, she had fought her way back to an insecure stability. Was it too late to achieve wholly the clear eye and the untroubled mind? And what, in that case, was she to do with one powerful fetter which still tied her ineluctably to the bitter past? What about Peter Wimsey?

During the past three years, their relations had been peculiar. Immediately after the horrible business that they had investigated together at Wilvercombe, Harriet – feeling that something must be done to ease a situation which was fast becoming intolerable – had carried out a long-cherished scheme, now at last made practicable by her increasing reputation and income as a writer. Taking a woman friend with her as companion and secretary, she had left England, and travelled slowly about Europe, staying now here, now there, as fancy dictated or a good background presented itself for a story. Financially the trip had been a success. She had gathered material for two full-length novels, the scenes laid respectively in Madrid and Carcassonne, and written a series of short stories dealing with detective adventures in Hitlerite Berlin, and also a number of travel articles; thus more than replenishing the treasury. Before her departure, she had asked Wimsey not to write. He had taken the prohibition with unexpected meekness.

'I see. Very well. *Vade in pacem*. If you ever want me, you will find the Old Firm at the usual stand.'

She had occasionally seen his name in the English papers, and that was all. At the beginning of the following June, she had returned home, feeling that, after so long a break, there should be little difficulty in bringing their relationship to a cool and friendly close. By this time he was probably feeling as much settled and relieved as she was. As soon as she got back to London, she moved to a new flat in Mecklenburg Square, and settled down to work at the Carcassonne novel.

A trifling incident, soon after her return, gave her the opportunity to test her own reactions. She went down to Ascot, in company with a witty young woman writer and her barrister husband – partly for fun and partly because she wanted to get local colour for a short story, in which an unhappy victim was due to fall suddenly dead in the Royal Enclosure, just at the exciting moment when all eyes were glued upon the finish of a race. Scanning those sacred precincts, therefore, from without the pale, Harriet became aware that the local colour included a pair of slim shoulders tailored to swooning-point and carrying a well-known parrot profile, thrown into prominence by the acute backward slant of a pale-grey topper. A froth of summer hats billowed about this apparition, so that it resembled a slightly grotesque but expensive orchid in a bouquet of roses. From the expressions of the parties, Harriet gathered that the summer hats were picking long-priced and impossible outsiders, and that the topper was receiving their instructions with an amusement amounting to hilarity. At any rate, his attention was well occupied.

'Excellent,' thought Harriet; 'nothing to trouble about there.' She came home rejoicing in the exceptional tranquillity of her own spirits. Three days later, while reading in the morning paper that among the guests at a literary luncheon-party had been seen 'Miss Harriet Vane, the well-known detective authoress,' she was interrupted by the telephone. A familiar voice said, with a curious huskiness and uncertainty:

'Miss Harriet Vane? . . . Is that you, Harriet? I saw you were back. Will you dine with me one evening?'

There were several possible answers; among them, the repressive and disconcerting 'Who is that speaking, please?' Being unprepared and naturally honest, Harriet feebly replied:

'Oh, thank you, Peter. But I don't know whether . . .'

'What?' said the voice, with a hint of mockery. '*Every* night booked from now till the coming of the Coqcigrues?'

'Of course not,' said Harriet, not at all willing to pose as the swollen-headed and much-run-after celebrity.

'Then say when.'

'I'm free to-night,' said Harriet, thinking that the shortness of the notice might force him to plead a previous engagement.

'Admirable,' said he. 'So am I. We will taste the sweets of freedom. By the way, you have changed your telephone number.'

'Yes; I've got a new flat.'

'Shall I call for you? Or will you meet me at Ferrara's at 7 o'clock?'

'At Ferrara's?'

'Yes. Seven o'clock, if that's not too early, Then we can go on to a show, if you care about it. Till this evening, then. Thank you.'

He hung up the receiver before she had time to protest. Ferrara's was not the place she would have chosen. It was both fashionable and conspicuous. Everybody who could get there, went there; but its charges were so high that, for the present at least, it could afford not to be crowded. That meant that if you went there you were seen. If one intended to break off a connection with anyone, it was perhaps not the best opening move to *afficher* one's self with him at Ferrara's.

Oddly enough, this would be the first time she had dined in the West End with Peter Wimsey. During the first year or so after her trial, she had not wanted to appear anywhere, even had she then been able to afford the frocks to appear in. In those days, he had taken her to

70

the quieter and better restaurants in Soho, or, more often, carried her off, sulky and rebellious, in the car to such roadside inns as kept reliable cooks. She had been too listless to refuse these outings, which had probably done something to keep her from brooding, even though her host's imperturbable cheerfulness had often been repaid only with bitter distressful words, Looking back, she was as much amazed by his patience as fretted by his persistence.

He received her at Ferrara's with the old, quick, side-long smile and ready speech, but with a more formal courtesy than she remembered in him. He listened with interest, and indeed with eagerness, to the tale of her journeyings abroad; and she found (as was to be expected) that the map of Europe was familiar ground to him. He contributed a few amusing incidents from his own experience, and added some well-informed comments on the conditions of life in modern Germany. She was surprised to find him so closely acquainted with the ins-and-outs of international politics, for she had not credited him with any great interest in public affairs. She found herself arguing passionately with him about the prospects of the Ottawa Conference, of which he appeared to entertain no very great hopes; and by the time they got to the coffee she was so eager to disabuse his mind of some perverse opinions about Disarmament that she had quite forgotten with what intentions (if any) she had come to meet him. In the theatre she contrived to remind herself from time to time that something decisive ought to be said; but the conversational atmosphere remained so cool that it was difficult to introduce the new subject.

The play being over, he put her into a taxi, asked what address he should give the driver, requested formal permission to see her home and took his seat beside her. This, to be sure, was the moment; but he was babbling pleasantly about the Georgian architecture of London. It was only as they were running along Guildford Street that he forestalled her by saying (after a pause, during which she had been making up her mind to take the plunge):

'I take it, Harriet, that you have no new answer to give me?'

'No, Peter. I'm sorry, but I can't say anything else.'

'All right. Don't worry. I'll try not to be a nuisance. But if you could put up with me occasionally, as you have done to-night, I should be very grateful to you.'

'I don't think that would be at all fair to you.'

'If that's the only reason, I am the best judge of that.' Then, with a return to his habitual self-mockery: 'Old habits die hard. I will not promise to reform altogether. I shall, with your permission, continue to propose to you, at decently regulated intervals – as a birthday treat, and on Guy Fawkes Day and on the Anniversary of the King's Accession. But consider it, if you will, as a pure formality. You need not pay the slightest attention to it.'

'Peter, it's foolish to go on like this.'

'And, of course, on the Feast of All Fools.'

'It would be better to forget all about it – I hoped you had.'

'I have the most ill-regulated memory. It does those things which it ought not to do and leaves undone the things it ought to have done, but it has not yet gone on strike altogether.'

The taxi drew up, and the driver peered round inquiringly. Wimsey handed her out and waited gravely while she disentangled her latch-key. Then he took it from her, opened the door for her, said good night and was gone.

Mounting the stone staircase, she knew that, as far as this situation was concerned, her flight had been useless. She was back in the old net of indecision and distress. In him, it appeared to have worked some kind of change; but it had certainly not made him any easier to deal with.

He had kept his promise, and troubled her very little. He had been out of Town a good deal, hard at work upon cases, some of which trickled through into newspaper columns, while others appeared to settle themselves in discreet obscurity. For six months he had himself been out of the country, offering no explanation except 'business.' One summer, he had been involved in an odd affair, which had led him to take a post in an Advertising Agency. He had found office life entertaining; but the thing had come to a strange and painful conclusion.

There had been an evening when he had turned up to keep a previously-made dinner appointment, but had obviously been unfit either to eat or talk. Eventually he had confessed to a splitting headache and a temperature and suffered himself to be personally conducted home. She had been sufficiently alarmed not to leave him till he was safely in his own flat and in the capable hands of Bunter. The latter had been reassuring: the trouble was nothing but reaction – of frequent occurrence at the end of a trying case, but soon over. A day or two later, the patient had rung up, apologised, and made a fresh appointment, at which he had displayed a quite remarkable effervescence of spirits.

On no other occasion had Harriet ever passed his threshold. Nor had he ever violated the seclusion of Mecklenburg Square. Two or three times, courtesy had moved her to invite him in; but he had always made some excuse, and she understood that he was determined to leave her that place, at least, free from any awkward associations. It was clear that he had no fatuous intention of making himself more valued by withdrawal: he had rather the air of trying to make amends for something. He renewed his offer of marriage on an average of once in three months, but in such a way as to afford no excuse for any outbreak of temperament on either side. One First of April, the question had arrived from Paris in a single Latin sentence, starting off dispiritedly, 'Num . . . ?' – a particle which notoriously 'expects the answer No.' Harriet, rummaging the Grammar book for 'polite negatives,' replied, still more briefly, 'Benigne.'

Looking back upon her visit to Oxford, Harriet found that it had had an unsettling effect. She had begun to take Wimsey for granted, as one might take dynamite for granted in a munitions factory. But the discovery that the mere sound of his name still had the power to provoke such explosions in herself – that she could so passionately resent, at one and the same time, either praise or blame of him on other people's lips – awakened a misgiving that dynamite was perhaps still dynamite, however harmless it might come to look through long custom.

On the mantelpiece of her sitting-room stood a note, in Peter's small and rather difficult writing. It informed her that he had been called away by Chief-Inspector Parker, who was in difficulties over a murder in the north of England. He must therefore regretfully cancel their appointment for that week. Could she oblige him by making use of the tickets, of which he had no time to dispose otherwise?

Harriet pinched her lips over that last cautious sentence. Ever since one frightful occasion, during the first year of their acquaintance, when he had ventured to send her a Christmas present and she, in an access of mortified pride, had returned it to him with a stinging rebuke, he had been careful never to offer anything that could possibly be looked upon as a material gift. Had he been wiped out of existence at any moment, there was nothing among her possessions to remind her of him. She now took up the tickets and hesitated over them. She could give them away, or she could go herself and take a friend. On the whole, she thought she would rather not sit through the performance with a kind of Banquo's ghost disputing possession of the next stall with somebody else. She put the tickets in an envelope, dispatched them to the married couple who had taken her to Ascot, and then tore the note across and deposited it in the waste-paper basket. Having thus disposed of Banquo, she breathed more freely, and turned to deal with the day's next nuisance.

This was the revision of three of her books for a new edition. The re-reading of one's own works is usually a dismal matter; and when she had completed her task she felt thoroughly jaded and displeased with herself. The books were all right, as far as they went; as intellectual exercises, they were even brilliant. But there was something lacking about them; they read now to her as though they had been written with a mental reservation, a determination to keep her own opinions and personality out of view. She considered with distaste a clever and superficial discussion between two of the characters about married life. She could have made a much better thing of that, if she had not been afraid of giving herself away. What hampered her was this sense of being in the middle of things, too close to things, pressed upon and bullied by reality. If she could succeed in standing aside from herself she would achieve self-confidence and a better control. That was the great possession in which – with all his limitations – the scholar could account himself blessed: the single eye, directed to the object, not dimmed nor distracted by private motes and beams. "Private, indeed?" muttered Harriet to herself, as she smacked her proofs irritably into brown paper.

'You not alone, when you are still alone,
O God, from you that I could private be!'

She was exceedingly glad that she had got rid of the theatre tickets.

So that when Wimsey eventually got back from his expedition north, she went to meet him in a belligerent spirit. He had asked her to dine with him. this time, at the Egotists' Club – an unusual venue. It was a Saturday night, and they had the room to themselves. She mentioned her Oxford visit and took the opportunity to recite to him a list of promising scholars, distinguished in their studies and subsequently extinguished by matrimony. He agreed mildly that such things did happen, far too often, and instanced a very brilliant painter who, urged on by a socially ambitious wife, had now become a slick machine for the production of Academy portraits.

'Sometimes, of course,' he went on dispassionately, 'the partner is merely jealous or selfish. But half the time it's sheer stupidity. They don't mean it. It's surprisin' how few people ever mean anything definite from one year's end to the other.'

'I don't think they could help it, whatever they meant. It's the pressure of other people's personalities that does the mischief.'

'Yes. Best intentions no security. They never are, of

course. You may say you won't interfere with another person's soul, but you do – merely by existing. The snag about it is the practical difficulty, so to speak, of not existing. I mean, here we all are, you know, and what are we to do about it?'

'Well, I suppose some people feel themselves called to make personal relationships their life-work. If so, it's all right for them. But what about the others?'

'Tiresome, isn't it?' he said, with a gleam of amusement that annoyed her. 'Do you think they ought to cut out human contacts altogether? It's not easy. There's always the butcher or the baker or the landlady or somebody one has to wrestle with. Or should the people with brains sit tight and let the people with hearts look after them?'

'They frequently do.'

'So they do.' For the fifth time he summoned the waiter to pick up Harriet's napkin for her. 'Why do geniuses make bad husbands, and all that? But what are you going to do about the people who are cursed with both hearts and brains?'

'I'm sorry I keep on dropping things; this silk's so slippery. Well, that's just the problem, isn't it? I'm beginning to believe they've got to choose.'

'Not compromise?'

'I don't think the compromise works.'

'That I should live to hear any person of English blood blaspheme against compromise!'

'Oh, I'm not all English. I've got some bits of Scotch and Irish tucked away somewhere.'

'That proves you're English. No other race ever boasts of being mongrel. I'm quite offensively English myself, because I'm one-sixteenth French, besides all the usual nationalities. So that compromise is in my blood.

However. Should you catalogue me as a heart or a brain?'

'Nobody,' said Harriet, 'could deny your brain.'

'Who denies it? And you may deny my heart, but I'm damned if you shall deny its existence.'

'You argue like an Elizabethan wit – two meanings under one word.'

'It was your word. You will have to deny something, if you intend to be like Cæsar's sacrifice.'

'Cæsar's . . .?'

'A beast without a heart. Has your napkin gone again?'

'No – it's my bag this time. It's just under your left foot.'

'Oh!' He looked round, but the waiter had vanished, 'Well,' he went on, without moving, 'it is the heart's office to wait upon the brain, but in view of—'

'Please don't trouble,' said Harriet, 'it doesn't matter in the least.'

'In view of the fact that I've got two cracked ribs, I'd better not try; because if I once got down I should probably never get up again.'

'Good gracious!' said Harriet. 'I thought you seemed a little stiff in your manner. Why on earth didn't you say so before, instead of sitting there like a martyr and inveigling me into misjudging you?'

'I don't seem able to do anything right,' he said plaintively.

'How did you manage to do it?'

'Fell off a wall in the most inartistic manner. I was in a bit of a hurry; there was a very plain-looking bloke on the other side with a gun. It wasn't so much the wall, as the wheelbarrow at the bottom. And it isn't really so much the ribs as the sticking-plaster. It's strapped as tight as hell and itches infernally.'

'How beastly for you. I'm so sorry. What became of the bloke with the gun?'

'Ah! I'm afraid personal complications won't trouble him any longer.'

'If luck had been the other way, I suppose they wouldn't have troubled *you* any longer?'

'Probably not. And then I shouldn't have troubled *you* any longer. If my mind had been where my heart was, I might have welcomed that settlement. But my mind being momentarily on my job, I ran away with the greatest rapidity, so as to live to finish the case.'

'We'll, I'm glad of that, Peter.'

'Are you? That shows how hard it is for even the most powerful brain to be completely heartless. Let me see. It is not my day for asking you to marry me, and a few yards of sticking-plaster are hardly enough to make it a special occasion. But we'll have coffee in the lounge, if you don't mind, because this chair is getting as hard as the wheelbarrow, and seems to be catching me in several of the same places.'

He got up cautiously. The waiter arrived and restored Harriet's bag, together with some letters which she had taken from the postman as she left the house and thrust into the outer pocket of the bag without reading. Wimsey steered his guest into the lounge, established her in a chair and lowered himself with a grimace into one corner of a low couch.

'Rather a long way down, isn't it?'

'It's all right when you get there. Sorry to be always presenting myself in such a decrepit state. I do it on purpose, of course, to attract attention and awaken sympathy; but I'm afraid the manoeuvre's getting rather obvious. Would you like a liqueur with the coffee or a brandy? Two old brandies, James.'

'Very good, my lord. This was found under the table in the dining-room, madam.'

'More of your scattered belongings?' said Wimsey, as she took the post-card; then, seeing her flush and frown of disgust. 'What it is?'

'Nothing,' said Harriet, pushing the ugly scrawl into her bag.

He looked at her.

'Do you often get that kind of thing?'

'What kind of thing?'

'Anonymous dirt.'

'Not very often now. I got one at Oxford. But they used to come by every post. Don't worry; I'm used to it. I only wish I'd looked at it before I got here. It's horrible of me to have dropped it about your club for the servants to read.'

'Careless little devil, aren't you? May I see it?'

'No, Peter; please.'

'Give it to me.'

She handed it to him without looking up. '*Ask your boy friend with the title if he likes arsenic in his soup. What did you give him to get you off?*' it inquired, disagreeably.

'God, what muck!' said he, bitterly. 'So that's what I'm letting you in for. I might have known it. I could hardly hope that it wasn't so. But you said nothing, so I allowed myself to be selfish.'

'It doesn't matter. It's just part of the consequences. You can't do anything about it.'

'I might have the consideration not to expose you to it. Heaven knows you've tried hard enough to get rid of me. In fact, I think you've used every possible lever to dislodge me, except that one.'

'Well, I knew you would hate it so. I didn't want to hurt you.'

'Didn't want to *hurt* me?'

She realised that this, to him, must sound completely lunatic.

'I mean that, Peter. I know I've said about every damnable thing to you that I could think of. But I have my limits.' A sudden wave of anger surged up in her. 'My God, do you really think that of me? Do you suppose there's no meanness I wouldn't stoop to?'

'You'd have been perfectly justified in telling me that I was making things more difficult for you by hanging round.'

'Should I? Did you expect me to tell you that you were compromising my reputation, when I had none to compromise? To point out that you'd saved me from the gallows, thank you very much, but left me in the pillory? To say, my name's mud, but kindly treat it as lilies? I'm not quite such a hypocrite as that.'

'I see. The plain truth is, that I am doing nothing but make life a little bitterer for you. It was generous of you not to say so.'

'Why did you insist on seeing that thing?'

'Because,' he said, striking a match and holding the flame to a corner of the post-card, 'while I am quite ready to take flight from plug-uglies with guns, I prefer to look other kinds of trouble in the face.' He dropped the burning paper on to the tray and crushed the ashes together, and she was again reminded of the message she had found in her sleeve. 'You have nothing to reproach yourself with – you didn't tell me this; I found it out for myself. I will admit defeat and say good-bye. Shall I?'

The club waiter set down the brandies. Harriet, with her eyes on her own hands, sat plaiting her fingers together. Peter watched her for some minutes, and then said gently:

'Don't look so tragic about it. The coffee's getting cold. After all, you know, I have the consolation that "not you but Fate has vanquished me." I shall emerge with my vanity intact, and that's something.'

'Peter, I'm afraid I'm not very consistent. I came here tonight with the firm intention of telling you to chuck it. But I'd rather fight my own battles. I – I –,' she looked up and went on quaveringly, 'I'm *damned* if I'll have you wiped out by plug-uglies or anonymous-letter writers!'

He sat up sharply, so that his exclamation of pleasure turned halfway into an anguished grunt.

'Oh, curse this sticking-plaster! . . . Harriet, you have got guts, haven't you? Give me your hand, and we'll fight on until we drop. Here! none of that. You can't cry in this club. It's never been done, and if you disgrace me like this, I shall get into a row with the Committee. They'll probably close the Ladies' Rooms altogether.'

'I'm sorry, Peter.'

'And *don't* put sugar in my coffee.'

Later in the evening, having lent a strong arm to extricate him, swearing loudly, from the difficult depths of the couch, and dispatched him to such rest as he might reasonably look for between the pains of love and sticking-plaster, she had leisure to reflect that if fate had vanquished either of them it was not Peter Wimsey. He knew too well the wrestler's trick of letting the adversary's own strength defeat itself. Yet she knew with certainty that if, when he had said, 'Shall I go?' she had replied with firm kindness, 'I'm sorry, but I think it would be better,' there would have been the desired end of the matter.

'I wish,' she said to the friend of the European trip, 'he would take a firm line of some kind.'

'But he has,' replied the friend, who was a clear-headed person. 'He knows what he wants. The trouble is that you don't. I know it isn't pleasant putting an end to things, but I don't see why he should do all your dirty work for you, particularly as he doesn't want it done. As for anonymous letters, it seems to me quite ridiculous to pay any attention to them.'

It was easy for the friend to say this, having no vulnerable points in her brisk and hard-working life.

'Peter says I ought to get a secretary and have them weeded out.'

'Well,' said the friend, 'that's a practical suggestion, anyway. But I suppose, since it's his advice, you'll find some ingenious reason for not taking it.'

'I'm not as bad as that,' said Harriet; and engaged the secretary.

So matters went on for some months. She made no further effort to discuss the conflicting claims of heart and brain. That line of talk led to a perilous exchange of personalities, in which he, with a livelier wit and better self-control, could always drive her into a corner without exposing himself. It was only by sheer brutal hacking that she could beat down his guard; and she was beginning to be afraid of those impulses to savagery.

She heard no news of Shrewsbury College in the interval, except that one day in the Michaelmas Term there was a paragraph in one of the more foolish London dailies about an 'Undergraduettes' Rag,' informing the world that somebody had made a bonfire of gowns in Shrewsbury Quad and that the 'Lady Head' was said to be taking disciplinary measures. Women, of course, were always news. Harriet wrote a tart letter to the paper, pointing out that either 'undergraduate' or 'woman student' would be seemlier English than 'undergraduette,' and that the correct method of describing Dr. Baring was 'the Warden.' The only result of this was to provoke a correspondence headed 'Lady Undergrads,' and a reference to 'sweet girl-graduates.'

She informed Wimsey – who happened to be the nearest male person handy for scarifying – that this kind of vulgarity was typical of the average man's attitude to women's intellectual interests. He replied that bad manners always made him sick; but was it any worse than headlining foreign monarchs by their Christian names, untitled?

About three weeks before the end of the Easter term, however, Harriet's attention was again called to college affairs in a way that was more personal and more disquieting.

February was sobbing and blustering its lachrymose way into March, when she received a letter from the Dean.

My dear Miss Vane,

I am writing to ask you whether you will be able to get up to Oxford for the opening of the New Library Wing by the Chancellor next Thursday. This, as you know, has always been the date for the official opening, though we had hoped that the buildings themselves would be ready for habitation at the beginning of this term. However, what with a dispute in the contractors' firm, and the unfortunate illness of the architect, we got badly held up, so that we shall only *just* be ready in time. In fact, the interior decoration of the ground floor isn't finished *yet*. – Still, we couldn't very well ask

Lord Oakapple to change the date, as he is such a busy man; and after all, the Library is the chief thing, and not the Fellows' sets, however badly they may need a home to go to, poor dears.

We are particularly anxious – I am speaking for Dr. Baring as well as myself – that you should come, if you *can* manage to find time, (though of course you have a lot of engagements). We should be very glad to have your advice about a most unpleasant thing that has been happening here. Not that one expects a detective novelist to be a practical policeman; but I know you have taken part in one real investigation, and I feel sure you know a lot more than we do about tracking down malefactors.

Don't think we are getting murdered in our beds! In some ways I'm not sure that a 'nice, clean murder' wouldn't be easier to deal with! The fact is, we are being victimised by a cross between a Poltergeist and a Poison-Pen, and you can imagine how disgusting it is for everybody. It seems that the letters started coming some time ago, but at first nobody took much notice. I suppose everyone gets vulgar anonymous communications from time to time; and though some of the beastly things didn't come by post, there's nothing in a place like this to prevent an outsider from dropping them at the Lodge or even inside the College. But wanton destruction of property is a different matter, and the last outbreak has been so abominable that something really must be done about it. Poor Miss Lydgate's *English Prosody* – you saw the colossal work in progress – has been defaced and mutilated in the most *revolting* manner, and some important manuscript portions completely destroyed, so that they will have to be done all over again. She was almost in tears, poor

85

dear – and the alarming thing is that it now looks as though somebody in college *must* be responsible. We suppose that some student must have a grudge against the S.C.R. – but it must be more than a grudge – it must be a very horrid kind of pottiness.

One can scarcely call in the police – if you'd seen some of the letters you'd realise that the less publicity the better, and you know how things get about. I dare say you noticed there was a wretched newspaper paragraph about that bonfire in the quad last November. We never discovered who did that, by the way; we thought, naturally, it was a stupid practical joke; but we are now beginning to wonder whether it wasn't all part of the same campaign.

So if you could possibly snatch time to give us the benefit of your experience, we should be exceedingly grateful. There must be *some* way of coping – this sort of persecution simply CAN'T GO ON. But it's an awfully difficult job to pin anything down in a place like this, with 150 students and all doors open everywhere night and day.

I am afraid this is rather an incoherent letter, but I'm feeling *that* put about, with the Opening looming ahead and *all* the entrance and scholarship papers blowing about me like leaves in Vallombrosa! Hoping very much to see you next Thursday,

Yours very sincerely,
LETITIA MARTIN.

Here was a pretty thing! Just the kind of thing to do the worst possible damage to University women – not only in Oxford, but everywhere. In any community, of course, one always ran the risk of harbouring somebody undesirable; but parents obviously would not care to send their young innocents to places where psychological oddities flourished unchecked. Even if the poison campaign led to no open disaster (and you never knew what people might be driven to under persecution) a washing of dirty linen in public was not calculated to do Shrewsbury any good. Because, though nine-tenths of the mud might not be thrown at random, the remaining tenth might quite easily be, as it usually was, dredged from the bottom of the well of truth, and would stick.

Who should know that better than herself? She smiled wryly over the Dean's letter. 'The benefit of your experience'; yes, indeed. The words had, of course been written in the most perfect innocence, and with no suspicion that they could make the galled jade wince. Miss Martin herself would never dream of writing abusive letters to a person who had been acquitted of murder, and it had undoubtedly never occurred to her that to ask the notorious Miss Vane for advice about how to deal with that kind of thing was to talk of rope in the house of the hanged. This was merely an instance of that kind of unworldly tactlessness to which learned and cloistered women were prone. The Dean would be horrified to know that Harriet was the last person who should, in charity, have been approached in the matter; and that, even in Oxford itself, in Shrewsbury College itself—

In Shrewsbury College itself: and at the Gaudy. That was the point. The letter she had found in her sleeve had been put there in Shrewsbury College *and at the Gaudy*. Not only that; there had been the drawing she had picked up in the quad. Was either, or were both of these, part only of her own miserable quarrel with the world? Or were they rather to be connected with the subsequent outbreak in the college itself? It seemed unlikely that Shrewsbury should have to harbour *two* dirty-minded lunatics in such quick succession. But if the two lunatics were one and the same lunatic, then the implication was an alarming one, and she herself must, at all costs, interfere at least so far as to tell what she knew. There did come moments when all personal felings had to be set aside in the interests of public service; and this looked like being one of them.

Reluctantly, she reached for the telephone and put a call through to Oxford. While she waited for it, she thought the matter over in this new light. The Dean had given no details about the poison letters, except that they suggested a grudge against the S.C.R. and that the culprit appeared to belong to the college. It was natural enough to attribute destructive ragging to the undergraduates; but then, the Dean did not know what Harriet knew. The warped and repressed mind is apt enough to turn and wound itself. 'Soured virginity' – 'unnatural life' – 'semi-demented spinsters' – 'starved appetites and suppressed impulses' – 'unwholesome atmosphere' – she could think of whole sets of epithets, ready-minted for circulation. Was this what lived in the tower set on the hill? Would it turn out to be like Lady Athaliah's tower in *Frolic Wind*, the home of frustration and perversion and madness? 'If thine eye be single, the whole body is full of light – but was it physically possible to have the single eye? 'What are you to do with the people who are cursed with both hearts and brains?' For them, stereoscopic vision was probably a necessity; as for whom was it not? (This was a foolish play on words, but it meant something.) Well, then, what about this business of choosing one way of life? Must one, after all, seek a compromise, merely to preserve one's sanity? Then one was doomed for ever to this miserable inner warfare, with confused noise and garments rolled in blood – and, she reflected drearily, with the usual war aftermath of a debased coinage, a lowered efficiency and unstable conditions of government.

At this point the Oxford call came through, with the Dean's voice sounding full of agitation. Harriet, after hurriedly disclaiming all pretence to detective ability in real life, expressed concern and sympathy and then asked the question that, to her, was of prime importance.

'How are the letters written?'

'That's *just* the difficulty. They're mostly done by pasting together bits out of newspapers. So, you see, there's no handwriting to identify.'

That seemed to settle it; there were not two anonymous correspondents, but only one. Very well, then:

'Are they merely obscene, or are they abusive or threatening too?'

'All three. Calling people names that poor Miss Lydgate, didn't know existed – the worst she knows being Restoration Drama – and threatening everything from public exposure to the gallows.'

Then the tower was Lady Athaliah's tower.

'Are they sent to anybody besides the S.C.R?'

'It's difficult to say, because people don't always come and tell you things. But I believe one or two of the students here have had them.'

'And they come sometimes by post and sometimes to the Lodge?'

'Yes. And they are beginning to come out on the walls now, and lately they've been pushed under people's doors at night. So it looks as though it *must* be somebody in college.'

'When did you get the first one?'

'The first one I *definitely* know about was sent to Miss de Vine last Michaelmas Term. That was her first term here, and of course, she thought it must be somebody who had a personal grudge against her. But several people got them shortly afterwards, so we decided it couldn't be that. We'd never had anything of that sort happening before, so just at present we're inclined to check up on the First Year students.'

The one set of people that it can't possibly be, thought Harriet. She only said, however:

'It doesn't do to take too much for granted. People may go on quite all right for a time, till something sets them off. The whole difficulty with these things is that the person generally behaves quite normally in other respects. It might be anybody.'

'That's true. I suppose it might even be one of ourselves. That's what's so horrible. Yes, I know – elderly virgins, and all that. It's awful to know that at any minute one may be sitting cheek by jowl with somebody who feels like that. Do you think the poor creature knows that she does it herself? I've been waking up with nightmares, wondering whether I didn't perhaps prowl round in my sleep, spitting at people. And my dear! I'm so terrified about next week! Poor Lord Oakapple, coming to open the Library, with venomous asps simply *dripping* poison over his boots! Suppose they send *him* something!'

'Well,' said Harriet, 'I think I'll come along next week. There's a very good reason why I'm not quite the right person to handle this, but on the other hand, I think I ought to come. I'll tell you why when we meet.'

'It's terribly good of you. I'm sure you'll be able to suggest something. I suppose you'll want to see all the specimens there are. Yes? Very well. Every fragment shall be cherished next our hearts. Do we handle them with the tongs for the better preservation of finger-prints?'

Harriet doubted whether finger-prints would be of much service, but advised that precautions should be taken on principle. When she had rung off, with the Dean's reiterated thanks still echoing from the other end of the line, she sat for a few moments with the receiver in her hand. Was there any quarter to which she might usefully turn for advice? There was; but she was not eager to discuss the subject of anonymous letters, still less the question of what lived in academic towers. She hung up resolutely, and pushed the instrument away.

She woke next morning with a change of heart. She had said that personal feeling ought not to stand in the way of public utility. And it should not. If Wimsey could be made useful to Shrewsbury College, she would use him. Whether she liked it or not, whether or not she had to put up with his saying 'I told you so,' she would put her pride in her pocket and ask him the best way to go about the job. She had her bath and dressed, glowing all the time with a consciousness of her own disinterested devotion to the cause of truth. She came into the sitting-room and enjoyed a good breakfast, still congratulating herself. As she was finishing her toast and marmalade, the secretary arrived, bringing in the morning's post. It contained a hurried note from Peter, sent off the previous evening from Victoria.

> Hauled off abroad again at a moment's notice. Paris first, then Rome. Then God knows. If you should want me – *per impossibile* – you can get me through the Embassies, or the post-office will forward letters from the Piccadilly address. In any case, you will hear from me on April 1st.
>
> P. D. B. W.

Post occasio calva. One could scarcely bombard the Embassies with letters about an obscure and complicated little affair in an Oxford college, especially when one's correspondent was urgently engaged in investigating something else all over Europe. The call must have been urgent, for the note was very ill and hastily written, and looked, in fact, as though it had been scribbled at the last moment in a taxi. Harriet amused herself with wondering whether the Prince of Ruritania had been shot, or the Master-Crook of the Continent had brought off a fresh *coup*, or whether this was the International Conspiracy to Wreck Civilisation with a Death-Ray – all those situations being frequent in her kind of fiction. Whatever it was all about, she would have to carry on unaided and find consolation in a proper independence of spirit.

5

Virginity is a fine picture, as *Bonaventure* calls it, a blessed thing in itself, and if you will believe a Papist, meritorious. And although there be some inconveniences, irksomeness, solitariness, etc., incident to such persons . . . yet they are but toys in respect, easily to be endured, if conferred to those frequent incumbrances of marriage. . . . And methinks sometime or other, amongst so many rich Bachelors, a benefactor should be found to build a monastical College for old, decayed, deformed, or discontented maids to live together in, that have lost their first loves, or otherwise miscarried, or else are willing howsoever to lead a single life. The rest, I say, are toys in respect, and sufficiently recompensed by those innumerable contents and incomparable privileges of Virginity.

ROBERT BURTON

HARRIET drove out to Oxford through a vile downpour of sleet that forced its way between the joints of the all-weather curtains and kept the windscreen-wiper hard at work. Nothing could have been less like her journey of the previous June; but the greatest change of all was in her own feelings. Then, she had been reluctant and uneasy; a prodigal daughter without the romantic appeal of husks and very uncertain of the fatted calf. Now, it was the College that had blotted its copybook and had called her in as one calls in a specialist, with little regard to private morals but a despairing faith in professional skill. Not that she cared much for the problem, or had very much hope of solving it; but she was able by now to look upon it as pure problem and a job to be done. In June, she had said to herself, at every landmark on the way: 'Plenty of time yet – thirty miles before I need begin to feel uncomfortable – twenty miles more respite – ten miles is still a good way to go.' This time, she was plainly and simply anxious to reach Oxford as quickly as possible – a state of mind for which the weather was perhaps largely responsible. She slithered down Headington Hill with no concern beyond a passing thought for possible skids, crossed Magdalen Bridge with only a caustic observation addressed to a shoal of push-cyclists, muttered 'Thank God!' as she reached the St. Cross Road gate, and said 'Good afternoon' cheerfully to Padgett the porter.

'Good afternoon, miss. Nasty day it's been. The Dean left a message, miss, as you was to be put in the Guest Room over at Tudor and she was out at a meeting but would be back for tea. Do you know the Guest Room, miss? That would be since your time, perhaps. Well, it's on the New Bridge, miss, between Tudor Building and the North Annexe where the Cottage used to be, miss, only of course that's all done away now and you has to go up by the main staircase past the West Lecture Room, miss, what used to be the Junior Common Room, miss, before they made the new entrance and moved the stairs, and then turn right and it's half-way along the corridor. You can't mistake it, miss. Any of the scouts would show you, miss, if you can find one about just now.'

'Thank you, Padgett. I'll find it all right. I'll just take the car round to the garage.'

'Don't you trouble, miss. Raining cats and dogs, it is. I'll take her round for you later on. She won't 'urt in the street for a bit. And I'll have your bag up in half a moment, miss; only I can't leave the gate till Mrs. Padgett comes back from running over to the Buttery, or I'm sure I'd show you the way myself.'

Harriet again begged him not to trouble.

'Oh, it's quite easy when you know, miss. But what with pulling down here and building up there and altering this and that, there's a many of our old ladies gets quite lost when they comes back to see us.'

'I won't get lost, Padgett.' And she had, in fact, no difficulty in finding the mysterious Guest Room by the shifting stair and the non-existent Cottage. She noticed that its windows gave her a commanding view over the Old Quad, though the New Quad was out of range and the greater part of the new Library Building hidden by the Annexe Wing of Tudor.

Having had tea with the Dean, Harriet found herself seated in the Senior Common Room at an informal meeting of the Fellows and Tutors, presided over by the Warden. Before her lay the documents in the case – a pitiful little heap of dirty imaginations. Fifteen or so of them had been collected for inspection. There were half-a-dozen drawings, all much of the same kind as the one she had picked up on the Gaudy night. There were a number of messages, addressed to various members of the S.C.R., and informing them, with various disagreeable epithets, that their sins would find them out, that they were not fit for decent society and that unless they left men alone, various unpleasing things would occur to them. Some of these missives had come by post; others had been found on window-sills or pushed under doors; all were made up of the same cut-out letters pasted on sheets of rough scribbling-paper. Two other messages had been sent to undergraduates: one, to the Senior Student, a very well-bred and inoffensive young woman who was reading Greats; the other to a Miss Flaxman, a brilliant Second-Year scholar. The latter was rather more definite than most of the letters, in that it mentioned a name: 'IF YOU DON'T LEAVE YOUNG FARRINGDON ALONE,' it said, adding an abusive term, 'IT WILL BE THE WORSE FOR YOU.'

The remaining items in the collection consisted, first, of a small book written by Miss Barton: *The Position of Women in the Modern State*. The copy belonged to the Library, and had been discovered one Sunday morning merrily burning on the fire in the Junior Common Room in Burleigh House. Secondly, there were the proofs and manuscript of Miss Lydgate's *English Prosody*. The history of these was as follows. Miss Lydgate had at length transferred all her corrections in the text to the final page-proof and destroyed all the earlier revises. She had then handed the proofs, together with the manuscript of the Introduction, to Miss Hillyard, who had undertaken to go through them with a view to verifying certain historical allusions. Miss Hillyard stated that she had received them on a Saturday morning and taken them to her own rooms (which were on Miss Lydgate's staircase and on the floor immediately above). She had subsequently taken them into the Library (that is to say, the Library in Tudor, now about to be superseded by the New Library), and had there worked upon them for some time with the aid of some reference books. She said she had been alone in the Library at the time, except for someone, whom she had never seen, who was moving about in the bay at the far end. Miss Hillyard had then gone out to lunch in Hall, leaving the papers on the Library table. After lunch, she had gone on the river to put a group of First-Year students through a sculling-test. On her return to the Library after tea to resume work, she found that the papers had disappeared from the table. She had at first supposed that Miss Lydgate had come in and, seeing them there, carried them off to make a few more of her celebrated corrections. She went to Miss Lydgate's rooms to ask about them, but Miss Lydgate was not there. She said she had been a little surprised that Miss Lydgate should have removed them without leaving a note to say what she had done; but she was not actually alarmed until, knocking again at Miss Lydgate's door shortly before Hall, she suddenly remembered that the English Tutor had said that she was leaving before lunch to spend a couple of nights in Town. An inquiry was, of course, immediately set on foot, but nothing had come of it until, on the Monday morning, just after Chapel, the missing proofs had been found sprawled over the table and floor of the Senior Common Room. The finder had been Miss Pyke, who had been the first don to enter the room that morning. The scout responsible for dusting the S.C.R. was confident that nothing of the kind had been there before Chapel; the appearance of the papers suggested that they had been tossed into the room by somebody passing the window, which would have been an easy enough thing for anybody to do. Nobody, however, had seen anything suspicious, though the entire college, particularly late-comers to Chapel and those students whose windows overlooked the S.C.R., had been interrogated.

The proofs, when found, had been defaced throughout with thick copying-ink. All the manuscript alterations in the margins had been heavily blacked out and on certain pages offensive epithets had been written in rough block capitals. The manuscript Introduction had been burnt, and a triumphant note to this effect pasted in large printed letters across the first sheet of the proofs.

This was the news with which Miss Hillyard had had to

face Miss Lydgate when the latter returned to College immediately after breakfast on the Monday. Some effort had been made to find out when, exactly, the proofs had been taken from the Library. The person in the far bay had been found, and turned out to have been Miss Burrows, the Librarian. She, however, said that she had not seen Miss Hillyard, who had come in after her and gone to lunch before her. Nor had she seen, or at any rate noticed, the proofs lying on the table. The Library had not been very much used on the Saturday afternoon; but a student who had gone in there at about 3 o'clock to consult Ducange's Late Latin Dictionary, in the bay where Miss Hillyard had been working, had said that she had taken the volume down and laid it on the table, and she *thought* that if the proofs had been there, she would have noticed them. This student was a Miss Waters, a Second-Year French student and a pupil of Miss Shaw's.

A slight awkwardness had been introduced into the situation by the Bursar, who had seen Miss Hillyard apparently entering the Senior Common Room just before Chapel on Monday morning. Miss Hillyard explained that she had only gone as far as the door, thinking that she had left her gown there; but remembering in time that she had hung it up in the cloak-room of Queen Elizabeth Building, had come out immediately without entering the S.C.R. She demanded, angrily, whether the Bursar suspected her of having done the damage herself. Miss Stevens said, 'Of course not, but if Miss Hillyard had gone in, she could have seen whether the proofs were already in the room, and so provided a *terminus a quo*, or alternatively *ad quem*, for that part of the investigation.'

This was really all the material evidence available, except that a large bottle of copying-ink had disappeared from the office of the College Secretary and Treasurer,

Miss Allison. The Treasurer had not had occasion to enter the office during Saturday afternoon or Sunday; she could only say that the bottle had been in its usual place at one o'clock on Saturday. She did not lock the door of her office at any time, as no money was kept there, and all important papers were locked up in a safe. Her assistant did not live in college and had not been in during the week-end.

The only other manifestation of any importance had been an outbreak of unpleasant scribbling on the walls of passages and lavatories. These inscriptions had, of course, been effaced as soon as noticed and were not available.

It had naturally been necessary to take official notice of the loss and subsequent disfigurement of Miss Lydgate's proofs. The whole college had been addressed by Dr. Baring and asked whether anybody had any evidence to bring forward. Nobody offered any; and the Warden had thereupon issued a warning against making the matter known outside the college, together with an intimation that anybody sending indiscreet communications to either the University papers or the daily press might find herself liable to severe disciplinary action. Delicate interrogation among the other Women's Colleges had made it fairly clear that the nuisance was, so far, confined to Shrewsbury.

Since nothing, so far, had come to light to show that the persecution had started before the previous October, suspicion rather naturally centred upon the First-Year students. It was when Dr. Baring had reached this point of her exposition that Harriet felt obliged to speak.

'I am afraid, Warden,' she said, 'that I am in a position to rule out the First Year, and in fact the majority of the present students altogether.'

And she proceeded, with some discomfort, to tell the meeting about the two specimens of the anonymous writer's work that she had discovered at and after the Gaudy.

'Thank you, Miss Vane,' said the Warden, when she had finished. 'I am extremely sorry that you should have had so unpleasant an experience. But your information of course narrows the field a great deal. If the culprit is someone who attended the Gaudy, it must have been either one of the few present students who were then waiting up for vivas, or one of the scouts, or – one of ourselves.'

'Yes. I'm afraid that is the case.'

The dons looked at one another.

'It cannot, of course,' went on Dr. Baring, 'be an old student, since the outrages have continued in the interim; nor can it be an Oxford resident outside the college, since we know that certain papers have been pushed under people's doors during the night, to say nothing of inscriptions on the walls which have been proved to have come into existence between, say, midnight and the next morning. We therefore have to ask ourselves who, among the comparatively small number of persons in the three categories I have mentioned can possibly be responsible.'

'Surely,' said Miss Burrows, 'it is far more likely to be one of the scouts than one of ourselves. I can scarcely imagine that a member of this Common Room would be capable of anything so disgusting. Whereas that class of persons—'

'I think that is a very unfair observation,' said Miss Barton. 'I feel strongly that we ought not to allow ourselves to be blinded by any sort of class prejudice.'

'The scouts are all women of excellent character, so far as I know,' said the Bursar, 'and you may be sure that I take very great care in engaging the staff. The scrubbing-women and others who come in by the day are, naturally, excluded from suspicion. Also, you will remember that the greater number of the scouts sleep in their own wing. The outer door of this is locked at night and the ground-floor windows have bars. Besides this, there are the iron gates which cut off the back entrance from the rest of the college buildings. The only possible communication at night would be by way of the buttery, which is also locked. The Head Scout has the keys. Carrie has been with us fifteen years, and is presumably to be trusted.'

'I have never understood,' said Miss Barton acidly, 'why the unfortunate servants should be locked up at night as though they were dangerous wild beasts, when everybody else is free to come and go at pleasure. However, as things are, it seems to be just as well for them.'

'The reason, as you very well know,' replied the Bursar, 'is that there is no porter at the tradesmen's entrance, and that it would not be difficult for un-authorised persons to climb over the outer gates. And I will remind you that *all* the ground-floor windows that open directly upon the street or the kitchen yard are barred, including those belonging to the Fellows. As for the locking of the buttery, I may say that it is done to prevent the students from raiding the pantry as they frequently did in my predecessor's time, or so I am informed. The precautions are taken quite as much against the members of the college as against the scouts.'

'How about the scouts in the other buildings?' asked the Treasurer.

'There are perhaps two or three occupying odd bed-rooms in each building,' replied the Bursar. 'They are all reliable women who have been in our service since before my time. I haven't the list here at the moment; but I think there are three in Tudor, three or four in Queen Elizabeth, and one in each of the four little dormer-rooms in the New Quad. Burleigh is all students' rooms. And there is, of course, the Warden's own domestic staff, besides the Infirmary maid who sleeps there with the Infirmarian.'

'I will take steps,' said Dr. Baring, 'to make sure that no member of my own household is at fault. You, Bursar, had better do the same by the Infirmary. And, in their own interests, the scouts sleeping in College had better be subjected to some kind of supervision.'

'Surely, Warden—' began Miss Barton hotly.

'In their own interests,' said the Warden, with quiet emphasis. 'I entirely agree with you, Miss Barton, that there is no greater reason for suspecting them than for suspecting one of ourselves. But that is the more reason why they should be cleared completely and at once.'

'By all means,' said the Bursar.

'As to the method used,' went on the Warden, 'to keep check upon the scouts, or upon anybody else, I feel strongly that the fewer people who know anything about that, the better. Perhaps Miss Vane will be able to put forward a good suggestion, in confidence to myself, or to . . .'

'Exactly,' said Miss Hillyard, grimly. 'To whom? So far as I can see, nobody among us can be taken on trust.'

'That is unfortunately quite true,' said the Warden, 'and the same thing applies to myself. While I need not say that I have every confidence in the senior members of the College, both jointly and severally, it appears to me that, exactly as in the case of the scouts, it is of the highest importance that we should be safeguarded, in our own interests. What do you say, Sub-Warden?'

'Certainly,' replied Miss Lydgate. 'There should be no

distinction made at all. I am perfectly willing to submit to any measure of supervision that may be recommended.'

'Well, you at least can scarcely be suspected,' said the Dean. 'You are the greatest sufferer.'

'We have nearly all suffered to some extent,' said Miss Hillyard.

'I am afraid,' said Miss Allison, 'we shall have to allow for what I understand is the well-known practice of these unfortunate – um, ah – anonymous-letter writers, of sending letters to themselves to distract suspicion. Isn't that so, Miss Vane?'

'Yes.' said Harriet, bluntly. 'It seems unlikely, on the face of it, that anybody would do herself the kind of material damage Miss Lydgate has received; but if we once begin to make distinctions it is difficult to know where to stop. I don't think anything but a plain alibi ought to be accepted as evidence.'

'And I have no alibi,' said Miss Lydgate. 'I did not leave College on the Saturday till after Miss Hillyard had gone to lunch. What is more, I went over to Tudor during lunch-time, to return a book to Miss Chilperic's room before I left; so that I might quite easily have taken the manuscript from the Library then.'

'But you have an alibi for the time when the proofs were put in the S.C.R.,' said Harriet.

'No,' said Miss Lydgate; 'not even that, I came by the early train and arrived when everybody was in Chapel. I should have had to be rather quick to run across and throw the proofs into the S.C.R. and be back in my rooms again before the discovery was made; but I suppose I *could* have done it. In any case, I would much rather be treated on the same footing as other people.'

'Thank you,' said the Warden. 'Is there anybody who does not feel the same?'

'I am sure we must all feel the same,' said the Dean. 'But there is one set of people we are overlooking.'

'The present students who were up at the Gaudy,' said the Warden, 'Yes; how about them?'

'I forget exactly who they were,' said the Dean, 'but I think most of them were Schools people, and have since gone down. I will look up the lists and see. Oh, and, of course, there was Miss Cattermole who was up for Responsions – for the second time of asking.'

'Ah!' said the Bursar. 'Yes. Cattermole.'

'And that woman who was taking Mods – what's her name? Hudson, isn't it? Wasn't she still up?'

'Yes,' said Miss Hillyard, 'she was.'

'They will be in their Second and Third Years now, I suppose,' said Harriet. 'By the way, is it known who "young Farringdon" is, in this note addressed to Miss Flaxman?'

'There's the point,' said the Dean. 'Young Farringdon is an undergraduate of – New College, I think it is – who was engaged to Cattermole when they both came up, but is now engaged to Flaxman.'

'Is he, indeed?'

'Mainly, I understand, or partly, in consequence of that letter. I am told that Miss Flaxman accused Miss Cattermole of sending it and showed it to Mr. Farringdon; with the result that the gentleman broke off the engagement and transferred his affections to Flaxman.'

'Not pretty,' said Harriet.

'No. But I don't think the Cattermole engagement was ever anything much more than a family arrangement, and that the new deal was not much more than an open recognition of the *fait accompli*. I gather there has been some feeling in the Second Year about the whole thing.'

'I see,' said Harriet.

'The question remains,' said Miss Pyke, 'what steps do we propose to take in the matter? We have asked Miss Vane's advice, and personally I am prepared to agree – particularly in view of what we have heard this evening – that it is abundantly necessary that some outside person should lend us assistance. To call in the police authorities is clearly undesirable. But may I ask whether, at this stage, it is suggested that Miss Vane should personally undertake an investigation? Or alternatively, would she propose our placing the matter in the hands of a private inquiry agent? Or what?'

'I feel I am in a very awkward position,' said Harriet. 'I am willing to give any help I can; but you do realise, don't you, that this kind of inquiry is apt to take a long time, especially if the investigator has to tackle it single-handed. A place like this, where people run in and out everywhere at all hours is almost impossible to police or patrol efficiently. It would need quite a little squad of inquiry agents – and even if you disguised them as scouts or students a good deal of awkwardness might arise.'

'Is there no material evidence to be obtained from an examination of the documents themselves?' asked Miss Pyke. 'Speaking for myself, I am quite ready to have my finger-prints taken or to undergo any other kind of pre-cautionary measure that may be considered necessary.'

'I'm afraid,' said Harriet, 'the evidence of finger-prints isn't quite so easy a matter as we make it appear in books. I mean, we could take finger-prints, naturally, from the S.C.R. and, possibly, from the scouts – though they wouldn't like it much. But I should doubt very much whether rough scribbling-paper like this would show distinguishable prints. And besides—'

'Besides,' said the Dean, 'every malefactor nowadays knows enough about finger-prints to wear gloves.'

'And,' said Miss de Vine, speaking for the first time, and with a slightly grim emphasis, 'if we didn't know before, we know it now.'

'Great Scott!' cried the Dean, impulsively, 'I'd forgotten all about it's being us.'

'You see what I meant,' said the Warden, 'when I said that it was better not to discuss methods of investigation too freely.'

'How many people have handled all these documents already?' inquired Harriet.

'Ever so many, I should think,' said the Dean.

'But could not a search be made for—' began Miss Chilperic. She was the most junior of the dons; a small, fair and timid young woman, assistant-tutor in English Language and Literature, and remarkable chiefly for being engaged to be married to a junior don at another college. The Warden interrupted her.

'Please, Miss Chilperic. That is the kind of suggestion that ought not to be made here. It might convey a warning.'

'This,' said Miss Hillyard, 'is an intolerable position.' She looked angrily at Harriet, as though she were responsible for the position; which, in a sense, she was.

'It seems to me,' said the Treasurer, 'that, now that we have asked Miss Vane to come and give us her advice, it is impossible for us to take it, or even to hear what it is. The situation is rather Gilbertian.'

'We shall have to be frank up to a point,' said the Warden. 'Do you advise the private inquiry agent, Miss Vane?'

'Not the ordinary sort,' said Harriet; 'you wouldn't like them at all. But I do know of an organisation where you could get the right type of person and the greatest possible discretion.'

For she had remembered that there was a Miss Katherine Climpson, who ran what was ostensibly a Typing Bureau but was in fact a useful organisation of women engaged in handling odd little investigations. The Bureau was self-supporting, though it had, she knew, Peter Wimsey's money behind it. She was one of the very few people in the Kingdom who did know that.

The Treasurer coughed.

'Fees paid to a Detective Agency,' she observed, 'will have an odd appearance in the Annual Audit.'

'I think that might be arranged,' said Harriet. 'I know the organisation personally. A fee might not be necessary.'

'That,' said the Warden, 'would not be right. The fees would, of course, have to be paid. I would gladly be personally responsible.'

'That would not be right either,' said Miss Lydgate. 'We certainly should not like that.'

'Perhaps,' suggested Harriet, 'I could find out what the fees were likely to be.' She had, in fact, no idea how this part of the business was worked.

'There would be no harm in inquiring,' said the Warden. 'In the meantime—'

'If I may make a suggestion,' said the Dean, 'I should propose, Warden, that the evidence should be handed over to Miss Vane, as she is the only person in this room who cannot possibly come under suspicion. Perhaps she would like to sleep upon the matter and make a report to you in the morning. At least, not in the morning, because of Lord Oakapple and the Opening; but at some time during to-morrow.'

'Very well,' said Harriet, in response to an inquiring look from the Warden. 'I will do that. And if I can think of any way in which I can be helpful, I'll do my best.'

The Warden thanked her. 'We all appreciate,' she added, 'the extreme awkwardness of the situation, and I am sure we shall all do what we can to co-operate in getting the matter cleared up. And I should like to say this: whatever any of us may think or feel, it is of the very greatest importance that we should dismiss, as far as possible, all vague suspicions from our minds, and be particularly careful how we may say anything that might be construed as an accusation against anybody at all. In a close community of this kind, nothing can be more harmful than an atmosphere of mutual distrust. I repeat that I have the very greatest confidence in every Senior Member of the College. I shall endeavour to keep an entirely open mind, and I shall look to all my colleagues to do the same.'

The dons assented; and the meeting broke up.

'*Well!*' said the Dean, as she and Harriet turned into the New Quad, 'that is the most uncomfortable meeting I have ever had to sit through. My dear, you *have* thrown a bombshell into our midst!'

'I'm afraid so. But what could I do?'

'You couldn't possibly have done anything else. Oh, dear! It's all very well for the Warden to talk about an open mind, but we shall all feel perfectly ghastly wondering what other people are thinking about us, and whether our own conversation doesn't sound a little potty. It's the pottiness, you know, that's so awful.'

'I know. By the way, Dean, I do absolutely refuse to suspect *you*. You're quite the sanest person I ever met.'

'I don't think that's keeping an open mind, but thank you all the same for those few kind words. And one can't possibly suspect the Warden or Miss Lydgate, can one? But I'd better not say even that. I suppose. Otherwise, by a process of elimination – oh, lord! For Heaven's sake can't we find some handy outsider with a cast-iron alibi ready for busting?'

'We'll hope so. And of course there are these two students and the scouts to be disposed of.' They turned in at the Dean's door. Miss Martin savagely poked up the fire in the sitting-room, sat down in an armchair and stared at the leaping flames. Harriet coiled herself on a couch and contemplated Miss Martin.

'Look here,' said the Dean; 'you had better not tell me too much about what *you* think, but there's no reason why any of us shouldn't tell *you* what *we* think, is there? No. Well. Here's the point. What is the object of all this persecution? It doesn't look like a personal grudge against anybody in particular. It's a kind of blind malevolence, directed against everybody in College. What's at the back of it?'

'Well, it might be somebody who thought the College as a body had injured her. Or it might be a personal grudge masking itself under a general attack. Or it might be just somebody with a mania for creating disturbance in order to enjoy the fun; that's the usual reason for this kind of outbreak, if you can call it a reason.'

'That's sheer pottiness, in that case. Like those tiresome children who throw furniture about and the servants who pretend to be ghosts. And, talking of servants, do you think there's anything in that idea that it's more likely to be somebody of that class? Of course, Miss Barton wouldn't agree; but after all, some of the words used are very coarse.'

'Yes,' said Harriet; 'but actually there isn't one that I, for example, don't know the meaning of. I believe, when you get even the primmest people under an anaesthetic, they are liable to bring the strangest vocabulary out of the subconscious – in fact, the primmer the coarser.'

'True. Did you notice that there wasn't a single spelling mistake in the whole bunch of messages?'

'I noticed that. It probably points to a fairly well educated person; though the converse isn't necessarily true. I mean, educated people often put in mistakes on purpose, so that spelling mistakes don't prove much. But an absence of mistakes is a more difficult thing to manage, if it doesn't come natural. I'm not putting this very clearly.'

'Yes, you are. A good speller could pretend to be a bad one; but a bad speller can't pretend to be a good one, any more than I could pretend to be a mathematician.'

'She could use a dictionary.'

'But then she would have to know enough to be dictionary-conscious – as the new slang would call it. Isn't our poison-pen rather silly to get all her spelling right?'

'I don't know. The educated person often fakes bad spelling rather badly; misspells easy words and gets quite difficult ones right. It's not so hard to tell when people are putting it on. I think it's probably cleverer to make no pretence about it.'

'I see. Does this tend to exclude the scouts? . . . But probably they spell far better than we do. They so often *are* better educated. And I'm sure they dress better. But that's rather off the point. Stop me when I dither.'

'You're not dithering,' said Harriet. 'Everything you say is perfectly true. At present I don't see how anybody is to be excluded.'

'And *what*,' demanded the Dean, 'becomes of the mutilated newspapers?'

'This won't do,' said Harriet; 'you're being a great deal too sharp about this. That's just one of the things I was wondering about.'

'Well, we've been into that,' said the Dean, in a tone of satisfaction. 'We've checked up on all the S.C.R. and J.C.R. papers ever since this business came to our notice – that is, more or less, since the beginning of this term. Before anything goes to be pulped, the whole lot are checked up with the list and examined to see that nothing has been cut out.'

'Who has been doing that?'

'My secretary, Mrs. Goodwin. I don't think you've met her yet. She lives in College during term. Such a nice girl – or woman, rather. She was left a widow, you know, very hard up, and she's got a little boy of ten at a prep. school. When her husband died – he was a schoolmaster – she set to work to train as a secretary and really did splendidly. She's simply invaluable to me, and most careful and reliable.'

'Was she here at Gaudy?'

'Of course she was. She – good gracious! You surely don't think – my dear, that's *absurd*! The *most* straight-forward and sane person. And she's very grateful to the College for having found her the job, and she certainly wouldn't want to run the risk of losing it.'

'All the same, she's got to go on the list of possibles. How long has she been here?'

'Let me see. Nearly two years. Nothing at all happened till the Gaudy, you know, and she'd been here a year before that.'

'But the S.C.R. and the scouts who live in College have been here still longer, most of them. We can't make exceptions along those lines. How about the other secretaries?'

'The Warden's secretary – Miss Parsons – lives at the Warden's Lodgings. The Bursar's and the Treasurer's secretaries both live out, so they can be crossed off.'

'Miss Parsons been here long?'

'Four years.'

Harriet noted down the names of Mrs. Goodwin and Miss Parsons.

'I think,' she said, 'for Mrs. Goodwin's own sake we'd better have a second check on those newspapers. Not that it really matters; because, if the poison-pen knows that the papers are being checked, she won't use those papers. And I suppose she must know, because of the care taken to collect them.'

'Very likely. That's just the trouble, isn't it?'

'How about people's private newspapers?'

'Well, naturally, we couldn't check them. We've kept an eye on the waste-paper baskets as well as we can. Nothing is ever destroyed, you know. It's all thriftily collected in sacks and sent to the paper-makers or who-ever it is that gives pence for old papers. The worthy Padgett is instructed to examine the sacks – but it's a terrific job. And then of course, since there are fires in all the rooms, why *should* anybody leave evidence in the W.P.B.?'

'How about the gowns that were burnt in the quad? That must have taken some doing. Surely more than one person would have been needed to work that.'

'We don't know whether that was part of the same business or not. About ten or a dozen people had left their gowns in various places – as they do, you know – before Sunday supper. Some were in the Queen Elizabeth portico, and some at the foot of the Hall stairs and so on. People bring them over and dump them, ready for evening Chapel.' (Harriet nodded; Sunday evening Chapel was held at a quarter to eight, and was compulsory; being also a kind of College Meeting for the giving-out of notices.) 'Well, when the bell started, these people couldn't find their gowns and so couldn't go in to Chapel. Everybody thought it was just a rag. But in the middle of the night somebody saw a blaze in the quad, and it turned out to be a merry little bonfire of bombazine. The gowns had all been soaked in petrol and they went up beautifully.'

'Where did the petrol come from?'

'It was a can Mullins keeps for his motor-cycle. You remember Mullins – the Jowett Lodge porter. His machine lies in a little outhouse in the Lodge garden. He didn't lock it up – why should he? He does *now*, but that doesn't help. Anybody could have gone and fetched it. He and his wife heard nothing, having retired to their virtuous rest. The bonfire happened bang in the middle of the Old Quad and burnt a nasty patch in the turf. Lots of people rushed out when the flare went up, and whoever did it probably mingled with the crowd. The victims were four M.A. gowns, two scholars' gowns and the rest commoners' gowns; but I don't suppose there was any selection; they just happened to be lying about.'

'I wonder where they were put in the interval between supper and the bonfire. Anybody carrying a whole bunch of gowns round College would be a bit conspicuous.'

'No; it was at the end of November, and it would be pretty dark. They could easily have been bundled into a lecture-room to be left till called for. There wasn't a proper organised search over college, you see. The poor victims who were left gownless thought somebody was having a joke; they were very angry, but not very efficient. Most of them rushed round to accuse their friends.'

'Yes; I don't suppose we can get much out of that episode at this time of day. Well – I suppose I'd better go and wash-and-brush-up for Hall.'

Hall was an embarrassed meal at the High Table. The conversation was valiantly kept to matters of academic and world interest. The undergraduates babbled noisily and cheerfully; the shadow that rested upon the college did not seem to have affected their spirits. Harriet's eye roamed over them.

'Is that Miss Cattermole at the table on the right? In a green frock, with a badly made-up face?'

'That's the young lady,' replied the Dean. 'How did you know?'

'I remember seeing her at Gaudy. Where is the all-conquering Miss Flaxman?'

'I don't see her. She may not be dining in Hall. Lots of them prefer to boil an egg in their rooms, so as to avoid the bother of changing. Slack little beasts. And that's Miss Hudson, in a red jumper, at the middle table. Black hair and horn rims.'

'She looks quite normal.'

'So far as I know, she is. So far as I know, we all are.'

'I suppose,' said Miss Pyke, who had overheard the last remark, 'even murderers look much like other people, Miss Vane. Or do you hold any opinions about the theories put forward by Lombroso? I understand that they are now to a considerable extent exploded.'

Harriet was quite thankful to be allowed to discuss murderers.

After Hall, Harriet felt herself rather at a loose end. She felt she ought to be doing something or interviewing somebody; but it was hard to know where to begin. The Dean had announced that she would be busy with some lists, but would be open to receive visitors later on. Miss Burrows the Librarian was to be engaged in putting the final touches to the Library before the Chancellor's visit;

she had been carting and arranging books the greater part of the day and had roped in a small band of students to assist her with the shelving of them. Various other dons mentioned that they had work to do; Harriet thought they seemed a little shy of one another's company.

Catching hold of the Bursar, Harriet asked whether it was possible to get hold of a plan of the college and a list of the various rooms and their occupants. Miss Stevens offered to supply the list and said she thought there was a plan in the Treasurer's office. She took Harriet across into the New Quad to get these things.

'I hope,' said the Bursar, 'you will not pay too much attention to the unfortunate remark of Miss Burrows' about the scouts. Nothing would please me more, personally, than to transfer all the maids to the Scouts' Wing out of reach of suspicion, if that were practicable; but there is no room for them there. Certainly I do not mind giving you the names of those who sleep in College, and I agree, certainly, that precautions should be taken. But to my mind, the episode of Miss Lydgate's proofs definitely rules out the scouts. Very few of them would be likely to know or care anything about proof-sheets; nor would the idea of mutilating manuscripts be likely to come into their heads. Vulgar letters – yes, possibly. But damaging those proofs was an educated person's crime. Don't you think so?'

'I'd better not say what I think,' said Harriet.

'No; quite right. But I can say what *I* think. I wouldn't say it to anybody but you. Still, I do not like this haste to make scapegoats of the scouts.'

'The thing that seems so extraordinary,' said Harriet, 'is that Miss Lydgate, of all people, should have been chosen as a victim. How could *anybody* – particularly one of her own colleagues – have a grudge against *her*? Doesn't it look rather as though the culprit knew nothing about the value of the proofs, and was merely making a random gesture of defiance to the world in general?'

'That's possible, certainly. I must say, Miss Vane, that your evidence to-day has made matters very complicated. I would rather suspect the scouts than the S.C.R., I admit; but when these hasty accusations are made by the last person known to have been in the same room with the manuscript, I can only say that – well, that it appears to me injudicious.'

Harriet said nothing to this. The Bursar, apparently feeling that she had gone a little too far, added:

'I have no suspicions of anybody. All I say is, that statements ought not to be made without proof.'

Harriet agreed, and, after marking off the relevant names upon the Bursar's list, went to find the Treasurer.

Miss Allison produced a plan of the College, and showed the positions of the rooms occupied by various people.

'I hope this means,' she said, 'that you intend to undertake the investigation yourself. Not, I suppose, that we ought to ask you to spare the time for any such thing. But I do most strongly feel that the presence of paid detectives in this college would be *most* unpleasant, however discreet they might be. I have served the College for a considerable number of years and I have its interests very much at heart. You know how undesirable it is that any outsider should be brought into a matter of this kind.'

'It is; very,' said Harriet. 'All the same, a spiteful or mentally deficient servant is a misfortune that might occur anywhere. Surely the important thing is to get to the bottom of the mystery as quickly as possible; and a trained detective or two would be very much more efficient than I should be.'

Miss Allison looked thoughtfully at her, and swayed her glasses to and fro slowly on their gold chain.

'I see you incline to the most comfortable theory. Probably we all do. But there is the other possibility. Mind you, I quite see that from your own point of view, you would not wish to take part in an exposure of a member of the Senior Common Room. But if it came to the point, I would put more faith in your tact than in that of an outside professional detective. And you start with a knowledge of the workings of the collegiate system, which is a great advantage.'

Harriet said that she thought she would know better what to suggest when she had made a preliminary review of all the circumstances.

'If,' said Miss Allison, 'you do undertake an inquiry, it is probably only fair to warn you that you may meet with some opposition. It has already been said – but perhaps I ought not to tell you this.'

'That is for you to judge.'

'It has already been said that the narrowing-down of the suspects within the limits mentioned at to-day's meeting rests only upon your assertion. I refer, of course, to the two papers you found at the Gaudy.'

'I see. Am I supposed to have invented those?'

'I don't think anybody would go as far as that. But you have said that you sometimes received similar letters on your own account. And the suggestion is that—'

'That if I found anything of the sort I must have brought it with me? That would be quite likely, only that the style of the things was so like the style of these others. However, I admit you have only my word for that.'

'*I'm* not doubting it for a moment. What is being said is that your experience in these affairs is – if anything – a disadvantage. Forgive me. That is not what *I* say.'

'That is the thing that made me very unwilling to have anything to do with the inquiry. It is absolutely true. I haven't lived a perfectly blameless life, and you can't get over it.'

'If you ask me,' said Miss Allison, 'some people's blameless lives are to blame for a good deal. I am not a fool, Miss Vane. No doubt my own life has been blameless as far as the more generous sins are concerned. But there are points upon which I should expect you to hold more balanced opinions than certain people here. I don't think I need say more than that, need I?'

Harriet's next visit was to Miss Lydgate; her excuse being to inquire what she should do with the mutilated proofs in her possession. She found the English Tutor patiently correcting a small pile of students' essays.

'Come in, come in,' said Miss Lydgate,, cheerfully. 'I have nearly done with these. Oh, about my poor proofs? I'm afraid they're not much use to me. They're really quite undecipherable. I'm afraid the only thing is to do the whole thing again. The printers will be tearing their hair, poor souls. I shan't have very much difficulty with the greater part of it, I hope. And I have the rough notes of the Introduction, so it isn't as bad as it might have been. The worst loss is a number of manuscript footnotes and two manuscript appendices that I had to put in at the last moment to refute what seemed to me some very ill-considered statements in Mr. Elkbottom's new book on *Modern Verse-Forms*. I stupidly wrote those in on the blank pages of the proofs and they are quite irrecoverable. I shall have to verify all the references again in Elkbottom. It's so tiresome, especially as one is always so busy towards the end of term. But it's all my own fault for not keeping a proper record of everything.'

'I wonder,' said Harriet, 'if I could be of any help to you in getting the proofs put together. I'd gladly stay up for a week or so if it would do any good, I'm quite used to juggling with proof-sheets, and I think I can remember enough of my Schools work to be reasonably intelligent about the Anglo-Saxon and Early English.'

'That would be a tremendous help!' exclaimed Miss Lydgate, her face lighting up. 'But wouldn't it be trespassing far too much on your time?'

Harriet said, No; she was well ahead with her own work and would enjoy putting in a little time on *English Prosody*. It was in her mind that if she really meant to pursue inquiries at Shrewsbury, Miss Lydgate's proofs would offer a convenient excuse for her presence in College.

The suggestion was left there for the moment. As regards the author of the outrages, Miss Lydgate could make no suggestions; except that, whoever it was, the poor creature must be mentally afflicted.

As she left Miss Lydgate's room, Harriet encountered Miss Hillyard, who was descending the staircase from her own abode.

'Well,' said Miss Hillyard, 'how is the investigation progressing? But I ought not to ask that. You have contrived to cast the Apple of Discord among us with a vengeance. However, as you are so well accustomed to the receipt of anonymous communications, you are no doubt the fittest person to handle the situation.'

'In my case,' said Harriet, 'I only got what was to some extent deserved. But this is a very different matter. It's not the same problem at all. Miss Lydgate's book could offend nobody.'

'Except some of the men whose theories she has attacked,' replied Miss Hillyard. 'However, circumstances seem to exclude the male sex from the scope of the inquiry. Otherwise, this mass-attack on a woman's college would suggest to me the usual masculine spite against educated women. But you, of course, would consider that ridiculous.'

'Not in the least. Plenty of men are very spiteful. But surely there are no men running about the college at night.'

'I wouldn't be too sure of that,' said Miss Hillyard, smiling sarcastically. 'It is quite ridiculous for the Bursar to talk about locked gates. What is to prevent a man from concealing himself about the grounds before the gates are locked and escaping again when they are opened in the morning? Or climbing the walls, if it comes to that?'

Harriet thought the theory far-fetched; but it interested her, as evidence of the speaker's prejudice, which amounted almost to obsession.

'The thing that in my opinion points to a man,' went on Miss Hillyard, 'is the destruction of Miss Barton's book, which is strongly pro-feminist. I don't suppose you have read it; probably it would not interest you. But why else should that book be picked out?'

Harriet parted from Miss Hillyard at the corner of the quad and went over to Tudor Building. She had not very much doubt who it was that was likely to offer opposition to her inquiries. If one was looking for a twisted mind, Miss Hillyard's was certainly a little warped. And, when one came to think of it, there was no evidence whatever that Miss Lydgate's proofs had ever been taken to the Library or ever left Miss Hillyard's hands at all. Also, she had undoubtedly been seen on the threshold of the S.C.R. before Chapel on the Monday morning. If Miss Hillyard was sufficiently demented to inflict a blow of this kind on Miss Lydgate, then she was fit for a lunatic asylum. But, indeed, this would apply to whoever it was.

She went into Tudor and tapped on Miss Barton's door, asking, when she was admitted, whether she might borrow a copy of *Woman's Place in the Modern State*.

'The sleuth at work?' said Miss Barton. 'Well, Miss Vane, here it is. By the way, I should like to apologise to you for some of the things I said when you were here last. I shall be very glad to see you handle this most unpleasant business, which can scarcely be an agreeable thing for you. I admire exceedingly anyone who can subordinate her own feelings to the common advantage. The case is obviously pathological – as all anti-social behaviour is, in my opinion. But here there is no question of legal proceedings, I imagine. At least, I hope not. I feel extremely anxious that it should *not* be brought into court; and on that account I am against hiring detectives of any kind. If you are able to get to the bottom of it, I am ready to give you any help I can.'

Harriet thanked the Fellow for her good opinion and for the book.

'You are probably the best psychologist here,' said Harriet. 'What do you think of it?'

'Probably the usual thing: a morbid desire to attract attention and create a public uproar. The adolescent and the middle-aged are the most likely suspects. I should very much doubt whether there is much more to it than that. Beyond, I mean, that the incidental obscenities point to some kind of sexual disturbance. But that is a common-place in cases of this kind. But whether you ought to look for a man-hater or a man-trap,' added

Miss Barton, with the first glimmer of humour Harriet had ever seen in her, 'I can't tell you.'

Having put away her various acquisitions in her own room, Harriet thought it was time to go and see the Dean. She found Miss Burrows with her, very tired and dusty after coping with the Library, and being refreshed with a glass of hot milk, to which Miss Martin insisted on adding just a dash of whisky to induce slumber.

'What new light one gets on the habits of the S.C.R. when one's an old student,' said Harriet. 'I always imagined that there was only one bottle of ardent spirits in the college, kept under lock and key by the Bursar for life-and-death emergencies.'

'It used to be so,' said the Dean, 'but I'm getting frivolous in my old age. Even Miss Lydgate cherishes a small stock of cherry brandy, for high-days and holidays. The Bursar is even thinking of laying down a little port for the College.'

'Great Scott!' said Harriet.

'The students are not supposed to imbibe alcohol,' said the Dean, 'but I shouldn't like to go bail for the contents of all the cupboards in College.'

'After all,' said Miss Burrows, 'their tiresome parents bring them up to have cocktails and things at home, so it probably seems ridiculous to them that they shouldn't do the same things here.'

'And what can one do about it? Make a police search through their belongings? Well, I flatly refuse. We can't keep the place like a gaol.'

'The trouble is,' said the Librarian, 'that everybody sneers at restrictions and demands freedom, till something annoying happens; then they demand angrily what has become of the discipline.'

'You can't exercise the old kind of discipline in these days,' said the Dean; 'it's too bitterly resented.'

'The modern idea is that young people should discipline themselves,' said the Librarian. 'But do they?'

'No; they won't. Responsibility bores 'em. Before the War they passionately had College Meetings about everything. Now, they won't be bothered. Half the old institutions like the College debates and the Third-Year Play, are dead or moribund. They don't want responsibility.'

'They're all taken up with their young men,' said Miss Burrows.

'Drat their young men,' said the Dean. 'In my day, we simply thirsted for responsibility. We'd all been sat on at school for the good of our souls, and came up bursting to show how brilliantly we could organise things when we were put in charge.'

'If you ask me,' said Harriet, 'it's the fault of the schools. Free discipline and so on. Children are sick to death of running things and doing prefect duty; and when they get up to Oxford they're tired out and only want to sit back and let somebody else run the show. Even in my time, the people from the up-to-date republican schools were shy of taking office, poor brutes.'

'It's all very different,' said Miss Burrows with a yawn. 'However, I did get my Library volunteers to do a job of work to-day. We've got most of the shelves decently filled, and the pictures hung and the curtains up. It looks very well. I hope the Chancellor will be impressed. They haven't finished painting the radiators downstairs, but I've bundled the paint-pots and things into a cupboard and hoped for the best. And I borrowed a squad of scouts to clean up, so as not to leave anything to be done to-morrow.'

'What time does the Chancellor arrive?' asked Harriet.

'Twelve o'clock; reception in the S.C.R. and show him round the College. Then lunch in Hall, and I hope he enjoys it. Ceremony at 2.30. And then push him off to catch the 3.45. Delightful man; but I am getting fed up with Openings. We've opened the New Quad, the Chapel (with choral service), the S.C.R. Dining-Room (with lunch to Former Tutors and Fellows), the Tudor Annexe (with Old Students' Tea), the Kitchens and Scouts' Wing (with Royalty), the Sanatorium (with address by the Lister Professor of Medicine), the Council-Chamber and the Warden's Lodgings, and we've unveiled the late Warden's Portrait, the Willettt Memorial Sundial and the New Clock. And now it's the Library. Padgett said to me last term, when we were making those alterations in Queen Elizabeth, "Excuse me, madam Dean, miss, but could you tell me, miss, the date of the Opening?" "What Opening, Padgett?" said I. "We aren't opening anything this term. What is there to open?" "Well, miss," says Padgett, "I was thinking of these here new lavatories, if you'll excuse me, madam Dean, miss. We've opened everything there was to open up to the present, miss, and if there was to be a Ceremony, miss, it would be convenient if I was to know in good time, on account of arranging for taxis and parking accommodation."'

'Dear Padgett!' said Miss Burrows. 'He's the brightest spot in this academy.' She yawned again. 'I'm dead.'

'Take her away to bed, Miss Vane,' said the Dean, 'and we'll call it a day.'

6

Often when they were gone to Bed, the inner doors were flung open, as also the Doors of a Cupboard which stood in the Hall; and this with a great deal of Violence and Noise. And one Night the Chairs, which when they went to Bed stood all in the Chimney-corner, were all removed and placed in the middle of the Room in very good order, and a Meal-sieve hung upon one cut full of Holes, and a Key of an inner Door upon another. And in the Day-time, as they sate in the House spinning, they could see the Barn-doors often flung open, but not by whom. Once, as *Alice* sate spinning the Rock or Distaff leapt several times out of the Wheel into the middle of the room . . . with much more such ridiculous stuff as this is, which would be tedious to relate.

WILLIAM TURNER

'PETER,' said Harriet. And with the sound of her own voice she came drowsing and floating up out of the strong circle of his arms, through a green sea of sun-dappled beech-leaves into darkness.

'Oh, damn,' said Harriet softly to herself. 'Oh, damn. And I didn't want to wake up.'

The clock in the New Quad struck three musically.

'This won't do,' said Harriet. 'This really will not do. My sub-conscious has a most treacherous imagination.' She groped for the switch of her bedside lamp. 'It's disquieting to reflect that one's dreams never symbolise

one's real wishes, but always something Much Worse.'
She turned the light on and sat up.

'If I really wanted to be passionately embraced by
Peter, I should dream of something like dentists or
gardening. I wonder what are the unthinkable depths
of awfulness that can only be expressed by the polite
symbol of Peter's embraces. Damn Peter! I wonder what
he would do about a case like this.'

This brought her mind back to the evening in the
Egotists' Club and the anonymous letter; and thence
back to his absurd fury with the sticking-plaster.

'. . . but my mind being momentarily on my job . . .'

You'd think he was quite bird-witted, sometimes, she
thought. But he does keep his mind on the job, when he's
doing it. One's mind on the job. Yes. What am I doing,
letting my mind stray all over the place. Is this a job, or
isn't it? . . . Suppose the Poison-Pen is on its rounds now,
dropping letters at people's doors . . . Whose door,
though? One can't watch all the doors . . . I ought to
be sitting up at the window, keeping an eye open for
creeping figures in the quad . . . Somebody ought to do it
– but who's to be trusted? Besides, dons have their jobs to
do; they can't sit up all night and work all day . . . The
job . . . keeping one's mind on the job . . .

She was out of bed now and pulling the window-
curtains aside. There was no moon, and nothing at all to
be seen. Not even a late essay-writer seemed to be
burning the midnight lamp.

Anybody could go anywhere on a dark night like this,
she thought to herself. She could scarcely see even the
outline of the roofs of Tudor on her right, or the dark
bulk of the New Library jutting out on her left from
behind the Annexe.

The Library; with not a soul in it.

She put on a dressing-gown and opened her door softly. It was bitterly cold. She found the wall-switch and went down the central corridor of the Annexe, past a row of doors behind which students were sleeping and dreaming of goodness knew what – examinations, sports, undergraduates, parties, all the queer jumble of things that are summed up as 'activities.' Outside their doors lay little heaps of soiled crockery for the scouts to collect and wash. Also shoes. On the doors were cards, bearing their names: Miss H. Brown, Miss Jones, Miss Colburn, Miss Szleposky, Miss Isaacson – so many unknown quantities. So many destined wives and mothers of the race; or, alternatively, so many potential historians, scientists, school-teachers, doctors, lawyers; as you liked to think one thing of more importance than the other. At the end of the passage was a large window, hygienically open at top and bottom. Harriet gently pushed up the bottom sash and looked out, shivering.

And suddenly she knew that whatever reason or instinct had led her to look at the Library had taken a very just view of the situation. The New Library should have been quite dark. It was not. One of the long windows was split from top to bottom by a narrow band of light.

Harriet thought rapidly. If this was Miss Burrows, carrying on legitimately (though at an unreasonable and sacrificial hour) with her preparations, why had she troubled to draw the curtains? The windows had been curtained, because a Library that faces south must have some protection against strong sunlight. But it would be absurd for the Librarian to protect herself and her proper functions from scrutiny in the middle of a dark March night. College authorities were not so secretive as all that. Something was up. Should one go and investigate on one's own, or rouse somebody else?

One thing was clear; if it was a member of the S.C.R. lurking behind those curtains, it would not be politic to bring a student to witness the discovery. What dons slept in Tudor? Without consulting the list, Harriet remembered that Miss Barton and Miss Chilperic had rooms there, but on the far side of the building. Here was an opportunity to check up on them, at any rate. With a last glance at the Library window, Harriet made her way quickly back past her own room on the Bridge and through into the main building. She cursed herself for not having a torch; she was delayed by fumbling with the switches. Along the corridor, past the stair-head and round to the left. No don on that floor; it must be on the floor below. Back, and down the stairs and along to the left again. She was leaving all the passage-lights burning behind her, and wondered whether they would arouse attention in other buildings. At last. A door on her left labelled 'Miss Barton.' And the door stood open.

She knocked at it sharply, and went in. The sitting-room was empty. Beyond it, the bedroom door stood open too. 'Gracious!' said Harriet. 'Miss Barton!' There was no reply; and looking in, she saw that the bedroom was as empty as the sitting-room. The bed-clothes were flung back and the bed had been slept in; but the sleeper had risen and gone.

It was easy to think of an innocent explanation. Harriet stood for a moment, considering; and then called to mind that the window of the room overlooked the quad. The curtains were drawn back; she looked out into the darkness The light still shone in the Library window; but while she looked, it went out.

She ran back to the foot of the stair and through the entrance-hall. The front door of the building was ajar. She pulled it open and ran out and across the quad. As she ran, something seemed to loom up ahead of her. She made for it and closed with it. It caught her in a muscular grip.

'Who's that?' demanded Harriet, fiercely.

'And who's *that*?'

The grip of one hand was released and a torch was switched on in Harriet's face.

'Miss Vane! What are you doing here?'

'Is that Miss Barton? I was looking for you. I saw a light in the New Library.'

'So did I. I've just been over to investigate. The door's locked.'

'Locked?'

'And the key inside.'

'Isn't there another way up?' asked Harriet.

'Yes, of course there is. I ought to have thought of that. Up through the Hall passage and the Fiction Library. Come along!'

'Wait a minute,' said Harriet. 'Whoever it is may be still there. You watch the main door, to see they don't get out that way. I'll go up through the Hall.'

'Very well. Good idea. Here! haven't you got a torch? You'd better take mine. You'll waste time turning on lights.'

Harriet snatched the torch and ran, thinking hard. Miss Barton's story sounded plausible enough. She had woken up (why?) seen the light (very likely she slept with her curtains drawn open) and gone out to investigate while Harriet was running about the upper floors hunting for the right room. In the meantime, the person in the Library had either finished what she was doing or, possibly, peeped out and been alarmed by seeing the lights go up in Tudor. She had switched out the light. She had not gone out by the main door; she was either still somewhere in the Hall-Library Wing, or she had crept out by the Hall stair while Miss Barton and Harriet were grappling with one another in the quad.

Harriet found the Hall stair and started up it, using her torch as little as possible and keeping the light low. It came forcibly into her mind that the person she was hunting was – must be – unbalanced, if not mad, and might possibly deliver a nasty swipe out of a dark corner. She arrived at the head of the stair, and pushed back the swinging glass double door that led to the passage between the Hall and the Buttery. As she did so, she fancied she heard a slight scuffling sound ahead, and almost simultaneously she saw the gleam of a torch. There ought to be a two-way switch just on the right, behind the door. She found it, and pressed it down. There was a quick flicker, and then darkness. A fuse? Then she laughed at herself. Of course not. The person at the other end of the passage had flicked the switch at the same moment as herself. She pushed the switch up again, and the lights flooded the passage.

On her left she saw the three doorways, with the serving-hatches between, that led into the Hall. On the right was the long blank wall between the passage and the kitchens. And ahead of her, at the far end of the passage, close to the Buttery door, stood somebody clutching a dressing-gown about her with one hand and a large jar in the other.

Harriet advanced swiftly upon this apparition, which came meekly enough to meet her. Its features seemed familiar, and in a moment she identified them. It was Miss Hudson, the Third Year student who had been up at Gaudy.

'What in the world are you doing here at this time of night?' demanded Harriet, severely. Not that she had any particular right to question students about their movements. Nor did she feel that her own appearance, in pyjamas and a jaeger dressing-gown, suggested dignity or authority. Miss Hudson, indeed, seemed quite flabbergasted at being thus accosted by a total stranger at three in the morning. She stared, speechless.

'Why shouldn't I be here?' said Miss Hudson, at last, defiantly. 'I don't know who you are. I've as much right to walk about as you have . . . Oh, gosh!' she added, and burst out laughing. 'I suppose you're one of the scouts. I didn't recognise you without your uniform.'

'No,' said Harriet, 'I'm an old student. You're Miss Hudson, aren't you? But your room isn't here. Have you been along to the Buttery?' Her eyes were on the jug; Miss Hudson blushed.

'Yes – I wanted some milk. I've got an essay.'

She spoke of it as though it were a disease. Harriet chuckled.

'So that still goes on, does it? Carrie's just as softhearted as Agnes was in my day.' She went up to the Buttery hatch and shook it, but it was locked. 'No, apparently she isn't.'

'I asked her to leave it open,' said Miss Hudson, 'but I expect she forgot. I say – don't give Carrie away. She's awfully decent.'

'You know quite well that Carrie isn't supposed to leave the hatch open. You ought to get your milk before ten o'clock.'

'I know. But one doesn't always know if one will want it. You've done the same thing in your time, I expect.'

'Yes,' said Harriet. 'Well, you'd better cut along. Wait a second. When did you come up here?'

'Just now. Just a few seconds before you did.'

'Did you meet anybody?'

131

'No.' Miss Hudson looked alarmed. 'Why? Has anything happened?'

'Not that I know of. Get along to bed.'

Miss Hudson escaped and Harriet tried the Buttery door which was as firmly locked as the hatch. Then she went on, through the Fiction Library, which was empty, and put her hand on the handle of the oak door that led to the New Library.

The door was immovable. There was no key in the lock. Harriet looked round the Fiction Library. On the windowsill lay a thin pencil, beside a book and a few papers. She pushed the pencil into the key-hole; it encountered no resistance.

She went to the window of the Fiction Library and pushed it up. It looked on to the roof of a small loggia. Two people were not enough for this game of hide-and-seek. She pulled a table across the Library door, so that if anybody tried to come out that way behind her back she should have notice of it; then she climbed out on to the loggia roof and leaned over the balcony. She could see nothing distinctly beneath her, but she pulled her torch from her pocket and signalled with it.

'Hullo!' said Miss Barton's voice, cautiously, from below.

'The other door's locked, and the key gone.'

'That's awkward. If either of us goes, somebody may come out. And if we yell for help there'll be an uproar.'

'That's about the size of it,' said Harriet.

'Well, listen; I'll try and get in through one of the ground-floor windows. They all seem to be latched, but I might break a pane of glass.'

Harriet waited. Presently she heard a faint tinkle. Then there was a pause, and presently the sound of a moving sash. There was a longer pause. Harriet came back into the Fiction Library and pulled the table away from the door. In about six or seven minutes' time she saw the door handle move and heard a tap on the other side of the oak. She stooped to the key-hole, and called: 'What's up?' and bent her ear to listen.

'Nobody here,' said Miss Barton's voice on the other side. 'Key's gone. And the most ghastly mess-up.'

'I'll come round.'

She hurried back through the Hall and round to the front of the Library. Here she found the window that Miss Barton had opened, climbed through and ran on up the stairs into the Library.

'Well!' said Harriet.

The New Library was a handsome, lofty room, with six bays on the South side, lit by as many windows running nearly from the floor to the ceiling. On the North side, the wall was windowless, and shelved to a height of ten feet. Above this was a space of blank wall, along which it would be possible, at some future time, to run an extra gallery when the books should become too many for the existing shelving. This blank space had been adorned by Miss Burrows and her party with a series of engravings, such as every academic community possesses, representing the Parthenon, the Colosseum, Trajan's Column and other topographical and classical subjects.

All the books in the room had been dragged out and flung on the floor, by the simple expedient of removing the shelves bodily. The pictures had been thrown down. And the blank wall-space thus exposed had been adorned with a frieze of drawings, roughly executed in brown paint, and with inscriptions in letters a foot high, all of the most unseemly sort. A pair of library steps and a pot of paint with a wide brush in it stood triumphantly in the midst of the wreckage, to show how the transformation had been accomplished.

'That's torn it,' said Harriet.

'Yes,' said Miss Barton. 'A very nice reception for Lord Oakapple.'

There was an odd note in her voice – almost of satisfaction. Harriet looked sharply at her.

'What are you going to do? What does one do? Go over the place with a magnifying glass? or send for the police?'

'Neither,' said Harriet. She considered for a moment.

'The first thing,' she said, 'is to send for the Dean. The next is to find either the original keys or a spare set. The third, is to clean off these filthy inscriptions before anybody sees them. And the fourth is to get the room straight before twelve o'clock. There's plenty of time. Will you be good enough to wake the Dean and bring her with you. In the meantime. I'll have a look round for clues. We can discuss afterwards who did the job and how she got out. Please make haste.'

'H'm!' said the Fellow. 'I like people who know their own minds.'

She went with surprising promptness.

'Her dressing-gown is all over paint,' said Harriet aloud to herself. 'But she may have got it climbing in.' She went downstairs and examined the open window. 'Yes, here's where she scrambled over the wet radiator. I expect I'm marked too. Yes, I am. Nothing to show whether it all came from there. Damp footmarks – hers and mine, no doubt. Wait a moment.'

She traced the damp marks up to the top of the stairs, where they grew faint and ceased. She could find no third set; but the footmarks of the intruder would probably have had time to dry. Whoever it was must have begun operations very soon after midnight at latest. The paint had splashed about a good deal; if it were possible to search the whole college for paint-stained clothing, well and good. But it would cause a terrific scandal. Miss Hudson – had she shown any marks of paint anywhere? Harriet thought not.

She looked about her again, and realised unexpectedly that she had the lights full on, and that the curtains were drawn open. If anybody was looking across from one of the other buildings, the interior of the room would show up like a lighted stage. She snapped the lights off, and drew the curtains again carefully before putting them on again.

'Yes,' she said. 'I see. That was the idea. The curtains were drawn while the job was done. Then the lights were turned off and the curtains opened. Then the artist escaped, leaving the door locked. In the morning, everything would look quite ordinary from the outside. Who would have been the first to try to come in? An early scout, to do a final clean round? She would find the door locked, think Miss Burrows had left it like that, and probably do nothing about it. Miss Burrows would probably have come up first. When? A little after Chapel, or a little before. She would not have been able to get in. Time would have been wasted hunting for the keys. When anybody did get in, it would have been too late to straighten things up. Everybody would have been about. The Chancellor—?

'Miss Burrows would have been the first to come up. She had also been the last to leave, and was the person who knew best where the paint pots had been put. Would she have wrecked her own job, any more than Miss Lydgate would have wrecked her own proofs? How far was that psychological premise sound? One would surely damage anything in the world, *except* one's own work. But on the other hand, if one were cunning enough to see that people would think exactly that, then one would promptly take the precaution of seeing that one's own work did suffer.'

Harriet moved slowly about the Library. There was a big splash of paint on the parquet. And at the edge of it – oh, yes! it would be very useful to hunt the place over for paint-stained clothes. But here was evidence that the culprit had worn no slippers. Why should she have worn anything? The radiators on this floor were working at full blast, and a complete absence of clothing would be not merely politic but comfortable.

And how had the person got away? Neither Miss Hudson (if she was to be trusted) nor Harriet had met anyone on the way up. But there had been plenty of time for escape, after the lights were put out. A stealthy figure creeping away under the Hall archway could not have been seen from the far side of the Old Quad. Or, if it came to that, there might quite well have been somebody lurking in the Hall while Harriet and Miss Hudson were talking in the passage.

'I've mucked it a bit,' said Harriet. 'I ought to have turned on the Hall lights to make sure.'

Miss Barton re-entered with the Dean, who took one look round and said 'Mercy!' She looked like a stout little mandarin, with her long red pigtail and quilted blue dressing-gown sprawled over with green-and-scarlet dragons. 'What *idiots* we were not to expect it. Of course, the *obvious* thing! If we'd only thought about it, Miss Burrows could have locked up before she went. And *what* do we do now?'

'My first reaction,' said Harriet, 'is turpentine. And the second is Padgett.'

'My dear, you are perfectly right. Padgett will cope. He always does. Like charity, he never fails. What a mercy you people spotted what was going on. As soon as we get these disgusting inscriptions cleaned off, we can put on a coat of quick-drying distemper or something, or paper the wall over, and – goodness! I don't know where the turpentine will come from, unless the painters have left a lot. It'll need a young bath. But Padgett will manage.'

'I'll run over and get him,' said Harriet, 'and at the same time I'll collar Miss Burrows. We'll have to get these books back into place. What's the time? Five to four, I think it can be done all right. Will you hold the fort till I come back?'

'Yes. Oh, and you'll find the main door open now. I had an extra key, fortunately. A beautiful *plated* key – all ready for Lord Oakapple. But we'll have to get a lock-smith to the other door, unless the builders have a spare.'

The most remarkable thing about that remarkable morning was the imperturbability of Padgett. He answered Harriet's summons attired in a handsome pair of striped pyjamas, and received her instructions with monumental stolidity.

'The Dean is sorry to say, Padgett, that somebody has been playing some very disagreeable tricks in the New Library.'

'Have they indeed, miss?'

'The whole place has been turned upside down, and some very vulgar words and pictures scrawled on the wall.'

'Very unfortunate, miss, that is.'

'In brown paint.'

'That's awkward, miss.'

'It will have to be cleaned at once, before anybody sees it.'

137

'Very good, miss.'

'And then we shall have to get hold of the decorators or somebody to paper or wash it over before the Chancellor arrives.'

'Very good, miss.'

'Do you think you can manage it, Padgett?'

'Just you leave it to me, miss.'

Harriet's next job was to collect Miss Burrows, who received the news with loud expressions of annoyance.

'How loathsome! And do you mean to say all those books have got to be done *again*? Now? Oh, lord, yes – I suppose there's no help for it. What a blessing I hadn't put the Folio Chaucer and the other valuables in the show-cases, Lord!'

The Librarian scrambled out of bed. Harriet looked at her feet. They were quite clean. But there was an odd smell in the bedroom. She traced it after a moment or two to the neighbourhood of the permanent basin.

'I say – is that turps?'

'Yes,' replied Miss Burrows, struggling into her stockings. 'I brought it across from the Library. I got paint on my hands when I moved those pots and things.'

'I wish you'd lend it me. We had to scramble in through the window over a wet radiator.'

'Yes, rather.'

Harriet went out, puzzled. Why should Miss Burrows have bothered to bring the can over to the New Quad, when she could have cleaned off the paint on the spot? But she could well understand that if anyone had wanted to remove paint from her feet, after being disturbed in the middle of a piece of dirty work, there might have been nothing for it but to snatch up the can and bolt for it.

Then she had another idea. The culprit could not have

left the Library with her bare feet. She would have put on her slippers again. If you put paint-stained feet into slippers, the slippers ought to show signs of it.

She went back to her own room and dressed. Then she returned to the New Quad. Miss Burrows had gone. Her bedroom slippers lay by the bed. Harriet examined them minutely, inside and out, but they were quite free from paint.

On her way back again, Harriet overtook Padgett. He was walking sedately across the lawn, carrying a large can of turpentine in each hand.

'Where did you rake that up, Padgett, so early in the morning?'

'Well, miss, Mullins went on his motor-bike and knocked up a chap he knows what lives over his own oil-shop, miss.'

As simple as that.

Some time later, Harriet and the Dean, decorously robed and gowned, found themselves passing along the East side of Queen Elizabeth Building in the wake of Padgett and the decorators' foreman.

'Young ladies,' Padgett was heard to say, 'will 'ave their larks, same as young gentlemen.'

'When I was a lad,' replied the foreman, 'young ladies was young ladies. And young gentlemen was young gentlemen. If you get my meaning.'

'Wot this country wants,' said Padgett, 'is a 'Itler.'

'That's right,' said the foreman. 'Keep the girls at 'ome. Funny kind 'o job you got 'ere, mate. Wot was you, afore you took to keepin' a 'en 'ouse?'

'Assistant camel 'and at the Zoo. Very interesting job it was, too.'

'Wot made you chuck it?'

139

'Blood-poison. I was bit in the arm,' said Padgett, 'by a female.'

'Ah' said the foreman decorator.

By the time Lord Oakapple arrived, the Library presented nothing unseemly to the eye, beyond a certain dampness and streakiness in its upper parts, where the new paper was drying unevenly. The glass had been swept up and the paint stains cleaned from the floor; twenty photographs of classical statuary had been unearthed from a store-cupboard to replace the Colosseum and the Parthenon; the books were back on their shelves, and the show-cases duly displayed the Chaucer Folio, the Shakespeare First Quarto, the three Kelmscott Morrises, the autographed copy of *The Man of Property*, and the embroidered glove belonging to the Countess of Shrewsbury.

The Dean hovered about the Chancellor like a hen with one chick, in a martyrdom of nervous apprehension lest some indelicate missive should drop from his table-napkin or flutter out unexpectedly from the folds of his robes; and when, in the Senior Common Room after lunch, he took out a bunch of notes from his pocket and riffled them over with a puzzled frown, the tension became so acute that she nearly dropped the sugar-basin. It turned out, however, that he had merely mislaid a Greek quotation. The Warden, though the history of the Library was known to her, displayed her usual serene poise.

Harriet saw nothing of all this. She spent the whole interval, after the decorators had done their part, in the Library, watching the movements of every one who came in or out, and seeing that they left nothing undesirable behind them.

Apparently, however, the College Poltergeist had shot its bolt. A cold lunch was brought up to the self-appointed invigilator. A napkin covered it; but nothing lurked beneath its folds beyond a plate of ham sandwiches and other such harmless matter. Harriet recognised the scout.

'It's Annie, isn't it? Are you on the kitchen staff now?'

'No. madam. I wait upon the Hall and Senior Common Room.'

'How are your little girls getting on? I think Miss Lydgate said you had two little girls?'

'Yes, madam. How kind of you to ask.' Annie's face beamed with pleasure. 'They're splendid. Oxford suits them, after living in a manufacturing town, where we were before. Are you fond of children, madam?'

'Oh, yes,' said Harriet. Actually, she did not care much about children; but one can scarcely say so, bluntly, to those possessed of these blessings.

'You ought to be married and have some of your own, madam. There! I oughtn't to have said that – it's not my place. But it seems to me a dreadful thing to see all these unmarried ladies living together. It isn't natural, is it?'

'Well, Annie, it's all according to taste. And one has to wait for the right person to come along.'

'That's very true, madam.' Harriet suddenly recollected that Annie's husband had been queer, or committed suicide, or something unfortunate, and wondered whether her commonplace had been a tactful one. But Annie seemed quite pleased with it. She smiled again; she had large, light blue eyes, and Harriet thought she must have been a good-looking woman before she got so thin and worried-looking. 'I'm sure I hope he'll come along for you – or perhaps you are engaged to be married?'

Harriet frowned. She had no particular liking for the

question, and did not want to discuss her private affairs with the college servants. But there seemed to be no impertinent intention behind the inquiry, so she answered pleasantly, 'Not just yet; but you never know. How do you like the new Library?'

'It's a very handsome room, isn't it, madam? But it seems a great shame to keep up this big place just for women to study books in. I can't see what girls want with books. Books won't teach them to be good wives.'

'What dreadful opinions!' said Harriet. 'Whatever made you take a job in a women's college, Annie?'

The scout's face clouded. 'Well, madam, I've had my misfortunes. I was glad to take what I could get.'

'Yes, of course; I was only joking. Do you like the work?'

'It's quite all right. But some of these clever ladies are a bit queer, don't you think, madam? Funny, I mean. No heart in them.'

Harriet remembered that there had been misunderstandings with Miss Hillyard.

'Oh, no,' she said briskly. 'Of course they are very busy people, and haven't much time for outside interests. But they are all very kind.'

'Yes, madam; I'm sure they mean to be. But I always think of what it says in the Bible, about "much learning hath made thee mad." It isn't a right thing.'

Harriet looked up sharply and caught an odd look in the scout's eyes.

'What do you mean by that, Annie?'

'Nothing at all, madam. Only funny things go on sometimes, but of course, being a visitor, you wouldn't know, and it's not my place to mention them – being only a servant, nowadays.'

'I certainly,' said Harriet, rather alarmed, 'wouldn't

mention anything of the kind you suggest to outside people or visitors. If you have any complaint to make, you should speak to the Bursar, or the Warden.'

'I haven't any complaint, madam. But you may have heard about rude words being written up on the walls, and about the things that were burnt in the Quad – why, there was a bit in the papers about that. Well you'll find, madam, they all happened since a certain person came into the college.'

'What person?' said Harriet sternly.

'One of these learned ladies, madam. Well, perhaps I'd better not say anything more about that. You write detective books, don't you, madam? Well, you'll find something in that lady's past, you may be sure of it. At least, that's what a good many people are saying. And it isn't a nice thing for anybody to be in the same place with a woman like that.'

'I feel quite sure you must be mistaken, Annie; I should be very careful how you spread about a tale of that kind. You'd better run along back to the Hall, now; I expect they'll be needing you.'

So that was what the servants were saying. Miss de Vine, of course; she was the 'learned lady' whose arrival had coincided with the beginning of the disturbances – coincided more exactly than Annie could know, unless she too had seen that drawing in the quad at the Gaudy. A curious woman, Miss de Vine, and undoubtedly with a varied experience behind those disconcerting eyes. But Harriet was inclined to like her, and she certainly did not look mad in the way that the 'Poison-Pen' was mad; though it would not be surprising to learn that she had a streak of fanaticism somewhere. What, by the way, had she been doing the previous night? She had rooms at the moment in the New Quad; there was probably little likelihood of proving an alibi for her now. Miss de Vine – well! she would have to be put on the same footing as everybody else.

The Opening of the Library took place without a hitch. The Chancellor unlocked the main door with the plated key, unaware that the same key had opened it, under curious circumstances, the night before. Harriet watched carefully the faces of the assembled dons and scouts; none of them showed any sign of surprise, anger or disappointment at the decorous appearance of the Library. Miss Hudson was present, looking cheerfully unconcerned; Miss Cattermole, too, was there. She looked as though she had been crying; and Harriet noticed that she stood in a corner by herself and talked to nobody until, at the conclusion of the ceremony, a dark girl in spectacles made her way through the crowd to her and they walked away together.

Later in the day, Harriet went to the Warden to make her promised report. She pointed out the difficulty of dealing with an outbreak like that of the previous night single-handed. A careful patrol of the quads and passages by a number of helpers would probably have resulted in the capture of the culprit; and the whole of the suspects could in any case have been checked up at an early moment. She strongly advised enlisting some women from Miss Climpson's Agency, the nature of which she explained.

'I see the point,' replied the Warden; 'but I find that at least two members of the Senior Common Room feel very strong objection to that course of action.'

'I know,' said Harriet. 'Miss Allison and Miss Barton. Why?'

'I think, too,' pursued the Warden, without answering this question, 'that the matter presents certain difficulties. What would the students think of these strangers prowling about the college at night? They will wonder why police duties cannot be undertaken by ourselves, and we can hardly inform them that we ourselves are particularly under suspicion. And to perform such duties as you suggest, properly, quite a large number would be required – if all the strategic points are to be held. Then these persons would be quite ignorant of the conditions of college life, and might easily make unfortunate mistakes by following and questioning the wrong people. I do not see how we could avoid a very unpleasant scandal and some complaints.'

'I see all that, Warden. But all the same, that is the quickest solution.'

The Warden bent her head over a handsome piece of tapestry-work on which she was engaged.

'I cannot feel it to be very desirable. I know you will say that the whole situation is undesirable. I quite agree with you.' She looked up. 'I suppose, Miss Vane, you could not yourself spare the time to assist us?'

'I could spare the time,' said Harriet slowly. 'But without help it is going to be very difficult. If there were only one or two people who were exonerated without a shadow of doubt, it would be very much easier.'

'Miss Barton assisted you very ably last night.'

'Yes,' said Harriet; 'but – how shall I put it? If I were writing a story about this, the person first on the spot would be the first to be suspected.'

The Warden selected an orange skein from her basket and threaded her needle deliberately.

'Will you explain that, please?'

Harriet explained carefully.

145

'That is very clearly put,' said Dr. Baring. 'I understand perfectly. Now, about this student, Miss Hudson. Her explanation does not seem to be satisfactory. She could not possibly have expected to get food from the Buttery at that hour; and in fact, she did not.'

'No,' said Harriet; 'but I know quite well that in my day it wasn't too difficult to get round the right side of the Head Scout to leave the hatch open all night. Then, if one had a late essay or anything and felt hungry, one went down and got what one wanted.'

'Dear me,' said the Warden.

'We were always quite honourable about it,' said Harriet, 'and entered it all on the slate, so that it figured in our battels at the end of term. Though,' she added thoughtfully, 'there were some items of cold meat and dripping that must have been camouflaged a bit. Still – I think Miss Hudson's explanation will pass muster.'

'Actually, the hatch was locked.'

'Actually, it was. As a matter of fact, I have seen Carrie, and she assures me that it was locked at 10.30 last night as usual. She admits that Miss Hudson asked her to leave it open, but says she didn't do so, because, only last night, the Bursar had given special instructions about the locking of the hatch and Buttery. That would be after the meeting, no doubt. She also says she has been more particular this term than she used to be, because of a little trouble there was over the same thing last term.'

'Well – I see there is no proof against Miss Hudson. I believe she is rather a lively young woman, however; so it may be as well to keep an eye on her. She is very able; but her antecedents are not particularly refined, and I dare say, it is possible that she might look upon even the disagreeable expressions found in the – er – the communications in the light of a joke. I tell you this, not to create any prejudice against the girl, but merely for whatever evidential value it may possess.'

'Thank you. Well, then, Warden; if you feel it is impossible to call in outside help, I suggest that I should stay in College for a week or so, ostensibly to help Miss Lydgate with her book and to do some research on my own account in Bodley. I could then make a few more investigations. If nothing decisive results by the end of the term, I really think the question of engaging professionals will have to be faced.'

'That is a very generous offer,' said the Warden. 'We shall all be exceedingly grateful to you.'

'I ought to warn you,' said Harriet, 'that one or two of the Senior Members do not approve of me.'

'That may make it a little more difficult. But if you are ready to put up with that unpleasantness in the interests of the College, it can only increase our sense of gratitude. I cannot too strongly emphasise how exceedingly important it is to avoid publicity. Nothing is more prejudicial to the College in particular and to University women in general than spiteful and ill-informed gossip in the press. The students, so far, seem to have been very loyal. If any of them had been indiscreet we should certainly have heard of it by now.'

'How about Miss Flaxman's young man at New College?'

'Both he and Miss Flaxman have behaved quite well. At first, naturally, it was taken to be a purely personal matter. When the situation developed, I spoke to Miss Flaxman, and received her assurance that she and her fiancé would keep the whole thing to themselves until it could be properly cleared up.'

'I see,' said Harriet. 'Well, we must do what we can. One thing I should like to suggest, and that is some of the passage-lights should be left on at night. It is difficult enough to patrol a large set of buildings in the light: in the dark, it is impossible.'

'That is reasonable,' replied Dr. Baring. 'I will speak to the Bursar about it.'

And with this unsatisfactory arrangement, Harriet was obliged to be content.

7

O my deare *Cloris* be not sad,
  Nor with these Furies daunted,
But let these female fooles be mad,
  With Hellish pride inchanted;
Let not thy noble thoughts descend
  So low as their affections,
Whom neither counsell can amend,
  Nor yet the Gods corrections.

MICHAEL DRAYTON

IT was a matter of mild public interest at Shrewsbury College that Miss Harriet Vane, the well-known detective novelist, was spending a couple of weeks in College, while engaged in research at the Bodleian upon the life and works of Sheridan Lefanu. The excuse was good enough; Harriet really was gathering material, in a leisurely way, for a study of Lefanu, though the Bodleian was not, perhaps, the ideal source for it. But there must be some reason given for her presence, and Oxford is willing enough to believe that the Bodleian is the hub of the scholar's universe. She was able to find enough references among the Periodical Publications to justify an optimistic answer to kindly inquiries about her progress; and if, in fact, she snoozed a great deal in the arms of Duke Humphrey by day, to make up for those hours of the night spent in snooping about the corridors, she was probably not the only person in Oxford to find the atmosphere of old leather and central heating favourable to slumber.

At the same time, she devoted a good many hours to establishing order among Miss Lydgate's chaotic proofs. The Introduction was rewritten, and the obliterated passages restored, from the author's capacious memory; the disfigured pages were replaced from fresh proof-sheets; fifty-nine errors and obscurities in the cross-references were eliminated; the rejoinder to Mr. Elkbottom was incorporated in the text and made more vigorous and conclusive; and the authorities at the Press began to speak quite hopefully about the date of publication.

Whether because Harriet's night prowlings, or perhaps the mere knowledge that the circle of suspects was so greatly narrowed, had intimidated the Poison-Pen, or for some other reason, there were few outbreaks during the next few days. One tiresome episode was the complete stopping-up of the lavatory basin drain in the S.C.R. cloak-room. This was found to be due to some torn fragments of material, which had been rammed firmly down through the grid with the help of a fine rod, and which, when the plumber had got them out, proved to be the remains of a pair of fabric gloves, stained with brown paint and quite unidentifiable as anybody's property. Another was the noisy emergence of the missing Library keys from the interior of a roll of photographs which Miss Pyke had left for half an hour in one of the lecture-rooms before using them to illustrate some remarks about the Parthenon Frieze. Neither of these episodes led to any discovery.

The Senior Common Room behaved to Harriet with that scrupulous and impersonal respect for a person's mission in life which the scholarly tradition imposes. It was clear to them that, once established as the official investigator, she must be allowed to investigate without interference. Nor did they hasten to her with protestations of innocence or cries of indignation. They treated the situation with a fine detachment, making little reference to it, and confining the conversation in Common Room to matters of general and University interest. In solemn and ritual order, they invited her to consume sherry or coffee in their rooms, and refrained from comment upon one another. Miss Barton, indeed, went out of her way to invite Harriet's opinions upon *Women in the Modern State* and to consult her on the subject of conditions in Germany. It is true that she flatly disagreed with many of the opinions expressed, but only objectively and without personal rancour; the vexed subject of the amateur's right to investigate crimes was decently shelved. Miss Hillyard also, setting aside animosity, took pains to interrogate Harriet about the technical aspects of such historical crimes as the murder of Sir Edmund Berry Godfrey and the alleged poisoning of Sir Thomas Overbury by the Countess of Essex. Such overtures might, of course, be policy; but Harriet was inclined to attribute them to a careful instinct for propriety.

With Miss de Vine she had many interesting conversations. The Fellow's personality attracted and puzzled her very much. More than with any other of the dons, she felt that with Miss de Vine the devotion to the intellectual life was the result, not of the untroubled following of a natural or acquired bias, but of a powerful spiritual call, over-riding other possible tendencies and desires. She felt inquisitive enough, without any prompting, about Miss de Vine's past life; but inquiry was difficult, and she always emerged from an encounter with the feeling that she had told more than she had learnt. She could guess at a history of conflict; but she found it difficult to believe that Miss de Vine was unaware of her own repressions or unable to control them.

With a view to establishing friendly relations with the Junior Common Room, Harriet further steeled herself to compose and deliver a 'talk' on 'Detection in Fact and Fiction' for a College literary society. This was perilous work. To the unfortunate case in which she had herself figured as the suspected party she naturally made no allusion; nor in the ensuing discussion was anybody so tactless as to mention it. The Wilvercombe murder was a different matter. There was no obvious reason why she should not tell the students about that, and it seemed unkind to deprive them of a legitimate thrill on the purely personal grounds that it was a bore to have to mention Peter Wimsey in every second sentence. Her exposition, though perhaps erring slightly on the dry and academic side, was received with hearty applause, and at the end of the meeting the Senior Student, one Miss Millbanks, invited her to coffee.

Miss Millbanks had her room in Queen Elizabeth, and had furnished it with a good deal of taste. She was a tall, elegant girl, obviously well-to-do, much better dressed than the majority of the students, and carrying her intellectual attainments easily. She held a minor scholarship without emoluments, declaring publicly that she was a scholar only because she would not be seen dead in the ridiculous short gown of a commoner. As alternatives to coffee, she offered Harriet the choice of madeira or a cocktail, politely regretting that the inadequacy of college arrangements made it impossible to provide ice for the shaker. Harriet, who disliked cocktails after dinner, and had consumed madeira and sherry on an almost wearisome number of occasions since her arrival in Oxford, accepted the coffee, and chuckled as cups and glasses were filled. Miss Millbanks inquired courteously what the joke was.

'Only,' said Harriet, 'that I gathered the other day from an article in the *Morning Star* that "undergraduettes," in the journalist's disgusting phrase, lived entirely on cocoa.'

'Journalists,' said Miss Millbanks, condescendingly, 'are always thirty years behind the times. Have you ever seen cocoa in College, Miss Fowler?'

'Oh, yes,' said Miss Fowler. She was a dark, thick-set Third Year, dressed in a very grubby sweater which, as she had previously explained, she had not had time to change, having been afflicted with an essay up to the moment of attending Harriet's talk. 'Yes, I've seen it in dons' rooms. Occasionally. But I've always looked on that as a kind of infantilism.'

'Isn't it a re-living of the heroic past?' suggested Miss Millbanks. '*O les beaux jours que ce siècle de fer*. And so on.'

'Groupists drink cocoa,' added another Third Year. She was thin, with an eager, scornful face, and made no apology for her sweater, apparently thinking such matters beneath her notice.

'But they are oh! so tender to the failings of others,' said Miss Millbanks. 'Miss Layton was "changed" once, but she has now changed back. It was good while it lasted.'

Miss Layton, curled on a pouffe by the fire, lifted a wicked little heart-shaped face alight with mischief.

'I did enjoy telling people what I thought of them. Too rapturous. Especially confessing in public the evil, evil thoughts I had had about that woman Flaxman.'

'Bother Flaxman,' said the dark girl, shortly. Her name was Haydock, and she was, as Harriet presently discov-

153

ered, considered to be a safe History First. 'She's setting the whole Second Year by the ears. I don't like her influence at all. And if you ask me, there's something véry wrong with Cattermole. Goodness knows, I don't want any of this business of being my brother's keeper – we had quite enough of that at school – but it'll be awkward if Cattermole is driven into doing something drastic. As Senior Student, Lilian, don't you think you could do something about it?'

'My dear,' protested Miss Millbanks, 'what can anybody do? I can't forbid Flaxman to make people's lives a burden to them. If I could, I wouldn't. You don't surely expect me to exercise authority? It's bad enough hounding people to College Meetings. The S.C.R. don't understand our sad lack of enthusiasm.'

'In their day,' said Harriet, 'I think people had a passion for meetings and organisation.'

'There are plenty of inter-collegiate meetings,' said Miss Layton. 'We discuss things a great deal, and are indignant about the Proctorial Rules for Mixed parties. But our enthusiasm for internal affairs is more restrained.'

'Well, I think,' said Miss Haydock bluntly, 'we sometimes overdo the *laisser-aller* side of it. If there's a big blow-up, it won't pay anybody.'

'Do you mean about Flaxman's cutting-out expeditions? Or about the ragging affair? By the way, Miss Vane, I suppose you have heard about the College Mystery.'

'I've heard something,' replied Harriet, cautiously. 'It seems to be all very tiresome.'

'It will be extremely tiresome if it isn't stopped,' said Miss Haydock. 'I say we ought to do a spot of private investigation ourselves. The S.C.R. don't seem to be making much progress.'

'Well, the last effort at investigation wasn't very satisfactory,' said Miss Millbanks.

'Meaning Cattermole? I don't believe it's Cattermole. She's too obvious. And she hasn't the guts. She could and does make an ass of herself, but she wouldn't go about it so secretively.'

'There's nothing against Cattermole,' said Miss Fowler, 'except that somebody wrote Flaxman an offensive letter on the occasion of her swiping Cattermole's young man. Cattermole was the obvious suspect then, but why should she do all these other things?'

'Surely,' Miss Layton appealed to Harriet, 'surely the obvious suspect is always innocent.'

Harriet laughed; and Miss Millbanks said:

'Yes; but I do think Cattermole is getting to the stage when she'd do almost anything to attract attention.'

'Well, I don't believe it's Cattermole,' said Miss Haydock. 'Why should she write letters to *me*?'

'Did you have one?'

'Yes; but it was only a kind of wish that I should plough in Schools. The usual silly thing made of pasted-up letters. I burnt it, and took Cattermole in to dinner on the strength of it.'

'Good for you,' said Miss Fowler.

'I had one too,' said Miss Layton. 'A beauty – about there being a reward in hell for women who went my way. So, acting on the suggestion given, I forwarded it to my future address by way of the fireplace.'

'All the same,' said Miss Millbanks, 'it is rather disgusting. I don't mind the letters so much. It's the rags, and the writing on the wall. If any snoopy person from outside happened to get hold of it, there'd be a public stink, and that would be a bore. I don't pretend to much public spirit, but I admit to some. We don't want to get

155

the whole College gated by way of reprisals. And I'd rather not have it said that we were living in a madhouse.'

'Too shame-making,' agreed Miss Layton; 'though of course, you may get an isolated queer specimen anywhere.'

'There are some oddities in the First Year all right,' said Miss Fowler. 'Why is it that every year seems to get shriller and scrubbier than the last?'

'They always did,' said Harriet.

'Yes,' said Miss Haydock, 'I expect the Third Year said the same about us when we first came up. But it's a fact that we had none of this trouble before we had this bunch of freshers in.'

Harriet did not contradict this, not wishing to focus suspicion on either the S.C.R. or on the unfortunate Cattermole who (as everybody would remember) was up during the Gaudy, waging simultaneous war against despised love and Responsions. She did ask, however, whether any suspicion had fallen upon other students besides Miss Cattermole.

'Not definitely, no,' replied Miss Millbanks. 'There's Hudson, of course – she came up from school with a bit of a reputation for ragging, but in my opinion she's quite sound. I should call the whole of our year pretty sound. And Cattermole really has only herself to thank. I mean, she's asking for trouble.'

'How?' asked Harriet.

'Various ways,' said Miss Millbanks, with a caution which suggested that Harriet was too much in the confidence of the S.C.R. to be trusted with details. 'She is rather inclined to break rules for the sake of it – which is all right if you get a kick out of it; but she doesn't.'

'Cattermole's going in off the deep end,' said Miss

Haydock. 'Wants to show young what's-his-name – Farringdon – he isn't the only pebble on the beach. All very well. But she's being a bit blatant. She's simply pursuing that lad Pomfret.'

'That fair-faced goop at Queen's?' said Miss Fowler. 'Well, she's going to be unlucky again, because Flaxman is steadily hauling him off.'

'Curse Flaxman!' said Miss Haydock. 'Can't she leave other people's men alone? She's bagged Farringdon; I do think she might leave Pomfret for Cattermole.'

'She hates to leave anybody anything,' said Miss Layton.

'I hope,' said Miss Millbanks, 'she has not been trying to collect your Geoffrey.'

'I'm not giving her the opportunity,' said Miss Layton, with an impish grin. 'Geoffrey's sound – yes, darlings, definitely sound – but I'm taking no chances. Last time we had him to tea in the J.C.R., Flaxman came undulating in – *so* sorry, she had no idea anybody was there, and she'd left a book behind. With the Engaged Label on the door as large as life. I did not introduce Geoffrey.'

'Did he want you to?' inquired Miss Haydock.

'Asked who she was. I said she was the Templeton Scholar and the world's heavyweight in the way of learning. That put him off.'

'What'll Geoffrey do when you pull off your First, my child?' demanded Miss Haydock.

'Well, Eve – it *will* be awkward if I do that. Poor lamb! I shall have to make him believe I only did it by looking fragile and pathetic at the viva.'

And Miss Layton did, indeed, contrive to look fragile and pathetic, and anything but learned. Nevertheless, on inquiry from Miss Lydgate, Harriet discovered that she was an extremely well-fancied favourite for the English

School, and was taking, of all things, a Language Special. If the dry bones of Philology could be made to live by Miss Layton, then she was a very dark horse indeed. Harriet felt a respect for her brains; so unexpected a personality might be capable of anything.

So much for Third-Year opinion. Harriet's first personal encounter with the Second Year was more dramatic.

The College had been so quiet for the last week that Harriet gave herself a holiday from police-duty and went to a private dance given by a contemporary of her own, who had married and settled in North Oxford. Returning between twelve and one, she garaged the car in the Dean's private garage, let herself quietly through the grille dividing the Traffic Entrance from the rest of College and began to cross the Old Quad towards Tudor. The weather had turned finer, and there was a pale glimmer of cloudy moonlight. Against that glimmer, Harriet, skirting the corner of Burleigh Building, observed something humped and strange about the outline of the eastern wall, close to where the Principal's private postern led out into St. Cross Road. It seemed clear that here, in the words of the old song, was 'a man where nae man should be.'

If she shouted at him, he would drop over on the outer side and be lost. She had the key of the postern with her – having been trusted with a complete set of keys for patrol purposes. Pulling her black evening cloak about her face and stepping softly, Harriet ran quickly down the grass path between the Warden's House and the Fellows' Garden, let herself silently out into St. Cross Road and stood beneath the wall. As she emerged, a second dark form stepped out from the shadows and said urgently, 'Oy!'

The gentleman on the wall looked round, exclaimed, 'Oh, hell!' and scrambled down in a hurry. His friend made off at a smart pace, but the wall-climber seemed to have damaged himself in his descent, and made but poor speed. Harriet, who was nimble enough, for all she was over nine years down from Oxford, gave chase and came up with him a few yards from the corner of Jowett Walk. The accomplice, now well away, looked back, hesitating.

'Clear out, old boy!' yelled the captive; and then, turning to Harriet, remarked with a sheepish grin, 'Well, it's a fair cop. I've bust my ankle or something.'

'And what were you doing on our wall, sir?' demanded Harriet. In the moonlight she beheld a fresh, fair and ingenuous face, youthfully rounded and, at the moment, disturbed by an expression of mingled apprehension and amusement. He was a very tall and very large young man; but Harriet had clasped him in a wiry grip that he could scarcely shake off without hurting her, and he showed no disposition to use violence.

'Just having a beano,' said the young man promptly. 'A bet, you know, and all that. Hang my cap on the tip-top branch of the Shrewsbury beeches. My friend there was the witness. I seem to have lost, don't I?'

'In that case,' said Harriet severely, 'where's your cap? And your gown, if it comes to that? And, sir, your name and college?'

'Well,' said the young man, impudently, 'if it comes to that, where and what are yours?'

When one's thirty-second birthday is no more than a matter of months away, such a question is flattering. Harriet laughed.

'My dear young man, do you take me for an under-graduate?'

'A don – a female don, God help us!' exclaimed the young man, whose spirits appeared to be sustained, though not unduly exalted, by spirituous liquors.

'Well?' said Harriet.

'I don't believe it,' said the young man, scanning her face as closely as he could in the feeble light. 'Not possible. Too young. Too charming. Too much sense of humour.'

'A great deal too much sense of humour to let you get away with that, my lad. And no sense of humour at all about this intrusion.'

'I say,' said the young man, 'I'm really most frightfully sorry. Mere light-heartedness and all that kind of thing. Honestly, we weren't doing any harm. Quite definitely not I mean, we were just winning the bet and going away quietly. I say, do be a sport. I mean, you're not the Warden or the Dean or anything. I know them. Couldn't you overlook it?'

'It's all very well,' said Harriet. 'But we can't have this kind of thing. It doesn't do. You must see that it doesn't do.'

'Oh, I do see,' agreed the young man. 'Absolutely. Definitely. Dashed silly thing to do. Open to misinterpretation.' He winced, and drew up one leg to rub his injured ankle. 'But when you do see a tempting bit of wall like that—'

'Ah, yes,' said Harriet, 'what *is* the temptation? Just come and show me, will you?' She led him firmly, despite his protests, towards the postern. 'Oh, I see, yes. A brick or two out of that buttress. Excellent foothold. You'd almost think they'd been knocked out on purpose, wouldn't you? And a handy tree in the Fellows' Garden.

The Bursar will have to see to it. Are you well acquainted with that buttress, young man?'

'It's known to exist,' admitted her captive. 'But, look here, we weren't – we weren't calling on anybody or anything of that kind, you know, if you know what I mean.'

'I hope not,' said Harriet.

'No, we were all on our own,' explained the young man eagerly. 'Nobody else involved. Good Heavens, no. And, look here, I've bust my ankle and we shall be gated anyhow, and, dear, kind lady—'

At this moment, a loud groan resounded from within the College wall. The young man's face became filled with agonised alarm.

'What's that?' asked Harriet.

'I really couldn't say,' said the young man.

The groan was repeated. Harriet grasped the undergraduate tightly by the arm and led him along to the postern.

'But look here,' said the gentleman, limping dolefully beside her, 'you mustn't – please don't think—'

'I'm going to see what's the matter,' said Harriet.

She unlocked the postern, drew her captive in with her, and relocked the gate. Under the wall, just beneath the spot where the young man had been perched, lay a huddled figure, which was apparently suffering acute internal agonies of some kind.

'Look here,' said the young man, abandoning all pretence. 'I'm most frightfully sorry about this. I'm afraid we were a bit thoughtless. I mean, we didn't notice. I mean , I'm afraid she isn't very well, and we didn't notice how it was, you know.'

'The girl's drunk,' said Harriet, uncompromisingly.

She had, in the bad old days, seen too many young

poets similarly afflicted to make any mistake about the symptoms.

'Well. I'm afraid – yes, that's about it,' said the young man. 'Rogers *will* mix 'em so strong. But look here, honestly, there's no harm done, and I mean—'

'H'm!' said Harriet. 'Well, don't shout. That house is the Warden's Lodgings.'

'Hell!' said the young man, for the second time. 'I say – are you going to be sporting?'

'That depends,' said Harriet. 'As a matter of fact, you've been extraordinarily lucky. I'm not one of the dons. I'm only staying in College. So I'm a free agent.'

'Bless you!' exclaimed the young man, fervently.

'Don't be in a hurry. You'll have to tell me about this. Who's the girl, by the way?'

The patient here gave another groan.

'Oh, dear!' said the undergraduate.

'Don't worry,' said Harriet. 'She'll be sick in a minute.' She walked over and inspected the sufferer. 'It's all right. You can preserve a gentlemanly reticence. I know her. Her name's Cattermole. What's yours?'

'My name's Pomfret – of Queen's.'

'Ah!' said Harriet.

'We threw a party round in my friend's rooms,' explained Mr. Pomfret. 'At least, it started as a meeting, but it ended as a party. Nothing wrong whatever. Miss Cattermole came along for a joke. All clean fun. Only there were a lot of us, and what with one thing and another we had a few too many, and then we found Miss Cattermole was rather under the weather. So we got her collected up, and Rogers and I—'

'Yes, I see,' said Harriet. 'Not very creditable, was it?'

'No, it's rotten,' admitted Mr. Pomfret.

'Had she got leave to attend the meeting? And late leave?'

'I don't know,' said Mr. Pomfret, disturbed. 'I'm afraid – look here! It's all rather tiresome. I mean, she doesn't belong to the Society—'

'What Society?'

'The Society that was meeting. I think she pushed in for a joke.'

'Gate-crashed you? H'm. That probably means no late leave.'

'Sounds serious,' said Mr. Pomfret.

'It's serious for *her*,' said Harriet. 'You'll get off with a fine or a gating, I suppose; but we have to be more particular. It's a nasty-minded world, and our rules have to remember that fact.'

'I know,' said Mr. Pomfret. 'As a matter of fact we were dashed worried. We had a devil of a job getting her along,' he burst out confidentially. 'Fortunately it was only from this end of Long Wall. Phew!'

He pulled out his handkerchief and wiped his forehead.

'Anyhow,' he went on, 'I'm thankful you aren't a don.'

'That's all very well,' said Harriet austerely; 'but I'm a Senior Member of College and I must feel responsibility. This isn't the kind of thing one wants.'

She turned a cold glance on the unfortunate Miss Cattermole, to whom the worst was happening.

'I'm sure *we* didn't want it,' said Mr. Pomfret, averting his eyes; 'but what could we do? It's no good trying to corrupt your porter,' he added ingenuously; 'it's been tried.'

'Indeed?' said Harriet. 'No; you wouldn't get much change out of Padgett. Was anybody else there from Shrewsbury?'

'Yes – Miss Flaxman and Miss Blake. But they had ordinary leave to come and went off at about eleven. So they're all right.'

'They ought to have taken Miss Cattermole with them.'

'Of course,' said Mr. Pomfret. He loked gloomier than ever. Obviously, thought Harriet, Miss Flaxman would not mind at all if Miss Cattermole got into trouble. Miss Blake's motives were more obscure; but she was probably only weak-minded. Harriet was fired with a quite unscrupulous determination that Miss Cattermole should not get into trouble if she could prevent it. She went across to the limp form and hauled it to its feet. Miss Cattermole groaned dismally. 'She'll do now,' said Harriet. 'I wonder where the little fool's room is. Do *you* know?'

'Well, as a matter of fact, I do,' replied Mr. Pomfret. 'Sounds bad, but there – people do show people their rooms, you know, all regulations notwithstanding and all that. It's somewhere over there, through that archway.'

He waved a vague hand towards the New Quad at the other end of nowhere.

'Heavens!' said Harriet, 'it would be. I'm afraid you'll have to give me a hand with her. She's a bit too much for me, and she can't stay here in the damp. If anybody sees us, you'll have to go through with it. How's the ankle?'

'Better, thanks,' said Mr. Pomfret. 'I think I can make shift to stagger a bit. I say, you're being very decent.'

'Get on with the job,' said Harriet, grimly, 'and don't waste time on speeches.'

Miss Cattermole was a thickly-built young woman, and no inconsiderable weight. She had also reached the stage of complete inertia. For Harriet, hampered by high-heeled shoes, and for Mr. Pomfret, afflicted with a game ankle, the progress across the quads was anything but triumphal. It was also rather noisy, what with the squeak of stone and gravel under their feet, and the grunts and shufflings of the limp figure between them. At every moment, Harriet expected to hear a window thrust up, or to see the shape of an agitated don come rushing out to demand some explanation of Mr. Pomfret's presence at that early hour of the morning. It was with very great relief that she at last found the right doorway and propelled Miss Cattermole's helpless form through it.

'What next?' inquired Mr. Pomfret in a hoarse whisper.

'I must let you out. I don't know where her room is, but I can't have you wandering all over College. Wait a minute. We'll deposit her in the nearest bathroom. Here you are. Round the corner. Easy does it.'

Mr. Pomfret again bent obligingly to the task.

'There!' said Harriet. She laid Miss Cattermole on her back on the bathroom floor, took the key from the lock and came out, securing the door behind her. 'She must stay there for the moment. Now we'll get rid of you. I don't think anybody saw us. If we're met on the way back, you were at Mrs. Heman's dance and saw me home. Get that? It's not very convincing, because you ought not to have done any such thing, but it's better than the truth.'

'I only wish I *had* been at Mrs. Heman's dance,' said the grateful Mr. Pomfret. 'I'd have danced every dance with you and all the extras. Do you mind telling me who you are?'

'My name's Vane. And you'd better not start being enthusiastic too soon. I'm not considering *your* welfare particularly. Do you know Miss Cattermole well?'

165

'Rather well. Oh, yes. Naturally. I mean, we know some of the same people and that sort of thing. As a matter of fact, she used to be engaged to an old school-fellow of mine – New College man – only that fell through and all that. No affair of mine; but you know how it is. One knows people and one kind of goes on knowing them. And there you are.'

'Yes, I see. Well, Mr. Pomfret, I am not anxious to get either you or Miss Cattermole into a row—'

'I knew you were a sport!' cried Mr. Pomfret.

'(Don't *shout*) – but this sort of thing cannot go on. There must be no more late parties and no more climbing over walls. You understand. Not with anybody. It's not fair. If I go to the Dean with this story, nothing much will happen to *you*, but Miss Cattermole will be lucky if she's not sent down. For God's sake, stop being an ass. There are much better ways of enjoying Oxford than fooling around at midnight with the women students.'

'I know there are. I think it's all rather rot, really.'

'Then why do it?'

'I don't know. Why does one do idiotic things?'

'Why?' said Harriet. They were passing the end of Chapel, and Harriet stood still to give emphasis to what she was saying. 'I'll tell you why, Mr. Pomfret. Because you haven't the guts to say No when somebody asks you to be a sport. That tom-fool word has got more people in trouble than all the rest of the dictionary put together. If it's sporting to encourage girls to break rules and drink more than they can carry and get themselves into a mess on your account, then I'd stop being a sport and try being a gentleman.'

'Oh, I say,' said Mr. Pomfret, hurt.

'I mean it,' said Harriet.

'Well, I see your point,' said Mr. Pomfret, shifting his

feet uneasily. 'I'll do my best about it. You've been dashed spor – I mean you've behaved like a perfect gentleman about all this—' He grinned – 'and I'll try to – good Lord! here's somebody coming.'

A quick patter of slippered feet along the passage between the Hall and Queen Elizabeth was approaching rapidly.

On an impulse, Harriet stepped back and pushed open the Chapel door.

'Get in,' she said.

Mr. Pomfret slipped hastily in behind her. Harriet shut the door on him and stood quietly in front of it. The footsteps came nearer, came opposite the porch and stopped suddenly. The night-walker uttered a little squeak.

'Ooh!'

'What is it?' said Harriet.

'Oh, miss, it's you! You gave me such a start. Did you see anything?'

'See what? Who is it, by the way?'

'Emily, miss. I sleep in the New Quad, miss, and I woke up, and I made sure I heard a man's voice in the quadrangle, and I looked out and there he was, miss, as plain as plain, coming this way with one of the young ladies. So I slipped on my slippers, miss. . . .'

'Damn!' said Harriet to herself. Better tell part of the truth, though.

'It's all right, Emily. It was a friend of mine. He came in with me and wanted very much to see the New Quad by moonlight. So we just walked across and back again.'

(A poor excuse, but probably less suspicious than a flat denial.)

'Oh, I see, miss. I beg your pardon. But I get that nervous, with one thing and another. And it's unusual, if you'll excuse me saying so, miss. . . .'

'Yes, very,' said Harriet, strolling gently away in the direction of the New Quad, so that the scout was bound to follow her. 'It was stupid of me not to think that it might disturb people. I'll mention it to the Dean in the morning. You did quite right to come down.'

'Well, miss, of course I didn't know who it was. And the Dean is so particular. And with all these queer things happening. . . .'

'Yes, absolutely. Of course. I'm really very sorry to have been so thoughtless. The gentleman has gone now, so you won't get woken up again.'

Emily seemed doubtful. She was one of those people who never feel they have said a thing till they have said it three times over. She paused at the foot of her staircase to say everything again. Harriet listened impatiently, thinking of Mr. Pomfret, fuming in the Chapel. At last she got rid of the scout and turned back.

Complicated, thought Harriet; silly situation, like a farce. Emily thinks she's caught a student: I think I've caught a Poltergeist. We catch each other. Young Pomfret parked in the Chapel. He thinks I'm kindly shielding him and Cattermole. Having carefully hidden Pomfret, I have to admit he was there. But if Emily *had* been the Poltergeist – and perhaps she is – then I couldn't have had Pomfret helping to chase her. This kind of sleuthing is very confusion-making.

She pushed open the Chapel door. The porch was empty.

'Damn!' said Harriet, irreverently. 'The idiot's gone. Perhaps he's gone inside, though.'

She looked in through the inner door and was relieved to see a dark figure faintly outlined against the pale oak of the stalls. Then, with a sudden, violent shock, she became aware of a second dark figure, poised strangely, it seemed, in mid-air.

'Hullo!' said Harriet. In the thin light of the South windows she saw the flash of a white shirt-front as Mr. Pomfret turned. 'It's only me. *What's that?*'

She took a torch from her handbag and recklessly switched it on. The beam showed a dismal shape dangling from the canopy above the stalls. It was swinging a little to and fro and turning slowly as it swung. Harriet darted forward.

'Morbid kind of imagination these girls have got, haven't they—' said Mr. Pomfret.

Harriet contemplated the M.A. cap and gown, arranged over a dress and bolster hitched by a thin cord on one of the terminals with which the architect had decorated the canopies.

'Bread-knife stuck through the tummy, too,' pursued Mr. Pomfret. 'Gave me quite a turn, as my aunt would say. Did you catch the young woman?'

'No. Was she in here?'

'Oh, definitely,' said Mr. Pomfret. 'Thought I'd retreat a bit farther, you know. So in I came. Then I saw that. So I came along to investigate and heard somebody scrambling out by the other door – over there.'

He pointed vaguely towards the north side of the building, where a door led into the vestry. Harriet hastened to look. The door was open, and the outer vestry door, though shut, had been unlocked from within. She peered out. All was quiet.

'Bother them and their rags,' said Harriet, returning. 'No, I didn't meet the lady. She must have got away while I was taking Emily back to the New Quad. Just my luck!' She muttered the last exclamation under her breath. It was really sickening to have had the Poltergeist under her hand like that, and to have been distracted by Emily. She went up to the dummy again, and saw that a paper was pinned to its middle by the bread-knife.

'Quotations from the classics,' said Mr. Pomfret, easily. 'Looks as though somebody had a grouse against your dons.'

'Silly young fools!' said Harriet: 'Very convincing bit of work, though, come to look at it. If we hadn't found it first, it would have created quite a sensation when we all filed into prayers. A little investigation is indicated. Well, now, it's time you went quietly home and were gated for the good of your soul.'

She led him down to the postern and let him out.

'By the way, Mr. Pomfret, I'd be obliged if you didn't mention this rag to anybody. It's not in the best of taste. One good turn deserves another.'

'Just as you say,' replied Mr. Pomfret. 'And, look here – may I push round to-morrow – at least, it's this morning, isn't it? – and make inquiries and all that? Only proper, you know. When shall you be in? Please!'

'No visitors in the morning,' said Harriet, promptly. 'I don't know what I shall be doing in the afternoon. But you can always ask at the Lodge.'

'Oh, I may? That's top-hole. I'll call – and if you're not there I'll leave a note. I mean, you must come round and have tea or a cocktail or something. And I do honestly promise it shan't happen again, if I can help it.'

'All right. By the way – what time did Miss Cattermole arrive at your friend's place?'

'Oh – about half-past nine, I think. Couldn't be sure. Why?'

'I only wondered whether her initials were in the porter's book. But I'll see to it. Good-night.'

'Good-night,' said Mr. Pomfret, 'and thanks frightfully.'

Harriet locked the postern behind him and returned across the quadrangle, feeling that, out of all this absurd tiresomeness, something had been most definitely gained. The dummy could scarcely have been put in position before 9.30; so that Miss Cattermole, through sheer folly, had contrived to give herself a cast-iron alibi. Harriet was so grateful to her for advancing the inquiry by even this small step that she determined the girl should, if possible, be let off the consequences of her escapade.

This reminded her that Miss Cattermole still lay on the bathroom floor, waiting to be dealt with. It would be awkward if she had come to her senses in the interval and started to make a noise. But on reaching the New Quad and unlocking the door, Harriet found her prisoner in the somnolent stage of her rake's progress. A little research along the corridors revealed that Miss Cattermole slept on the first floor. Harriet opened the door of the room, and as she did so the door next it opened also, and a head popped out.

'Is that you, Cattermole?' whispered the head. 'Oh, I'm sorry.' It popped in again.

Harriet recognised the girl who had gone up and spoken to Miss Cattermole after the Opening of the Library. She went to her door, which bore the name of 'C. I. Briggs,' and knocked gently. The head reappeared.

'Were you expecting to see Miss Cattermole come in?'

'Well,' said Miss Briggs. 'I heard somebody at her door – oh! it's Miss Vane, isn't it?'

'Yes. What made you sit up and wait for Miss Cattermole?'

Miss Briggs, who was wearing a woolly coat over her pyjamas, looked a little alarmed.

'I had some work to do. I was sitting up in any case. Why?'

Harriet looked at the girl. She was short and sturdily built, with a plain, strong, sensible face. She appeared trustworthy.

'If you're a friend of Miss Cattermole's,' said Harriet, 'you'd better come and help me upstairs with her. She's down in the bathroom. I found her being helped over the wall by a young man, and she's rather under the weather.'

'Oh, dear!' said Miss Briggs. 'Tight?'

'I'm afraid so.'

'She *is* a fool,' said Miss Briggs. 'I knew there'd be trouble some day. All right, I'll come.'

Between them they lugged Miss Cattermole up the noisy, polished stairs and dumped her upon her bed. In grim silence they undressed her and put her between the sheets.

'She'll sleep it off now,' said Harriet. 'I think, by the way, a little explanation wouldn't be a bad idea. How about it?'

'Come into my room,' said Miss Briggs. 'Would you like any hot milk or Ovaltine or coffee, or anything?'

Harriet accepted hot milk. Miss Briggs put a kettle on the ring in the pantry opposite, came in, stirred up the fire and sat down on a pouffe.

'Please tell me,' said Miss Briggs, 'what has happened.'

Harriet told her, omitting the names of the gentlemen concerned. But Miss Briggs promptly supplied the omission.

'That was Reggie Pomfret, of course,' she observed. 'Poor blighter. He *always* gets left with the baby. After all, what is the lad to do, if people go chasing him.'

'It's awkward,' said Harriet. 'I mean, you need some

172

knowledge of the world to get out of it gracefully. Does the girl really care for him?'

'No,' said Miss Briggs. 'Not really. She just wants somebody or something. You know. She got a nasty knock when her engagement was broken. You see, she and Lionel Farringdon had been childhood friends and so on, and it was all settled before she came up. Then Farringdon got collared by our Miss Flaxman, and there was a frightful bust-up. And there were complications. And Violet Cattermole has gone all unnerved.'

'I know,' said Harriet. 'Sort of desperate feeling – I must have a man of my own – that kind of thing.'

'Yes. Doesn't matter who he is. I think it's a sort of inferiority complex, or something. One must do idiotic things and assert one's self. Am I making myself clear?'

'Oh, yes. I understand that perfectly. It happens so often. One just has to make one's self out no end of a little devil. . . . Has this kind of thing happened often?'

'Well,' confessed Miss Briggs, 'more often than I like. I've tried to keep Violet reasonable, but what's the good of preaching to people? When they get into that worked-up state you might as well talk to the man in the moon. And though it's very tiresome for young Pomfret, he's awfully decent and safe. If he were strong-minded, of course he'd get out of it. But I'm rather thankful he's not, because, if it wasn't for him it might be some frightful tick or other.'

'Is anything likely to come of it?'

'Marriage, do you mean? No-o. I think he has enough sense of self-protection to avoid that. And besides— Look here, Miss Vane, it really is an awful shame. Miss Flaxman simply cannot leave anybody alone, and she's trying to get Pomfret away too, though she doesn't want him. If only she'd leave poor Violet alone, the whole thing would probably work itself out quite quietly. Mind you, I'm very fond of Violet. She's a decent sort, and she'd be absolutely all right with the right kind of man. She's no business to be up at Oxford at all, really. A nice domestic life with a man to be devoted to is what she really wants. But he'd have to be a solid, decided kind of man, and frightfully affectionate in a firm kind of way. But not Reggie Pomfret, who is a chivalrous young idiot.'

Miss Briggs poked the fire savagely.

'Well,' said Harriet, 'something has got to be done about all this. I don't want to go to the Dean, but—'

'Of course, something must be done,' said Miss Briggs. 'It's extraordinarily lucky it should have been you who spotted it and not one of the dons. I've been almost wishing that *something* might happen. I've been frightfully worried about it. It isn't the kind of thing I know how to cope with at all. But I had to stand by Violet more or less – otherwise I should simply have lost her confidence altogether and goodness knows what stupid thing she'd have done then.'

'I think you're quite right,' said Harriet. 'But now, perhaps I can have a word with her and tell her to mind her step. After all, she has got to give some guarantee of sensible behaviour if I'm not to report her to the Dean. A spot of benevolent blackmail is indicated, I fancy.'

'Yes,' agreed Miss Briggs. 'You can do it. It's exceedingly decent of you. I'll be thankful to be relieved of the responsibility. It's all rather wearing – and it does upset one's work. After all, work's what one's here for. I've got Honour Mods next term, and it's frightfully upsetting, never knowing what's going to happen next.'

'I expect Miss Cattermole relies on you a lot.'

'Yes,' said Miss Briggs, 'but listening to people's confidences does take such a time, and I'm not awfully good at wrestling with fits of temperament.'

'The confidante has a very heavy and thankless task,' said Harriet. 'It's not surprising if she goes mad in white linen. It's more surprising if she keeps sane and sensible like you. But I agree that you ought to have the burden taken off your shoulders. Are you the only one?'

'Pretty well. Poor old Violet lost a lot of friends over the uproar.'

'And the business of the anonymous letters?'

'Oh, you've heard about that? Well, of course, it wasn't Violet. That's ridiculous. But Flaxman spread the story all over the college, and once you've started an accusation like that, it takes a lot of killing.'

'It does. Well, Miss Briggs, you and I had better go to bed. I'll come along and see Miss Cattermole after breakfast. Don't worry too much. I dare say this upset will be a blessing in disguise. Well, I'll be going now. Can you lend me a strong knife?'

Miss Briggs, rather astonished, produced a stout pen-knife and said good-night. On her way over to Tudor, Harriet cut down the dangling dummy and carried it away with her for scrutiny and action at a later hour. She felt she badly needed to sleep on the situation.

She must have been weary, for she dropped off as soon as she was in bed, and dreamed neither of Peter Wimsey nor of anything else.

8

Tho marking him with melting eyes
A thrilling throbbe from her hart did aryse,
And interrupted all her other speache.
With some old sorowe that made a newe breache
Seeme shee sawe in the younglings face
The old lineaments of his fathers grace.

EDMUND SPENSER

'THE fact remains,' said Miss Pyke, 'that I have to lecture at nine. Can anybody lend me a gown?'

A number of the dons were breakfasting in the S.C.R. dining-room. Harriet entered in time to hear the request, formulated in a high and rather indignant tone.

'Have you lost your gown, Miss Pyke?'

'You could have mine with pleasure, Miss Pyke,' said little Miss Chilperic, mildly, 'but I'm afraid it wouldn't be nearly long enough.'

'It isn't safe to leave *anything* in the S.C.R. cloakroom these days,' said Miss Pyke. 'I *know* it was there after dinner, because I saw it.'

'You can have mine,' suggested Miss Burrows, 'if you can get it back to me by 10 o'clock.'

'Ask Miss de Vine or Miss Barton,' said the Dean. 'They have no lectures. Or Miss Vane – hers would fit you.'

'Certainly,' said Harriet, carelessly. 'Do you want a cap as well?'

'The cap *has* gone as well,' replied Miss Pyke. 'I don't need it for the lecture; but it would be convenient to know where my property has gone to.'

'It's surprising the way things disappear,' said Harriet, helping herself to scrambled eggs. 'People are very thoughtless. Who, by the way, owns a black semi-evening crêpe-de-chine, figured with bunches of red and green poppies, with a draped cross-over front, deep hip-yoke and flared skirt and sleeves about three years out of date?'

She looked round the dining-room, which was by now fairly well filled with dons. 'Miss Shaw – you have a very good eye for a frock. Can you identify it?'

'I might if I saw it,' said Miss Shaw. 'I don't recollect one like it from your description.'

'Have you found one?' asked the Bursar.

'Another chapter in the mystery?' suggested Miss Barton.

'I'm sure none of my students has one like it,' said Miss Shaw. 'They like to come and show me their frocks. I think it's a good thing to take an interest in them.'

'I don't remember a frock like that in the Senior Common Room,' said the Bursar.

'Didn't Miss Wrigley have a black figured crêpe-de-chine?' asked Mrs. Goodwin.

'Yes,' said Miss Shaw. 'But she's left. And anyhow, hers had a square neck and no hip-yoke. I remember it very well.'

'Can't you tell us what the mystery is, Miss Vane?' inquired Miss Lydgate. 'Or is it better that you shouldn't say anything?'

'Well,' said Harriet, 'I don't see any reason why I shouldn't tell you. When I came in last night after my dance I-er went the rounds a bit—'

'Ah!' said the Dean. 'I thought I heard somebody going to and fro outside my window. And whispering.'

'Yes – Emily came out and caught me. I think she thought I was the Practical Joker. Well – I happened to go into the Chapel.'

She told her story, omitting all mention of Mr. Pomfret, and merely saying that the culprit had apparently left by the vestry door.

'And,' she concluded, 'as a matter of fact, the cap and gown were yours, Miss Pyke, and you can have them any time. The bread-knife was taken from the Hall, presumably, or from here. And the bolster – I can't say where they got that.'

'I think I can guess,' said the Bursar. 'Miss Trotman is away. She lives on the ground floor of Burleigh. It would be easy to nip in and bag her bolster.'

'Why is Trotman away?' asked Miss Shaw. 'She never told me.'

'Father taken ill,' said the Dean. 'She went off in a hurry yesterday afternoon.'

'I can't think why she shouldn't have told me,' said Miss Shaw. 'My students always come to me with their troubles. It's rather upsetting, when you think your pupils value your sympathy—'

'But you were out to tea,' said the Treasurer practically.

'I put a note in your pigeon-hole,' said the Dean.

'Oh,' said Miss Shaw. 'Well, I didn't see it. I knew nothing about it, It's very odd that nobody should have mentioned it.'

'Who *did* know it?' asked Harriet.

There was a pause; during which everybody had time to think it strange and improbable that Miss Shaw should not have received the note or heard of Miss Trotman's departure.

'It was mentioned at the High last night, I think,' said Miss Allison.

'I was out to dinner,' said Miss Shaw. 'I shall go and see if that note's there.'

Harriet followed her out; the note was there – a sheet of paper folded together and not sealed in an envelope.

'Well,' said Miss Shaw; 'I never saw it.'

'Anybody might have read that and put it back,' said Harriet.

'Yes – including myself, you mean.'

'I didn't say that, Miss Shaw. Anybody.'

They returned gloomily to the Common Room.

'The-er-the joke was perpetrated between dinner-time, when Miss Pyke lost her gown, and about a quarter to one, when I found it out,' said Harriet. 'It would be convenient if anybody could produce a watertight alibi for the whole of that time. Particularly for the time after 11.15. I suppose I can find out whether any students had late leave till midnight. Anybody coming in then might have seen something.'

'I have a list,' said the Dean. 'And the porter could show you the names of those who came in after nine.'

'That will be a help.'

'In the meantime,' said Miss Pyke, pushing away her plate and rolling her napkin, 'the ordinary duties of the day must be proceeded with. Could I have my gown – or *a* gown?'

She went over to Tudor with Harriet, who restored the gown and displayed the crêpe-de-chine frock.

'I have never seen that dress to my knowledge before,' said Miss Pyke; 'but I cannot pretend to be observant in these matters. It appears to be made for a slender person of medium height.'

'There's no reason to suppose it belongs to the person

who put it there,' said Harriet, 'any more than your gown.'

'Of course not,' said Miss Pyke; 'no.' She gave Harriet an odd, swift glance from her sharp, black eyes. 'But the owner might provide some clue to the thief. Would it not – pardon me if I am trespassing upon your province – would it not be possible to draw some deduction from the name of the shop where it was bought?'

'Obviously it would have been,' said Harriet; 'the tab has been removed.'

'Oh,' said Miss Pyke. 'Well; I must go to my lecture. As soon as I can find leisure I will endeavour to provide you with a time-table of my movements last night. I fear, however, it will scarcely be illuminating. I was in my room after dinner and in bed by half-past ten.'

She stalked out, carrying her cap and gown. Harriet watched her go, and then took out a piece of paper from a drawer. The message upon it was pasted up in the usual way, and ran

tristius haud illis monstrum nec saevior ulla pestis et ira deum Stygiis sese extulit undis. Virginei volucrum vultus foedissima ventris proluvies uncaeque manus et pallida semper ora fame.

'Harpies,' said Harriet aloud. 'Harpies. That seems to suggest a train of thought. But I'm afraid we can't suspect Emily or any of the scouts of expressing their feelings in Virgilian hexameters.'

She frowned. Matters were looking rather bad for the Senior Common Room.

Harriet tapped on Miss Cattermole's door, regardless of the fact that it bore a large notice: HEADACHE – DO NOT DISTURB. It was opened by Miss Briggs, whose brow was anxious, but cleared when she saw who the visitor was.

'I was afraid it might be the Dean,' said Miss Briggs.

'No,' said Harriet, 'so far I have held my hand. How is the patient?'

'Not too good,' said Miss Briggs.

'Ah! "His lordship hath drunk his bath and gone to bed again." That's about it, I suppose.' She strode across to the bed and looked down at Miss Cattermole, who opened her eyes with a groan. They were large, light, hazel eyes, set in a plump face that ought to have been of a pleasant rose-leaf pink. A quantity of fluffy brown hair tumbled damply about her brow, adding to the general impression of an Angora rabbit that had gone on the loose and was astonished at the result.

'Feeling bloody?' inquired Harriet, with sympathy.

'Horrible,' said Miss Cattermole.

'Serve you right,' said Harriet. 'If you must take your drink like a man, the least you can do is to carry it like a gentleman. It's a great thing to know your own limitations.'

Miss Cattermole looked so woebegone that Harriet began to laugh 'You don't seem to be a very practised hand at this kind of thing. Look here; I'll get you something to pull you together and then I'm going to talk to you.'

She went out briskly and nearly fell over Mr. Pomfret in the outer doorway.

'You here?' said Harriet. 'I told you, no visitors in the morning. It makes a noise in the quad and is contrary to regulations.'

'I'm not a visitor,' said Mr. Pomfret, grinning, 'I've been attending Miss Hillyard's lecture on Constitutional Developments.'

'God help you!'

'And seeing you cross the quad in this direction, I turned in that direction like the needle to the North. Dark,' said Mr. Pomfret, with animation, 'and true and tender is the North. That's a quotation. It's very nearly the only one I know, so it's a good thing it fits.'

'It does not fit. I am not feeling tender.'

'Oh! . . . how's Miss Cattermole?'

'Bad hang-over. As you might expect.'

'Oh! . . . sorry . . . No row, I hope?'

'No.'

'Bless you!' said Mr. Pomfret. 'I was lucky too. Friend of mine has a dashed good window. All quiet on the Western Front. So – look here! I wish there was something I could do to—'

'You shall,' said Harriet. She twitched his lecture note-book from under his arm and scribbled in it.

'Get that made up at the chemist's and bring it back. I'm damned if I want to go myself and ask for a recipe for hobnailed liver.'

Mr. Pomfret looked at her with respect.

'Where did you learn that one?' said he.

'Not at Oxford. I may say I have never had occasion to taste it; I hope it's nasty. The quicker you can get it made up, the better, by the way.'

'I know, I know,' said Mr. Pomfret, disconsolately. 'You're fed up with the sight of me, and no wonder. But I do wish you'd come round some time and meet old Rogers. He's incredibly penitent. Come and have tea. Or a drink or something. Come this afternoon. Do. Just to show there's no ill-feeling.'

Harriet was opening her mouth to say No, when she looked at Mr. Pomfret, and her heart softened. He had the appeal of a very young dog of a very large breed – a kind of amiable absurdity.

'All right,' said Harriet. 'I will. Thank you very much.'

Mr. Pomfret exhausted himself in expressions of delight, and, still vocal, allowed himself to be shepherded to the gate, where, almost in the act of stepping out, he had to step back to allow the entrance of a tall, dark student wheeling a bicycle.

'Hullo, Reggie!' cried the young woman, 'looking for me?'

'Oh, good morning,' said Mr. Pomfret, rather taken aback. Then, catching sight of a handsome leonine head over the student's shoulder, he added with more assurance, 'Hullo, Farringdon!'

'Hullo, Pomfret!' cried Mr. Farringdon. The adjective 'Byronic' fitted him well enough, thought Harriet. He had an arrogant profile, a mass of close chestnut curls, hot brown eyes and sulky mouth, and looked less pleased to see Mr. Pomfret than Mr. Pomfret to see him.

Mr. Pomfret presented Mr. Farringdon of New College to Harriet, and murmured that of course Miss Flaxman was known to her. Miss Flaxman stared coolly at Harriet and said how much she had enjoyed her detective talk the other night.

'We're throwing a party at 6 o'clock,' went on Miss Flaxman to Mr. Pomfret. She pulled off her scholar's gown and stuffed it unceremoniously into her bicycle-basket. 'Care to come? In Leo's room. Six o'clock. I think we've room for Reggie, haven't we, Leo?'

'I suppose so,' said Mr. Farringdon, rather ungraciously. 'There'll be an awful crowd anyway.'

'Then we can always stuff in one more,' said Miss Flaxman. 'Don't mind, Leo, Reggie; he's mislaid his manners this morning.'

Mr. Pomfret appeared to think that somebody else's manners had also been mislaid, for he replied with more spirit than Harriet had expected of him:

'I'm sorry; I'm afraid I'm engaged. Miss Vane is coming to tea with me.'

'Another time will do for that,' said Harriet.

'Oh, no,' said Mr. Pomfret.

'Couldn't you both come along, then, afterwards?' said Mr. Farringdon. 'Always room for one more, as Catherine says.' He turned to Harriet. 'I hope you will come, Miss Vane. We should be delighted.'

'Well—' said Harriet. It was Miss Flaxman's turn to look sulky.

'I say,' said Mr. Farringdon, suddenly putting two and two together, 'are you *the* Miss Vane, the novelist . . .? You *are*! Then, look here, you simply *must* come. I shall be the most envied man in New College. We're all detective fans there.'

'What about it?' said Harriet, deferring to Mr. Pomfret.

It was so abundantly clear that Miss Flaxman did not want Harriet, that Mr. Farringdon did not want Mr. Pomfret, and that Mr. Pomfret did not want to go, that she felt the novelist's malicious enjoyment in a foolish situation. Since none of the party could now very well get out of the situation without open rudeness, the invitation was eventually accepted. Mr. Pomfret stepped into the street to join Mr. Farringdon; Miss Flaxman could scarcely get out of accompanying Miss Vane back through the quadrangle.

'I didn't know you knew Reggie Pomfret,' said Miss Flaxman.

'Yes, we have met,' said Harriet. 'Why didn't you bring Miss Cattermole home with you last night? Especially as you must have seen she was unwell.'

Miss Flaxman looked startled.

'It was nothing to do with me,' she said. 'Was there a row?'

'No; but did you do anything to prevent it? You might have done, mightn't you?'

'I can't be Violet Cattermole's guardian.'

'Anyway,' said Harriet, 'you may be glad to know that some good has come of this stupid business. Miss Cattermole is now definitely cleared of all suspicion about the anonymous letters and other disturbances. So it would be quite a good idea to behave decently to her, don't you think?'

'I tell you,' said Miss Flaxman, 'that I don't care one way or the other about it.'

'No; but you started the rumours about her; it's up to you to stop them, now you know. I think it would be only fair to tell Mr. Farringdon the truth. If you do not, I shall.'

'You seem to be very much interested in my affairs, Miss Vane.'

'They seem to have aroused a good deal of general interest,' said Harriet bluntly. 'I don't blame you for the original misunderstanding, but now that it is cleared up – and you can take my word for it that it is – I am sure you will see it is unfair that Miss Cattermole should be made a scapegoat. You can do a lot with your own year. Will you do what you can?'

Miss Flaxman, perplexed and annoyed, and obviously not quite clear what status she was to accord to Harriet, said, rather grudgingly:

'Of course, if she didn't do it, I'm glad. Very well. I'll tell Leo.'

'Thank you very much,' said Harriet.

*   *   *

Mr. Pomfret must have run very fast both ways, for the prescription appeared in a remarkably short space of time, along with a large bunch of roses. The draught was a potent one, and enabled Miss Cattermole not only to appear in the Hall, but to eat her lunch. Harriet pursued her as she was leaving and carried her off to her own room.

'Well,' said Harriet, 'you are a young idiot, aren't you?'

Miss Cattermole dismally agreed.

'What's the sense of it?' said Harriet. 'You have contrived to commit every crime in the calendar and got dashed little fun out of it, haven't you? You've attended a meeting in a man's rooms after Hall without leave, and you oughtn't to have got leave, because you gatecrashed the meeting. That's a social crime as well as a breach of rules. In any case, you were out after nine, without putting your initials in the book. That would cost you two bob. You came back to College after 11.15 without extra leave – which would be five shillings. You returned, in fact, after midnight, which would be ten shillings, even if you had had leave. You climbed the wall, for which you ought to be gated; and finally, you came in blotto, for which you ought to be sent down. Incidentally, that's another social crime. What have you got to say, prisoner at the bar? Is there any reason why sentence should not be passed upon you? Have a cigarette.'

'Thank you,' said Miss Cattermole, faintly.

'If,' said Harriet, 'you hadn't, by this silly piece of work, contrived to clear yourself of the suspicion of being the College lunatic, I should go to the Dean. As it is, the episode has had its usefulness, and I'm inclined to be merciful.'

Miss Cattermole looked up.

'Did something happen while I was out?'

'Yes, it did.'

'Oh-h-h!' said Miss Cattermole, and burst into tears.

Harriet watched her for a few minutes and then brought out a large clean handkerchief from a drawer and silently handed it over.

'You can forget all that,' said Harriet, when the victim's sobs had died down a little. 'But do chuck all this nonsense. Oxford isn't the place for it. You can run after young men any time – God knows the world's full of them. But to waste three years which are unlike anything else in one's lifetime is ridiculous. And it isn't fair to College. It's not fair to other Oxford women. Be a fool if you like – I've been a fool in my time and so have most people – but for Heaven's sake do it somewhere where you won't let other people down.'

Miss Cattermole was understood to say, rather incoherently, that she hated College and loathed Oxford, and felt no responsibility towards those institutions.

'Then why,' said Harriet, 'are you here?'

'I don't want to be here; I never did. Only my parents were so keen. My mother's one of those people who work to get things open to women – you know – professions and things. And father's a lecturer in a small provincial University. And they've made a lot of sacrifices and things.'

Harriet thought Miss Cattermole was probably the sacrificial victim.

'I didn't mind coming up, so much,' went on Miss Cattermole; 'because I was engaged to somebody, and he was up, too, and I thought it would be fun and the silly old Schools wouldn't matter much. But I'm not engaged to him any more and how on earth can I be expected to bother about all this dead-and-gone History?'

'I wonder they bothered to send you to Oxford, if you didn't want to go, and were engaged.'

'Oh! but they said that didn't make any difference. Every woman ought to have a University education, even if she married. And *now*, of course, they say what a good thing it is I still have my College career. And I can't make them understand that I *hate* it! They can't see that being brought up with everybody talking education all round one is enough to make one loathe the sound of it. I'm sick of education.'

Harriet was not surprised.

'What should you have liked to do? I mean, supposing the complication about your engagement hadn't happened?'

'I think,' said Miss Cattermole, blowing her nose in a final manner and taking another cigarette, 'I think I should have liked to be a cook. Or possibly a hospital nurse, but I think I should have been better at cooking. Only, you see, those are two of the things Mother's always trying to get people out of the way of thinking women's sphere ought to be restricted to.'

'There's a lot of money in good cooking,' said Harriet.

'Yes – but it's not an educational advance. Besides, there's no school of Cookery at Oxford, and it had to be Oxford, you see, or Cambridge, because of the opportunity of making the right kind of friends. Only I haven't made any friends. They all hate me. Perhaps they won't so much, now that the beastly letters—'

'Quite so,' said Harriet, hastily, fearing a fresh outburst. 'How about Miss Briggs? She seems to be a very good sort.'

'She's awfully kind. But I'm always having to be

grateful to her. It's very depressing. It makes me want to bite.'

'How right you are,' said Harriet, to whom this was a direct blow over the solar plexus. 'I know. Gratitude is simply damnable.'

'And now,' said Miss Cattermole, with devastating candour, 'I've got to be grateful to *you*.'

'You needn't be. I was serving my own ends as much as yours. But I'll tell you what I'd do. I'd stop trying to do sensational things, because it's apt to get you into positions where you have to be grateful. And I'd stop chasing undergraduates, because it bores them to tears and interrupts their work. I'd tackle the History and get through Schools. And then I'd turn round and say, "Now I've done what you want me to, and I'm going to be a cook." And stick to it.'

'Would you?'

'I expect you want to be very truly run after, like Old Man Kangaroo. Well, good cooks are. Still, as you've started here on History, you'd better worry on at it. It won't hurt you, you know. If you learn how to tackle one subject – any subject – you've learnt how to tackle all subjects.'

'Well,' said Miss Cattermole, in rather an unconvinced tone, 'I'll try.'

Harriet went away in a rage and tackled the Dean.

'Why do they send these people here? Making themselves miserable and taking up the place of people who *would* enjoy Oxford? *We* haven't got room for women who aren't and never will be scholars. It's all right for the men's colleges to have hearty passmen who gambol round and learn to play games, so that they can gambol and game in Prep. Schools. But this dreary little devil isn't even hearty. She's a wet mess.'

'I *know*,' said the Dean impatiently. 'But schoolmistresses and parents are such jugginses. We do our best, but we can't always weed out their mistakes. And here's my secretary – called away, because her tiresome little boy's got chicken-pox at his infuriating school. Oh, dear! I oughtn't to talk like that, because he's a delicate child and naturally children must come first, but it is *too* crushing!'

'I'll be off,' said Harriet. 'It's a shame you should have to be working of an afternoon and a shame of me to interrupt. By the way, I may as well tell you that Cattermole had an alibi for last night's affair.'

'Had she? Good! That's something. Though I suppose it means *more* suspicion on our miserable selves. Still, facts are facts. Miss Vane, what *was* the noise in the quad last night? And who was the young man you were bear-leading? I didn't ask this morning in Common-Room, because I had an idea you didn't want me to.'

'I didn't,' said Harriet.

'And you don't?'

'As Sherlock Holmes said on another occasion: "I think we must ask for an amnesty in that direction."'

The Dean twinkled shrewdly at her.

'Two and two make four. Well, I trust you.'

'But I was going to suggest a row of revolving spikes on the wall of the Fellows' Garden.'

'Ah!' said the Dean. 'Well, I don't *want* to know things. And most of it's sheer cussedness. They want to make heroes and heroines of themselves. Last week of term's the worst for wall-climbing. They make bets. Have to work 'em off before the end of term. Tiresome little cuckoos. All the same, it can't be allowed.'

'It won't happen again, I fancy, with this particular lot.'

'Very well. I'll speak to the Bursar – in a general way – about spikes.'

Harriet changed her frock, pondering on the social absurdities of the party to which she was invited. Clearly Mr. Pomfret clung to her as a protection against Miss Flaxman, and Mr. Farringdon, as a protection against Mr. Pomfret, while Miss Flaxman, who was apparently her hostess, did not want her at all. It was a pity that she could not embark on the adventure of annexing Mr. Farringdon, to complete a neat little tail-chasing circle. But she was both too old and too young to feel any thrill over the Byronic profile of Mr. Farringdon; there was more amusement to be had out of remaining a buffer state. She did, however, feel sufficient resentment against Miss Flaxman for her handling of the Cattermole affair, to put on an exceedingly well-cut coat and skirt and a hat of unexceptionable smartness, before starting out for the first item in her afternoon's programme.

She had little difficulty in finding Mr. Pomfret's staircase, and none whatever in finding Mr. Pomfret. As she wound her way up the dark and ancient stairs, past the shut door of one Mr. Smith, the sported oak of one Mr. Banerjee, and the open door of one Mr. Hodges, who seemed to be entertaining a large and noisy party of male friends, she became aware of an altercation going on upon the landing above, and presently Mr. Pomfret himself came into view, standing in his own doorway and arguing with a man whose back was turned towards the stairs.

'You can go to the devil,' said Mr. Pomfret.

'Very good, sir,' said the back; 'but how about me going to the young lady? If I was to go and tell her that I seen you a-pushing of her over the wall—'

'Blast you!' exclaimed Mr. Pomfret. '*Will* you shut up?'

At this point, Harriet set her foot upon the top stair, and encountered the eye of Mr. Pomfret.

'Oh!' said Mr. Pomfret, taken aback. Then, to the man, 'Clear off now; I'm busy. You'd better come again.'

'Quite a man for the ladies, ain't you, sir?' said the man, disagreeably.

At these words, he turned, and, to her amazement, Harriet recognised a familiar face.

'Dear me, Jukes,' said she. 'Fancy seeing you here!'

'Do you know this blighter?' said Mr. Pomfret.

'Of course I do,' said Harriet. 'He was a porter at Shrewsbury, and was sacked for petty pilfering. I hope you're going straight now, Jukes. How's your wife?'

'All right,' said Jukes, sulkily. 'I'll come again.'

He made a move to slip down the staircase, but Harriet had set her umbrella so awkwardly across it as to bar the way pretty effectively.

'Hi!' said Mr. Pomfret. 'Let's hear about this. Just come back here a minute, will you?' He stretched out a powerful arm, and yanked the reluctant Jukes over the threshold.

'You can't get me on that old business,' said Jukes, scornfully, as Harriet followed them in, shutting oak and door after her with a bang. 'That's over and done with. It ain't got nothing to do with that other little affair what I mentioned.'

'What's that?' asked Harriet.

'This nasty piece of work,' said Mr. Pomfret, 'has had the blasted neck to come here and say that if I don't pay him to keep his blasted mouth shut, he'll lay an information about what happened last night.'

'Blackmail,' said Harriet, much interested. 'That's a serious offence.'

'I didn't mention no money,' said Jukes, injured. 'I only told this gentleman as I seen something as didn't ought to have happened and was uneasy in my mind about it. He says I can go to the devil, so I says in this case I'll go to the lady, being troubled in my conscience, don't you see.'

'Very well,' said Harriet. 'I'm here. Go ahead.'

Mr. Jukes stared at her.

'I take it,' said Harriet, 'you saw Mr. Pomfret help me in over the Shrewsbury wall last night when I'd forgotten my key. What were you doing out there, by the way? Loitering with intent? You then probably saw me come out again, thank Mr. Pomfret and ask him to come in and see the College Buildings by moonlight. If you waited long enough, you saw me let him out again. What about it?'

'Nice goings-on, I don't think,' said Jukes, disconcerted.

'Possibly,' said Harriet. 'But if Senior Members choose to enter their own college in an unorthodox way, I don't see who's to prevent them. Certainly not you.'

'I don't believe a word of it,' said Jukes.

'I can't help that,' said Harriet. 'The Dean saw Mr. Pomfret and me, so she will. Nobody's likely to believe you. Why didn't you tell this man the whole story at once, Mr. Pomfret, and relieve his conscience? By the way, Jukes, I've just told the Dean she ought to have that wall spiked. It was handy for us, but it really isn't high enough to keep out burglars and other undesirables. So it's not much good your loitering about there any more. One or two things have been missed from people's rooms lately,' she added, with some truth, 'it might be as well to have that road specially policed.'

'None of that,' said Jukes. 'I ain't a-going to have my character took away. If it's as you say, then I'm sure I'd be the last to want to make trouble for a lady like yourself.'

'I hope you'll bear that in mind,' said Mr. Pomfret. 'Perhaps you'd like to have something to remember it by.'

'No assault!' cried Jukes, backing towards the door. 'No assault! Don't you go to lay 'ands on me!'

'If ever you show your dirty face here again,' said Mr. Pomfret, opening the door, 'I'll kick you downstairs and right through the quad. Get that? Then get out!'

He flung the oak back with one hand and propelled Jukes vigorously through it with the other. A crash and a curse proclaimed that the swiftness of Jukes' exit had carried him over the head of the stairs.

'Whew!' exclaimed Mr. Pomfret returning. 'By jove! that was great! That was marvellous of you. How did you come to think of it?'

'It was fairly obvious. I expect it was all bluff, really. I don't see how he could have known who Miss Catter-mole was. I wonder how he got on to you.'

'He must have followed me back when I came out. But I didn't go in through this window – obviously – so how did he—? Oh! yes, when I knocked Brown up I believe he stuck his head out and said "That you, Pomfret?" Careless blighter. I'll talk to him. . . . I say, you do seem to be everybody's guardian angel, don't you. It's marvellous, being able to keep your wits about you like that.'

He gazed at her with dog-like eyes. Harriet laughed, as Mr. Rogers and the tea entered the room together.

Mr. Rogers was in his third year – tall, dark, lively and full of an easy kind of penitence.

'All this running around and busting rules is rot,' said Mr. Rogers. 'Why do we do it? Because somebody says it is fun, and one believes it. Why should one believe it? I can't imagine. One should look at these things more objectively. Is the thing beautiful in itself? No. Then let us not do it. By the way, Pomfret, have you been approached about debagging Culpepper?'

'I am all for it,' said Mr. Pomfret.

'True, Culpepper is a wart. He is a disgusting object. But would he look any better debagged? No, Socrates, he would not. He would look much worse. If anybody is to be debagged, it shall be somebody with legs that will stand exposure – your own, Pomfret, for example.'

'You try, that's all,' said Mr. Pomfret.

'In any case,' pursued Mr. Rogers, 'debagging is otiose and out of date. The modern craze for exposing unaesthetic legs needs no encouragement from me. I shall not be a party to it. I intend to be a reformed character. From now on, I shall consider nothing but the value of the Thing-in-Itself, unmoved by any pressure of public opinion.'

Having, in this pleasant manner, confessed his sins and promised amendment, Mr. Rogers gracefully led the conversation to topics of general interest, and, about 5 o'clock, departed, murmuring something in an apologetic way about work and his tutor, as though they were rather indelicate necessities. At this point, Mr. Pomfret suddenly went all solemn as a very young man occasionally does when alone with a woman older than himself, and told Harriet a good deal about his own view of the meaning of life. Harriet listened with as much intelligent sympathy as she could command; but was slightly relieved when three young men burst in to borrow Mr. Pomfret's beer and remained to argue over their host's head about Komisarjevsky. Mr. Pomfret seemed faintly annoyed, and eventually asserted his right to his own guest by announcing that it was time to pop round to New College for old Farringdon's party. His friends let him go with mild regret and, before Harriet and her escort were well out of the room, took possession of their armchairs and continued the argument.

'Very able fellow, Marston,' said Mr. Pomfret, amiably enough. 'Great noise on O.U.D.S. and spends his vacations in Germany. I don't know how they contrive to get so worked up about plays. I like a good play, but I don't understand all this stuff about stylistic treatment and planes of vision. I expect you do though.'

'Not a word,' said Harriet, cheerfully. 'I dare say they don't either. Anyhow, I know I don't like plays in which all the actors have to keep on tumbling up and down flights of steps, or where the lighting's so artistically done that you can't see anything, or where you keep on wondering all the time what the symbolic whirligig in the centre of the stage is going to be used for, if anything. It distracts me. I'd rather go to the Holborn Empire and have my fun vulgar.'

'Would you?' said Mr. Pomfret, wistfully. 'You wouldn't come and do a show with me in Town in the vac, would you?'

Harriet made a vague kind of promise, which seemed to delight Mr. Pomfret very much, and they presently found themselves in Mr. Farringdon's sitting-room, packed like sardines among a mixed crowd of undergraduates and struggling to consume sherry and biscuits without moving their elbows.

The crowd was such that Harriet never set eyes on Miss Flaxman from first to last. Mr. Farringdon did, however, struggle through to them, bringing with him a bunch of young men and women who wanted to talk about detective fiction. They appeared to have read a good deal of this kind of literature, though very little of anything else. A School of Detective Fiction would, Harriet thought, have a fair chance of producing a goodly crop of Firsts. The fashion for psychological analysis had, she decided, rather gone out since her day; she was instinctively aware that a yearning for action and the concrete was taking its place. The pre-War solemnity and the post-War exhaustion were both gone; the desire now was for an energetic doing of something definite, though the definitions differed. The detective story, no doubt, was acceptable, because in it something definite was done, the 'what' being comfortably decided beforehand by the author. It was borne in upon Harriet that all these young men and women were starting out to hoe a hardish kind of row in a very stony ground. She felt rather sorry for them.

Something definite done. Yes, indeed. Harriet, reviewing the situation next morning, felt deeply dissatisfied. She did not like this Jukes business at all. He could scarcely, she supposed, have anything to do with the anonymous letters: where could he have got hold of that passage from the Aeneid? But he was a man with a grudge, a nasty-minded man, and a thief; it was not pleasant that he should make a habit of hanging round the College walls after dark.

Harriet was alone in the Senior Common Room, everybody else having departed to her work. The S.C.R. scout came in, carrying a pile of clean ash-trays, and Harriet suddenly remembered that her children lodged with the Jukeses.

'Annie,' she said impulsively, 'what does Jukes come down into Oxford for, after dark?'

The woman looked startled. 'Does he, madam? For no good, I should think.'

'I found him loitering in St. Cross Road last night, in a place where he might easily get over. Is he keeping honest, do you know?'

'I couldn't say, I'm sure, madam, but I have my doubts. I like Mrs. Jukes very much, and I'd be sorry to add to her troubles. But I never have trusted Jukes. I've been thinking I ought to put my little girls somewhere else. He might be a bad influence on them, don't you think?'

'I certainly do think so.'

'I'm the last person to wish to put difficulties in the way of a respectable married woman,' went on Annie, slapping an ash-tray smartly down, 'and naturally she's right to stick by her husband. But one's own children must come first, mustn't they?'

'Of course,' said Harriet, rather inattentively. 'Oh, yes. I should find somewhere else for them. I suppose you haven't ever heard either Jukes or his wife say anything to suggest that he – well, that he was stealing from the College or cherished bad feelings against the dons.'

'I don't have much to say to Jukes, madam, and if Mrs. Jukes knew anything, she wouldn't tell me. It wouldn't be right if she did. He's her husband, and she has to take his part. I quite see that. But if Jukes is behaving dishonestly, I shall have to find somewhere else for the children. I'm much obliged to you for mentioning it, madam. I shall be going round there on Wednesday, which is my free afternoon, and I'll take the opportunity to give notice. May I ask if you have said anything to Jukes, madam?'

'I have spoken to him, and told him that if he hangs round here any more he will have to do with the police.'

'I'm very glad to hear that, madam. It isn't right at all that he should come here like that. If I'd known about it, I really shouldn't have been able to sleep. I feel sure it ought to be put a stop to.'

'Yes, it ought. By the way, Annie, have you ever seen anybody in the College in a dress of this description?'

Harriet picked up the black figured crêpe-de-chine from the chair beside her. Annie examined it carefully.

'No, madam, not to my recollection. Perhaps one of the maids that's been here longer than me might know. There's Gertrude in the dining-room; should you like to ask her?'

Gertrude, however, could give no help. Harriet asked them to take the dress and catechise the rest of the staff. This was done, but with no result. An inquiry among the students produced no identification, either. The dress was brought back, still unclaimed and unrecognised. One more puzzle. Harriet concluded that it must actually be the property of the Poison-Pen; but if so, it must have been brought to College and kept in hiding till the moment of its dramatic appearance in Chapel; for if it had ever been worn in College, it was almost inconceivable that no one should be able to recognise it.

The alibis produced, meekly enough, by the members of the S.C.R. were none of them water-tight. That was not surprising; it would have been more surprising if they had been. Harriet (and Mr. Pomfret, of course) alone knew the exact time for which the alibi was required; and though many people were able to show themselves covered up to midnight or thereabouts, all had been, or claimed to have been, virtuously in their own rooms and beds by a quarter to one. Nor, though the porter's book and late-leave tickets had been examined, and all students interrogated who might have been about the quad at midnight, had anybody seen any suspicious behaviour with gowns or bolsters or bread-knives. Crime was too easy in a place like this. The College was too big, too open. Even if a form had been seen crossing the quad with a bolster, or indeed for that matter a complete set of bedding and a mattress, nobody would ever think anything of it. Some hardy fresh-air fiend sleeping out; that would be the natural conclusion.

Harriet, exasperated, went over to Bodley and plunged into her researches upon Lefanu. There, at least, one did know what one was investigating.

She felt so much the need of a soothing influence that, in the afternoon, she went down to Christ Church to hear service at the Cathedral. She had been shopping – purchasing, among other things, a bag of meringues for the entertainment of some students she had asked to a small party in her room that evening – and it was only when her arms were already full of parcels that the idea of Cathedral suggested itself. It was rather out of her way; but the parcels were not heavy. She dodged across Carfax, angrily resenting its modern bustle of cars and complications of stop-and-go lights, and joined the little sprinkling of foot-passengers who were tripping down St. Aldate's and through Wolsey's great unfinished quadrangle, bound on the same pious errand as herself.

It was quiet and pleasant in Cathedral. She lingered in her seat for some little time after the nave had emptied and until the organist had finished the voluntary. Then she came slowly out, turning left along the plinth with a vague idea of once more admiring the great staircase and the Hall, when a slim figure in a grey suit shot with such velocity from a dark doorway that he cannoned full tilt against her, nearly knocking her down, and sending her bag and parcels flying in disorder along the plinth.

'Hell!' said a voice which set her heart beating by its unexpected familiarity, 'have I hurt you? Me all over – bargin' and bumpin' about like a bumble-bee in a bottle. Clumsy lout! I say, do say I haven't hurt you. Because, if I have, I'll run straight across and drown myself in Mercury.'

He extended the arm that was not supporting Harriet in a vague gesture towards the pond.

'Not in the least, thank you,' said Harriet, recovering herself.

'Thank God for that. This is my unlucky day. I've just had a most unpleasant interview with the Junior Censor. Was there anything breakable in the parcels? Oh, look! your bag's opened itself wide and all the little oojahs have gone down the steps. Please don't move. You stand there, thinkin' up things to call me, and I'll pick 'em all up one by one on my knees sayin' "meâ culpâ" to every one of 'em.'

He suited the action to the words.

'I'm afraid it hasn't improved the meringues.' He looked up apologetically. 'But if you'll say you forgive me, we'll go and get some new ones from the kitchen – the real kind – *you* know – speciality of the House, and all that.'

'Please don't bother,' said Harriet.

It wasn't he, of course. This was a lad of twenty-one or two at the most, with a mop of wavy hair tumbling over his forehead and a handsome, petulant face, full of charm, though ominously weak about the curved lips and upward-slanting brows. But the colour of the hair was right – the pale yellow of ripe barley; and the light drawling voice, with its clipped syllables and ready babble of speech; and the quick, sidelong smile; and above all, the beautiful, sensitive hands that were gathering the 'oojahs' deftly up into their native bag.

'You haven't called me any names yet,' said the young man.

'I believe I could almost put a name to you,' said Harriet. 'Isn't it – are you any relation of Peter Wimsey's?'

'Why, of course,' said the young man, sitting up on his heels. 'He's my uncle; and a dashed sight more accommodating than the Jewish kind,' he added, as though struck by a melancholy association of ideas. 'Have I met you somewhere? Or was it pure guesswork? You don't think I'm like him, do you?'

'When you spoke, I thought you were your uncle for the moment. Yes, you're very like him, in some ways.'

'That'll break my mater's heart, all right,' said the young man, with a grin. 'Uncle Peter's not approved. I wish to God he was here, though. He'd come in uncommonly handy at the moment. But he seems to have beetled off somewhere as usual. Mysterious old tom-cat, isn't he? I take it you know him – I forget the proper bromide about how small the world is, but we'll take it as read. Where *is* the old blighter?'

'I believe he's in Rome.'

'He *would* be. That means a letter. It's awfully hard to be persuasive in a letter, don't you think? I mean, it all takes so much explaining, and the famous family charm doesn't seem to go over so well in black and white.'

He smiled at her with engaging frankness as he recaptured a last straying copper.

'Do I gather,' said Harriet, with some amusement, 'that you anticipate an appeal to Uncle Peter's better feelings?'

'That's about it,' said the young man. 'He's quite human, really, you know, if you go about him the right way. Besides, you see, I've got the bulge on Uncle Peter. If the worst comes to the worst, I can always threaten to cut my throat and land him with the strawberry leaves.'

'With the what?' said Harriet, fancying that this must be the latest Oxford version of giving the raspberry.

'The strawberry leaves,' said the young man. 'The balm, the sceptre, and the ball. Four rows of moth-eaten ermine. To say nothing of that dashed great barracks down at Denver, eating its mouldy head off.' Seeing that Harriet still looked blankly at him, he explained further: 'I'm sorry; I forgot. My name's Saint-George and the Governor forgot to provide me with any brothers. So the minute they write d.s.p. after me, Uncle Peter's for it. Of course, my father might outlive him; but I don't believe Uncle Peter's the sort to die young, unless one of his pet criminals manages to bump him off.'

'That might easily happen,' said Harriet, thinking of the plug-ugly.

'Well, that makes it all the worse for him,' said Lord Saint-George, shaking his head. 'The more risks he takes, the quicker he's got to toe the line for the matrimonial stakes. No more bachelor freedom with old Bunter in a Piccadilly flat. *And* no more spectacular Viennese singers. So you see, it's as much as his life's worth to let anything happen to me.'

'Obviously,' said Harriet, fascinated by this new light on the subject.

'Uncle Peter's weakness,' went on Lord Saint-George, carefully disentangling the squashed meringues from their paper, 'is his strong sense of public duty. You mightn't think it to look at him, but it's there. (Shall we try these on the carp? I don't think they're really fit for human consumption.) He's kept out of it so far – he's an obstinate old devil. Says he'll have the right wife or none.'

'But suppose the right one says No.'

'That's the story he puts up. I don't believe a word of it. Why should anybody object to Uncle Peter? He's no beauty and he'd talk the hind leg off a donkey; but he's dashed well-off and he's got good manners and he's in the stud-book.' He balanced himself on the edge of Mercury and peered into its tranquil waters. 'Look! there's a big one. Been here since the foundation, by the looks of him – see him go? Cardinal Wolsey's particular pet.' He tossed a crumb to the great fish, which took it with a quick snap and submerged again.

'I don't know how well you know my uncle,' he proceeded, 'but if you do get a chance, you might let him know that when you saw me I was looking rather unwell and hag-ridden and hinted darkly at felo-de-se.'

'I'll make a point of it,' said Harriet. 'I will say you seemed scarcely able to crawl and, in fact, fainted into my arms, accidentally crushing all my parcels. He won't believe me, but I'll do my best.'

'No – he isn't good at believing things, confound him. I'm afraid I shall have to write, after all, and produce the evidence, Still, I don't know why I should bore you with my personal affairs. Come on down to the kitchen.'

The Christ Church cook was well pleased to produce meringues from the ancient and famous College oven; and when Harriet had duly admired the vast fireplace with its shining spits and heard statistics of the number of joints roasted and the quantities of fuel consumed per week in term-time, she followed her guide out into the quadrangle again with all proper expressions of gratitude.

'Not at all,' said the Viscount. 'Not much return, I'm afraid, after banging you all over the place and throwing your property about. May I know, by the way, whom I have had the honour of inconveniencing?'

'My name's Harriet Vane.'

Lord Saint-George stood still, and smote himself heavily over the forehead.

'My God, what have I done? Miss Vane, I do beg your pardon – and throw myself abjectly on your mercy. If my uncle hears about this he'll never forgive me, and I *shall* cut my throat. It is borne in upon me that I have said every possible thing I should not.'

'It's my fault,' said Harriet, seeing that he looked really alarmed, 'I ought to have warned you.'

'As a matter of fact, I've no business to say things like that to anybody. I'm afraid I've inherited my uncle's tongue and my mother's want of tact. Look here, for God's sake forget all that rot. Uncle Peter's a dashed good sort, and as decent as they come.'

'I've reason to know it.' said Harriet.

'I suppose so. By the way – hell! I seem to be putting my foot in it all round, but I ought to explain that I've never heard him talk about you. I mean, he's not that sort. It's my mother. She says all kinds of things. Sorry, I'm making things worse and worse.'

'Don't worry,' said Harriet. 'After all, I *do* know your uncle, you know – well enough, anyhow, to know what sort he is. And I certainly won't give you away.'

'For Heaven's sake, don't. It isn't only that I'd never get anything more out of him – and I'm in a devil of a mess – but he makes one feel such an appalling tick. I don't suppose you've ever been given the wrong side of my uncle's tongue – naturally not. But of the two, I recommend skinning.'

'We're both in the same boat. I'd no business to listen. Good-bye – and many thanks for the meringues.'

She was half-way up St. Aldate's when the viscount caught her up.

'I say – I've just remembered. That old story I was ass enough to rake up—'

'The Viennese dancer?'

'Singer – music's his line. Please forget that. I mean, it's got whiskers on it – it's six years old, anyway. I was a kid at school and I dare say it's all rot.'

Harriet laughed, and promised faithfully to forget the Viennese singer.

9

Come hether freind, I am ashamed to hear that what I hear of you. . . . You have almost attayned to the age of nyne yeeres, at least to eight and a halfe, and seeing that you knowe your dutie, if you neglect it you deserve greater punishment then he which through ignorance doth it not. Think not that the nobilitie of your Ancestors doth free you to doe all that you list, contrarywise, it bindeth you more to followe vertue.

PIERRE ERONDELL

'So,' said the Bursar, coming briskly up to the High Table for lunch on the following Thursday; 'Jukes has come to grief once more. . . .'

'Has he been stealing again?' asked Miss Lydgate. 'Dear me, how disappointing!'

'Annie tells me she's had her suspicions for some time, and yesterday being her half-day she went down to tell Mrs. Jukes she would have to place the children somewhere else – when lo, and behold! in walked the police and discovered a whole lot of things that had been stolen a fortnight ago from an undergraduate's rooms in Holywell. It was most unpleasant for her – for Annie, I mean. They asked her a lot of questions.'

'I always thought it was a mistake to put those children there,' said the Dean.

'So that's what Jukes did with himself at night,' said Harriet. 'I heard he'd been seen outside the College here.

As a matter of fact, I gave Annie the tip. It's a pity she couldn't have removed the children earlier.'

'I thought he was doing quite well,' said Miss Lydgate. 'He had a job – and I know he kept chickens – and there was the money for the little Wilsons, Annie's children, I mean – so he ought not to have needed to steal, poor man. Perhaps Mrs. Jukes is a bad manager.'

'Jukes is a bad lot,' said Harriet. 'A nasty bit of business altogether. He's much best out of the way.'

'Had he taken much?' inquired the Dean.

'I gather from Annie,' said the Bursar, 'that they rather think they can trace a lot of petty thieving to Jukes. I understand it's a question of finding out where he sold the things.'

'He'd dispose of them through a fence, I suppose,' said Harriet; 'some pawnbroker or somebody of that kind. Has he been inside – in prison – before?'

'Not that I know of,' said the Dean; 'though he *ought* to have been.'

'Then I suppose he'll get off lightly as a first offender.'

'Miss Barton will know all about that. We'll ask her. I do hope poor Mrs. Jukes isn't involved,' said the Bursar.

'Surely not,' cried Miss Lydgate, 'she's such a nice woman.'

'She must have known about it,' said Harriet, 'unless she was a perfect imbecile.'

'What a dreadful thing, to know your husband was a thief!'

'Yes,' said the Dean. 'It would be very uncomfortable to have to live on the proceeds.'

'Terrible,' said Miss Lydgate. 'I can't imagine anything more dreadful to an honest person's feelings.'

'Then,' said Harriet, 'we must hope, for Mrs. Jukes' sake, she was as guilty as he was.'

'What a horrible hope!' exclaimed Miss Lydgate.

'Well, she's got to be either guilty or unhappy,' said Harriet, passing the bread to the Dean with a twinkle in her eye.

'I dissent altogether,' said Miss Lydgate. 'She must either be innocent and unhappy or guilty and unhappy – I don't see how she can be happy, poor creature.'

'Let us ask the Warden next time we see her,' said Miss Martin, 'whether it is possible for a guilty person to be happy. And if so, whether it is better to be happy or virtuous.'

'Come, Dean,' said the Bursar, 'we can't allow this sort of thing. Miss Vane, a bowl of hemlock for the Dean, if you please. To return to the subject under discussion, the police have not, so far, taken up Mrs. Jukes, so I suppose there's nothing against her.'

'I'm very glad of that,' said Miss Lydgate; and, Miss Shaw arriving at that moment, full of woe about one of her pupils who was suffering from perpetual headache, and an incapacity to work, the conversation wandered into other channels.

Term was drawing to a close, and the investigation seemed little farther advanced; but it appeared possible that Harriet's mightly perambulationus and the frustration of the Library and Chapel scandals had exercised a restraining influence on the Poltergeist, for there was no further outbreak of any kind, not so much as an inscription in a lavatory or an anonymous letter, for three days. The Dean, exceedingly busy, was relieved by the respite, and also cheered by the news that Mrs. Goodwin the secretary would be back on the Monday to cope with the end-of-term rush. Miss Cattermole was seen to be more cheerful, and wrote a quite respectable paper for Miss

Hillyard about the naval policy of Henry VIII. Harriet asked the enigmatic Miss de Vine to coffee. As usual, she had intended to lay bare Miss de Vine's soul, and, as usual, found herself laying bare her own.

'I quite agree with you,' said Miss de Vine, 'about the difficulty of combining intellectual and emotional interests. I don't think it affects women only; it affects men as well. But when men put their public lives before their private lives, it causes less outcry than when a woman does the same thing, because women put up with neglect better than men, having been brought up to expect it.'

'But suppose one doesn't quite know which one wants to put first. Suppose,' said Harriet, falling back on words which were not her own, 'suppose one is cursed with both a heart and a brain?'

'You can usually tell,' said Miss de Vine, 'by seeing what kind of mistakes you make. I'm quite sure that one never makes *fundamental* mistakes about the thing one really wants to do. Fundamental mistakes arise out of lack of genuine interest. In my opinion, that is.'

'I made a very big mistake once,' said Harriet, 'as I expect you know. I don't think that arose out of lack of interest. It seemed at the time the most important thing in the world.'

'And yet you made the mistake. Were you really giving all your mind to it, do you think? Your *mind*? Were you really being as cautious and exacting about it as you would be about writing a passage of fine prose?'

'That's rather a difficult sort of comparison. One can't, surely, deal with emotional excitements in that detached spirit.'

'Isn't the writing of good prose an emotional excitement?'

210

'Yes, of course it is. At least, when you get the thing dead right and know it's dead right, there's no excitement like it. It's marvellous. It makes you feel like God on the Seventh Day – for a bit, anyhow.'

'Well, that's what I mean. You expend the trouble and you don't make any mistake – and *then* you experience the ecstasy. But if there's any subject in which you're content with the second-rate, then it isn't really your subject.'

'You're dead right,' said Harriet after a pause. 'If one's genuinely interested one knows how to be patient, and let time pass, as Queen Elizabeth said. Perhaps that's the meaning of the phrase about genius being eternal patience, which I always thought rather absurd. If you truly want a thing, you don't snatch; if you snatch, you don't really want it. Do you suppose that, if you find yourself taking pains about a thing, it's a proof of its importance to you?'

'I think it is, to a large extent. But the big proof is that the thing comes right, without those fundamental errors. One always makes surface errors, of course. But a fundamental error is a sure sign of not caring. I wish one could teach people nowadays that the doctrine of snatching what one thinks one wants is unsound.'

'I saw six plays this winter in London,' said Harriet, 'all preaching the doctrine of snatch. I agree that they left me with the feeling that none of the characters knew what they wanted.'

'No,' said Miss de Vine. 'If you are once sure what you do want, you find that everything else goes down before it like grass under a roller – all other interests, your own and other people's. Miss Lydgate wouldn't like my saying that, but it's as true of her as of anybody else. She's the kindest soul in the world, in things she's indifferent about, like the peculations of Jukes. But she hasn't the slightest mercy on the prosodical theories of Mr. Elkbottom. She wouldn't countenance those to save Mr. Elkbottom from hanging. She'd say she couldn't. And she couldn't, of course. If she actually saw Mr. Elkbottom writhing in humiliation she'd be sorry, but she wouldn't alter a paragraph. That would be treason. One can't be pitiful where one's own job is concerned. You'd lie cheerfully, I expect, about anything except – what?'

'Oh, anything!' said Harriet, laughing. 'Except saying that somebody's beastly book is good when it isn't. I can't do that. It makes me a lot of enemies, but I can't do it.'

'No, one can't,' said Miss de Vine. 'However painful it is, there's always one thing one has to deal with sincerely, if there's any root to one's mind at all. I ought to know, from my own experience. Of course, the one thing may be an emotional thing; I don't say it mayn't. One may commit all the sins in the calendar, and still be faithful and honest towards one person. If so, then that one person is probably one's appointed job. I'm not despising that kind of loyalty; it doesn't happen to be mine, that is all.'

'Did you discover that by making a fundamental mistake?' asked Harriet, a little nervously.

'Yes,' said Miss de Vine. 'I once got engaged to somebody. But I found I was always blundering – hurting his feelings, doing stupid things, making quite elementary mistakes about him. In the end I realised that I simply wasn't taking as much trouble with him as I should have done over a disputed reading. So I decided he wasn't my job.' She smiled. 'For all that, I was fonder of him than he was of me. He married an excellent woman who is devoted to him and does make him her job. I should think he was a full-time job. He is a painter and usually on the verge of bankruptcy; but he paints very well.'

'I suppose one oughtn't to marry anybody, unless one's prepared to make him a full-time job.'

'Probably not; though there are a few rare people, I believe, who don't look on themselves as jobs but as fellow-creatures.'

'I should think Phœbe Tucker and her husband were like that,' said Harriet. 'You met her at the Gaudy. That collaboration seems to work. But what with the wives who are jealous of their husbands' work and the husbands who are jealous of their wives' interests, it looks as though most of us imagined ourselves to be jobs.'

'The worst of being a job,' said Miss de Vine, 'is the devastating effect it has on one's character. I'm very sorry for the person who is somebody else's job; he (or she, of course) ends by devouring or being devoured, either of which is bad for one. My painter has devoured his wife, though neither of them knows it; and poor Miss Cattermole is in great danger of being identified with her parents' job and being devoured.'

'Then you're all for the impersonal job?'

'I am,' said Miss de Vine.

'But you say you don't despise those who make some other persons their job?'

'Far from despising them,' said Miss de Vine; 'I think they are dangerous.'

Christ Church,
Friday.

Dear Miss Vane,

If you can forgive my idiotic behaviour the other day, will you come and lunch with me on Monday at 1 o'clock? Please do. I am still feeling suicidal, so it would really be a work of charity all round. I hope the meringues got home safely.

Very sincerely yours,
SAINT-GEORGE.

My dear young man, thought Harriet, as she wrote an acceptance of this naïve invitation, if you think I can't see through that, you're mightily mistaken. This is not for me, but for *les beaux yeux de la cassette de l'oncle Pierre.* But there are worse meals than those that come out of the House kitchen, and I will go. I should like to know how much money you're managing to get through, by the way. The heir of Denver should be rich enough in his own right without appealing to Uncle Peter. Gracious! when I think that I was given my college fees and my clothes and five pounds a term to make whoopee on! You won't get much sympathy or support from me, my lord.

Still in this severe mood, she drove down St. Aldate's on Monday and inquired of the porter beneath Tom Tower for Lord Saint-George; only to be told that Lord Saint-George was not in College.

'Oh!' said Harriet, disconcerted, 'but he asked me to lunch.'

'What a pity you weren't let know, miss. Lord Saint-George was in a nasty motor-accident on Friday night. He's in the Infirmary. Didn't you see it in the papers?'

'No, I missed it. Is he badly hurt?'

'Injured his shoulder and cut his head open pretty badly, so we hear,' said the porter, with regret, and yet, with a slight relish at the imparting of bad news. 'He was unconscious for twenty-four hours; but we are informed that his condition is now improving. The Duke and Duchess have left for the country again.'

'Dear me!' said Harriet. 'I'm sorry to hear this. I'd better go round and inquire. Do you know whether he is allowed to see anybody yet?'

The porter looked her over with a paternal eye, which somehow suggested to her that if she had been an undergraduate the answer would have been No.

'I believe, miss,' said the porter, 'that Mr. Danvers and Lord Warboys were permitted to visit his lordship this morning. I couldn't say further than that. Excuse me – there is Mr. Danvers just crossing the quadrangle. I will ascertain.'

He emerged from his glass case and pursued Mr. Danvers, who immediately came running to the lodge.

'I say,' said Mr. Danvers, 'are you Miss Vane? Because poor old Saint-George has only just remembered about you. He's terribly sorry, and I was to catch you and give you some grub. No trouble at all – a great pleasure. We ought to have let you know, but he was knocked clean out, poor old chap. And then, what with the family fussing round – do you know the Duchess? – No? – Ah! Well, she went off this morning, and then I was allowed to go round and got my instructions. Terrific apologies and all that.'

'How did it happen?'

'Driving a racing car to the danger of the public,' said Mr. Danvers, with a grimace. 'Trying to make it before the gates were shut. No police on the spot, as it happened, so we don't know exactly what *did* happen. Nobody killed, fortunately. Saint-George took a telegraph pole in his stride, apparently, went out head first and pitched on his shoulder. Lucky he had the windscreen down, or he'd have had no face to speak of. The car's a total wreck, and I don't know why he isn't. But all those Wimseys have as many lives as cats. Come along in. These are my rooms. I hope you can eat the usual lamb cutlets – there wasn't time to think up anything special. But I had particular orders to hunt out Saint-George's Niersteiner '23 and mention Uncle Peter in connection with it. Is that right? I don't know whether Uncle Peter bought it or recommended it or merely enjoyed it, or what he had to do with it, but that's what I was told to say.'

Harriet laughed. 'If he did any of those things, it'll be all right.'

The Niersteiner was excellent, and Harriet heartlessly enjoyed her lunch, finding Mr. Danvers a pleasant host.

'And do go up and see the patient.' said Mr. Danvers, as he escorted her at length to the gate. 'He's quite fit to receive company, and it'll cheer him up no end. He's in a private ward, so you can get in any time.'

'I'll go straight away,' said Harriet.

'Do,' said Mr. Danvers. 'What's that?' he added turning to the porter, who had come out with a letter in his hand. 'Oh, something for Saint-George. Right. Yes. I expect the lady will take it up, if she's going now. If not, it can wait for the messenger.'

Harriet looked at the superscription. 'The Viscount Saint-George, Christ Church, Oxford, Inghilterra.' Even without the Italian stamp, there was no mistaking where that came from. 'I'll take it,' she said – 'it might be urgent.'

Lord Saint-George, with his right arm in a sling, his forehead and one eye obscured by bandages and the other eye black and bloodshot, was profuse in welcome and apology.

'I hope Danvers looked after you all right. It's frightfully decent of you to come along.'

Harriet asked if he was badly hurt.

'Well, it might be worse. I fancy Uncle Peter had a near squeak of it this time, but it's worked out at a cut head and a busted shoulder. And shock and bruises and all that. Much less than I deserve. Stay and talk to me. It's dashed dull being all alone, and I've only got one eye and can't see out of that.'

'Won't talking make your head ache?'

'It can't ache worse than it does already. And you've got a nice voice. Do be kind and stay.'

'I've brought a letter for you from College.'

'Some dashed dun or other, I suppose.'

'No. It's from Rome.'

'Uncle Peter. Oh, God! I suppose I'd better know the worst.'

She put it into his left hand, and watched his fingers fumble across the broad red seal.

'Ugh! Sealing-wax and the family crest. I know what that means. Uncle Peter at his stuffiest.'

He struggled impatiently with the tough envelope.

'Shall I open it for you?'

'I wish you would. And, look here – be an angel and read it to me. Even with two good eyes, his fist's a bit of a strain.'

Harriet drew out the letter and glanced at the opening words.

'This looks rather private.'

'Better you than the nurse. Besides, I can bear it better with a spot of womanly sympathy. I say, is there any enclosure?'

'No enclosure. No.'

The patient groaned.

'Uncle Peter turns to bay. That's torn it. How does it start? If it's "Gherkins" or "Jerry," or even "Gerald," there's hope yet.'

'It starts, "My dear Saint-George." '

'Oh gosh! Then he's really furious. And signed with all the initials he can rake up, what?'

Harriet turned the letter over.

'Signed with all his names in full.'

'Unrelenting monster! You know, I had a sort of feeling he wouldn't take it very well. I don't know what the devil I'm going to do now.'

He looked so ill that Harriet said, rather anxiously:

'Hadn't we better leave it till to-morrow?'

'No. I must know where I stand. Carry on. Speak gently to your little boy. Sing it to me. It'll need it.'

My dear Saint-George,

If I have rightly understood your rather incoherent statement of your affairs, you have contracted a debt of honour for a sum which you do not possess. You have settled it with a cheque which you had no money to meet. As cover for this, you have borrowed from a friend, giving him a post-dated cheque which you have no reason to suppose will be met either. You suggest that I should accommodate you by backing your bill at six months; failing which, you will either (a) 'try Levy again,' or (b) blow your brains out. The former alternative would, as you admit, increase your ultimate liability; the second, as I will myself venture to point out, would not reimburse your friend but merely add disgrace to insolvency.

Lord Saint-George shifted restlessly upon his pillows. 'Nasty clear-headed way he has of putting things.'

You are good enough to say that you approach me
rather than your father, because I am, in your opinion,
more likely to be sympathetic to this dubious piece of
finance. I cannot say I feel flattered by your opinion.

'I didn't mean that, exactly,' groaned the viscount. 'He
knows quite well what I mean. The Governor would fly
right off the handle. Damn it, it's his own fault! He
oughtn't to keep me so short. What does he expect?
Considering the money *he* got through in his giddy
youth, he should know something about it. And Uncle
Peter's rolling – it wouldn't hurt him to cough up a bit.'
'I don't think it's the money so much as the dud
cheques, is it?'
'That's the trouble. Well, why the devil does he go
barging off to Rome just when he's wanted? He knows I
wouldn't have given a dud if I could have got cover for it.
But I couldn't get him if he wasn't there. Well, read on.
Let's hear the worst.'

I am quite aware that your premature decease would
leave me heir-presumptive to the title—

'Heir-presumptive? . . . Oh, I see. My mother might
peg out and my father marry again. Calculating brute.'

—heir presumptive to the title and estate. Tedious as
such an inheritance might be, you will forgive me for
suggesting that I might prove a more honest steward
than yourself.

'Hell! That's one in the eye,' said the viscount. 'If that
line of defence has gone, it's all up.'

You remind me that when you attain your majority
next July, you will receive an increased allowance.
Since, however the sum you have mentioned amounts

to about a year's income on the higher scale of payment, your prospect of redeeming your bill in six months' time seems to be remote; nor do I understand what you propose to live on when you have anticipated your income to this extent. Further, I do not for one moment suppose that the sum in question represents the whole of your liabilities.

'Damned thought-reader!' growled his lordship. 'Of course it doesn't. But how does *he* know?'

In the circumstances, I must decline to back your bill or to lend you money.

'Well, that's flat. Why didn't he say so at once?'

Since, however, you have put your name to a cheque, and that name must not be dishonoured, I have instructed my bankers—

'Come! that sounds a bit better. Good old Uncle Peter! You can always get him on the family name.'

—instructed my bankers to arrange to cover your cheque—

'Cheque, or cheques?'
'Cheques, in the plural; quite distinctly.'

—cover your cheques from now until the time of my return to England when I shall come and see you. This will probably be before the end of the Trinity Term. I will ask you to see to it that the whole of your liabilities are discharged by that time, including your outstanding Oxford debts and your obligations to the children of Israel.

'First gleam of humanity,' said the viscount.

May I offer you, in addition, a little advice? Bear in mind that the amateur professional is peculiarly rapacious. This applies both to women and to people who play cards. If you must back horses, back them at a reasonable price and both ways. And, if you insist on blowing out your brains, do it in some place where you will not cause mess and inconvenience.

Your affectionate Uncle,
PETER DEATH BREDON WIMSEY.

'Whew!' said Lord Saint-George, 'that's a stinker! I fancy I detect a little softening in the last paragraph. Otherwise, I should say that a nastier kind of letter never came to soothe the sufferer's aching brow. What do you think?'

Harriet privately agreed that it was not the kind of letter she would care to receive. It displayed, in fact, almost everything that she resented most in Peter; the condescending superiority, the arrogance of caste and the generosity that was like a blow in the face. However:—

'He's done far more than you asked him,' she pointed out. 'So far as I can see, there's nothing to prevent you from drawing a cheque for fifty thousand and blueing the lot.'

'That's the devil of it. He's got me by the short hairs. He's trusted me with the whole dashed outfit. I did think he might offer to settle up for me, but he's left me to do it and hasn't even asked for an account. That means it'll have to be done. I don't see how I can get out of it. He has the most ingenious ways of making a fellow feel a sweep. Oh, hell! my head's splitting.'

'You'd better keep quiet and try to go to sleep. You've nothing to worry about now.'

'No. Wait a minute. Don't go away. The cheque's all right, that's the chief thing. Just as well, because I'd have had a job to raise the wind elsewhere, laid up like this. There's one thing about it – I can't use this arm, so I shan't have to write a long screed full of grateful penitence.'

'Does he know about your accident?'

'Not unless Aunt Mary's written to him. My Grandmother's on the Riviera, and I don't suppose it would occur to my sister. She's at school. The Governor never writes to anybody, and my Mother certainly wouldn't bother with Uncle Peter. Look here, I must do something. I mean, the old boy's been thoroughly decent, really. Couldn't you write a line for me, explaining all about it? I don't want to let my family in on this.'

'I'll do that, certainly.'

'Tell him I'll settle the blasted debts as soon as I can produce a recognisable signature. I say! think of having a free hand with Uncle Peter's pile and not being able to sign a cheque. Enough to make a cat laugh, isn't it? Say I – what's the phrase? – appreciate his confidence and won't let him down. Here! You might give me a spot of the stuff in that jug, would you? I feel like Dives in what's-his-name.'

He gulped the iced drink down gratefully.

'No, damn it! I must do something. The old boy's really worried. I think I can work these fingers after a fashion. Find me a pencil and paper and I'll have a shot.'

'I don't think you'd better.'

'Yes, I had better. And I will if it kills me. Find me something, there's a darling.'

She found writing materials, and held the paper in

place while he scrawled a few staggering words. The pain made him sweat; a shoulder joint which has been dislocated and returned to position is no cushion of ease the day after; but he set his teeth and went through with it gamely.

'There,' he said, with a faint grin, 'that looks dashed pathetic. Now it's up to you. Do your best for me, won't you?'

Perhaps, thought Harriet, Peter knew the right way with his nephew. The boy was unblushingly ready to consider other people's money his own; and probably, if Peter had simply backed his bill, he would have thought his uncle easy game and proceeded to issue more paper on the same terms. As it was, he seemed inclined to stop and think. And he had, what she herself lacked, the grace of gratitude. His facile acceptance of favours might be a sign of shallowness; still, it had cost him something to scribble that painful note.

It was only when, in her own room after Hall, she set about writing to Peter, that she realised how awkward her own task was going to be. To put down a brief explanation of her own acquaintance with Lord Saint-George and a reassuring account of his accident was child's play. The difficulties began with the matter of the young man's finances. Her first draft ran easily; it was slightly humorous and rather gave the benefactor to understand that his precious balms were calculated to break the recipient's head, where other agents had not already broken it. She rather enjoyed writing this one. On reading it over, she was disappointed to find that it had an air of officious impertinence. She tore it up.

The students were making a vast noise of trampling

and laughter in the corridor. Harriet briefly cursed them and tried again.

The second draft began stiffly: 'Dear Peter – I am writing on behalf of your nephew, who has unfortunately—'

This one, when finished, conveyed the impression that she disapproved strongly of uncle and nephew alike, and was anxious to dissociate herself as far as possible from their affairs.

She tore it up, cursed the students again and made a third draft.

This, when completed, turned out to be a moving, and, indeed, powerful piece of special pleading on the young sinner's behalf, but contained remarkably little of the gratitude and repentance which she had been instructed to convey. The fourth draft, erring in the opposite direction, was merely fulsome.

'What the devil is the matter with me?' she said aloud. '(Damn those noisy brats!) Why can't I write a straightforward piece of English on a set subject?'

When she had once formulated the difficulty in this plain question, the detached intellect bent meekly to its academic task and produced the answer.

'Because, however you put it, all this is going to hurt his pride damnably.'

Answer adjudged correct.

What she had to say, stripped of its verbiage, was: Your nephew has been behaving foolishly and dishonestly, and I know it; he gets on badly with his parents, and I know that, too; he has taken me into his confidence and, what is more, into yours, where I have no right to be; in fact, I know a great many things you would rather I did not know, and you can't lift a hand to prevent it.

In fact, for the first time in their acquaintance, she had

the upper hand of Peter Wimsey, and could rub his aristocratic nose in the dirt if she wanted to. Since she had been looking for such an opportunity for five years, it would be odd if she did not hasten to take advantage of it.

Slowly and with extreme pains, she started on Draft No. 5.

Dear Peter,

I don't know whether you know that your nephew is in the Infirmary, recovering from what might have been a nasty motor accident. His right shoulder is dislocated and his head badly cut; but he is getting on all right and is lucky not to have been killed. Apparently he skidded into a telegraph pole. I don't know the details; perhaps you have already heard from his people. I met him by chance a few days ago, and only heard of the accident to-day, when I went round to see him.

So far, so good; now for the awkward bit.

One of his eyes was bandaged up and the other badly swollen, so he asked me to read him a letter he had just that moment received from you. (Please don't think his sight is damaged – I asked the nurse, and it's only cuts and bruises.) There was nobody else to read it to him, as his parents left Oxford this morning. As he can't write much himself, he asks me to send you the enclosed and to say he thanks you very much and is sorry. He appreciates your confidence and will do exactly as you ask him, as soon as he is well enough.

She hoped there was nothing there that could offend. She had started to write 'honourably do as you ask,' and then erased the first word: to mention honour was to suggest its opposite. Her consciousness seemed to have

225

become all one exposed nerve-centre, sensitive to the lightest breath of innuendo in her own words.

I didn't stay long, as he was really a good bit under the weather, but they assure me he is doing very well. He insisted on writing this note himself, though I suppose I oughtn't to have let him. I'll look him up again before I leave Oxford – entirely for my own sake, because he is perfectly charming. I hope you don't mind my saying so, though I'm sure you don't need to be told it.

Yours,
HARRIET D. VANE.

I seem to be taking a lot of trouble about this she thought, as she carefully re-read it. If I believed Miss de Vine, I might begin to imagine – *damn* those students! – Would anybody believe it could take one two hours to write a simple letter?

She put the letter resolutely into an envelope, and addressed and stamped it. Nobody, having put on a twopenny-halfpenny stamp, was ever known to open the envelope again. That was *done*. For a couple of hours now she would devote herself to the affairs of Sheridan Lefanu.

She worked away happily till half-past ten; the racket in the passage calmed down; words flowed smoothly. From time to time, she looked up from her paper, hesitating for a word, and saw through the window the lights of Burleigh and Queen Elizabeth burning back across the quad, counterparts of her own. Many of them, no doubt, illuminated cheerful parties, like the one in the Annexe; others lent their aid to people who, like herself, were engaged in the elusive pursuit of knowledge, covering paper with ink and hesitating now and again over a word. She felt herself to be a living part of a community engaged in a common purpose. 'Wilkie Collins,' wrote Harriet, 'was always handicapped in his treatment of the supernatural by the fatal itch' (could one be handicapped by an itch? Yes, why not? Let it go, anyway, for the moment) 'the fatal itch to explain everything. His legal training—' Bother! Too long. '. . . was handicapped by the lawyer's fatal habit of explaining everything. His ghaisties and ghoulies' – No; worn-out humour— 'His dream-phantasms and apparitions are too careful to tuck their shrouds neatly about them and leave no loose ends to trouble us. It is in Lefanu that we find the natural maker of – natural master of – the master of the uncanny whose mastery comes by nature. If we compare—'

Before the comparison could be instituted, the lamp went suddenly out.

'Curse!' said Harriet. She rose and pressed down the wall-switch. Nothing happened. 'Fused!' said Harriet, opening the door to investigate. The corridor was in darkness, and a lamentable outcry on either side proclaimed that the lights were out in the whole of Tudor.

Harriet snatched her torch from the table and turned right towards the main block of the building. She was soon swept into a crowd of students, some with torches and some clinging to those that had them, all clamouring and wanting to know what was wrong with the lights.

'Shut *up*!' said Harriet, peering behind the barrier of the torch-lights to find anybody she recognised. 'The main fuse must have gone. Where's the fuse-box?'

'I think it's under the stairs,' said somebody.

'Stay where you are,' said Harriet. 'I'll go and see.'

Nobody, naturally, stayed where she was. Everybody came helpfully and angrily downstairs.

'It's the Poltergeist,' said somebody.

'Let's catch her this time,' said somebody else.

'Perhaps it's only blown,' suggested a timid voice out of the darkness.

'Blown be blowed!' exclaimed a louder voice, scornfully. 'How often does a main fuse blow?' Then, in an agitated whisper, 'Hellup, it's the Chilperic. Sorry I spoke.'

'Is that you, Miss Chilperic?' said Harriet, glad to round up one member of the Senior Common Room. 'Have you met Miss Barton anywhere?'

'No, I've only just got out of bed.'

'Miss Barton isn't there,' said a voice from the hall below, and then another voice chimed in:

'Somebody's pulled out the main fuse and taken it away!'

And then, in a shrill cry from someone at the end of the lower corridor: 'There she goes! Look! running across the quad!'

Harriet was carried down the stairs with a rush of twenty or thirty students into the midst of those already milling in the hall. There was a cram in the doorway. She lost Miss Chilperic and was left behind in the struggle. Then, as she thrust her way through on to the terrace, she saw under the dim sky a string of runners stretched across the quad. Voices were calling shrilly. Then, as the first half-dozen or so of the pursuers were outlined against the blazing lower windows of Burleigh, those lights too were blacked out.

She ran, desperately – not to Burleigh, where the uproar was repeating itself, but to Queen Elizabeth, which, she judged, would be the next point of attack.

The side-doors would, she knew, be locked. She dashed past the hall stair and through to the portico, where she flung herself upon the main door. That was locked also. She stepped back and shouted through the nearest window: 'Look out! There's somebody in here playing tricks. I'm coming in.' A student put out a tousled head. Other heads appeared. 'Let me get past,' said Harriet, flinging the sash up, and hauling herself up over the sill. 'They're putting out all the lights in College. Where's your fuse-box?'

'I'm sure I don't know,' said the student, as Harriet plunged across the room.

'Of course you wouldn't!' said Harriet, unreasonably, She flung the door open and burst out – into Stygian blackness. By this time the hue-and-cry had reached Queen Elizabeth, Somebody found the front door and unlocked it, and the tumult increased, those within surging out and those outside surging in. A voice said: 'Somebody came through my room and went out of the window, just after the lights went out.' Torches appeared. Here and there a face – mostly unfamiliar – was momentarily lit up. Then the lights in the New Quad began to go out also, beginning on the South side. Everybody was running aimlessly. Harriet, dashing along the plinth, cannoned full tilt into somebody and flashed the torch in her face. It was the Dean.

'Thank God!' said Harriet. 'Here's somebody in the right place.' She held on to her.

'What's happening?' said the Dean.

'Stand still,' said Harriet: 'I'll have an alibi for you if I die for it.' As she spoke, the lights on the North-East went out. 'You're all right,' said Harriet. 'Now then! make for the West Staircase and we'll catch her.'

The same idea seemed to have occurred to a number of

other people, for the entrance to the West staircase was blocked with a crowd of students, while a crowd of scouts, released by Carrie from their own Wing, added to the congestion. Harriet and the Dean forced a pathway through them, and found Miss Lydgate standing bewildered, and clasping her proof-sheets to her bosom, being determined that this time nothing should happen to them. They scooped her up with them – 'like playing "Staggie"' thought Harriet – and made their way to the fuse-boxes under the stairs. There they found Padgett, grimly on guard, with his trousers hastily pulled on over his pyjamas and a rolling-pin in his hand.

'They don't get this,' said Padgett. 'You leave it to me, madam Dean, miss. Just turning into my bed, I was, all the late-leave ladies being in. My wife's telephoning across to Jackson to fetch over some new fuses. Have you seen the boxes, miss? Wrenched open with a chisel, they was, or summat of that. A nice thing to happen. But they won't get this.'

Nor did 'they.' In the West side of the New Quad, the Warden's House, the Infirmary, and the Scouts' Wing entrenched behind its relocked grille, the lights burned on steadily. But when Jackson arrived with the new fuses, every darkened building showed its trail of damage. While Padgett had sat by the mousehole, waiting for the mouse that did not come, the Poltergeist had passed through the college, breaking ink-bottles, flinging papers into the fire, smashing lamps and crockery and throwing books through the window-panes. In the Hall, where the main fuse had also been taken, the silver cups on the High Table had been hurled at the portraits, breaking the glass, and the plaster bust of a Victorian benefactor pitched down the stone stair, to end in a fragmentary trail of detached side-whiskers and disintegrated features.

'*Well!*' said the Dean, surveying the wreckage. 'That's *one* thing to be grateful for. We've seen the last of the Reverend Melchisedek Entwistle, But, oh, *lord*!'

10

Some say thy fault is youth, some wantonness,
Some say thy grace is youth and gentle sport;
Both grace and faults are loved of more and less;
Thou makst faults graces that to thee resort.

WILLIAM SHAKESPEARE

IT would seem, at first sight, as though, in an episode witnessed by so many people and lasting altogether about an hour (counting, that is, from the first alarm in Tudor to the refitting of the final fuse) it should have been easy to find alibis for all the innocent. In practice, it was not so at all, chiefly owing to the stubborn refusal of human beings to stay where they are put. It was the very multiplicity of witnesses that made the difficulty; for it seemed likely that the culprit had mixed with the crowd over and over again in the dark. Some alibis were established for certain: Harriet and the Dean had been standing together when the lights were extinguished on the Northeast angle of the New Quad; the Warden had not left her own house till after the uproar had started, as her household staff could attest; the two porters were vouched for by their respective wives, and had, in fact, never been suspected, since on various earlier occasions disturbances had occurred while they were at their posts; the Infirmarian and the Infirmary maid had also been together the whole time. Miss Hudson, the student who had been considered a 'possible,' had been at a coffee-party when the trouble began, and was clear; Miss Lydgate also, to Harriet's great relief, had been in Queen Elizabeth,, enjoying the hospitality of a party of Third Years; she had just risen to say good night, remarking that it was past her usual time, when the lights had gone out. She had then been caught up in the throng and, as soon as she could free herself, had run hastily up to her own room to rescue her proofs.

Other members of the S.C.R. were less fortunately placed. The case of Miss Barton was exciting and mysterious. According to her own account, she had been sitting working when the fuse was pulled out in Tudor. After trying the wall-switch, she had looked out of the window, seen the figure hastening across the quad, and gone immediately in pursuit. The figure had dodged her round Burleigh twice, and had then suddenly come upon her from behind, flung her against the wall 'with extraordinary strength' and knocked her torch from her hand. Before she could recover herself, the evil-doer had extinguished the Burleigh lights and gone again. Miss Barton could give no description of this person, except that it wore 'something dark' and ran very fast. She had not seen its face. The only proof of this story was that Miss Barton certainly had received a heavy bruise on the side of the face where, so she said, she had been flung against an angle of the building. She had remained where she lay for a few minutes after receiving the blow; by that time the excitement had spread to the New Quad. Here she had certainly been seen for a few seconds together by a pair of students. She had then run to look for the Dean, found her room empty, run out again and joined Harriet and the rest in the West Staircase.

Miss Chilperic's story was equally difficult of proof. When the cry of 'There she goes!' had been raised at

Tudor, she had been among the first to run out, but, having no torch, and being too much excited to notice where she was going, she had tripped and fallen down the steps of the terrace, twisting her foot slightly. This had made her late in arriving on the scene. She had come up with the crowd at Queen Elizabeth, been carried in with it through the portico and run straight into the New Quadrangle Buildings. She had thought she heard footsteps scurrying along to her right, and had followed them, when the lights had gone out and, not knowing the building at all well, she had wandered about in some confusion, till at last she found the way out into the quad. Nobody seemed able to remember seeing Miss Chilperic at all after she left Tudor; she was that kind of person.

The Treasurer had been sitting up at work on the term's accounts. The lights in her building had been the last to go out, and her windows looked outward upon the road and not upon the quad, so that she had known nothing about the affair till a late stage in the proceedings. When the darkness fell on her she went (so she said) to the Bursar's set opposite, electrical replacements being in the Bursar's department. The Bursar was not in her bedroom or office; but as Miss Allison came out from looking for her, she emerged from the place where the fuse-boxes were, to announce the disappearance of the main fuse. Treasurer and Bursar had then joined the crowd in the quadrangle.

The account given by Miss Pyke of her movements seemed to be the most incredible of all. She lived above the Treasurer and had been working at an article for a learned Society's transactions. When her lights had gone out, she had said, 'Bother!', taken a pair of candles from a stock which she kept for such emergencies, and gone quietly on working.

Miss Burrows asserted that she had been having a bath when the Burleigh Building Lights failed, and, by an extraordinary coincidence, had found, on getting hastily out of it, that she had left her towel in her bedroom. She did not possess a self-contained set with a private bath-room and so was obliged to grope, with her dressing-gown clutched about her dripping body, along the pas-sage to her bedroom, and there dry and dress herself in the dark. This had taken a surprisingly long time and, when she came up with the main party, most of the fun was over. No proof, except the undoubted presence of soapy water in a bathroom on her floor.

Miss Shaw's set was over the Bursar's, and her bed-room looked out on St. Cross Road. She had gone to bed and to sleep, being very tired, and knew nothing about it till it was all over. The same story was told by Mrs. Goodwin, who had returned to College only that day, rather exhausted by sick-nursing. As for Miss Hillyard and Miss de Vine, living above Miss Lydgate; their lights had never gone out at all, and, their windows facing on the road, they had never known that anything was wrong, putting down a vague noise in the quad to the natural cussedness of undergraduates.

It had only been after Padgett had sat for about five minutes in vain at the mouse-hole, that Harriet had done what she should have done earlier, and attempted to make a count of the Senior Common Room. She had then found them all in the places where, by their sub-sequent accounts of themselves, they should have been. But to collect them all into one lighted room and keep them there was not so easy. She established Miss Lydgate in her own room and went to look for the rest, asking them to go straight down to Miss Lydgate's room and stay there. The Warden, meanwhile, had arrived and was addressing the students, imploring them also to stay where they were and keep quiet. Unfortunately, just as it began to seem possible to make sure of everybody's whereabouts, some inquisitive person, who had broken away from the rest and gone roaming through the Old Quad, arrived, breathless, to announce the tale of damage in the Hall. Instantly, pandemonium broke loose again. Dons who were trotting like lambs into the sheepfold suddenly lost their heads and raced with the students into the darkness. Miss Burrows screamed 'The Library!' and tore away, and the Bursar, with an anguished cry for the College property, dashed after her. The Dean called, 'Stop them!' and Miss Pyke and Miss Hillyard, taking the command to themselves, rushed out and disappeared. In the resulting confusion, everybody got lost twenty times over; and by the time the fuses were replaced and the community at last gathered and numbered, the damage had all been done.

It is surprising how much can be done in a very few minutes. Harriet calculated that the Hall had probably been wrecked first of all, being in a detached wing, where noise was not likely to attract much attention; all that was done there could have been done in a couple of minutes. From the extinguishing of the first lights in Tudor to that of the last lights in the New Quad, rather less than ten, minutes had elapsed. The third, and longest part of the business – the wrecking of the rooms in the darkened buildings, had taken anything from a quarter to half an hour.

The Warden addressed the College after Chapel, again enjoining discretion, begging the culprit to come forward, and promising that all possible measure should be taken to identify her in case she did not confess.

'I have no intention,' said Dr. Baring, 'of inflicting any restriction or punishment upon the college in general for the act of one irresponsible person. I will ask any one who has any suggestion to make or any evidence to offer with regard to the identity of this foolish practical joker to come privately, either to the Dean or myself, and make the communication in strict confidence.'

She added a few words about the solidarity of the College and departed with a grave face, her gown floating behind her.

The glaziers were already at work restoring damaged window-panes. In the Hall, the Bursar was affixing neat cards in the places of portraits whose glass had been broken: 'Portrait of Miss Matheson: Warden 1899–1912. Removed for cleaning.' Broken crockery was being swept from the grass of the Old Quad. The College was engaged in presenting a serene face to the world.

It did not improve anybody's temper to discover a printed message, consisting of 'HA! HA!' and a vulgar epithet, pasted across the mirror in the Senior Common Room, shortly before lunch. The Common Room had been empty from 9 o'clock onwards, so far as was known. The Common Room maid, going in at lunch-time with the coffee-cups, had been the first to see the notice; and it had by then dried hard. The Bursar, who had missed her pot of Gloy after the night's excitement, found it placed neatly in the centre of the S.C.R. mantelpiece.

The feeling in the Senior Common Room after this episode underwent a subtle alteration. Tongues were sharpened; the veneer of detachment began to wear thin;

the uneasiness of suspicion began to make itself felt; only Miss Lydgate and the Dean, being proved innocent, remained unmoved.

'Your bad luck seems to have repeated itself, Miss Barton,' observed Miss Pyke, acidly, 'Both in the Library affair and in this last outbreak, you seem to have been first on the spot and yet unhappily prevented from securing the culprit.'

'Yes,' said Miss Barton. 'It's very unfortunate. If next time my gown gets taken as well, the College sleuth will begin to smell a rat.'

'Very trying for you, Mrs. Goodwin,' said Miss Hillyard, 'to come back to all this upset, just when you needed a rest. I trust your little boy is better. It is particularly tiresome, because all the time you were away we had no disturbance at all.'

'It's most annoying,' said Mrs. Goodwin. 'The poor creature who does these things must be quite demented. Of course these disorders do tend to occur in celibate, or chiefly celibate communities. It is a kind of compensation, I suppose, for the lack of other excitements.'

'The great mistake,' said Miss Burrows, 'was, of course, our not keeping together. Naturally I wanted to see if any damage had been done in the Library – but why so many people should have come pelting after me—'

'The Hall was my concern,' said the Bursar.

'Oh! you *did* get to the Hall? I completely lost sight of you in the quad.'

'That,' said Miss Hillyard, 'was exactly the catastrophe I was trying to avoid when I pursued you. I called loudly to you to stop. You *must* have heard me.'

'There was too much noise to hear anything,' said Miss Stevens.

'I came to Miss Lydgate's room,' said Miss Shaw, 'the moment I could get dressed, understanding that everybody was to be there. But there was really nobody. I thought I must have misunderstood, so I tried to find Miss Vane, but she seemed to have gone off into the Ewigkeit.'

'It must have taken you a remarkably long time to dress,' said Miss Burrows. 'Anybody could run three times round College in the time it takes you to pull your stockings on.'

'Somebody,' said Miss Shaw, 'apparently *did*.'

'They're beginning to get fractious,' said Harriet to the Dean.

'What *can* you expect? The silly cuckoos! If they'd *only* sat tight on their little behinds last night, we could have cleared the whole business up. It's not *your* fault. You couldn't be everywhere at once. *How* we can expect discipline from the students, when a whole bunch of middle-aged seniors behave like a flock of *hens* in a crisis, I can't think. Who's that out there, conducting that strident conversation with a top window? Oh! I think it's Baker's young man. Well, discipline must be observed, I suppose. Give me the house telephone, would you? Thanks. I don't see how we're to prevent this last outbreak from getting – Oh! Martha! The Dean's compliments, if you please, to Miss Baker, and will she kindly bear in mind the rule about morning visitors – And the students are getting rather annoyed about the destruction of their property. I think they're actually getting worked up to calling a J.C.R. meeting, and it's very unfair on them, poor lambs, to let *them* go on suspecting one another, but what *can* we do about it? Thank God, it's the last week of term! I suppose we're not making a ghastly mistake? It must be one of us, and not a student or a scout.'

'We seem to have eliminated the students – unless it's a conspiracy between two of them. It might be that. Hudson and Cattermole together. But as for the scouts – I can show you this, now, I suppose. Would any of the scouts quote Virgil?'

'No,' said the Dean, examining the 'Harpy' passage. 'No; it doesn't seem likely. Oh, dear!'

The reply to Harriet's letter arrived by return.

My dear Harriet,

It is exceedingly good of you to be bothered with my graceless nephew. I am afraid the episode must have left you with an unfortunate impression of both of us.

I am very fond of the boy, and he is, as you say, attractive; but he is rather easily led, and my brother is not, in my opinion, handling him in the wisest way. Considering his expectations, Gerald is kept absurdly short of money, and naturally he feels he has a right to anything he can lay hands on. Still, he must learn to draw the line between carelessness and dishonesty. I have offered to augment his allowance myself, but the suggestion was not well received at home. His parents, I know, feel that I am stealing his confidence from them; but if I refused to help him, he would go elsewhere and get himself into worse trouble. Though I do not like the position into which I am forced of 'Codlin is the friend, not Short,' I still think it better that he should turn to me than to an outsider. I call this family pride; it may be mere vanity; I know it is vexation of spirit.

Let me assure you that so far, when I have trusted Gerald with anything, he has not let me down. He is amenable to some of the shibboleths. But he is not amenable to a discipline of alternate indulgence and severity; and indeed I do not know who is.

I must again apologise for troubling you with our family affairs. What on earth are you doing in Oxford? Have you retired from the world to pursue the contemplative life? I will not attempt to dissuade you now, but shall address you on the subject in the usual form on the 1st April next.

Yours in all gratitude,

P.D.B.W.

I had forgotten to say, thank-you for telling me about the accident and reassuring me as to its results. It was the first I had heard of it – as old James Forsyte says, 'Nobody ever tells me anything.' I will oblige with a few kind words.

'Poor old Peter!' said Harriet.

The remark probably deserves to be included in an anthology of Great First Occasions.

Lord Saint-George, when she went to pay him a parting visit, was considerably improved in appearance; but his expression was worried. His bed strewn with untidy papers, he seemed to be trying to cope with his affairs, and to be making but heavy weather of it. He brightened up considerably at sight of Harriet.

'Oh, look! You're just the person I've been praying for. I've no head for this kind of thing, and all the beastly bills keep sliding off the bed. I can write my name pretty well, but I can't keep track of things. I'm sure I've paid some of these brutes twice over.'

'Let me help; can I?'

'I hoped you'd say that. It's so nice of you to spoil me, isn't it? I can't think how things mount up so. They rook one shockingly at these places. But one must have something to eat, mustn't one? And belong to a few clubs. And play a game or two. Of course polo comes a bit expensive, but it's rather done just now. It's nothing, really. Of course, the mistake was going round with that bunch in Town last vac. Mother imagines they're O.K. because they're in the studbook, but they're pretty hot, really. She'll be no end surprised if they end up in gaol, and her white-headed boy with them. Sad degeneracy of old landed families, and that kind of thing. Solemn rebuke by learned judge. I somehow got behindhand with things about the New Year, and never caught up again. It looks to me as though Uncle Peter was going to get a bit of a shock. He's written, by the way. Much more like himself.'

He tossed the letter over.

Dear Jerry,

Of all the thundering nuisances that ever embittered the lives of their long-suffering relatives, you are the worst. For God's sake put down that bloody Alfa before you kill yourself; strange as it may appear, I still retain some lingering remnants of affection for you. I hope they take your licence away for life, and I hope you feel like hell. You probably do. Don't worry any more about the money.

I am writing to thank Miss Vane for her kindness to you. She is a person whose good opinion I value, so be merciful to my feelings as a man and an uncle.

Bunter has just found three silver threads among the gold. He is incredibly shocked. He begs to tender you his respectful commiserations, and advises scalp-massage (for me, I mean).

When you can manage it, send a line to report progress to your querulous and rapidly-decaying uncle,

P.W.

'He'll get a whole crop of silver threads when he realises that I hadn't paid up the insurance,' said the viscount, callously, as he took the letter back.

'What!'

'Fortunately there was nobody else involved, and the police weren't on the spot. But I suppose I shall hear from the Post Office about their blasted telegraph pole. If I have to go before the magistrates and the Governor hears of it, he'll be annoyed. It'll cost a bit to get the car put right. I'd throw the damned thing away, only Dad gave it to me in one of his generous fits. And of course, about the first thing he asked when I came out from under was whether the insurance was all right. And being in no state to argue, I said Yes. If only it doesn't get into the papers about the insurance, we're all right – only the repairs will make a nice little item in Uncle Peter's total.'

'Is it fair to make him pay for that?'

'Damned unfair,' said Lord Saint-George, cheerfully. 'The Governor ought to pay the insurance himself. He's like the Old Man of Thermopylæ – never does anything properly. If you come to that, it isn't fair to make Uncle Peter pay for all the horses that fall down when one backs them. Or for all the rotten little gold-diggers one carts around, either – I shall have to lump *them* together under "Sundries." And he'll say, "Ah yes! Postage stamps, telephone calls and live wires." And then I shall lose my head and say, "Well, Uncle—" I hate those sentences that start with "Well, Uncle." They always seem to go on and on and lead anywhere.'

'I don't suppose he'll ask for details, if you don't volunteer them. Look! I've got all these bills sorted. Shall I write out the cheques for you to sign?'

'I wish you would. No, he won't ask. He'll only sit looking harmless till I tell him. I suppose that's the way he gets criminals to come across with it. It's not a nice characteristic. Have you got that note from Levy? That's the main thing. And there's a letter from a chap called Cartwright that's rather important. I borrowed a bit from him up in Town once or twice. What's he make it come to? . . . Oh, rot! It can't be as much as that . . . Let's see . . . Well, I suppose he's right . . . and Archie Campbell – he's my bookmaker – God! what a lot of screws! they oughtn't to allow the poor beasts out. And the odds-and-ends here? What a marvellously neat way you have with these things, haven't you? Shall we tot them all up and see where we get to? Then if I faint, you can ring the bell for Nurse.'

'I'm not very good at arithmetic. You'd better check this up. It looks a bit unlikely, but I can't make it come any less.'

'Add on, say a hundred and fifty, estimated repairs to car, and then we'll see. Oh, hell! what have we here?'

'The portrait of a blinking idiot,' said Harriet, irresistibly.

'Amazin' fellow, Shakespeare. The apt word for all occasions. Yes; there's a "Well Uncle" look about this, all right. Of course, I get my quarter's allowance at the end of the month, but there's the vac, to get through and all next term. One thing, I'll have to go home and be good; can't get about the place much like this. The

Governor more or less hinted that I ought to pay my own doctor's bill, but I wasn't taking the hint. Mother blames Uncle Peter for the whole thing.

'Why on earth?'

'Setting me a bad example of furious driving. He is a bit hot, of course, but he never seems to get my foul luck.'

'Can he possibly be a better driver?'

'Darling Harriet, that's unkind. You don't mind my calling you Harriet?'

'As a matter of fact, I do, rather.'

'But I can't keep on saying "Miss Vane" to a person who knows all my hideous secrets. Perhaps I'd better accustom myself to saying "Aunt Harriet" . . . What's wrong with that? You simply can't refuse to be an adopted aunt to me. My Aunt Mary has gone all domestic and hasn't time for me, and my mother's sisters are the original gorgons. I'm dreadfully unappreciated and quite auntless for all practical purposes.'

'You deserve neither aunts nor uncles, considering how you treat them. Do you mean to finish these cheques to-day? Because, if not, I have other things to do.'

'Very well. We will continue to rob Peter to pay all. It's wonderful what a good influence you have over me. Unbending devotion to duty. If you'd only take me in hand I might turn out quite well after all.'

'Sign, please.'

'But you don't seem very susceptible. Poor Uncle Peter!'

'It will be poor Uncle Peter by the time you've finished.'

'That's what I mean. Fifty-three, nineteen, four – it's shocking the way other people smoke one's fags, and I'm sure my scout bags half of them. Twenty-six, twelve, eight. Nineteen, seven, two. A hundred quid gone before

245

you've time to look at it. Thirty-one, fourteen. Twelve, nine, six. Five, fifteen, three. What's all this tale about ghosts playing merry hell in Shrewsbury?'

Harriet jumped. 'Damn! which of our little beasts told you about that?'

'None of 'em told *me*. I don't encourage women students. Nice girls, no doubt, but too grubby. There's a chap on my staircase who came up to-day with a story. . . . I forgot, he told me not to mention it. What's it all about? And why the hush-hush?'

'Oh, dear! and they were implored not to talk. They never think of the harm this kind of thing does to the College.'

'Well, but it's only a rag, isn't it?'

'I'm afraid it's a bit more than that. Look here, if I tell you why it's hush-hush, will you promise not to pass it on?'

'Well,' said Lord Saint-George, candidly, 'you know how my tongue runs away with me. I'm not very dependable.'

'Your uncle says you are.'

'Uncle Peter? Good lord! he must be potty. Sad to see a fine brain going to rack and ruin. Of course, he's not as young as he was. . . . You're looking very sober about it.'

'It is rather grim, really. We're afraid the trouble's caused by somebody who's not quite right in her head. Not a student – but of course we can't very well tell the students that, especially when we don't know who it is.'

The viscount stared. 'Good lord! How beastly for you! I quite see your point. Naturally you don't want a thing like that to get about. Well, I'll not say a word – honestly, I won't. And if anybody mentions it I'll register a concentrated expression of no enthusiasm. I say! Do you know, I wonder if I've seen your ghost.'

'Met her?'

'Yes. I certainly met somebody who didn't seem quite all there. It scared me a bit. You'll be the first person I've told about it.'

'When was this? Tell me about it.'

'End of last term. I was awfully short of cash, and I'd had a bet with a man that I'd get into Shrewsbury and—' He stopped and looked up at her with the smile that was so uncannily not his own. 'What do you know about that?'

'If you mean that bit of the wall by the private gate, it's having a set of spikes put on it. The revolving sort.'

'Ah! all is known. Well, it wasn't an awfully good night for it – full moon and all that – but it seemed about the last chance to get that ten quid, so I hopped over. There's a bit of a garden there.'

'The Fellows' Garden. Yes.'

'Yes. Well, I was just pushing along there, when somebody hopped out from behind a bush and grabbed me. My heart nearly shot right out of my mouth on to the lawn. I wanted to do a bunk.'

'What was the person like?'

'It was in black and had a bit of black stuff sort of twisted round its head. I couldn't see anything but its eyes, and they looked beastly. So I said, "Oh, gosh!" and she said, "Which of 'em do you want?" in a horrid voice, like glue. Well, that wasn't nice and not what I expected. I don't pretend to be a good boy, but such were not my intentions at the time. So I said, "Nothing of that sort; I only made a bet I wouldn't be caught, and I have been caught, so I'll go away and I'm sorry." So she said, "Yes, go away. We murder beautiful boys like you and eat their hearts out." So I said, "Good God! how very unpleasant!" I didn't like it a bit.'

'Are you making all this up?'

'Honestly, I'm not. Then she said, "The other one had fair hair, too." And I said, "No, did he really?" And she said something, I forget what – it seemed to me she had a kind of hungry look about her, if you know what I mean – and anyhow, it was all most uncomfortable, and I said, "Excuse me, I think I'd better be getting along," and I pulled free (she was uncommonly strong in the wrists) and legged it over the wall like one, John Smith.'

Harriet looked at him, but he appeared to be perfectly serious.

'How tall was she?'

'About your height, I should think, or a bit less. Honestly, I was too scared to notice much. I couldn't recognise her again, I don't think. She didn't give me the impression of being a young thing, and that's about all I can tell you.'

'And you say you've kept this remarkable story to yourself?'

'Yes. Doesn't sound like me, does it? But there was something about it – I don't know. If I'd told any of the men, they'd have thought it howlingly funny. But it wasn't. So I didn't mention it. It didn't seem the right thing, somehow.'

'I'm glad you didn't want it laughed at.'

'No. The boy has quite nice instincts. Well, that's all. Twenty-five, eleven, nine; that blasted car simply eats oil and petrol – all those big engines do. It's going to be awfully awkward about that insurance. Please, dear Aunt Harriet, need I do any more of these? They depress me.'

'You can leave them till I've gone, and write all the cheques and envelopes yourself.'

'Slave-driver. I shall burst into tears.'

'I'll fetch you a handkerchief.'

'You are the most unwomanly woman I ever met. Uncle Peter has my sincere sympathy. Look at this! Sixty-nine, fifteen – account rendered; I wonder what it was all about.'

Harriet said nothing, but continued to make out the cheques.

'One thing, there doesn't seem to be much at Black-well's. A mere trifle of six pounds twelve.'

'One halfpennyworth of bread to this intolerable deal of sack.'

'Did you catch that habit of quotation from Uncle Peter?'

'You needn't lay any *more* burdens on your Uncle's shoulders.'

'Must you rub it in? There's practically nothing at the wine-merchant's either. Hard drinking has quite gone out. Isn't that satisfactory? Of course, the Governor obliges with a bottle or two from time to time. Did you like that Niersteiner the other day? Uncle Peter obliged with that. How many more of these things are there?'

'Quite a few.'

'Oh! My arm aches horribly.'

'If you're really too tired—'

'No. I can manage.'

Half an hour later, Harriet said. 'That's the lot.'

'Thank God! Now talk prettily to me.'

'No; I must get back now. I'll post these on my way.'

'You're not really going? Right away?'

'Yes; right away to London.'

'Wish I was you. Shall you be up next term?'

'I don't know.'

'Oh, dear, oh, dear! Well, kiss me good-bye nicely.'

Since she could think of no form of refusal that might not provoke some nerve-shattering comment, Harriet sedately complied. She was turning to go, when the nurse arrived to announce another visitor. This was a young woman, dressed in the more foolish extreme of the current fashion, with an intoxicated-looking hat and bright purple finger-nails, who advanced, crying sympathetically:

'Oh, darling Jerry! How too ruinously shattering!'

'Good lord, Gillian!' said the viscount, without very much enthusiasm. 'How did you—?'

'My lamb! You don't sound very pleased to see me.'

Harriet escaped, and found the nurse in the passage, putting an armful of roses in a bowl.

'I hope I haven't tired your patient too much with all that business.'

'I'm glad you came to help him out with it; it was on his mind. Aren't these roses beautiful? The young lady brought them from London. He gets a lot of visitors. But you can't wonder, can you? He's a dear boy, and the things he says to Sister! It's as much as one can do to keep a straight face. He's looking a lot better now, don't you think? Mr. Whybrow's made a beautiful job of the cut on his head. He's got his stitches out now – oh, yes! it'll hardly show at all. It *is* a mercy, isn't it? Because he's ever so handsome.'

'Yes; he's a very good-looking young man.'

'He takes after his father. Do you know the Duke of Denver? He's ever so handsome, too. I shouldn't call the Duchess good-looking; more distinguished. She was terribly afraid he might be disfigured for life, and it *would* have been a pity. But Mr. Whybrow's a splendid surgeon. You'll see he'll be quite all right. Sister's ever so pleased – we tell her she's quite lost her heart to Number

Fifteen. I'm sure we shall all be sorry to say good-bye to him; he keeps us all lively.'

'I expect he does.'

'And the way he pulls Matron's leg. Impudent young monkey, she calls him, but she can't help laughing at his ways. Oh, dear! there's Number Seventeen ringing again. I expect she wants a bed-pan. You know your way out, don't you?'

Harriet departed; feeling that it might be rather an onerous position to be aunt to Lord Saint-George.

'Of course,' said the Dean, 'if anything should happen in vacation—'

'I rather doubt if it will,' said Harriet. 'Not a big enough audience. A public scandal is the thing aimed at, I imagine. But if another episode should occur, it will narrow the field.'

'Yes; most of the S.C.R. will be away. Next term, what with the Warden, Miss Lydgate and myself definitely clear of suspicion, we ought to be able to patrol the place better. What are you going to do?'

'I don't know. I've been rather thinking of coming back to Oxford altogether for a time, to do some work. This place gets you. It's so completely uncommercial. I think I'm getting a little shrill in my mind. I need a mellowing.'

'Why not work for a B.Litt.?'

'That would be rather fun. I'm afraid they wouldn't accept Lefanu, would they? It would have to be somebody duller. I should enjoy a little dullness. One would have to go on writing novels for bread and butter, but I'd like an academic and meaty egg to my tea for a change.'

'Well, I hope you'll come back for part of next term,

anyway. You can't leave Miss Lydgate now till those proofs are in the printer's hands.'

'I'm almost afraid to set her loose this vac. She is dissatisfied with her chapter on Gerard Manley Hopkins; she feels she may have attacked him from the wrong angle altogether.'

'Oh, *no*!'

'I'm afraid it's Oh, yes! . . . Well, I'll cope with that, anyway. And the rest – well, we shall see what happens.'

Harriet left Oxford just after lunch. As she was putting her suit-case in the car, Padgett came up to her.

'Excuse me, miss, but the Dean thinks you would like to see this, miss. In Miss de Vine's fireplace it was found this morning, miss.'

Harriet looked at the half-burnt sheet of crumpled newspaper. Letters had been cut out from the advertising columns.

'Is Miss de Vine still in College?'

'She left by the 10.10, miss.'

'I'll keep this, Padgett, thank you. Does Miss de Vine usually read the *Daily Trumpet*?'

'I shouldn't think so, miss. It would be more likely the *Times* or *Telegraph*. But you could easy find out.'

'Of course, anybody might have dropped this in the fireplace. It proves nothing. But I'm very glad to have seen it. Good afternoon, Padgett.'

'Good afternoon, miss.'

11

Leave me, O Love, which reachest but to dust
And thou, my mind, aspire to higher things;
Grow rich in that which never taketh rust,
Whatever fades, but fading pleasures brings.
Draw in thy beams, and humble all they might
To that sweet yoke where lasting freedoms be;
Which breaks the clouds, and opens forth the light
That doth both shine and give us sight to see.

SIR PHILIP SIDNEY

TOWN seemed remarkably empty and uninteresting. Yet a lot of things were going on. Harriet saw her agent and publisher, signed a contract for serial rights, heard the inner history of the quarrel between Lord Gobbersleigh the newspaper proprietor and Mr. Adrian Cloot the reviewer, entered warmly into the triangular dispute raging among Gargantua Colour-Talkies Ltd., Mr. Garrick Drury the actor and Mrs. Snell-Wilmington author of *Passion-flower Pie*, and into the details of Miss Sugar Toobin's monstrous libel action against the *Daily Headline*, and was, of course, passionately interested to learn that Jacqueline Squills had made a malicious exposé of her second divorced husband's habits and character in her new novel *Gas-Filled Bulbs*.

Yet, somehow, these distractions failed to keep her amused. To make matters worse, her new mystery novel had got somehow stuck. She had five suspects, neatly confined in an old water-mill with no means of entrance or egress except by a plank bridge, and all provided with motives and alibis for a pleasantly original kind of murder. There seemed to be nothing fundamentally wrong with the thing. But the permutations and combinations of the five people's relationships were beginning to take on an unnatural, an incredible symmetry. Human beings were not like that; human problems were not like that; what you really got was two hundred or so people running like rabbits in and out of a college, doing their work, living their lives, and actuated all the time by motives unfathomable even to themselves, and then, in the midst of it all – not a plain, understandable murder, but an unmeaning and inexplicable lunacy.

How could one, in any case, understand other people's motives and feelings, when one's own remained mysterious? Why did one look forward with irritation to the receipt of a letter on April 1st, and then feel alarmed and affronted when it did not arrive by the first post? Very likely the letter had been sent to Oxford. There was no possible urgency about it, since one knew what it would contain and how it had to be answered; but it was annoying to sit about, expecting it.

Ring. Enter secretary with telegram (this was probably it). Wordy and unnecessary cable from American magazine representative to say she was shortly arriving in England and very anxious to talk to Miss Harriet Vane about a story for their publication. Cordially. What on earth did these people want to talk about? You did not write stories by talking about them.

Ring. Second post. Letter with Italian stamp. (Slight delay in sorting, no doubt.) Oh, thank you, Miss Bracey. Imbecile, writing very bad English, was eager to translate Miss Vane's works into Italian. Could Miss Vane inform the writer of what books she had composed? Translators were all like that – no English, no sense, no backing. Harriet said briefly what she thought of them, told Miss Bracey to refer the matter to the agent and returned to her dictation.

'Wilfrid stared at the handkerchief. What was it doing there in Winchester's bedroom? With a curious feeling of . . .'

Telephone. Hold on a moment, please. (It couldn't very well be that; it would be ridiculous to put through an expensive foreign call.) Hullo! Yes. Speaking. Oh?

She might have known it. There was a kind of mild determination about Reggie Pomfret. Would Miss Vane, could Miss Vane put up with his company for dinner and the new show at the Palladium? That night? The next night? Any night? That very night? Mr. Pomfret was inarticulate with pleasure. Thank you. Ring off. Where were we, Miss Bracey?

'With a curious feeling of— Oh, yes, Wilfrid. Very distressing for Wilfrid to find his young woman's handkerchief in the murdered man's bedroom. Agonising. A curious feeling of— What should you feel like under the circumstances. Miss Bracey?'

'I should think the laundry had made a mistake, I expect.'

'Oh, Miss Bracey! Well – we'll better say it was a lace handkerchief. *Winchester* couldn't have mistaken a lace handkerchief for one of his own, whatever the laundry sent him.'

'But would Ada have used a lace handkerchief, Miss Vane? Because she's been made rather a boyish, out-door person. And it's not as if she was in evening dress, because it was so important she should turn up in a tweed costume.'

'That's true. Well – well, better make the handkerchief small, but not lace. Plain but good. Turn back to the description of the handkerchief . . . Oh, dear! No, I'll answer it Yes? *Yes?* Yes! . . . No, I'm afraid I can't possibly. No, really. Oh? Well, you had better ask my agents. Yes, that's right. Good-bye . . . Some club wanting a debate on 'Should Genius Marry?' The question's not likely to concern any of their members personally, so why do they bother? . . . Yes, Miss Bracey? Oh, yes, Wilfrid. Bother Wilfrid! I'm taking quite a dislike to the man.'

By tea-time, Wilfrid was behaving so tiresomely that Harriet put him away in a rage and sallied out to attend a literary cocktail party. The room in which it was held was exceedingly hot and crowded, and all the assembled authors were discussing (*a*) publishers (*b*) agents, (*c*) their own sales (*d*) other people's sales, and (*e*) the extraordinary behaviour of the Book at the Moment selectors in awarding their ephemeral crown to Tasker Hepplewater's *Mock Turtle*. 'I finished this book,' one distinguished adjudicator had said, 'with tears running down my face.' The author of *Serpent's Fang* confided to Harriet over a *petite saucisse* and a glass of sherry that they must have been tears of pure boredom; but the author of *Dust and Shiver* said, No – they were probably tears of merriment, called forth by the unintentional humour of the book; had she ever met Hepplewater? A very angry young woman, whose book had been passed over, declared that the whole thing was a notorious farce. The Book of the Moment was selected from each publisher's list in turn, so that her own *Ariadne Adams* was automatically excluded from benefit, owing to the mere fact that her publisher's imprint had been honoured in the previous January. She had, however, received private assurance that the critic of the *Morning Star* had sobbed like a child over the last hundred pages of *Ariadne*, and would probably make it his Book of the Fortnight, if only the publisher could be persuaded to take advertising space in the paper. The author of *The Squeezed Lemon* agreed that advertising was at the bottom of it: had they heard how the *Daily Flashlight* had tried to blackmail Humphrey Quint into advertising with them? And how, on his refusal, they had said darkly, 'Well, you know what will happen, Mr. Quint?' And how no single Quint book had received so much as a review from the *Flashlight* ever since? And how Quint had advertised that fact in the *Morning Star* and sent up his net sales 50 per cent in consequence? Well, by some fantastic figure anyhow. But the author of *Primrose Dalliance* said that with the Book of the Moment crowd, what counted was Personal Pull – surely they remembered that Hepplewater had married Walton Strawberry's latest wife's sister. The author of *Jocund Day* agreed about the Pull, but thought that in this instance it was political, because there was some powerful anti-Fascist propaganda in *Mock Turtle* and it was well known that you could always get old Sneep Fortescue with a good smack at the Blackshirts.

'But what's *Mock Turtle* about?' inquired Harriet.

On this point the authors were for the most part vague; but a young man who wrote humorous magazines stories, and could therefore afford to be wide-minded about novels, said he had read it and thought it rather interesting, only a bit long. It was about a swimming instructor at a watering place, who had contracted such an unfortunate anti-nudity complex through watching so many bathing-beauties that it completely inhibited all his natural emotions. So he got a job on a whaler and fell in love at first sight with an Eskimo, because she was such a beautiful bundle of garments. So he married her and brought her back to live in a suburb, where she fell in love with a vegetarian nudist. So then the husband went slightly mad and contracted a complex about giant turtles, and spent all his spare time staring into the turtle-tank at the Aquarium, and watching the strange, slow monsters swimming significantly round in their encasing shells. But of course a lot of things came into it – it was one of those books that reflect the author's reactions to Things in General. Altogether, significant was, he thought, the word to describe it.

Harriet began to feel that there might be something to be said even for the plot of *Death 'twixt Wind and Water*. It was, at least, significant of nothing in particular.

Harriet went back, irritated to Mecklenburg Square. As she entered the house, she could hear her telephone ringing apoplectically on the first floor. She ran upstairs hastily – one never knew with telephone calls. As she thrust her key into the lock, the telephone stopped dead.

'Damn!' said Harriet. There was an envelope lying inside the door. It contained press cuttings. One referred to her as Miss Vines and said she had taken her degree at Cambridge; a second compared her work unfavourably with that of an American thriller-writer; a third was a belated review of her last book, which give away the plot; a fourth attributed somebody else's thriller to her and stated that she 'adopted a sporting outlook on life' (whatever that might mean). 'This,' said Harriet, much put out, 'is one of those days! April the First, indeed! And now I've got to dine with this dashed undergraduate, and be made to feel the burden of incalculable age.'

To her surprised, however, she enjoyed both the

dinner and the show. There was a refreshing lack of complication about Reggie Pomfret. He knew nothing about literary jealousies; he had no views about the comparative importance of personal and professional loyalties; he laughed heartily at obvious jokes; he did not expose your nerve-centres or his own; he did not use words with double meanings; he did not challenge you to attack him and then suddenly roll himself into an arma-dillo-like ball, presenting a smooth, defensive surface of ironical quotations; he had no overtones of any kind; he was a good-natured, not very clever, young man, eager to give pleasure to some one who had shown him a kind-ness. Harriet found him quite extraordinarily restful.

'Will you come up for a moment and have a drink or anything?' said Harriet, on her own doorstep.

'Thanks awfully.' said Mr. Pomfret, 'if it isn't too late.'

He instructed the taxi to wait and galumphed happily up. Harriet opened the door of the flat and switched the light on. Mr. Pomfret stooped courteously to pick up the letter lying on the mat.

'Oh, thank you,' said Harriet.

She preceded him into the sitting-room and let him remove her cloak for her. A moment or two later, she became aware that she was still holding the letter in her hand and that her guest and she was still standing.

'I beg your pardon. Do sit down.'

'Please—' said Mr. Pomfret, with a gesture that in-dicated, 'Read it and don't mind me.'

'It's nothing,' said Harriet, tossing the envelope on the table. 'I know what's in it. What will you have? Will you help yourself?'

Mr. Pomfret surveyed such refreshments as offered themselves and asked what he might mix for her. The drink question being settled, there was a pause.

'Er – by the way,' said Mr. Pomfret, 'is Miss Cattermole all right? I haven't seen very much of her since – since that night when I made your acquaintance, you know. Last time we met she said she was working rather hard.'

'Oh, yes. I believe she is. She's got Mods next term.'

'Oh, poor girl! She has a great admiration for you.'

'Has she? I don't know why. I seem to remember ticking her off rather brutally.'

'Well, you were fairly firm with me. But I agree with Miss Cattermole. Absolutely, I mean, we agree about having a great admiration for you.'

'How nice of you,' said Harriet, inattentively.

'Yes, really. Rather. I'll never forget the way you tackled that fellow Jukes. Did you see he got himself into trouble only a week or so later?'

'Yes. I'm not surprised.'

'No. A most unpleasant wart. Thoroughly scaly.'

'He always was.'

'Well, here's to a long stretch for comrade Jukes. Not a bad show to-night, don't you think?'

Harriet pulled herself together. She was all at once tired of Mr. Pomfret and wished he would go; but it was monstrous of her not to behave politely to him. She exerted herself to talk with bright interest of the entertainment to which he had kindly taken her and succeeded so well that it was nearly fifteen minutes before Mr. Pomfret remembered his waiting taxi, and took himself off in high spirits.

Harriet took up the letter. Now that she was free to open it, she did not want to. It had spoilt the evening for her.

Dear Harriet,

I send in my demand notes with the brutal regularity of the income-tax commissioners; and probably you say when you see the envelopes 'Oh, God! I know what this is.' The only difference is that, some time or other, one *has* to take notice of the income-tax.

Will you marry me? – It's beginning to look like one of those lines in farce – merely boring till it's said often enough; and after that, you get a bigger laugh every time it comes.

I should like to write you the kind of words that burn the paper they are written on – but words like that have a way of being not only unforgettable but unforgivable. You will burn the paper in any case; and I would rather there should be nothing in it that you cannot forget if you want to.

Well, that's over. Don't worry about it.

My nephew (whom you seem, by the way, to have stimulated to the most extraordinary diligence) is cheering my exile by dark hints that you are involved in some disagreeable and dangerous job of work at Oxford about which he is in honour bound to say nothing. I hope he is mistaken. But I know that, if you have put anything in hand, disagreeableness and danger will not turn you back, and God forbid they should. Whatever it is, you have my best wishes for it.

I am not my own master at the moment, and do not know where I shall be sent next or when I shall be back – soon, I trust. In the meantime may I hope to hear from time to time that all is well with you?

Yours, more than my own,
PETER WIMSEY.

After reading that letter, Harriet knew that she could not rest till it was answered. The bitter unhappiness of its opening paragraphs was readily explained by the last two. He probably thought – he could not possibly help thinking – that she had known him all these years, only to confide in the end, not in him, but in a boy less than half his age and his own nephew, whom she had known only a couple of weeks and had little reason to trust. He had made no comment and asked no questions – that made it worse. More generously still, he had not only refrained from offers of help and advice which she might have resented; he had deliberately acknowledged that she had the right to run her own risks. 'Do be careful of yourself'; 'I hate to think of your being exposed to unpleasantness'; 'If only I could be there to protect you'; any such phrase would express the normal male reaction. Not one man in ten thousand would say to the woman he loved, or to any woman: 'Disagreeableness and danger will not turn you back, and God forbid they should.' That was an admission of equality, and she had not expected it of him. If he conceived of marriage along those lines, then the whole problem would have to be reviewed in that new light; but that seemed scarcely possible. To take such a line and stick to it, he would have to be, not a man but a miracle. But the business about Saint-George must be cleared up immediately. She wrote quickly, without stopping to think too much.

Dear Peter,

No. I can't see my way to it. But thank you all the same. About the Oxford business – I would have told you all about it long ago, only that it is not my secret. I wouldn't have told your nephew, only that he had stumbled on part of it and I had to trust him with the rest to keep him from making unintentional mischief: I wish I could tell you; I should be very glad of your help; if ever I get leave to, I will. It is rather disagreeable but not dangerous, I hope. Thank you for not telling me to run away and play – that's the best compliment you ever paid me.

I hope your case, or whatever it is, is getting on all right. It must be a tough one to take so long.

HARRIET.

Lord Peter Wimsey read this letter while seated upon the terrace of an hotel overlooking the Pincian Gardens, which were bathed in brilliant sunshine. It astonished him so much that he was reading it for the fourth time, when he became aware that the person standing beside him was not the waiter.

'My dear Count! I beg your pardon. What manners! My head was in the clouds. Do me the favour to sit down and join me. *Servitore!*'

'I beg you will not apologise. It is my fault for interrupting you. But fearing that last night might have somewhat entangled the situation—'

'It is foolish to talk so long and so late. Grown men behave like tired children who are allowed to sit up till midnight. I admit that we were all very fractious, myself not least.'

'You are always the soul of amiability. That is why I thought that a word with you alone— We are both reasonable men.'

'Count, Count, I hope you have not come to persuade me to anything. I should find it too difficult to refuse you.' Wimsey folded the letter away in his pocket-book. 'The sun is shining, and I am in the mood to make mistakes through over-confidence.'

'Then, I must take advantage of the good moment.' The Count set his elbows on the table and leaned forward, thumb-tip to thumb-tip and little finger-tip to little finger-tip, smiling, irresistible. Forty minutes later, he took his leave, still smiling, having ceded, without noticing it, rather more than he had gained, and told in ten words more than he had learned in a thousand.

But of this interlude Harriet naturally knew nothing. On the evening of the same day, she was dining alone, a little depressed, at Romano's. She had nearly finished, when she saw a man, just leaving the restaurant, who was sketching a vague gesture of recognition. He was in the forties, going a little bald, with a smooth, vacant face and a dark moustache. For a moment she could not place him; then something about his languid walk and impeccable tailoring brought back an afternoon at Lord's. She smiled at him, and he came up to her table.

'Hullo—ullo! Hope I'm not bargin' in. How's all the doings and all that?'

'Very well, thanks.'

'That's grand. Thought I must just ooze over and pass the time of day. Or night. Only I was afraid you wouldn't remember me, and might think I was bein' a nuisance.'

'Of course I remember you. You're Mr. Arbuthnot – the Honourable Frederick Arbuthnot – and you're a friend of Peter Wimsey's, and I met you at the Eton and Harrow match two years ago, and you're married and have two children. How are they?'

'Fair to middlin', thanks. What a brain you've got! Yes, ghastly hot afternoon that was, too. Can't think why harmless women should be dragged along to be bored while a lot of little boys play off their Old School Ties. (That's meant for a joke.) You were frightfully well-behaved, I remember.'

Harriet said sedately that she always enjoyed a good cricket match.

'Do you? I thought it was politeness. It's pretty slow work, if you ask me. But I was never any good at it myself. It's all right for old Peter. He can always work himself into a stew thinking how much better he'd have done it himself.'

Harriet offered him coffee.

'I didn't know anybody ever got into a stew at Lord's. I thought it wasn't done.'

'Well, the atmosphere doesn't exactly remind one of the Cup Final; but mild old gentlemen do sometimes break out into a spot of tut-tuttery. How about a brandy? Waiter, two liqueur brandies. Are you writing any more books?'

Suppressing the rage that this question always rouses in a professional writer, Harriet admitted that she was.

'It must be splendid to be able to write,' said Mr. Arbuthnot. 'I often think I could spin a good yarn myself if I had the brains. About the odd things that happen, you know. Queer deals, and that kind of thing.'

A dim recollection of something Wimsey had once said lit up the labyrinth of Harriet's mind. Money. That was the connection between the two men. Mr. Arbuthnot, moron as he might be in other respects, had a flair for money. He knew what that mysterious commodity was going to do; it was the one thing he did know, and he only knew that by instinct. When things were preparing to go up or down, they rang a little warning bell in what Freddy Arbuthnot called his mind, and he acted on the warning without being able to explain why. Peter had money, and Freddy understood money; that must be the common interest and bond of mutual confidence that explained an otherwise inexplicable friendship. She admired the strange nexus of interests that unites the male half of mankind into a close honeycomb of cells, each touching the other on one side only, and yet constituting a tough and closely adhering fabric.

'Funny kind of story popped up the other day,' went on Mr. Arbuthnot. 'Mysterious business. Couldn't make head or tail of it. It would have amused old Peter. How is old Peter, by the way?'

'I haven't seen him for some time. He's in Rome. I don't know what he's doing there, but I suppose he's on a case of some kind.'

'No. I expect he's left his country for his country's good. It's usually that. I hope they manage to keep things quiet. The exchanges are a bit nervy.'

Mr. Arbuthnot looked almost intelligent.

'What's Peter got to do with the exchange?'

'Nothing. But if anything blows up, it's bound to affect the exchange.'

'This is Greek to me. What is Peter's job out there?'

'Foreign Office. Didn't you know?'

'I hadn't the slightest idea. He's not permanently attached there, is he?'

'In Rome, do you mean?'

'To the Foreign Office.'

'No; but they sometimes push him out when they think he's wanted. He gets on with people.'

'I see. I wonder why he never mentioned it.'

'Oh, everybody knows; it's not a secret. He probably thought it wouldn't interest you.' Mr. Arbuthnot balanced his spoon across his coffee-cup in an abstracted way. 'I'm damned fond of old Peter,' was his next, rather irrelevant, contribution. 'He's a dashed good sort. Last time I saw him, I thought he seemed a bit under the weather . . . Well, I'd better be toddling.'

He got up, a little abruptly, and said good night.

Harriet thought how humiliating it was to have one's ignorance exposed.

Ten days before the beginning of term, Harriet could bear London no longer. The final touch was put to her disgust by the sight of an advance notice of *Death 'twixt Wind and Water*, embodying an exceptionally fulsome blurb. She developed an acute homesickness for Oxford and for the *Study of Lefanu* – a book which would never have any advertising value, but of which some scholar might some day moderately observe, 'Miss Vane has handled her subject with insight and accuracy.' She rang up the Bursar, discovered that she could be accommodated at Shrewsbury, and fled back to Academe.

College was empty, but for herself, the Bursar and Treasurer, and Miss Barton, who vanished daily into the Radcliffe Camera and was only seen at meals. The Warden was up, but remained in her own house.

April was running out, chilly and fickle, but with the promise of good things to come; and the city wore the withdrawn and secretive beauty that wraps her about in vacation. No clamour of young voices echoed along her ancient stones; the tumult of flying bicycles was stilled in the narrow strait of the Turl; in Radcliffe Square the Camera slept like a cat in the sunshine, disturbed only by the occasional visit of a slow-footed don; even in the High, the roar of car and charabanc seemed minished and brought low, for the holiday season was not yet; punts and canoes, new-fettled for the summer term, began to put forth upon the Cherwell like the varnished buds upon the horse-chestnut tree, but as yet there was no press of traffic upon the shining reaches; the mellow bells, soaring and singing in tower and steeple, told of time's flight through an eternity of peace; and Great

Tom, tolling his nightly hundred-and-one, called home only the rooks from off Christ Church Meadow.

Mornings in Bodley, drowsing among the worn browns and tarnished gilding of Duke Humphrey, snuffing the faint, musty odour of slowly perishing leather, hearing only the discreet tippety-tap of Agag-feet along the padded floor; long afternoons, taking an outrigger up the Cher, feeling the rough kiss of the sculls on unaccustomed palms, listening to the rhythmical and satisfying ker-klunk of the rowlocks, watching the play of muscle on the Bursar's sturdy shoulders at stroke, as the sharp spring wind flattened the thin silk shirt against them; or, if the day were warmer, flicking swiftly in a canoe under Magdalen walls and so by the twisting race at King's Mill by Mesopotamia to Parson's Pleasure; then back, with mind relaxed and body stretched and vigorous, to make toast by the fire; and then, at night, the lit lamp and the drawn curtain, with the flutter of the turned page and soft scrape of pen on paper the only sounds to break the utter silence between quarter and quarter chime. Now and again, Harriet took out the dossier of the poison-pen and looked it over; yet, viewed by that solitary lamp, even the ugly, printed scrawls looked harmless and impersonal, and the whole dismal problem less important than the determining of a first edition date or the settlement of a disputed reading.

In that melodious silence, something came back to her that had lain dumb and dead ever since the old, innocent undergraduate days. The singing voice, stifled long ago by the pressure of the struggle for existence, and throttled into dumbness by that queer, unhappy contact with physical passion, began to stammer a few uncertain notes. Great golden phrases, rising from nothing and leading to nothing, swam up out of her dreaming mind like the huge, sluggish carp in the cool water of Mercury. One day she climbed up Shotover and sat looking over the spires of the city, deep-down, fathom-drowned, striking from the round bowl of the river-basin, improbably remote and lovely as the towers of Tir-nan-Og beneath the green sea-rollers. She held on her knee the loose-leaf note-book that contained her notes upon the Shrewsbury scandal; but her heart was not in that sordid inquiry. A detached penta-meter, echoing out of nowhere, was beating in her ears – seven marching feet – a pentameter and a half:—

To that still centre where the spinning world
Sleeps on its axis—

Had she made it or remembered it? It sounded familiar, but in her heart she knew certainly that it was her own, and seemed familiar only because it was inevitable and right.

She opened the note-book at another page and wrote the words down. She felt like the man in the *Punch* story: 'Nice little barf-room, Liza – what shall we do with it?' Blank verse? . . . No . . . it was part of the octave of a sonnet . . . it had the feel of a sonnet. But what a rhyme-sound! Curled? furled? . . . she fumbled over rhyme and metre, like an unpractised musician fingering the keys of a disused instrument.

Then, with many false starts and blank feet, returning and filling and erasing painfully as she went, she began to write again, knowing with a deep inner certainty that somehow, after long and bitter wandering, she was once more in her own place.

Here, then, at home . . .

the centre, the middle sea, the heart of the labyrinth . . .

Here, then, at home, by no more storms distrest,
Stay we our steps – course – flight – hands folded and
wings furled

Here, then, at home, by no more storms distrest,
Folding laborious hands we sit, wings furled;
Here in close perfume lies the rose-leaf curled,
Here the sun stands and knows not east nor west,
Here no tide runs; we have come, last and best,
From the wide zone through dizzying circles hurled,
To that still centre where the spinning world
Sleeps on its axis, to the heart of rest.

Yes; there was something there, though the metre
halted monotonously, lacking a free stress-shift, and
the chime 'dizzying-spinning' was unsatisfactory. The
lines swayed and lurched in her clumsy hands, uncontrollable. Still, such as it was, she had an octave.

And there it seemed to end. She had reached the full
close, and had nothing more to say. She could find no
turn for the sestet to take, no epigram, no change of
mood. She put down a tentative line or two and crossed
them out. If the right twist would not come of itself, it
was useless to manufacture it. She had her image – the
world sleeping like a great top on its everlasting spindle –
and anything added to that would be mere verse-making.
Something might come of it some day. In the meanwhile
she had got her mood on to paper – and this is the release
that all writers, even the feeblest, seek for as men seek for
love; and, having found it, they doze off happily into
dreams and trouble their heads no further.

She shut up the note-book, scandal and sonnet together, and began to make her way slowly down the
steep path. Half-way down, she met a small party coming

up: two small, flaxen-haired girls in charge of a woman whose face seemed at first vaguely familiar. Then, as they came close, she realised that it was Annie, looking strange without her cap and apron, taking the children for a walk.

As in duty bound, Harriet greeted them and asked where they were living now.

'We've found a very nice place in Headington, madam, thank you. I'm stopping there myself for my holiday. These are my little girls. This one's Beatrice and this is Carola. Say how-do-you-do to Miss Vane.'

Harriet shook hands gravely with the children and asked their ages and how they were getting on.

'It's nice for you having them so close.'

'Yes, madam. I don't know what I should do without them.' The look of quick pride and joy was almost fiercely possessive. Harriet got a glimpse of a fundamental passion that she had, as it were, forgotten when she made her reckoning; it blazed across the serenity of her sonnet-mood like an ominous meteor.

'They're all I have – now that I've lost their father.'

'Oh, dear, yes,' said Harriet, a little uncomfortably. 'Has he – how long ago was that, Annie?'

'Three years, madam. He was driven to it. They said he did what he ought not, and it preyed on his mind. But I didn't care. He never did any harm to anybody, and a man's first duty is to his wife and family, isn't it? I'd have starved with him gladly, and worked my fingers to the bone to keep the children. But he couldn't get over it. It's a cruel world for anyone with his way to make and so much competition.'

'Yes, indeed,' said Harriet. The elder child, Beatrice, was looking up at her mother with eyes that were too intelligent for her eight years. It would be better to get off the subject of the husband's wrongs and iniquities, whatever they might be. She murmured that the children must be a great comfort.

'Yes, madam. There's nothing like having children of your own. They make life worth living. Beatrice here is her father's living image, aren't you, darling? I was sorry not to have a boy; but now I'm glad. It's difficult to bring up boys without a father.'

'And what are Beatrice and Carola going to be when they grow up?'

'I hope they'll be good girls, madam, and good wives and mothers – that's what I'll bring them up to be.'

'I want to ride a motor-cycle when I'm bigger,' said Beatrice, shaking her curls assertively.

'Oh, no darling. What things they say, don't they, madam?'

'Yes, I do,' said Beatrice. 'I'm going to have a motor-cycle and keep a garage.'

'Nonsense,' said her mother, a little sharply. 'You mustn't talk so. That's a boy's job.'

'But lots of girls do boys' jobs nowadays,' said Harriet.

'But they ought not, madam. It isn't fair. The boys have hard enough work to get jobs of their own. Please don't put such things into her head madam. You'll never get a husband, Beatrice, if you mess about in a garage, getting all ugly and dirty.'

'I don't want one,' said Beatrice, firmly. 'I'd rather have a motor-cycle.'

Annie looked annoyed; but laughed when Harriet laughed.

'She'll find out some day, won't she, madam?'

'Very likely she will,' said Harriet. If the woman took the view that any husband was better than none at all, it was useless to argue. And she had rather got into the habit of shying at all discussion that turned upon men and marriage. She said good-afternoon pleasantly and strode on, a little shaken in her mood, but not unduly so. Either one liked discussing these matters or one did not. And when there were ugly phantoms lurking in the corners of one's mind, skeletons that one dared not show to anybody, even to Peter—

Well, of course not to Peter; he was the last person. And he at any rate, had no niche in the grey stones of Oxford. He stood for London, for the swift, rattling, clattering, excitable and devilishly upsetting world of strain and uproar. Here, at the still centre (yes, that line was definitely good), he had no place. For a whole week, she had scarcely given him a thought.

And then the dons began to arrive, full of their vacation activities and ready to take up the burden of the most exacting, yet most lovable term of the academic year, Harriet watched them come, wondering which of those cheerful and determined faces concealed a secret. Miss de Vine had been consulting a library in some ancient Flemish town, where was preserved a remarkable family correspondence dealing with trade conditions between England and Flanders under Elizabeth. Her mind was full of statistics about wool and pepper, and it was difficult to get her to think back to what she had done on the last day of the Hilary Term. She had undoubtedly burnt some old papers – there might have been newspapers among them – certainly she never read the *Daily Trumpet* – she could throw no light on the mutilated newspaper found in the fireplace.

Miss Lydgate – as Harriet had expected – had contrived in a few short weeks to make havoc of her proofs. She was apologetic. She had spent a most interesting long week-end with Professor Somebody, who was a great authority upon Greek quantitative measures; and he had discovered several passages that contained inaccuracies and thrown an entirely fresh light upon the argument of Chapter Seven. Harriet groaned dismally.

Miss Shaw had taken five of her students for a reading-party, had seen four new plays and bought a rather exciting summer outfit. Miss Pyke had spent an enthralling time assisting the curator of a local museum to put together the fragments of three figured pots and a quantity of burial-urns that had been dug up in a field in Essex. Miss Hillyard was really glad to be back in Oxford; she had had to spend a month at her sister's house while the sister was having a baby; looking after her brother-in-law seemed to have soured her temper. The Dean, on the other hand, had been helping to get a niece married and had found the whole business full of humour, 'One of the bridesmaids went to the wrong church and only turned up when it was all over, and there were at *least* two hundred of us squeezed into a room that would only hold fifty, and I only got half a glass of champagne and no wedding-cake, my tummy was flapping against my spine; and the bridegroom lost his hat at the last moment, and my *dear*! would you believe it? people *still* give plated biscuit-barrels!' Miss Chilperic had gone with her fiancé and his sister to a number of interesting places to study mediæval domestic sculpture. Miss Burrows had spent most of her time playing golf. There arrived also a reinforcement in the person of Miss Edwards, the Science tutor, just returned from taking a term's leave. She was a young and active woman, square in face and shoulder, with bobbed hair and a stand-no-nonsense manner. The only member missing from the Senior Common Room was Mrs. Goodwin, whose small son (a most unfortunate child) had come out with measles immediately upon his return to school and again required his mother's nursing.

'Of course she can't help it,' said the Dean, 'but it's a very great nuisance, just at the beginning of the Summer Term. If I'd only known, I could have come back earlier.'

'I don't see,' observed Miss Hillyard, grimly, 'what else you can expect, if you give jobs to widows with children. You have to be prepared for these perpetual interruptions. And for some reason, these domestic pre-occupations always have to be put before the work.'

'Well,' said the Dean, 'one must put work aside in a case of serious illness.'

'But all children get measles.'

'Yes; but he's not a very strong child, you know. His father was tubercular, poor man – in fact, that's what he died of – and if measles should turn to pneumonia, as it so often does, the consequences might be serious.'

'But *has* it turned to pneumonia?'

'They're afraid it may. He's got it very badly. And, as he's a nervous little creature, he naturally likes to have his mother with him. And in any case, she'd be in quarantine.'

'The longer she stays with him, the longer she'll *be* in quarantine.'

'It's very tiresome, of course,' put in Miss Lydgate, mildly. 'But if Mrs. Goodwin had isolated herself and come back at the earliest possible moment – as she very bravely offered to do – she would have been suffering a great deal of anxiety.'

'A great many of us have to suffer from anxiety in one way or another,' said Miss Hillyard, sharply. 'I have been very anxious about my sister. It is always an anxious business to have a first baby at thirty-five. But if the event

275

had happened to occur in term-time, it would have had to take place without my assistance.'

'It is always difficult to say which duty one should put first,' said Miss Pyke. 'Each case must be decided individually. I presume that, in bringing children into the world one accepts a certain responsibility towards them.'

'I'm not denying it,' said Miss Hillyard. 'But if the domestic responsibility is to take precedence of the public responsibility, then the work should be handed over to some one else to do.'

'But the children must be fed and clothed,' said Miss Edwards.

'Quite so. But the mother should not take a resident post.'

'Mrs. Goodwin is an excellent secretary,' said the Dean. 'I should be very sorry to lose her. And it's nice to think that we are able to help her in her very difficult position.'

Miss Hillyard lost patience.

'The fact is, though you will never admit it, that everybody in this place has an inferiority complex about married women and children. For all your talk about careers and independence, you all believe in your hearts that we ought to abase ourselves before any woman who has fulfilled her animal functions.'

'That is absolute nonsense,' said the Bursar.

'It is natural, I suppose, to feel that married women lead a fuller life,' began Miss Lydgate.

'And a more useful one,' retorted Miss Hillyard. 'Look at the fuss that's made over "Shrewsbury grandchildren"! Look how delighted you all are when old students get married! As if you were saying "Aha! education doesn't unfit us for real life after all!" And when a really brilliant scholar throws away all her prospects to marry a curate, you say perfunctorily, "What a pity! But of course her own life must come first."'

'I've *never* said such a thing,' cried the Dean indignantly. 'I always say they're perfect *fools* to marry.'

'I shouldn't mind,' said Miss Hillyard, unheeding, 'if you said openly that intellectual interests were only a second-best; but you pretend to put them first in theory and are ashamed of them in practice.'

'There's no need to get so heated about it,' said Miss Barton, breaking in upon the angry protest of Miss Pyke. 'After all, *some* of us may have deliberately chosen not to marry. And, if you will forgive my saying so—'

At this ominous phrase, always the prelude to something quite unforgivable, Harriet and the Dean broke hastily into the discussion.

'Considering that we are devoting our whole lives—'

'Even for a man, it is not always easy to say—'

Their common readiness confronted their good intention. Each broke off and begged the other's pardon, and Miss Barton went on unchecked:

'It is not altogether wise – or convincing – to show so much animus against married women. It was the same unreasonable prejudice that made you get that scout removed from your staircase—'

'I object,' said Miss Hillyard, with a heightened colour, 'to this preferential treatment. I do not see why we should put up with slackness on duty because a servant or a secretary happens to be a widow with children. I do not see why Annie should be given a room to herself in the Scouts' Wing, and charge over a corridor, when servants who have been here for longer than she has have to be content to share a room. I do not—'

'Well,' said Miss Stevens, 'I think she is entitled to a

little consideration. A woman who has been accustomed to a nice home of her own—'

'Very likely,' said Miss Hillyard. 'At any rate, it was not *my* lack of consideration that led to her precious children being placed in the charge of a common thief.'

'I was always against that,' said the Dean.

'And why did you give in? Because poor Mrs. Jukes was such a nice woman and had a family to keep. She *must* be considered and rewarded for being fool enough to marry a scoundrel. What's the good of pretending that you put the interests of the College first, when you hesitate for two whole terms about getting rid of a dishonest porter, because you're so sorry for his family?'

'There,' said Miss Allison, 'I entirely agree with you. The College ought to come first in a case like that.'

'It ought always to come first. Mrs. Goodwin ought to see it, and resign her post if she can't carry out her duties properly.' She stood up, 'Perhaps, however, it is as well that she should be away and stay away. You may remember that, *last* time she was away, we had no trouble from anonymous letters or monkey-tricks.'

Miss Hillyard put down her coffee-cup and stalked out of the room. Everybody looked uncomfortable.

'Bless my heart!' said the Dean.

'Something very wrong there,' said Miss Edwards, bluntly.

'She's so prejudiced,' said Miss Lydgate. 'I always think it's a very great pity she never married.'

Miss Lydgate had a way of putting into language that a child could understand, things which other people did not say, or said otherwise.

'I should be sorry for the man, I must say,' observed Miss Shaw; 'but perhaps I am showing an undue consideration for the male sex. One is almost afraid to open one's mouth.'

'Poor Mrs. Goodwin!' exclaimed the Bursar. 'The very last person!'

She got up angrily and went out. Miss Lydgate followed her. Miss Chilperic, who had said nothing, but looked quite alarmed, murmured that she must get along to work. The Common Room slowly cleared, and Harriet was left with the Dean.

'Miss Lydgate has the most terrifying way of hitting the nail on the head,' said Miss Martin; 'because it is obviously much more likely that—'

'A great deal more likely,' said Harriet.

Mr. Jenkyn was a youngish and agreeable don whom Harriet had met the previous term at a party in North Oxford – the same party, in fact, which had led to her acquaintance with Mr. Reginald Pomfret. He resided at Magdalen, and was incidentally one of the pro-Proctors. Harriet had happened to say something to him about the Magdalen May-day ceremony, and he had promised to send her a ticket for the Tower. Being a scientist and a man of scrupulously exact mind, he remembered his promise; and the ticket duly arrived.

None of the Shrewsbury S.C.R. was going. Most of them had been up on May mornings before. Miss de Vine had not; but though she had been offered tickets, her heart would not stand the stairs. There were students who had received invitations; but they were not students whom Harriet knew. She therefore set off alone, well before sunrise, having made an appointment to meet Miss Edwards when she came down and take an outrigger down to the Isis for a pipe-opener before having breakfast on the river.

*   *   *

The choristers had sung their hymn. The sun had risen, rather red and angry, casting a faint flush over the roofs and spires of the waking city. Harriet leaned over the parapet, looking down upon the heart-breaking beauty of the curved High Street, scarcely disturbed as yet by the roar of petrol-driven traffic. Under her feet, the tower began to swing to the swinging of the bells. The little group of bicyclists and pedestrians far below began to break up and move away. Mr. Jenkyn came up, said a few pleasant words, remarked that he had to hurry off to go bathing with a friend at Parson's Pleasure; there was no need for her to hurry – could she get down the stairs all right alone?

Harriet laughed and thanked him, and he took leave of her at the stair-head. She moved to the East side of the tower. There lay the river and Magdalen Bridge, with its pack of punts and canoes. Among them, she distinguished the sturdy figure of Miss Edwards, in a bright orange jumper. It was wonderful to stand so above the world, with a sea of sound below and an ocean of air above, all mankind shrunk to the proportions of an ant-heap. True, a cluster of people still lingered upon the tower itself – her companions in this airy hermitage. They too, spell-bound with beauty—

Great Scott! What was that girl trying to do?

Harriet made a dive at the young woman who was just placing one knee on the stonework and drawing herself up between two crenellations of the parapet.

'Here!' she said, 'you mustn't do that. It's dangerous.'

The girl, a thin, fair, frightened-looking child, desisted at once.

'I only wanted to look over.'

'Well, that's very silly of you. You might get giddy. You'd better come along down. It would be very unpleasant for the Magdalen authorities if anyone fell over. They might have to stop letting people come up.'

'I'm so sorry. I didn't think.'

'Well, you should think. Is anybody with you?'

'No.'

'I'm going down now; you'd better come too.'

'Very well.'

Harriet shepherded the girl down the dark spiral. She had no proof of anything but rash curiosity, but she wondered. The girl spoke with a slightly common accent, and Harriet would have put her down for a shop-assistant, but for the fact that tickets for the Tower were more likely to be restricted to University people and their friends. She might be an undergraduate, come up with a County Scholarship. In any case, one was perhaps attaching too much importance to the incident.

They were passing the bell-chamber now, and the brazen clamour was loud and insistent. It reminded her of a story that Peter Wimsey had told her, years ago now, one day when only a resolute determination to talk on and on had enabled him to prevent a most unfortunate outing from ending in a quarrel. Something about a body in a belfry, and a flood, and the great bells bawling the alarm across three counties.

The noise of the bells died down behind her as she passed, and the recollection with it; but she had paused for a moment in the awkward descent, and the girl, whoever she was, had got ahead of her. When she reached the foot of the stair and came out into clear daylight, she saw the slight figure scurrying off through the passage into the quad. She was doubtful whether to pursue it or not. She followed at a distance, watched it turn townwards up the High, and suddenly found herself almost in the arms of Mr. Pomfret, coming down from

Queen's in a very untidy grey flannel suit, with a towel over his arm.

'Hullo!' said Mr. Pomfret. 'You been saluting the sunrise?'

'Yes. Not a very good sunrise, but a good salute.'

'*I* think it's going to rain,' said Mr. Pomfret. 'But I said I would bathe and I am bathing.'

'Much the same here,' said Harriet. 'I said I'd scull, and I'm sculling.'

'Aren't we a pair of heroes?' said Mr. Pomfret. He accompanied her to Magdalen Bridge, was hailed by an irritable friend in a canoe, who said he had been waiting for half an hour, and went off up-river, grumbling that nobody loved him and that he knew it was going to rain.

Harriet joined Miss Edwards, who said, on hearing about the girl:

'Well, you might have got her name, I suppose. But I don't see what one could do about it. It wasn't one of our people, I suppose?'

'I didn't recognise her. And she didn't seem to recognise me.'

'Then it probably wasn't. Pity you didn't get the name, all the same. People oughtn't to do that kind of thing. Inconsiderate. Will you take bow or stroke?'

12

As a Tulipant to the Sun (which our herbalists call *Narcissus*) when it shines, is *admirandus flos ad radios solis se pandens*, a glorious Flower exposing itself; but when the Sun sets, or a tempest comes, it hides itself, pines away, and hath no pleasure left . . . do all Enamoratoes to their Mistress.

ROBERT BURTON

The mind most effectually works upon the body, producing by his passions and perturbations miraculous alterations, as melancholy, despair, cruel diseases, and sometimes death itself. . . . They that live in fear are never free, resolute, secure, never merry, but in continual pain. . . . It causeth oft-times sudden madness.

IBID

THE arrival of Miss Edwards, together with the rearrangements of residences due to the completion of the Library Building, greatly strengthened the hands of authority at the opening of the Trinity Term. Miss Barton, Miss Burrows and Miss de Vine moved into the three new sets on the ground-floor of the Library; Miss Chilperic was transferred to the New Quad, and a general redistribution took place; so that Tudor and Burleigh Buildings were left entirely denuded of dons. Miss Martin, Harriet, Miss Edwards and Miss Lydgate established a system of patrols, by which the New Quad,

Queen Elizabeth and the Library Building could be visited nightly at irregular intervals and an eye kept on all suspicious movements.

Thanks to this arrangement, the more violent demonstrations of the Poison-Pen received a check. It is true that a few anonymous letters continued to arrive by post, containing scurrilous insinuations and threats of revenge against various persons. Harriet was carefully docketing as many of these as she could hear of or lay hands on – she noticed that by this time every member of the S.C.R. had been persecuted, with the exception of Mrs. Goodwin and Miss Chilperic; in addition, the Third Year taking Schools began to receive sinister prognostications about their prospects, while Miss Flaxman was presented with an ill-executed picture of a harpy tearing the flesh of a gentleman in a mortar-board. Harriet had tried to eliminate Miss Pyke and Miss Burrows from suspicion, on the ground that they were both fairly skilful with a pencil, and would therefore be incapable of producing such bad drawings, even by taking thought; she discovered, however, that, though both were dexterous, neither of them was ambidexterous, and that their left-handed efforts were quite as bad as anything produced by the Poison-Pen, if not worse. Miss Pyke, indeed, on being shown the Harpy picture, pointed out that it was, in several respects, inconsistent with the classical conception of this monster; but there again it was clearly easy enough for the expert to assume ignorance; and perhaps the eagerness with which she drew attention to the incidental errors told as much against her as in her favour.

Another trifling but curious episode, occurring on the third Monday in term, was the complaint of an agitated and conscientious First-Year that she had left a harmless modern novel open upon the table in the Fiction Library, and that on her return to fetch it after an afternoon on the river, she had found several pages from the middle of the book – just where she was reading – ripped out and strewn about the room. The First-Year, who was a County Council Scholar, and as poor as a church mouse, was almost in tears; it really wasn't her fault; should she have to replace the book? The Dean, to whom the question was addressed, said No; it certainly didn't seem to be the First-Year's fault. She made a note of the outrage: 'The Search by C. P. Snow, pp. 327 to 340 removed and mutilated, May 13th,' and passed the information on to Harriet, who incorporated it in her diary of the case, together with such items as: 'March 7 – abusive letter by post to Miss de Vine,' 'March 11, do, to Miss Hillyard and Miss Layton,' 'April 29 – Harpy drawing to Miss Flaxman,' of which she had now quite a formidable list.

So the Summer Term set in, sun-flecked and lovely, a departing April whirled on wind-spurred feet towards a splendour of May. Tulips danced in the Fellows' Garden; a fringe of golden green shimmered and deepened upon the secular beeches; the boats put out upon the Cher between the budding banks, and the wide reaches of the Isis were strenuous with practising eights. Black gowns and summer frocks fluttered up and down the streets of the city and through the College gates, making a careless heraldry with the green of smooth turf and the silver-sable of ancient stone; motor-car and bicycle raced perilously side by side through narrow turnings and the wail of gramophones made hideous the water-ways from Magdalen Bridge to far above the new By-pass. Sunbathers and untidy tea-parties desecrated Shrewsbury Old Quad, newly-whitened tennis-shoes broke out like strange, unwholesome flowers along plinth and window-ledge, and the Dean was forced to issue a ukase in the matter of the bathing-dresses which flapped and fluttered, flag-fashion, from every coign of vantage. Solicitous tutors began to cluck and brood tenderly over such ripening eggs of scholarship as were destined to hatch out damply in the Examination Schools after their three-years' incubation; candidates, realising with a pang that they had no fewer than eight weeks in which to make up for cut lectures and misspent working hours, went flashing from Bodley to lecture-room and from Camera to coaching; and the thin trickle of abuse from the Poison-Pen was swamped and well-nigh forgotten in that stream of genial commination always poured out from the lips of examinees elect upon examining bodies. Nor, in the onset of Schools Fever, was a lighter note lacking to the general delirium. The draw for the Schools' Sweep was made in the Senior Common Room, and Harriet found herself furnished with the names of two 'horses,' one of whom, a Miss Newland, was said to be well fancied. Harriet asked who she was, having never to her knowledge seen or heard of her.

'I don't suppose you have,' said the Dean. 'She's a shy child. But Miss Shaw thinks she's pretty safe for a First.'

'She isn't looking well this term, though,' said the Bursar. 'I hope she isn't going to have a break-down or anything. I told her the other day she ought not to cut Hall so often.'

'They *will* do it,' said the Dean. 'It's all very well to say they can't be bothered to change when they come off the river and prefer pyjamas and an egg in their rooms; but I'm sure a boiled egg and a sardine aren't sustaining enough to do Schools on.'

'And the mess it all makes for the scouts to clear up,' grumbled the Bursar. 'It's almost impossible to get the rooms done by eleven when they're crammed with filthy crockery.'

'It isn't being out on the river that's the matter with Newland,' said the Dean. 'That child works.'

'All the worse,' said the Bursar. 'I distrust the candidate who swots in her last term. I shouldn't be a bit surprised if your horse scratched, Miss Vane. She looks nervy to me.'

'That's very depressing,' said Harriet. 'Perhaps I'd better sell half my ticket while the price is good. I agree with Edgar Wallace, "Give me a good stupid horse who will eat his oats." Any offers for Newland?'

'What's that about Newland?' demanded Miss Shaw, coming up to them. They were having coffee in the Fellows' Garden at the time. 'By the way, Dean, couldn't you put up a notice about sitting on the grass in the New Quad? I have had to chase two parties off. We cannot have the place looking like Margate Beach.'

'Certainly not. They know quite *well* it isn't allowed. *Why* are women undergraduates so sloppy?'

'They're always exceedingly anxious to be like the men,' said Miss Hillyard, sarcastically, 'but I notice the likeness doesn't extend to showing respect for the College grounds.'

'Even you must admit that men have some virtues,' said Miss Shaw.

'More tradition and discipline, that's all,' said Miss Hillyard.

'I don't know,' said Miss Edwards. 'I think women are messier by nature. They are naturally picnic-minded.'

'It's nice to sit in the open air in this lovely weather,' suggested Miss Chilperic, almost apologetically (for her student days were not far behind her) 'and they don't think how awful it looks.'

'In hot weather,' said Harriet, moving her chair back into the shade, 'men have the common sense to stay indoors, where it's cooler.'

'Men,' said Miss Hillyard, 'have a passion for frowst.'

'Yes,' said Miss Shaw, 'but what were you saying about Miss Newland? You weren't offering to sell your chance, Miss Vane, were you? Because, take it from me, she's a hot favourite. She's the Latymer Scholar, and her work's brilliant.'

'Somebody suggested she was off her feed and likely to be a non-starter.'

'That's very unkind,' said Miss Shaw, with indignation. 'Nobody's any right to say such things.'

'I think she looks harassed and on edge,' said the Bursar. 'She's too hard-working and conscientious. She hasn't got the wind-up about Schools, has she?'

'There's nothing wrong with her work,' said Miss Shaw. 'She does look a little pale, but I expect it's the sudden heat.'

'Possibly she's worried about things at home,' suggested Mrs. Goodwin. She had returned to College on the 9th May, her boy having taken a fortunate turn for the better, though he was still not out of the wood. She looked anxious and sympathetic,

'She'd have told me if she had been,' said Miss Shaw. 'I encourage my students to confide in me. Of course she's a very reserved girl, but I have done my best to draw her out, and I feel sure I should have heard if there was anything on her mind,'

'Well,' said Harriet, 'I must see this horse of mine before I decide what to do about my sweep-stake ticket. Somebody must point her out.'

'She's up in the Library at this moment, I fancy,' said the Dean; 'I saw her stewing away there just before dinner – cutting Hall as usual. I nearly spoke to her. Come and stroll through, Miss Vane. If she's there, we'll chase her out for the good of her soul. I want to look up a reference anyhow.'

Harriet got up, laughing, and accompanied the Dean.

'I sometimes think,' said Miss Martin, 'that Miss Shaw would get more real confidence from her pupils if she wasn't always probing into their little insides. She likes people to be fond of her, which I think is rather a mistake. Be kind, but leave 'em alone, is my motto. The shy ones shrink into their shells when they're poked, and the egotistical ones talk a lot of rubbish to attract attention. However, we all have our methods.'

She pushed open the Library door, halted in the end bay to consult a book and verify a quotation, and then led the way through the long room. At a table near the centre, a thin, fair girl was working amid a pile of reference books. The Dean stopped.

'You still here, Miss Newland? Haven't you had any dinner?'

'I'll have some later, Miss Martin. It was so hot, and I want to get this language paper done.'

The girl looked startled and uneasy. She pushed the damp hair back from her forehead. The whites of her eyes showed like those of a fidgety horse.

'Don't you be a little juggins,' said the Dean. 'All work and no play is simply silly in your Schools term. If you go on like this, we'll have to send you away for a rest-cure and forbid work altogether for a week or so. Have you got a headache? You look as if you had.'

'Not very much, Miss Martin.'

'For goodness' sake,' said the Dean, 'chuck that perishing old Ducange and Meyer-Lübke or whoever it is and go away and play. I'm always having to chase the

Schools people off to the river and into the country,' she added, turning to Harriet, 'I wish they'd all be like Miss Camperdown – she was after your time. She frightened Miss Pyke by dividing the whole of her Schools term between the river and the tennis-courts, and she ended up with a First in Greats.'

Miss Newland looked more alarmed than ever.

'I don't seem able to think,' she confessed. 'I forget things and go blank.'

'Of course you do,' said the Dean, briskly. 'Sure sign you're doing too much. Stop it at once. Get up now and get yourself some food and then take a nice novel or something, or find somebody to have a knock-up with you.'

'Please don't bother, Miss Martin. I'd rather go on with this. I don't feel like eating and I don't care about tennis – I *wish* you wouldn't bother!' she finished, rather hysterically.

'All right,' said the Dean; 'bless you, *I* don't want to fuss. But do be sensible.'

'I will, really, Miss Martin. I'll just finish this paper. I couldn't feel comfortable if I hadn't. I'll have something to eat then and go to bed. I promise I will.'

'That's a good girl.' The Dean passed on, out of the Library, and said to Harriet:

'I don't like to see them getting into that state. What do you think of your horse's chance?'

'Not much,' said Harriet. 'I do know her. That is, I've seen her before. I saw her last on Magdalen Tower.'

'What?' said the Dean. 'Oh, lord!'

Of Lord Saint-George, Harriet had not seen very much during that first fortnight of term. His arm was out of a sling; but a remaining weakness in it had curbed his sporting activities, and when she did see him, he informed her that he was working. The matter of the telegraph pole and the insurance had been safely adjusted, and the parental wrath avoided. 'Uncle Peter,' to be sure, had had something to say about it, but Uncle Peter, though scathing, was safe as houses. Harriet encouraged the young gentleman to persevere with his work and refused an invitation to dine and meet 'his people.' She had no particular wish to meet the Denvers, and had hitherto successfully avoided doing so.

Mr. Pomfret had been assiduously polite. He and Mr. Rogers had taken her on the river, and had included Miss Cattermole in the party. They had all been on their best behaviour, and a pleasant time had been enjoyed by all, the mention of previous encounters having, by common consent, been avoided. Harriet was pleased with Miss Cattermole; she seemed to have made an effort to throw off the blight that had settled upon her, and Miss Hillyard's report had been encouraging. Mr. Pomfret had also asked Harriet to lunch and to play tennis; on the former occasion she had truthfully pleaded a previous engagement and, on the second, had said, with rather less truth, that she had not played for years, was out of form and was not really keen. After all, one had one's work to do (*Lefanu*, *'Twixt Wind and Water*, and the *History of Prosody* among them made up a fairly full programme), and one could not spend all one's time idling with undergraduates.

On the evening after her formal introduction to Miss Newland, however, Harriet encountered Mr. Pomfret accidentally. She had been to see an old Shrewsburian who was attached to the Somerville Senior Common Room, and was crossing St. Giles on her way back, shortly before midnight, when she was aware of a group of young men in evening dress, standing about one of the trees which adorn that famous thoroughfare. Being naturally inquisitive, Harriet went to see what was up. The street was practically deserted, except for through traffic of the ordinary kind. The upper branches of the tree were violently agitated, and Harriet, standing on the outskirts of the little group beneath, learned from their remarks that Mr. Somebody-or-the-other had undertaken, in consequence of an after-dinner bet, to climb every tree in St. Giles without interference from the Proctor. As the number of trees was large and the place public, Harriet felt the wager to be rather optimistic. She was just turning away to cross the street in the direction of the Lamb and Flag, when another youth, who had evidently been occupying an observation-post, arrived, breathless, to announce that the Proggins was just coming into view round the corner of Broad Street. The climber came down rather hastily, and the group promptly scattered in all directions – some running past her, some making their way down side-streets, and a few bold spirits fleeing towards the small enclosure known as the Fender, within which (since it belongs not to the Town but to St. John's) they could play at tig with the Proctor to their hearts' content. One of the young gentlemen darting in this general direction passed Harriet close, stopped with an exclamation, and brought up beside her.

'Why, it's you!' cried Mr. Pomfret, in an excited tone.

'Me again,' said Harriet. 'Are you always out without your gown at this time of night?'

'Practically always,' said Mr. Pomfret, falling into step beside her. 'Funny you should always catch me at it. Amazing luck, isn't it . . . ? I say, you've been avoiding me this term. Why?'

'Oh, no,' said Harriet; 'only I've been rather busy.'

'But you *have* been avoiding me,' said Mr. Pomfret. 'I know you have. I suppose it's ridiculous to expect you to take any particular interest in me. I don't suppose you ever think about me. You probably despise me.'

'Don't be so absurd, Mr. Pomfret. Of course I don't do anything of the sort. I like you very much, but—'

'Do you? . . . Then why won't you let me see you? Look here, I *must* see you. There's something I've got to tell you. When can I come and talk to you?'

'What about?' said Harriet, seized with a sudden and awful qualm.

'What *about*? Hang it, don't be so unkind. Look here, Harriet— No, stop, you've got to listen. Darling, wonderful Harriet—'

'Mr. Pomfret, please—'

But Mr. Pomfret was not to be checked. His admiration had run away with him, and Harriet, cornered in the shadow of the big horse-chestnut by the Lamb and Flag, found herself listening to as eager an avowal of devotion as any young gentleman in his twenties ever lavished upon a lady considerably his senior in age and experience.

'I'm frightfully sorry, Mr. Pomfret. I never thought— No, really, it's quite impossible. I'm at least ten years older than you are. And besides—'

'What does that matter?' With a large and clumsy gesture Mr. Pomfret swept away the difference of age and plunged on in a flood of eloquence, which Harriet, exasperated with herself and him, could not stop. He loved her, he adored her, he was intensely miserable, he could neither work nor play games for thinking of her, if she refused him he didn't know what he should do with himself, she must have seen, she must have realised – he wanted to stand between her and all the world—

Mr Pomfret was six feet three and broad and strong in proportion.

'Please don't do that,' said Harriet, feeling as though she were feebly saying 'Drop it, Cæsar,' to somebody else's large and disobedient Alsatian. 'No, I mean it. I can't let you—' And then in a different tone:

'Look out, juggins! Here's the Proctor.'

Mr. Pomfret, in some consternation, gathered himself together and turned as to flee. But the Proctor's bull-dog, who had been having a lively time with the tree-climbers in St. Giles, and were now out for blood, had come through the archway at a smart trot, and, seeing a young gentleman not only engaged in nocturnal vaga-tion without his gown but actually embracing a female *(mulier vel meretrix, cujus consortio Christianis prorsus interdictum est)* leapt gleefully upon him, as upon a lawful prey.

'Oh, blast!' said Mr. Pomfret. 'Here, you—'

'The Proctor would like to speak to you, sir,' said the Bulldog, grimly.

Harriet debated with herself whether it might not be more tactful to depart, leaving Mr. Pomfret to his fate. But the Proctor was close on the heels of his men; he was standing within a few yards of her and already demand-ing to know the offender's name and college. There seemed to be nothing for it but to face the matter out.

'Just a moment, Mr. Proctor,' began Harriet, strug-gling, for Mr. Pomfret's sake, to control a rebellious uprush of laughter. 'This gentleman is with me, and you can't— Oh! good evening, Mr. Jenkyn.'

It was, indeed, that amiable pro-Proctor. He gazed at Harriet, and was struck dumb with embarrassment.

'I say,' broke in Mr. Pomfret, awkwardly, but with a gentlemanly feeling that some explanation was due from him; 'it was entirely my fault. I mean, I'm afraid I was annoying Miss Vane. She–I—'

'You can't very well prog him, you know,' said Harriet, persuasively, 'can you now?'

'Come to think of it,' replied Mr. Jenkyn, 'I suppose I can't. You're a Senior Member, aren't you?' He waved his bulldogs to a distance. 'I beg your pardon,' he added, a little stiffly.

'Not at all,' said Harriet. 'It's a nice night. Did you have good hunting in St. Giles?'

'Two culprits will appear before their dean to-morrow,' said the pro-Proctor, rather more cheerfully. 'I suppose nobody came through here?'

'Nobody but ourselves,' said Harriet; 'and I can assure you that we haven't been climbing trees.'

A wicked facility in quotation tempted her to add 'except in the Hesperides'; but she respected Mr. Pomfret's feelings and restrained herself.

'No, no,' said Mr. Jenkyn. He fingered his hands nervously and hitched his gown with its velvet facings protectively about his shoulders. 'I had better be away in pursuit of those that have.'

'Good night,' said Harriet.

'Good night,' said Mr. Jenkyn, courteously raising his square cap. He turned sharply upon Mr. Pomfret. 'Good night, sir.'

He stalked away with brisk steps between the posts into Museum Road, his long liripipe sleeves agitated and fluttering. Between Harriet and Mr. Pomfret there occurred one of those silences into which the first word spoken falls like the stroke of a gong. It seemed equally impossible to comment on the interruption or to resume the interrupted conversation. By common consent, however, they turned their backs upon the pro-Proctor and moved out once more into St. Giles. They had turned left and were passing through the now-deserted Fender before Mr. Pomfret found his tongue.

'A nice fool I look,' said Mr. Pomfret, bitterly.

'It was very unfortunate,' said Harriet, 'but I must have looked much the more foolish. I very nearly ran away altogether. However, all's well that ends well. He's a very decent sort and I don't suppose he'll think twice about it.'

She remembered, with another disconcerting interior gurgle of mirth, an expression in use among the irreverent: 'to catch a Senior girling.' 'To boy' was presumably the feminine equivalent of the verb 'to girl'; she wondered whether Mr. Jenkyn would employ it in Common Room next day. She did not grudge him his entertainment; being old enough to know that even the most crashing social bricks make but a small ripple in the ocean of time, which quickly dies away. To Mr. Pomfret, however, the ripple must inevitably appear of the dimensions of a maelstrom. He was muttering sulkily something about a laughing-stock.

'Please,' said Harriet, 'don't worry about it. It's of no importance. I don't mind one bit.'

'Of course not,' said Mr. Pomfret. 'Naturally, you can't take me seriously. You're treating me like a child.'

'Indeed I'm not. I'm very grateful – I'm very much honoured by everything you said to me. But really and truly, it's quite impossible.'

'Oh, well, never mind,' said Mr. Pomfret, angrily.

It was too bad, thought Harriet. To have one's young affections trampled upon was galling enough; to have been made an object of official ridicule as well was almost unbearable. She must do something to restore the young gentleman's self-respect.

'Listen, Mr. Pomfret. I don't think I shall ever marry anybody. Please believe that my objection isn't personal at all. We have been very good friends. Can't we—?'

Mr. Pomfret greeted this fine old bromide with a dreary snort.

'I suppose,' he said, in a savage tone, 'there's somebody else.'

'I don't know that you've any right to ask that.'

'Of course not,' said Mr. Pomfret, affronted. 'I've no right to ask you anything. I ought to apologise for asking you to marry me. And for making a scene in front of the Proggins – in fact, for existing. I'm exceedingly sorry.'

Very clearly, the only balm that could in the least soothe the wounded vanity of Mr. Pomfret would be the assurance that there *was* somebody else. But Harriet was not prepared to make any such admission; and besides, whether there was anybody else or not, nothing could make the notion of marrying Mr. Pomfret anything but preposterous. She begged him to take a reasonable view of the matter; but he continued to sulk; and indeed, nothing that could possibly be said could mitigate the essential absurdity of the situation. To offer a lady one's chivalrous protection against the world in general, and to be compelled instead to accept her senior standing as a protection for one's self against the just indignation of the Proctor is, and remains, farcical.

Their ways lay together. In resentful silence they paced the stones, past the ugly front of Balliol and the high iron gates of Trinity, past the fourteen-fold sneer of the Cæsars and the top-heavy arch of the Clarendon Building, till they stood at the junction of Cat Street and Holywell.

'Well,' said Mr. Pomfret, 'if you don't mind, I'd better cut along here. It's just going twelve.'

'Yes. Don't bother about me. Good night . . . And thank you again very much.'

'Good night.'

Mr. Pomfret ran hurriedly in the direction of Queen's College pursued by a yelping chorus of chimes.

Harriet went on down Holywell. She could laugh now if she wanted to; and she did laugh. She had no fear of any permanent damage to Mr. Pomfret's heart; he was far too cross to be suffering in anything but his vanity. The incident had that rich savour of the ludicrous which neither pity nor charity can destroy. Unfortunately, she could not in decency share it with anybody; she could only enjoy it in lonely ecstasies of mirth. What Mr. Jenkyn must be thinking of her she could scarcely imagine. Did he suppose her to be an unprincipled cradle-snatcher? or a promiscuous sexual maniac? or a disappointed woman eagerly grasping at the rapidly disappearing skirts of opportunity? or what? The more she thought about her own part in the episode, the funnier it appeared to her. She wondered what she should say to Mr. Jenkyn if she ever met him again.

She was surprised to find how much Mr. Pomfret's simple-minded proposal had elated her. She ought to have been thoroughly ashamed of herself. She ought to be blaming herself for not having seen what was happening to Mr. Pomfret and taken steps to stop it. Why hadn't she? Simply, she supposed, because the possibility of such a thing had never occurred to her. She had taken it for granted that she could never again attract any man's fancy, except the eccentric fancy of Peter Wimsey. And to him she was, of course, only the creature of his making and the mirror of his own magnanimity. Reggie Pomfret's devotion, though ridiculous, was at least single-minded; *he* was no King Cophetua; she had not to be humbly obliged to *him* for kindly taking notice of her. And that reflection, after all, was pleasurable. However loudly we may assert our own unworthiness, few of us are really offended by hearing the assertion contradicted by a disinterested party.

In this unregenerate mood she reached the College, and let herself in by the postern. There were lights in the Warden's Lodgings, and somebody was standing at the gate, looking out. At the sound of Harriet's footsteps, this person called out, in the Dean's voice:

'Is that you, Miss Vane. The Warden wants to see you.'

'What's the matter, Dean?'

The Dean took Harriet by the arm.

'Newland hasn't come in. You haven't seen her anywhere?'

'No – I've been round at Somerville. It's only just after twelve. She'll probably turn up. You don't think—?'

'We don't know what to think. It's not like Newland to be out without leave. And we've found things.'

She led Harriet into the Warden's sitting-room. Dr. Baring was seated at her desk, her handsome face stern and judicial.In front of her stood Miss Haydock, with her hands thrust into her dressing-gown pockets; she looked excited and angry. Miss Shaw, curled dismally in a corner of the big couch, was crying; while Miss Millbanks the Senior Student, half-frightened and half-defiant, hovered uneasily in the background. As Harriet came in with the Dean, everybody looked hopefully towards the door and then away again.

'Miss Vane,' said the Warden, 'the Dean tells me that you saw Miss Newland behaving in a peculiar manner on Magdalen Tower last May-Day. Can you give me any more exact details about that?'

Harriet told her story again.

'I am sorry,' she added in conclusion, 'that I didn't get her name at the time; but I didn't recognise her as one of our students. As a matter of fact, I don't remember ever noticing her at all, until she was pointed out to me yesterday by Miss Martin.'

'That's quite right,' said the Dean. 'I'm not at all surprised you shouldn't have known her. She's very quiet and shy and seldom comes in to Hall or shows herself anywhere. I think she works nearly all day at the Radcliffe. Of course, when you told me about the May-Day business, I decided that somebody ought to keep an eye on her. I informed Dr. Baring and Miss Shaw, and I asked Miss Millbanks whether any of the Third Year had noticed that she seemed to be in any trouble.'

'I can't understand it,' cried Miss Shaw. 'Why couldn't she have come to me about it? I always encourage my pupils to give me their full confidence. I asked her again and again. I really thought she had a real affection for me . . .'

She sniffed hopelessly into a damp handkerchief.

'I knew something was up,' said Miss Haydock, bluntly, 'But I didn't know what it was. The more questions you asked, the less she'd tell you – so I didn't ask many.'

'Has the girl no friends?' asked Harriet.

'I thought she looked on me as a friend,' complained Miss Shaw.

'She didn't make friends,' said Miss Haydock.

'She's a very reserved child,' said the Dean. 'I don't think anybody could make much out of her. I know I couldn't.'

'But what has happened, exactly?' asked Harriet.

'When Miss Martin spoke to Miss Millbanks about

her,' said Miss Haydock, cutting in without respect of persons upon the Warden's reply, 'Miss Millbanks mentioned the matter to me, saying she couldn't see that we could be expected to do anything.'

'But I scarcely knew her . . .' began Miss Millbanks.

'Nor did I,' said Miss Haydock. 'But I thought something had better be done about it. I took her out on the river this afternoon. She said she ought to work, but I told her not to be an idiot, or she'd crack up. We took a punt up over the Rollers and had tea along by the Parks. She seemed all right then. I brought her back and persuaded her to come and dine properly in Hall. After that, she said she wanted to go and work at the Radder. I had an engagement, so I couldn't go with her – besides, I thought she'd think it funny if I trailed after her all day. So I told Miss Millbanks that somebody else had better carry on.'

'Well, I carried on myself,' said Miss Millbanks, rather defiantly. 'I took my own work across there. I sat in a desk where I could see her. She was there till half-past nine. I came away at ten and found she'd gone.'

'Didn't you see her go?'

'No. I was reading and I suppose she slipped out. I'm sorry; but how was I to know? I've got Schools this term. It's all very well to say I oughtn't to have taken my eyes off her, but I'm not a nurse or anything—'

Harriet noticed how Miss Millbank's self-assurance had broken down. She was defending herself angrily and clumsily like a schoolgirl.

'On returning,' pursued the Warden, 'Miss Millbanks—'

'But has anything been done about it?' interrupted Harriet, impatient with this orderly academic exposition. 'I suppose you asked whether she's been up to the gallery of the Radcliffe.'

'I thought of that later on,' replied the Warden, 'and suggested that a search should be made there. I understand that it has been made, without result. However, a subsequent—'

'How about the river?'

'I am coming to that. Perhaps I had better continue in chronological order. I can assure you that no time has been wasted.'

'Very well, Warden.'

'On returning,' said the Warden, taking up her tale exactly where she had left it, 'Miss Millbanks told Miss Haydock about it, and they ascertained that Miss Newland was not in College. They then, very properly, informed the Dean, who instructed Padgett to telephone through as soon as she came in. At 11.15 she had not returned, and Padgett reported that fact. He mentioned at the same time that he had himself been feeling uneasy about Miss Newland. He had noticed that she had taken to going about alone, and that she looked strained and nervous.'

'Padgett is pretty shrewd,' said the Dean. 'I often think he knows more about the students than any of us.'

'Up till to-night,' wailed Miss Shaw, 'I should have said I knew all my pupils intimately.'

'Padgett also said he had seen several of the anonymous letters arrive at the Lodge for Miss Newland.'

'He ought to have reported that,' said Harriet.

'No,' said the Dean. 'It was after you came last term that we instructed him to report. The ones he saw came before that.'

'I see.'

'By that time,' said the Warden, 'we were beginning to feel alarmed, and Miss Martin rang up the police. In the meantime, Miss Haydock made a search in Miss Newland's room for anything that might throw light on her state of mind; and found – these.'

She took a little sheaf of papers from her desk and handed them to Harriet, who said 'Good God!'

The Poison-Pen, this time, had found a victim ready made to her hand. There were the letters, thirty or more of them ('and I don't suppose that's the lot, either,' was the Dean's comment) – menacing, abusive, insinuating – all hammering remorselessly upon the same theme. 'You needn't think you will get away with it' – 'What will you do when you fail in Schools?' – 'You deserve to fail and I shall see that you do' – then more horrible suggestions: 'Don't you feel your brain going?' – 'If they see you are going mad they will send you down' – and finally, in a sinister series: 'You'd better end it now' – 'Better dead than in the loony-bin' – 'In your place I should throw myself out of the window' – 'Try the river' – and so on; the continuous, deadly beating on weak nerves that of all things is hardest to resist.

'If only she had shown them to me!' Miss Shaw was crying.

'She wouldn't of course,' said Harriet. 'You have to be very well balanced to admit that people think you're going mad. That's what's done the mischief.'

'Of all the wicked things—' said the Dean. 'Think of that unfortunate child collecting all these horrors and brooding over them! I'd like to kill whoever it is!'

'It's a definite effort at murder,' said Harriet. 'But the point is, has it come off?'

There was a pause. Then the Warden said in an expressionless voice:

'One of the boat-house keys is missing.'

'Miss Stevens and Miss Edwards have gone up-stream in the Water-fly,' said the Dean, 'and Miss Burrows and

Miss Barton have taken the other sculler down to the Isis. The police are searching too. They've been gone about three-quarters of an hour. We didn't discover till then that the key was gone.'

'Then there's not much we can do,' said Harriet, suppressing the angry comment that the boat-house keys should have been checked the moment Miss Newland's absence had been remarked. 'Miss Haydock – did Miss Newland say anything to you – anything at all – while you were out, that might suggest where she was likely to go in case she wanted to drown herself?'

The blunt phrase, spoken openly for the first time, shook everybody. Miss Haydock put her head in her hands.

'Wait a minute,' she said. 'I do remember something. We were well up through the Parks – Yes – It was after tea, and went a bit farther before turning. I struck a bad bit of water and nearly lost the pole. I remember saying it would be a nasty place to go in, because of the weeds. It's a bad bottom – all mud with deep holes in it. Miss Newland asked if that wasn't the place where a man had been drowned last year. I said I didn't know, but I thought it was near there. She didn't say anything more, and I'd forgotten it till this moment.'

Harriet looked at her watch.

'Half-past nine, she was last seen. She'd have to get to the boat-house. Had she a bicycle? No? Then it would take her nearly half an hour. Ten. Say another forty minutes to the Rollers, unless she was very quick—'

'She's not a quick punter. She'd take a canoe.'

'She'd have the wind and stream against her. Say 10.45. And she'd have to get the canoe over the Rollers by herself. That takes time. But she would still have over an hour. We may be too late, but it's just worth trying.'

304

'But she might have gone in anywhere.'

'Of course she might. But there's just the chance. People get an idea and stick to it. And they don't always make their minds up instantly.'

'If I know anything of the girl's psychology,' began Miss Shaw.

'What's the good of arguing?' said Harriet. 'She's either dead or alive and we've got to risk a guess. Who'll come with me? I'll get the car – we shall go quicker by road than by river. We can commandeer a boat somewhere above the Parks – if we have to break open a boathouse. Dean—'

'I'm with you,' said Miss Martin.

'We want torches and blankets. Hot coffee. Brandy. Better get the police to send up a constable to meet us at Timms's. Miss Haydock, you're a better oar than I am—'

'I'll come,' said Miss Haydock. 'Thank God for something to do.'

Lights on the river. The splash of sculls. The steady chock of the rowlocks.

The boat crept slowly down-stream. The constable, crouched in the bows, swept the beam of a powerful torch from bank to bank. Harriet, holding the rudder-lines, divided her attention between the dark current and the moving light ahead. The Dean, setting a slow and steady stroke, kept her eyes before her and her wits on the job.

At a word from the policeman, Harriet checked the boat and let her drift down towards a dismal shape, black and slimy on the black water. The boat lurched as the man leaned out. In the silence came the answering groan, splash, chuck of oars on the far side of the next bend.

'All right,' said the policeman. 'Only a bit o' sacking.'
'Ready? Paddle!'

The sculls struck the water again.

'Is that the Bursar's boat coming up?' said the Dean.

'Very likely,' said Harriet.

Just as she spoke, someone in the other boat gave a shout. There was a heavy splash and a cry ahead, and an answering shout from the constable:

'There she goes!'

'Pull like blazes,' said Harriet. As she drew on the rudder-lines to bring their nose round the bend, she saw, across stroke's shoulder in the beam of the torch, the thing they had come to find – the shining keel of a canoe adrift in mid-stream, with the paddles floating beside it; and all around it the water ran, ringed and rippling with the shock of the plunge.

'Look out, ladies. Don't run her down. She can't be far off.'

'Easy!' said Harriet. And then, 'Back her! Hold her!'

The stream chuckled and eddied over the reversed oar-blades. The constable shouted to the up-coming sculler, and then pointed away towards the left bank.

'Over by the willow there.'

The light caught the silver leaves, dripping like rain towards the river. Something swirled below them, pale and ominous.

'Easy. Paddle. One on bow. Another on bow. Another. Easy. Paddle. One. Two. Three. Easy. Paddle on stroke, backwater on bow. One. Two. Easy. Look out for your bow oars.'

The boat swung across the stream and turned, following the policeman's signal. He was kneeling and peering into the water on the bow side. A white patch glimmered up to the surface and sank again.

'Fetch her round a bit more, miss.'

'Ready? One on stroke, paddle. Another. Easy. Hold her.' He was leaning out, groping with both hands among the ribbon-weed. 'Back a little. Easy. Keep those bow oars out of the water. Trim the boat. Sit over to stroke. Have you got her?'

'I've got her – but the weeds are cruel strong.'

'Mind you don't go over or there'll be two of you. Miss Haydock – ready, ship! See if you can help the constable. Dean – paddle one very gentle stroke and sit well over.'

The boat rocked perilously as they heaved and tore at the clinging weeds, razor-sharp and strong as gravebands. The Water-fly had come up now and was pulling across the stream. Harriet yelled to Miss Stevens to keep her sculls out of mischief. The boats edged together. The girl's head was out of the water, dead-white and lifeless, disfigured with black slime and dark stripes of weed. The constable was supporting the body. Miss Haydock had both hands in the stream, slashing with a knife at the ribbon-weed that was wrapped viciously about the legs. The other boat, hampered by its own lightness, was heeling over to stroke with gunwales awash, as her passengers reached and grappled.

'Trim your boat, damn you!' said Harriet, not pleased at the idea of having two fresh corpses to see to, and forgetting in her wrath to whom she was speaking. Miss Stevens paid no attention; but Miss Edwards threw her weight over; and as the boat lifted the body lifted too. Harriet, keeping her torch steady so that the rescuers could see what they were doing, watched the reluctant weeds loose their last coils and slip back.

'Better get her in here,' said the constable. Their boat had the less room in it, but the stronger arms and the better balance. There was a strong heave and a violent lurch as the dead weight was hauled over the side and rolled in a dripping heap at Miss Haydock's feet.

The constable was a capable and energetic young man. He took the first-aid measures in hand with admirable promptness. The women, gathered on the bank, watched with anxious faces. Other help had now arrived from the boat-house. Harriet took it upon herself to stem the stream of questions.

'Yes. One of our students. Not a good waterman. Alarmed to think she had taken a canoe out alone. Reckless. Yes, we were afraid there might be an accident. Wind. Strong current. Yes. No. Quite against the rules.' (If there was going to be an inquest, other explanations might have to be made there. But not here. Not now.) 'Very unwise. High spirits. Oh, yes. Most unfortunate. Taking risks . . .'

'She'll do now,' said the constable.

He sat up and wiped the sweat from his eyes.

Brandy. Blankets. A melancholy little procession along the fields to the boat-house, but less melancholy than it might have been. Then an orgy of telephoning. Then the arrival of the doctor. Then Harriet found herself, suddenly shaking with nerves, being given whisky by some kindly person. The patient was better. The patient was quite all right. The capable policeman and Miss Haydock and Miss Stevens were having their hands dressed, where the sharp weeds had slashed them to the bone. People were talking; Harriet hoped they were not talking foolishly.

'Well,' said the Dean in her ear, 'we *are* having a night!'

'Who's with Miss Newland?'

'Miss Edwards. I've warned her not to let the child say

anything if she can help it. And I've muzzled that nice policeman. Accident, my dear, accident. It's quite all right. We've taken your cue. You kept your head wonderfully. Miss Stevens lost hers a bit, though. Started to cry and talk about suicide. I soon shut *her* up'.

'Damn!' said Harriet. 'What did she want to do that for?'

'What indeed? You'd think she *wanted* to make a scandal.'

'Somebody obviously does.'

'You don't think Miss Stevens—? She did her bit with the rescue-work, you know.'

Yes, I know. All right, Dean. I don't think. I won't try to think. I thought she and Miss Edwards would have that boat over between them.'

'Don't let's discuss it now. Thank Heaven the worst hasn't happened. The girl's safe and that's all that matters. What we've got to do now is to put the best face on it.'

It was nearly five in the morning when the rescuers, weary and bandaged, sat once again in the Warden's house. Everybody was praising everybody else.

'It was so clever of Miss Vane,' said the Dean, 'to realise that the wretched child would go up to that particular place. What a mercy that we arrived just when we did.'

'I'm not so sure about that,' said Harriet. 'We may have done more harm than good. Do you realise that it was only when she saw us coming that she made up her mind to do it?'

'Do you mean she mightn't have done it at all if we hadn't gone after her?'

'Difficult to say. She was putting it off, I think. What

really sent her in was that shout from the other boat. Who shouted, by the way?'

'I shouted,' said Miss Stevens. 'I looked over my shoulder and saw her. So I shouted.'

'What was she doing when you saw her?'

'Standing up in the canoe.'

'No, she wasn't,' said Miss Edwards. 'I looked round when you shouted, and she was just getting to her feet then.'

'You're quite mistaken,' contradicted Miss Stevens. 'I say she was standing up when I saw her, and I shouted to stop her. You couldn't have seen past me.'

'I saw perfectly plainly,' said Miss Edwards. 'Miss Vane is quite right. It was when she heard the shout that she got up.'

'I know what I saw,' said the Bursar, obstinately.

'It's a pity you didn't take somebody to cox,' said the Dean. 'Nobody can see clearly what's going on behind her back.'

'It is hardly necessary to argue about it,' said the Warden, a little sharply. 'The tragedy has been prevented, and that is all that matters. I am exceedingly grateful to everybody.'

'I resent the suggestion,' said Miss Stevens, 'that I drove the unfortunate girl to destroy herself. And as for saying that we ought not to have gone in search of her—'

'I never said that,' said Harriet, wearily. 'I only said that *if* we had not gone it *might* not have happened. But of course we had to go.'

'What does Newland say herself?' demanded the Dean.

'Says, why couldn't we leave her alone?' replied Miss Edwards. 'I told her not to be an inconsiderate little ass.'

'Poor child!' said Miss Shaw.

'If I were you,' said Miss Edwards, 'I shouldn't be too soft with these people. Bracing up is what does them good. You let them talk too much about themselves—'

'But she didn't talk to me,' said Miss Shaw. 'I tried very hard to make her.'

'They'd talk much more if you'd only leave them alone.'

'I think we'd better all go to bed,' said Miss Martin.

'What a night,' said Harriet, as she rolled, dog-weary, between the, sheets. 'What a gaudy night!' Her memory, thrashing round her brain like a cat in a sack, brought up the images of Mr. Pomfret and the pro-Proctor. They seemed to belong to another existence.

13

My sad hurt it shall releeve,
When my thoughts I shall disclose,
For thou canst not chuse but greeve,
When I shall recount my woes;
There is nothing to that friend,
To whose close uncranied breast,
We our secret thoughts may send,
And there safely let it rest;
And thy faithfull counsell may
My distressed case assist,
Sad affliction else may sway
Me a woman as it list.

MICHAEL DRAYTON

'You must see,' said Harriet, 'that it's impossible to go
on like this. You've got to call in expert help and risk the
consequences. Any scandal is better than a suicide and an
inquest.'

'I think you are right,' said the Warden.

Only Miss Lydgate, the Dean and Miss Edwards sat
with Dr. Baring in the Warden's sitting-room. The brave
pretence at confidence had been given up. In the Senior
Common Room, members averted their eyes from one
another and set a guard upon their lips. They were no
longer angry and suspicious. They were afraid.

'The girl's parents are not likely to keep quiet about it,'
went on Harriet, remorselessly. 'If she had succeeded in

drowning herself, we should have the police and the reporters in at this moment. Next time, the attempt may come off.'

'Next time—' began Miss Lydgate.

'There will be a next time,' said Harriet. 'And it may not be suicide; it may be open murder. I told you at the beginning that I did not think the measures adequate. I now say that I refuse to take any further share in the responsibility. I have tried, and I have failed, every time.'

'What could the police do?' asked Miss Edwards. 'We did have them in once – about those thefts, you remember, Warden. They made a great deal of fuss and arrested the wrong person. It was a very troublesome business.'

'I don't think the police are the right people at all,' said the Dean. 'Your idea was a firm of private detectives, wasn't it?'

She turned to Harriet.

'Yes; but if anybody else has anything better to suggest—'

Nobody had any very helpful suggestion. The discussion went on. In the end:

'Miss Vane,' said the Warden, 'I think your idea is the best. Will you get into communication with these people?'

'Very well, Warden. I will ring up the head of the firm.'

'You will use discretion.'

'Of course,' said Harriet. She was becoming a little impatient; the time for discretion seemed to her to be past. 'If we call people in, we shall have to give them a free hand, you know,' she added.

This was obviously an unpalatable reminder, though its force had to be admitted. Harriet could foresee endless hampering restrictions placed upon the investigators, and felt the difficulties that went with a divided authority. The police were answerable to nobody but themselves, but paid private detectives were compelled to do more or less as they were told. She looked at Dr. Baring, and wondered whether Miss Climpson or any of her underlings was capable of asserting herself against that formidable personality.

'And now,' said the Dean, as she and Harriet crossed the quad together, 'I've got to go and tackle the Newlands. I'm *not* looking forward to it. They'll be terribly upset, poor things. He's a very minor civil servant, and their daughter's career means everything to them. Quite apart from the personal side of it, it'll be a frightful blow if this ruins her Schools. They're very poor and hardworking, and so proud of her—'

Miss Martin made a little despairing gesture, squared her shoulders and went to face her task.

Miss Hillyard, in her gown, was making for one of the lecture-rooms. She looked hollow-eyed and desperate, Harriet thought. Her glance shot from side to side, as though she were pursued.

From an open window on the ground floor of Queen Elizabeth came the voice of Miss Shaw, giving a coaching:

'You might have quoted also from the essay *De la Vanité*. You remember the passage. *Je me suis couché mille fois chez moi, imaginant qu'on me trahirait et assomeroit cette nuit-là* – his morbid preoccupation with the idea of death and his—'

The academic machine was grinding on. At the entrance leading to their offices, the Bursar and Treasurer stood together, their hands full of papers. They seemed to be discussing some question of finance. Their glances were secretive and mutually hostile; they looked like sullen dogs, chained together and forced into a grumbling amity by the reprimand of their master.

Miss Pyke came down her staircase and passed them without a word. Still without a word, she passed Harriet and turned along the plinth. Her head was held high and defiantly. Harriet went in and along to Miss Lydgate's room. Miss Lydgate, as she knew, was lecturing; she could use her telephone undisturbed. She put her call through to London.

A quarter of an hour later, she hung up the receiver with a sinking heart. Why she should be surprised to learn that Miss Climpson was absent from Town 'engaged on a case' she could not have said. It seemed vaguely monstrous that this should be so; but it was so. Would she like to speak to anyone else? Harriet had asked for Miss Murchison, the only other member of the firm who was personally known to her. Miss Murchison had left a year ago to be married. Harriet felt this as almost a personal affront. She did not like to pour all the details of the Shrewsbury affair into the ears of a complete stranger. She said she would write, rang off, and sat feeling curiously helpless.

It is all very well to take a firm line about things, and rush to the telephone, determined to 'do something' without delay; other people do not sit with folded hands waiting upon the convenience even of our highly interesting and influential selves. Harriet laughed at her own annoyance. She had made up her mind to instant action, and now she was furious because a business firm had affairs of its own to attend to. Yet to wait any longer was impossible. The situation was becoming a nightmare. Faces had grown sly and distorted overnight; eyes fearful; the most innocent words charged with suspicion. At any moment some new terror might break bounds and carry all before it.

She was suddenly afraid of all these women; *horti conclusi, fontes signati*, they were walled in, sealed down, by walls and seals that shut her out. Sitting there in the clear light of morning, staring at the prosaic telephone on the desk, she knew the ancient dread of Artemis, moon-goddess, virgin-huntress, whose arrows are plagues and death.

It struck her then as a fantastic idea that she should fly for help to another brood of spinsters; even if she succeeded in getting hold of Miss Climpson, how was she to explain matters to that desiccated and elderly virgin? The very sight of some of the poison letters would probably make her sick, and the whole trouble would be beyond her comprehension. In this, Harriet did the lady less than justice; Miss Climpson had seen many strange things in sixty-odd years of boarding-house life, and was as free from repressions and complexes as any human being could very well be. But in fact, the atmosphere of Shrewsbury was getting on Harriet's nerves. What she wanted was someone with whom she did not need to mince her words, somebody who would neither show nor feel surprise at any manifestation of human eccentricity, somebody whom she knew and could trust.

There were plenty of people in London – both men and women – to whom the discussion of sexual abnormalities was a commonplace; but most of them were very little to be trusted. They cultivated normality till it stood out of them all over in knobs, like the muscles upon professional strong men, and scarcely looked normal at all. And they talked interminably and loudly. From their bouncing mental health ordinary ill-balanced mortals shrank in alarm. She ran over various names in her mind, but found none that would do.

'The fact is,' said Harriet to the telephone, 'I don't know whether I want a doctor or a detective. But I've got to have somebody.'

She wished – and not for the first time – that she could have got hold of Peter Wimsey. Not, of course, that this was the kind of case he could very suitably have investigated himself; but he would probably have known the right person. He at least would be surprised at nothing, shocked at nothing; he had far too wide an experience of the world. And he was completely to be trusted. But he was not there. He had vanished from view at the very moment when the Shrewsbury affair had first come to her notice; it seemed almost pointed. Like Lord Saint-George, she began to feel that Peter really had no right to disappear just when he was wanted. The fact that she had spent five years angrily refusing to contract further obligations towards Peter Wimsey had no weight with her now; she would readily have contracted obligations towards the devil himself, if she could have been sure that the prince of darkness was a gentleman of Peter's kidney. But Peter was as far beyond reach as Lucifer.

Was he? There was the telephone at her elbow. She could speak to Rome as easily as to London – though at a trifle more expense. It was probably only the financial modesty of the person whose income is all earned by work that made it seem more momentous to ring somebody up across a continent than across a city. At any rate, it could do no harm to fetch Peter's last letter and find the telephone number of his hotel. She went out quickly, and encountered Miss de Vine.

'Oh!' said the Fellow. 'I was coming to look for you. I thought I had better show you this.'

She held out a piece of paper; the sight of the printed letters was odiously familiar:

YOUR TURN'S COMING

'It's nice to be warned,' said Harriet, with a lightness she did not feel. 'Where? when? and how?'

'It fell out of one of the books I'm using,' said Miss de Vine, blinking behind her glasses at the question, 'just now.'

'When did you use the book last?'

'That,' said Miss de Vine, blinking again, 'is the odd thing about it. I didn't. Miss Hillyard borrowed it last night, and Mrs. Goodwin brought it back to me this morning.'

Considering the things Miss Hillyard had said about Mrs. Goodwin, Harriet was faintly surprised that she should have chosen her to run her errands. But in certain circumstances the choice might, of course, be a wise one.

'Are you sure the paper wasn't there yesterday?'

'I don't think it could have been. I was referring to various pages, and I think I should have seen it.'

'Did you give it directly into Miss Hillyard's own hands?'

'No; I put it in her pigeon-hole before Hall.'

'So that anybody might have got hold of it.'

'Oh, yes.'

Exasperating. Harriet took possession of the paper and passed on. It was now not even clear against whom the threat was directed, much less from whom it came. She fetched Peter's letter, and discovered that in the interval she had made up her mind. She had said she would ring up the head of the firm; and so she would. If he was not technically the head, he was certainly the brains of it. She put the call through. She did not know how long it would take, but left instructions at the Lodge that when it came she was to be searched for and found without fail. She felt abominably restless.

The next piece of news was that a violent quarrel had taken place between Miss Shaw and Miss Stevens, who were normally the closest of friends. Miss Shaw, having heard the full story of the previous night's adventure, had accused Miss Stevens of frightening Miss Newland into the river; Miss Stevens had in turn accused Miss Shaw of deliberately playing on the girl's feelings, so as to work her up into a state of nerves.

The next disturber of the peace was Miss Allison. As Harriet had discovered the previous term. Miss Allison had a way of passing on to people the things other people had said of them. In a spirit of candour she had now chosen to pass on to Mrs. Goodwin the hints thrown out by Miss Hillyard. Mrs. Goodwin had tackled Miss Hillyard about it; and there had been a most unpleasant scene, in which Miss Allison, the Dean and poor little Miss Chilperic, who had been drawn into the discussion by malignant chance, took sides with Mrs. Goodwin against Miss Pyke and Miss Burrows, who, though they thought Miss Hillyard had spoken ill-advisedly, resented any aspersions cast against the unmarried state as such. This unpleasantness took place in the Fellows' Garden.

Finally, Miss Allison had further inflamed the situation by passing on a vivid account of the matter to Miss Barton, who had gone away indignantly to tell Miss Lydgate and Miss de Vine exactly what she thought of the psychology both of Miss Hillyard and Miss Allison.

It was not an agreeable morning.

*　　*　　*

Between the married (or about-to-be-married) and the unmarried, Harriet felt herself to be like Æsop's bat between the birds and beasts; an odd result, she felt, of having sown her wild oats in public. Lunch was a strained meal. She came into Hall rather late, to find that the High Table had sorted itself out into opposing camps, with Miss Hillyard at one end and Mrs. Goodwin at the other. She found an empty chair between Miss de Vine and Miss Stevens, and amused herself by drawing them and Miss Allison, who was next to Miss de Vine on the other side, into a discussion of currency and inflation. She knew nothing of the subject, but they, naturally, knew a good deal, and her tact was rewarded. Conversation spread; the table presented a less sullen front to the assembled students; and Miss Lydgate beamed approval. Things were moving nicely when a scout, leaning between Miss Allison and Miss de Vine, murmured a message.

'From Rome?' said Miss de Vine. 'Who can that be, I wonder?'

'Telephoning from Rome?' said Miss Allison, in piercing accents. 'Oh, one of your correspondents, I suppose. He must be better off than most historians.'

'I think it's for me,' said Harriet, and turned to the scout. 'Are you sure they said de Vine and not Vane?'

The scout was not very sure.

'If you're expecting it, it must be for you,' said Miss de Vine. Miss Allison made some rather sharp observation about writers of international celebrity and Harriet left the table, flushing uncomfortably and angry with herself for doing so.

As she went down to the public call-box in Queen Elizabeth, to which the call had been put through, she tried to arrange in her own mind what to say. A brief sentence of apology; another brief sentence of explanation and a request for advice; into whose hands should the case be put? There was, surely, nothing difficult about that.

The voice from Rome spoke English very well. It did not think Lord Peter Wimsey was in his hotel, but would inquire. A pause, during which she could hear feet passing to and fro on the other side of the continent. Then the voice again, suave and apologetic.

'His lordship left Rome three days ago.'

Oh! Did they know, for what destination?

They would inquire. Another pause, and voices speaking Italian. Then the same voice again. 'His lordship left for Warsaw.'

'Oh! Thank you very much,'

And that was that.

At the thought of ringing up the British Embassy at Warsaw, her heart failed her. She replaced the receiver and went upstairs again. She did not seem to have gained very much by taking a firm line.

Friday afternoon. Crises always, thought Harriet, occurred at the week-end, when there were no posts. If she wrote now to London and they replied by return, she would still, in all probability, be able to take no action till Monday. If she wrote to Peter, there might be an Air-Mail – but suppose he wasn't at Warsaw after all. He might by now have gone on to Bucharest or Berlin. Could she possibly ring up the Foreign Office and demand to know his whereabouts? Because, if the letter got to him over the week-end and he wired a reply, she would not be losing so very much time. She was not sure if she would be very good at dealing with the Foreign Office. Was there anybody who could? How about the Hon. Freddy?

It took a little time to locate Freddy Arbuthnot, but eventually she ran him down, by 'phone, at an office in Throgmorton Street. He was definitely helpful. He had no idea where old Peter was, but he would take steps to find out, and if she liked to send a letter care of him (Freddy) he would see that it was forwarded on at the earliest possible moment. No trouble at all. Charmed to be of use.

So the letter was written, and despatched so as to reach Town first post on the Saturday morning. It contained a brief outline of the case, and finished up:

'Can you tell me whether you think Miss Climpson's people could handle it? And who, in her absence, is the most competent person there? Or, if not, can you suggest anybody else I could ask? Perhaps it should be a psychologist and not a detective. I know that anybody you recommend will be trustworthy. Would you mind wiring as soon as you get this? I should be immensely grateful. We are all getting rather worked up, and I'm afraid something drastic may happen if we don't cope with it quickly.'

She hoped that last sentence did not sound as panicky as she felt.

'I rang up your hotel in Rome and they said you had gone on to Warsaw. As I don't know where you may be by this time, I'm getting Mr. Arbuthnot to forward this through the Foreign Office.'

That sounded faintly reproachful, but it couldn't be helped. What she really wanted to say was, 'I wish to God you were here and could tell me what to do'; but she felt that that might make him feel uncomfortable, since he obviously couldn't be there. Still, it could do no harm

322

to ask 'How soon do you think you will be back in England?' And with this addition, the letter was finished and posted.

'And to put the lid on things,' said the Dean, 'there's this man coming to dinner.'

'This man' was Dr. Noel Threep, a very worthy and important man, a Fellow of a distinguished college and a member of the Council by which Shrewsbury was governed. Friends and benefactors of this kind were not infrequently entertained in College, and as a rule the High Table was glad of their presence. But the moment was scarcely auspicious. However, the engagement had been made early in the term, and it was quite impossible to put Dr. Threep off. Harriet said she thought this visit might be a good thing, and help to keep the minds of the S.C.R. off their troubles.

'We'll hope so,' said the Dean. 'He's a very nice man, and talks very interestingly. He's a political economist.'

'Hard-boiled or soft-boiled?'

'Hard, I think.'

This question had no reference to Dr. Threep's politics or economics, but only to his shirt-front. Harriet and the Dean had begun to collect shirt-fronts. Miss Chilperic's 'young man' had started the collection. He was extremely tall and thin and rather hollow-chested; by way of emphasising this latter defect, he always wore a soft pleated dress-shirt, which made him look (according to the Dean) like the scooped-out rind of a melon. By way of contrast, there had been an eminent and ample professor of chemistry – a visitor from another university – who had turned up in a front of intense rigidity, which stood out before him like the chest of a pouter pigeon, bulging out of all control and displaying a large area of the parent shirt at either side. A third variety of shirt fairly common among the learned was that which escaped from the centre stud and gaped in the middle; and one never-to-be-forgotten happy day a popular poet had arrived to give a lecture on his methods of composition and the -future of poetry, whereby, at every gesticulation (and he had used a great many) his waistcoat had leapt in the air, allowing a line of shirt, adorned with a little tab, to peep out, rabbit-like, over the waistline of the confining trouser. On this occasion, Harriet and the Dean had disgraced themselves badly.

Dr. Threep was a large, agreeable, talkative person, who at first sight appeared to present no loophole for sartorial criticism. But he had not been seated at table three minutes before Harriet realised that he was doomed to form one of the most notable additions to the collection. For he popped. When he bent over his plate, when he turned to pass the mustard, when he courteously inclined himself to catch what his neighbour was saying, his shirt-front exploded with a merry little report like the opening of ginger-beer. The clamour in Hall seemed louder than usual that night, so that the poppings were inaudible beyond a few places to right and left of him; but the Warden and the Dean, who sat beside him, heard them, and Harriet, sitting opposite, heard them; she dared not catch the Dean's eye. Dr. Threep was too well-bred, or perhaps too much embarrassed, to allude to the matter; he talked on imperturbably, raising his voice more and more to be heard above the din of the undergraduates. The Warden was frowning.

'—the excellent relations between the Women's Colleges and the University,' said Dr. Threep. 'All the same—'

The Warden summoned a scout, who presently went

down to the Junior High and thence to the other tables, with the usual message:

'The Warden's compliments, and she would be obliged if there could be rather less noise.'

'I beg your pardon, Dr. Threep. I didn't quite catch.'

'All the same,' repeated Dr. Threep, with a polite bend and pop, 'it is curious to see how traces of the old prejudice linger. Only yesterday the Vice-Chancellor showed me a remarkably vulgar anonymous letter sent to him that very morning . . .'

The noise in Hall was dying down gradually; it was like a lull in the intervals of a storm.

'. . . making the most absurd accusations – oddly enough against your own Senior Common Room in particular. Accusations of murder, of all things. The Vice-Chancellor . . .'

Harriet missed the next few words; she was watching how, as Dr. Threep's voice rang out in the comparative quiet, the heads at the High Table jerked towards him, as though pulled by wires.

'. . . pasted on paper – quite ingenious. I said, 'My dear Mr. Vice-Chancellor, I doubt whether the police can do much; it is probably the work of some harmless crank.' But is it not curious that such peculiar delusions should exist – and *persist* – at this day?'

'Very curious indeed,' said the Warden, with stiff lips.

'So I advised against police interference – for the moment, at any rate. But I said I would put the matter before you, since Shrewsbury was particularly mentioned. I defer, of course, to your opinion.'

The dons sat spell-bound; and in that moment, Dr. Threep, bowing to the Warden's decisions, popped – with so loud and violent an explosion that it resounded from end to end of the table, and the major embarrassment was swallowed up in the minor. Miss Chilperic suddenly broke out into a spasm of high, nervous laughter.

How dinner ended, Harriet could never properly recall. Dr. Threep went over to have coffee with the Warden, and Harriet found herself in the Dean's room, helpless between mirth and alarm.

'It's really very serious,' said Miss Martin.

'Horribly. "I said to the Vice-Chancellor—"'

'Pop!'

'No; but honestly, what are we to do about it?'

'I defer to your opinion.'

'Pop!'

'I can't imagine what makes shirts do that. Can you?'

'I've no idea. And I meant to be so clever this evening. Here, said I, is a Man come among us; I will watch everybody's reactions – and then it all went Pop!'

'It's no good watching reactions to Dr. Threep,' said the Dean. 'Everyone's too used to him. And anyhow, he has half a dozen children. But it's going to be very awkward if the Vice-Chancellor—'

'Very.'

Saturday dawned dull and lowering.

'I believe it's going to thunder,' said Miss Allison.

'Rather early in the year for that,' said Miss Hillyard.

'Not at all,' retorted Mrs. Goodwin; 'I've known plenty of thunderstorms in May.'

'There is certainly something electrical in the atmosphere,' said Miss Lydgate.

'I agree with you,' said Miss Barton.

Harriet had slept badly. She had, in fact, been walking about College half the night, a prey to imaginary alarms. When at length she had gone to bed, she had had the tiresome dream about trying to catch a train, hampered all the time by a quantity of luggage which she strove vainly to pack in misty and unmanageable suit-cases. In the morning, she struggled desperately with the proofs of Miss Lydgate's chapter on Gerald Manley Hopkins, finding it as unmanageable as the suitcases and nearly as misty. In the intervals of disentangling the poet's own system of sprung, counterpoint and logaœdic rhythm, with its rove-over lines and outrides, from Miss Lydgate's rival system of scansion (which required five alphabets and a series of pothooks for its expression), she wondered whether Freddy Arbuthnot had succeeded in doing what he had promised and whether she ought to leave it at that or do something else: in which case, what? In the afternoon, she could bear herself no longer and set out, under a threatening sky, to wander about Oxford, and walk herself, if possible, into exhaustion. She started up the High, pausing for a few moments to stare into the window of an Antique shop; there was a set of carved ivory chessmen there, for which she had conceived an unreasonable affection. She even played with the idea of going boldly in and buying them; but she knew they would cost too much. They were Chinese, and each piece was a complicated nest of little revolving balls, delicate as fine lace. It would be jolly to handle them, but idiotic to buy them; she was not even a good chess-player, and in any case, one couldn't play chess comfortably with pieces like that. She put temptation aside and moved on. There was a shop full of wooden objects embellished with the painted shields of colleges: book-ends, match-stands, pens shaped like oars and horribly top-heavy, cigarette-boxes, inkpots and even powder-compacts. Did it add a zest to facial repairs to have them watched over by the lions of Oriel or the martlets of Worcester? To be reminded during the process that one had a betrothed among the tripping stags of Jesus or a brother nourished by the pious pelican of Corpus? She crossed the street before she came to Queen's (for Mr. Pomfret might conceivably pop out of the gate, and she was rather avoiding an encounter with Mr. Pomfret) and went on up the other side. Books and prints – fascinating at most times, but insufficiently exciting to hold her attention. Robes and gowns, colourful, but too academic for her mood. A chemist's shop. A stationer's, with more college bric-à-brac, this time in glass and pottery. A tobacconist's, with more coats of arms, on ash-rays and tobacco-jars. A jeweller's, with college arms on spoons and brooches and napkin-rings. She grew weary of college arms and turned down a side-street into Merton Street. In this untouched and cobbled thoroughfare there should be peace, if anywhere. But peace is in the mind, and not in streets, however old and beautiful. She passed through the iron gate into Merton Grove, and so, crossing over Dead Man's Walk, into the Broad Walk of Christ Church and along this and round to the towing path where the New Cut meets the Isis. And there to her horror, she was hailed by a well-known voice. Here, by special interposition of all the powers of evil, was Miss Schuster-Slatt, whose presence in Oxford she had till that moment mercifully forgotten, convoying a party of American visitors, all eager for information. Miss Vane was the very person to tell them everything. Did she know which of these barges belonged to which college? Were those cute little blue-and-gold heads griffins or phœnixes and were there three of them to symbolise the Trinity or was that just accident? Were those the Magdalen lilies? If so, why was there the initial 'W' painted all round the barge and what did it stand for? Why did

Pembroke have the English rose and the Scotch thistle at the top of the shield? Were the roses of New College English roses, too? Why was it called New when it was so old, and why mustn't you call it 'New' but always 'New College'? Oh! look, Sadie – are those geese flying across? Swans? How interesting! Were there many swans on the river? Was it true that all the swans in England belonged to the King? Was that a swan on that barge? Oh, an eagle. Why did some barges have figure-heads and some not? Did the boys ever have tea-parties on the barges? Could Miss Vane explain about those bumping races, because nobody had been able to understand from Sadie's description. Was that the University barge? Oh, the University *College* barge. Was the University College the place where all the classes were held?

And so forth and so on – all along the towing path, all the way up the long avenue to the Meadow Buildings and all the way round Christ Church, from Hall to Kitchen, from Cathedral to Library, from Mercury to Great Tom, while all the time the sky brooded lower and the weather became more oppressive, until Harriet, who had started out feeling as though her skull were stuffed with wool, ended up with a raging headache.

The storm held off till after Hall, except for threatenings and grumblings of thunder. At 10 o'clock the first great flash went across the sky like a searchlight, picking out roof and tree-top violet-blue against the blackness, and followed by a clap that shook the walls. Harriet flung her window open and leaned out. There was a sweet smell of approaching rain. Another flash and crash; a swift gust of wind; and then the swish and rush of falling water, the gurgle of overflowing gutters, and peace.

14

Truce gentle love, a parly now I crave,
Me thinks, 'tis long since first these wars begun
Nor thou nor I, the better yet can have:
Bad is the match where neither party won.
I offer free conditions of faire peace,
My hart for hostage, that it shall remaine,
Discharge our forces heere, let malice cease,
So for my pledge, thou give me pledge againe.

MICHAEL DRAYTON

'IT was a good storm,' said the Dean.

'First-class,' said the Bursar, dryly, 'for those that like it and don't have to cope with those that don't. The scouts' quarters were a pandemonium; I had to go over. There was Carrie in hysterics, and Cook thinking her last hour had come, and Annie shrieking to Heaven that her darling children would be terrified and wanting to rush off to Headington then and there to comfort them—'

'I wonder you didn't send her there at once in the best car available,' put in Miss Hillyard in sarcastic tones.

'—and one of the kitchen-maids having an outbreak of religious blues,' went on Miss Stevens, 'and confessing her sins to an admiring circle. I can't think why people have so little self-control.'

'I'm horribly afraid of thunder,' said Miss Chilperic.

'The wretched Newland was all upset again,' said the Dean. 'The Infirmarian was quite frightened about her.

Said the Infirmary maid was hiding in the linen-cupboard and she didn't like to be left alone with Newland. However, Miss Shaw obligingly coped.'

'Who were the four students who were dancing in the quad in bathing-dresses?' inquired Miss Pyke. 'They had quite a ritual appearance. I was reminded of the cere-monial dances of the—'

'I was afraid the beeches were going to be struck,' said Miss Burrows. 'I sometimes wonder whether it's safe to have them so near the buildings. If they came down—'

'There's a bad leak in my ceiling, Bursar,' said Mrs. Goodwin. 'The rain came in like a water-spout – just over my bed. I had to move all the furniture, and the carpet is quite—'

'Anyhow,' repeated the Dean, 'it was a good storm, and it's cleared the air. Look at it. Could anybody want a better and brighter Sunday morning?'

Harriet nodded. The sun was brilliant on the wet grass and the wind blew fresh and cool.

'It's taken my headache away, thank goodness! I'd like to do something calm and cheerful and thoroughly Oxonian. Isn't everything a lovely colour? Like the blues and scarlets and greens in an illuminated missal!'

'I'll tell you what we'll do,' said the Dean, brightly. 'We'll toddle along like two good little people and hear the University Sermon. I can't think of anything more soothingly normal and academic than that. And Dr. Armstrong's preaching. He's always interesting.'

'The University Sermon?' said Harriet, amused. 'Well, that's the last thing I should have thought of for myself. But it's an idea; definitely an idea. Well go.'

Yes; the Dean was right; here was the great Anglican compromise at its most soothing and ceremonial. The solemn procession of doctors in hood and habit; the Vice-Chancellor bowing to the preacher; and the bedels tripping before them; the throng of black gowns and the decorous gaiety of the summer-frocked wives of dons; the hymn and the bidding-prayer; the gowned and hooded preacher austere in cassock and bands; the quiet discourse delivered in a thin, clear, scholarly voice, and dealing gently with the relations of the Christian philosophy to atomic physics. Here were the Universities and the Church of England kissing one another in righteousness and peace, like the angels in a Botticelli Nativity: very exquisitely robed, very cheerful in a serious kind of way, a little mannered, a little conscious of their fine mutual courtesy. Here, without heat, they could discuss their common problem, agreeing pleasantly or pleasantly agreeing to differ. Of the grotesque and ugly devil-shapes sprawling at the foot of the picture these angels had no word to say. What solution could either of them produce, if challenged, for the Shrewsbury problem? Other bodies would be bolder: the Church of Rome would have its answer, smooth, competent and experienced; the queer, bitterly-jarring sects of the New Psychology would have another, ugly, awkward, tentative and applied with a passionate experimentalism. It was entertaining to imagine a Freudian University indissolubly wedded to a Roman Establishment: they certainly would not live so harmoniously together as the Anglican Church and the School of Litteræ Humaniores. But it was delightful to believe, if only for an hour, that all human difficulties could be dealt with in this detached and amiable spirit. 'The University is a Paradise' – true, but – 'then saw I that there was a way to hell even from the gates of Heaven' . . .

*   *   *

The blessing was given; the voluntary rolled out – something fugal and pre-Bach; the procession re-formed and dispersed again, passing out south and north; the congregation rose to their feet and began to stream away in an orderly disorder. The Dean, who was fond of early fugues, remained quietly in her place and Harriet sat dreamily beside her, with eyes fixed on the softly-tinted saints in the rood-screen. At length they both rose and made their way to the door. A mild, clear gust of wind met them as they passed between the twisted columns of Dr. Owen's porch, making the Dean clutch at the peak of her rebellious cap and bellying out their gowns into wide arcs and volutes. The sky, between pillow and pillow of rounded cloud, was pale and transparent blue of aquamarine.

Standing at the comer of Cat Street was a group of gowns, chatting with animation-among them, two Fellows of All Souls and a dignified figure which Harriet recognised as that of the Master of Balliol. Beside him was another M.A. who, as Harriet and the Dean went by, conversing of counterpoint, turned suddenly and lifted his mortar-board.

For a long moment, Harriet simply could not believe her eyes. Peter Wimsey. Peter, of all people. Peter, who was supposed to be in Warsaw, planted placidly in the High as though he had grown there from the beginning. Peter, wearing cap and gown like any orthodox Master of Arts, presenting every appearance of having piously attended the University Sermon, and now talking mild academic shop with two Fellows of All Souls and the Master of Balliol.

'And why not?' thought Harriet, after the first second of shock. 'He is a Master of Arts. He was at Balliol. Why shouldn't he talk to the Master if he likes? But how did he get here? And why? And when did he come? And why didn't he let me know?'

She found herself confusedly receiving introductions and presenting Lord Peter to the Dean.

'I rang up yesterday from Town,' Wimsey was saying, 'but you were out.' And then more explanations – something about flying over from Warsaw, and 'my nephew at the House,' and 'the Master's kind hospitality,' and sending a note round to College. Then, out of the jumble of polite nothings, a sentence she grasped clearly.

'If you are free and in College during the next half-hour or so, may I come round and look you up?'

'Yes, do,' said Harriet, lamely, 'that would be delightful.' She pulled herself together. 'I suppose it's no good asking you to lunch?'

It appeared that he was lunching with the Master, and that one of the All Souls men was lunching also. In fact, a little lunch-party with, she gathered, some kind of historical basis, mention of somebody's article for the Proceedings of Something or Other, which Wimsey was going to 'step into All Souls and look at – it won't take you ten minutes,' and references to the printing and distribution of Reformation polemical pamphlets – to Wimsey's expert knowledge – to the other man's expert knowledge – and to the inexpert pretence at knowledge of some historian from another university.

Then the whole group broke up. The Master raised his cap and drifted away, reminding Wimsey and the historian that lunch would be at 1.15; Peter said something to Harriet about being 'round in twenty minutes,' and then vanished with the two Fellows into All Souls, and Harriet and the Dean were walking together again.

'Well!' said the Dean, 'so that's the man.'

'Yes,' said Harriet weakly, 'that's him.'

'My dear, he's perfectly charming. You never said he was coming to Oxford.'

'I didn't know. I thought he was in Warsaw. I knew he was supposed to be coming up some time this term to see his nephew, but I'd no idea he could get away so soon. As a matter of fact, I wanted to ask him – only I don't suppose he could have got my letter—'

She felt that her efforts at explanation were only darkening counsel. In the end she made a clean breast of the whole affair to the Dean.

'I don't know whether he got my letter and knows already, or whether, if he doesn't, I ought to tell him. I know he's absolutely safe. But whether the Warden and the S.C.R.— I didn't expect him to turn up like this.'

'I should think it was the wisest thing you could have done,' said Miss Martin. 'I shouldn't say too much at College. Bring him along, if he'll come, and let him turn the whole lot of us inside out. A man with manners like that could twist the whole High Table round his little finger. What a mercy he's a historian – that will put him on the right side of Miss Hillyard.'

'I never thought of him as a historian.'

'Well, he took a First, anyway . . . didn't you know?'

She had not known. She had not even troubled to wonder. She had never consciously connected Wimsey and Oxford in her mind. This was the Foreign Office business all over again. If he had realised her thought-lessness it must have hurt him. She saw herself as a monster of callous ingratitude.

'I'm told he was looked upon as one of the ablest scholars of his year,' pursued the Dean. 'A. L. Smith thought highly of him. It's a pity, in a way, he didn't stick to History – but naturally, his chief interests wouldn't be academic.'

'No,' said Harriet.

So the Dean had been making inquiries. Naturally, she would. Probably the whole S.C.R. could by now give her detailed information about Wimsey's University career. That was comprehensible enough: they thought along those lines. But she herself might surely have found the energy for two minutes' study of the Calendar.

'Where shall I put him when he comes? I suppose if I take him off to my own room it will set a bad example to the students. And it is a bit cramped.'

'You can have my sitting-room. Much better than any of the public rooms, if you're going to discuss this beastly business. I wonder if he *did* get that letter. Perhaps the eager interest behind that penetrating eye was due to his suspicions of me. And I put it all down to my personal fascination! The man's dangerous, though he doesn't look it.'

'That's why he's dangerous. But if he read my letter, he'll know that it isn't you.'

Some minor confusions were cleared up when they reached College and found a note from Peter in Harriet's pigeon-hole. It explained that he had reached London early on Saturday afternoon and found Harriet's letter waiting for him at the Foreign Office. 'I tried to ring you, but left no name, as I did not know whether you wanted me to appear personally in this matter.' He had been engaged in London that afternoon, motored to Oxford for dinner, been captured by some Balliol friends and kindly invited by the Master to stay the night, and would call 'some time to-morrow' in the hope of finding her in.

So she waited in the Dean's room, idly watching the summer sun play through the branches of the plane-tree in the New Quad and make a dancing pattern upon the plinth, until she heard his knock. When she said 'Come in!' the commonplace formula seemed to take on a startling significance. For good or evil, she had called in something explosive from the outside world to break up the ordered tranquillity of the place; she had sold the breach to an alien force; she had sided with London against Oxford and with the world against the cloister.

But when he entered, she knew that the image had been a false one. He came into the quiet room as though he belonged there, and had never belonged to any other place.

'Hullo—ullo!' he said, with a faint echo of the old, flippant manner. Then he stripped off his gown and tossed it on the couch beside her own, laying his mortar-board on the table.

'I found your note when I got back. So you did get my letter?'

'Yes; I'm sorry you should have had all this bother. It seemed to me, as I was coming to Oxford in any case, I had better push along and see you. I meant to come round yesterday evening, but I got tied up with people – and I thought perhaps I had better announce myself first.'

'It was good of you to come. Sit down.'

She pulled an arm-chair forward, and he dropped into it rather heavily. She noticed, with a curious little prick of anxiety, how the clear light picked out the angles of the skull on jaw and temple.

'Peter! You look tired to death. What have you been doing with yourself?'

'Talking,' he said, discontentedly. 'Words, words, words. All these interminable weeks. I'm the professional funny man of the Foreign Office. You didn't know that? Well, I am. Not often, but waiting in the wings if wanted.

Some turn goes wrong – some Under-Secretary's secretary with small discretion and less French uses an ill-considered phrase in an after-dinner speech, and they send on the patter-comedian to talk the house into a good humour again. I take people out to lunch and tell them funny stories and work them up to mellowing point. God! what a game!'

'I didn't know this, Peter. I've just discovered that I've been too selfish even to try and know anything. But it isn't like you to sound so dreadfully discouraged. You look—'

'Spare me, Harriet. Don't say I'm getting to look my age. That won't do. An eternal childishness is my one diplomatic asset.'

'You only look as though you hadn't slept for weeks.'

'I'm not sure that I have, now you mention it. I thought – at one point we all thought – something might be going to happen. All the old filthy uproar. I got as far as saying to Bunter one night: "It's coming; it's here; back to the Army again, sergeant. . . ." But in the end, you know, it made a noise like a hoop and rolled away – for the moment.'

'Thanks to the comic cross-talk?'

'Oh, no. Great Scott, no. Mine was a very trivial affair. Slight frontier skirmish. Don't get it into your head that I'm the man who saved the Empire.'

'Then who did?'

'Dunno. Nobody knows. Nobody ever does know, for certain. The old bus wobbles one way, and you think, 'That's done it'! and then it wobbles the other way and you think, 'All serene'; and then, one day, it wobbles over too far and you're in the soup and can't remember how you got there.'

'That's what we're all afraid of, inside ourselves.'

'Yes. It terrifies me. It's a relief to get back and find you here – and all this going on as it used to do. Here's where the real things are done, Harriet – if only those bunglers out there will keep quiet and let it go on. God! how I loathe haste and violence and all that ghastly, slippery cleverness. Unsound, unscholarly, insincere – nothing but propaganda and special pleading and "what do we get out of this?" No time, no peace, no silence; nothing but conferences and newspapers and public speeches till one can't hear one's self think . . . If only one could root one's self in here among the grass and stones and do something worth doing, even if it was only restoring a lost breathing for the love of the job and nothing else.'

She was astonished to hear him speak with so much passion.

'But Peter, you're saying exactly what I've been feeling all this time. But can it be done?'

'No; it can't be done. Though there are moments when one comes back and thinks it might.'

' "Ask for the old paths, where is the good way, and walk therein, and ye shall find rest for your souls." '

'Yes,' said he bitterly, 'and it goes on: "But they said: we will not walk therein." Rest? I had forgotten there was such a word.'

'So had I.'

They sat silent for a few minutes. Wimsey offered her his cigarette-case and struck a match for them both.

'Peter, it's queer we should sit here and talk like this. Do you remember that horrible time at Wilvercombe when we could find nothing to throw at one another but cheap wit and spiteful remarks? At least, I was spiteful: you never were.'

'It was the watering-place atmosphere,' said Wimsey. 'One is always vulgar at watering-places. It is the one haunting terror of my life that some day some perfectly irresistible peach of a problem will blossom out at Brighton or Blackpool, and that I shall be weak-minded enough to go and meddle with it.' The laughter had come back to his voice and his eyes were tranquil. 'Thank Heaven, it's extremely difficult to be cheap in Oxford – after one's second year, at any rate. Which reminds me that I haven't yet properly thanked you for being so kind to Saint-George.'

'Have you seen him yet?'

'No; I have threatened to descend on him on Monday, and show him a damned disinheriting countenance. He has gone off somewhere to-day with a party of friends. I know what that means. He's getting thoroughly spoilt.'

'Well, Peter, you can't wonder. He's terribly good-looking.'

'He's a precocious little monkey,' said his uncle, without enthusiasm. 'Though I can't blame him for that; it runs in the blood. But it's characteristic of his impudence that he should have gate-crashed your acquaintance, after you had firmly refused to meet any of my people.'

'I found him for myself, you see, Peter.'

'Literally, or so he says. I gather that he nearly knocked you down, damaged your property and generally made a nuisance of himself, and that you instantly concluded he must be some relation to me.'

'That's – if he said that, you know better than to believe it. But I couldn't very well miss the likeness.'

'Yet people have been known to speak slightingly of my personal appearance! I congratulate you on a perception worthy of Sherlock Holmes at his keenest.'

It amused and touched her to discover this childish streak of vanity in him. But she knew that he would see through her at once if she tried to pander to it by saying anything more flattering than the truth.

'I recognised the voice before I looked at him at all. And he has your hands; I shouldn't think anybody has ever spoken slightingly about those.'

'Confound it, Harriet! My one really shameful weakness. My most jealously guarded bit of personal conceit. Dragged into the light of day and remorsely exposed. I am idiotically proud of having inherited the Wimsey hands. My brother and my sister both missed them, but they go back in the family portraits for three hundred years.' His face clouded for a moment. 'I wonder all the strength hasn't been bred out of them by this time; our sands are running down fast. Harriet, will you come with me one day to Denver and see the place before the new civilisation grows in on it like the jungle? I don't want to go all Galsworthy about it. They'll tell you I don't care a damn for the whole outfit, and I don't know that I do. But I was born there, and I shall be sorry if I live to see the land sold for ribbon-building and the Hall turned over to a Hollywood Colour-Talkie king.'

'Lord Saint-George wouldn't do that, would he?'

'I don't know, Harriet. Why shouldn't he? Our kind of show is dead and done for. What the hell good does it do anybody these days? But he may care more than he thinks he does.'

'You care, don't you, Peter?'

'It's very easy for me to care, because I'm not called upon to do a hand's turn in the matter. I am the usual middle-aged prig, with an admirable talent for binding heavy burdens and laying them on other men's shoulders. Don't think I envy my nephew his job. I'd rather live at peace and lay my bones in the earth. Only I have a cursed hankering after certain musty old values, which I'm coward enough to deny, like my namesake of the Gospels. I never go home if I can help it, and I avoid coming here; the cocks crow too long and too loudly.'

'Peter, I'd no idea you felt like that. I'd like to see your home.'

'Would you? Then we'll go, one of these days. I won't inflict the family on you – though I think you'd like my Mother. But we'll choose a time when they're all away – except a dozen or so harmless dukes in the family vault. All embalmed, poor devils, to linger on dustily to the Day of Judgment. Typical, isn't it, of a family tradition that it won't even let you rot.'

Harriet could find nothing to say to him. She had fought him for five years, and found out nothing but his strength; now, within half an hour he had exposed all his weaknesses, one after the other. And she could not in honesty say: 'Why didn't you tell me before?' because she knew perfectly well what the answer ought to be. Fortunately, he did not seem to expect any comment.

'Great Scott!' was his next remark, 'Look at the time! You've let me maunder on, and we've never said a word about your problem.'

'I've been only too thankful to forget it for a bit.'

'I dare say you have,' he said, looking thoughtfully at her. 'Listen, Harriet, couldn't we make to-day a holiday? You've had enough of this blasted business. Come and be bothered with me for a change. It'll be a relief for you – like getting a nice go of rheumatism in exchange for toothache. Equally damnable, but different. I've got to go to this lunch-party, but it needn't take too long. How about a punt at 3 o'clock from Magdalen Bridge?'

'There'll be an awful crowd on the river. The Cher-well's not what it was, especially on a Sunday. More like

Bank Holiday at Margate, with gramophones and bath-ing-dresses and everybody barging into everybody else.'

'Never mind. Let's go and do our bit of barging along with the happy populace. Unless you'd rather come in the car and fly with me to the world's end. But the roads will be worse than the river. And if we find a quiet spot, either I shall make a pest of myself or else we shall start on the infernal problem. There's safety in publicity.'

'Very well, Peter. We'll do exactly as you like.'

'Then we'll say Magdalen Bridge at three. Trust me, I'm not shirking the problem. If we can't see our way through it together, we'll find somebody who can. There are no seas innavigable nor lands unhabitable.'

He got up and held out a hand.

'Peter, what a rock you are! The shadow of a great rock in a weary land. My dear, what are you thinking about? One doesn't shake hands at Oxford.'

'The elephant never forgets.' He kissed her fingers gently. 'I have brought my formal cosmopolitan courtesy with me. My God! talk of courtesy – I'm going to be late for lunch.'

He snatched up cap and gown and was gone before she had time even to think of seeing him down to the Lodge.

'But it's just as well,' she thought, watching him run across the quad like an undergraduate, 'he hasn't too much time as it is. Bless the man, if he hasn't taken my gown instead of his own! Oh, well, it doesn't matter. We're much of a height and mine's pretty wide on the shoulders, so it's exactly the same thing.'

And then it struck her as strange that it should be the same thing.

Harriet smiled to herself as she went to change for the river. If Peter was keen on keeping up decayed traditions he would find plenty of opportunity by keeping to a pre-War standard of watermanship, manners and dress. Especially dress. A pair of grubby shorts or a faded regulation suit rolled negligently about the waist was the modern version of Cherwell fashions for men; for women, a sun-bathing costume with (for the tender-footed) a pair of gaily-coloured beach sandals. Harriet shook her head at the sunshine, which was now hot as well as bright. Even for the sake of startling Peter, she was not prepared to offer a display of grilled back and mosquito-bitten legs. She would go seemly and comfortable.

The Dean, meeting her under the beeches, gazed with exaggerated surprise at her dazzling display of white linen and pipe-clay.

'If this were twenty years ago I should say you were going on the river.'

'I am. Hand in hand with a statelier past.'

The Dean groaned gently. 'I'm afraid you are making yourself conspicuous. That kind of thing is not done. You are clothed, clean and cool. On a Sunday afternoon, too. I am ashamed of you. I hope, at least, the parcel under your arm contains the records of crooners.'

'Not even that,' said Harriet.

Actually, it contained her diary of the Shrewsbury scandal. She had thought that the best thing would be to let Peter take it away and study it for himself. Then he could decide what was best to be done about it.

She was punctual at the bridge, but found Peter there before her. His obsolete politeness in this respect was emphasised by the presence of Miss Flaxman and another Shrewsburian, who were sitting on the raft, apparently waiting for their escort, and looking rather hot and irritable. It amused Harriet to let Wimsey take charge of her parcel, hand her ceremoniously into the punt and arrange the cushions for her, and to know, by his ironical eyes, that he perfectly well understood the reason of her unusual meekness.

'Is it your pleasure to go up or down?'

'Well, going up there's more riot but a better bottom; going down you're right as far as the fork, and then you choose between thick mud and the Corporation dump.'

'It appears to be altogether a choice of evils. But you have only to command. My ear is open like a greedy shark to catch the tunings of a voice divine.'

'Great heavens! Where did you find that?'

'That, though you might not believe it, is the crashing conclusion of a sonnet by Keats. True, it is a youthful effort; but there are some things that even youth does not excuse.'

'Let us go down-stream. I need solitude to recover from the shock.'

He turned the punt out into the stream and shot the bridge accurately. Then:

'Admirable woman! You have allowed me to spread the tail of vanity before that pair of deserted Ariadnes. Would you now prefer to be independent and take the pole? I admit it is better fun to punt than to be punted, and that a desire to have all the fun is nine-tenths of the law of chivalry.'

'Is it possible that you have a just and generous mind? I will not be outdone in generosity. I will sit like a perfect lady and watch you do the work. It's nice to see things well done.'

'If you say that, I shall get conceited and do something silly.'

He was, in fact, a pretty punter to watch, easy in action and quite remarkably quick. They picked their way at surprising speed down the crowded and tortuous stream until, in the narrow reach above the ferry, they were checked by another punt, which was clumsily revolving in mid-stream and cramming a couple of canoes rather dangerously against the bank.

'Before you come on this water,' cried Wimsey, thrusting the offenders off with his heel and staring offensively at the youth in charge (a stringy young man, naked to the waist and shrimp-pink with the sun) 'you should learn the rule of the river. Those canoes have the right of way. And if you can't handle a pole better than that, I recommend you to retire up the back-water and stay there till you know what God gave you feet for.'

Whereat a middle-aged man, whose punt was moored a little way farther on, turned his head sharply and cried in ringing tones:

'Good lord! Wimsey of Balliol!'

'Well, well, well,' said his lordship, abandoning the pink youth, and ranging up alongside the punt. 'Peake of Brasenose, by all that's holy. What brings you here?'

'Dash it,' said Mr. Peake, 'I live here. What brings *you* here is more to the point. You haven't met my wife – Lord Peter Wimsey, my dear – the cricket blue, you know. The rest is my family.'

He waved his hand vaguely over a collection of assorted offspring.

'Oh, I thought I'd look the old place up,' said Peter, when the introductions were completed all round. 'I've got a nephew here and all that. What are you doing? Tutor? Fellow? Lecturer?'

'Oh, I coach people. A dog's life, a dog's life. Dear me! A lot of water has flowed under Folly Bridge since we last met. But I'd have known your voice anywhere. The moment I heard those arrogant, off-hand, go-to-blazes tones I said, "Wimsey of Balliol." Wasn't I right?'

Wimsey shipped the pole and sat down.

'Have pity, old son, have pity! Let the dead bury their dead.'

'You know,' said Mr. Peake to the world at large, 'when we were up together – shocking long time ago that is – never mind! If anyone got landed with a country cousin or an American visitor who asked, as these people will, 'What is this thing called the Oxford manner?' we used to take 'em round and show 'em Wimsey of Balliol. He fitted in very handily between St. John's Gardens and the Martyrs' Memorial.'

'But suppose he wasn't there, or wouldn't perform?'

'That catastrophe never occurred. One never failed to find Wimsey of Balliol planted in the centre of the quad and laying down the law with exquisite insolence to somebody.'

Wimsey put his head between his hands.

'We were accustomed to lay bets,' went on Mr. Peake, who seemed to have preserved an undergraduate taste in humour, owing, no doubt, to continuous contact with First-Year mentality, 'upon what they would say about him afterwards. The Americans mostly said, "My, but isn't he just the perfect English aristocrat!" but some of them said, "Does he need that glass in his eye or is it just part of the costoom?"'

Harriet laughed, thinking of Miss Schuster-Slatt.

'My dear—' said Mrs. Peake, who seemed to have a kindly nature.

'The country cousins,' said Mr. Peake remorselessly, 'invariably became speechless and had to be revived with coffee and ices at Buol's.'

'Don't mind me,' said Peter, whose face was invisible except for the tip of a crimson ear.

'But you're wearing very well, Wimsey,' pursued Mr.

Peake, benevolently. 'Kept your waist-line. Still good for a sprint between the wickets? Can't say I'm much use now, except for the Parents' Match, eh, Jim? That's what marriage does for a man – makes him fat and lazy. But *you* haven't changed. Not an atom. Not a hair. Absolutely unmistakable. And you're quite right about these louts on the river. I'm sick and tired of being barged into and getting their beastly punts over my bows. They don't even know enough to apologise. Think it's dashed funny. Stupid oafs. And gramophones bawling in your ears. And look at 'em! Just look at 'em! Enough to make you sick. Like the monkey-house at the Zoo!'

'Noble and nude and antique!' suggested Harriet.

'I don't mean that. I mean the pole-climbing. Watch that girl – hand over hand, up she goes! And turning round to shove as if she was trying to clear a drain. She'll be in if she isn't careful.'

'She's dressed for it.' said Wimsey.

'I'll tell you what,' said Mr. Peake, confidentially. 'That's the real reason for the costume. They *expect* to fall in. It's all right to come out with those beautiful creases down your flannels, but if you do go in it makes it all the funnier.'

'How true that is. Well, we're blocking the river. We'd better be getting on. I'll look you up one day, if Mrs. Peake will allow me. So long.'

The punts parted company.

'Dear me,' said Peter, when they were out of earshot; 'it's pleasant to meet old friends. And very salutary.'

'Yes; but don't you find it depressing when they go on making the same joke they were making about a hundred years ago?'

'Devilish depressing. It's the one great drawback to living in this place. It keeps you young. Too young.'

'It's rather pathetic, isn't it?'

The river was wider here, and by way of answer he bent his knees to the stroke, making the punt curtsey and the water run chuckling under the bows.

'Would you have your youth back if you could, Harriet?'

'Not for the world.'

'Nor I. Not for anything you could give me. Perhaps that's an exaggeration. For one thing you could give me I might want twenty years of my life back. But not the same twenty years. And if I went back to my twenties, I shouldn't be wanting the same thing.'

'What makes you so sure of that?' said Harriet, suddenly reminded of Mr. Pomfret and the pro-Proctor.

'The vivid recollection of my follies . . . Harriet! Are you going to tell me that all young men in their twenties are not fools?' He stood, trailing the pole, and looking down at her; his raised eyebrows lent his face a touch of caricature.

'Well, well, well. . . . I hope it is not Saint-George, by the way. That would be a most unfortunate domestic complication.'

'No, not Saint-George.'

'I thought not; his follies are less ingenuous. But somebody. Well, I refuse to be alarmed, since you have sent him about his business.'

'I like the rapidity of your deductions.'

'You are incurably honest. If you had done anything drastic you would have told me so in your letter. You would have said, "Dear Peter, I have a case to submit to you; but before doing so I think it only right to inform you that I am engaged to Mr. Jones of Jesus." Should you not?'

'Probably. Should you have investigated the case all the same?'

'Why not? A case is a case. What is the bottom like in the Old River?'

'Foul. You're pulled back two strokes for every stroke you make.'

'Then we will stick to the New Cut. Well, Mr. Jones of Jesus has my sincere sympathy. I hope his troubles will not affect his class.'

'He is only in his Second Year.'

'Then he has time to get over it. I should like to meet him. He is probably the best friend I have in the world.'

Harriet said nothing. Peter's intelligence could always make rings round her own more slowly-moving wits. It was quite true that the spontaneous affections of Reggie Pomfret had, somehow, made it easier to believe that Peter's own feelings might be something more than an artist's tenderness for his own achievement. But it was indecent of Peter to reach that conclusion so rapidly. She resented the way in which he walked in and out of her mind as if it was his own flat.

'Good God!' said Peter, suddenly. He peered with an air of alarm into the dark green water. A string of oily bubbles floated slowly to the surface, showing where the pole had struck a patch of mud; and at the same moment their nostrils were assaulted by a loathsome stench of decay.

'What's the matter?'

'I've struck something horrible. Can't you smell it? It's scandalous the way corpses pursue me about. Honestly, Harriet . . .'

'My dear idiot, it's only the corporation garbage dump.'

His eyes followed her pointing hand to the farther bank, where a cloud of flies circled about a horrid mound of putrefaction.

'Well, of all the—! What the devil do they mean by doing a thing like that?' He passed a wet hand across his forehead. 'For a moment I really thought I *had* run across Mr. Jones of Jesus. I was beginning to be sorry I had spoken so light-heartedly about the poor chap. Here! Let's get out of this!'

He drove the punt vigorously forward.

'The Isis for me. There is *no* romance left on this river.'

15

Do but consider what an excellent thing sleep is: it is so
inestimable a jewel that, if a tyrant would give his
crown for an hour's slumber, it cannot be bought: of
so beautiful a shape is it, that though a man lie with an
Empress, his heart cannot beat quite till he leaves her
embracements to be at rest with the other: yea, so
greatly indebted are we to this kinsman of death, that
we owe the better tributary, half of our life to him: and
there is good cause why we should do so: for sleep is
that golden chain that ties health and our bodies
together. Who complains of want? of wounds? of
cares? of great men's oppressions? of captivity? whilst
he sleepeth? Beggars in their beds take as much pleasure
as kings: can we therefore surfeit on this delicate
Ambrosia? Can we drink too much of that whereof
to taste too little tumbles us into a churchyard, and to
use it but indifferently throws us into Bedlam? No, no,
look upon Endymion, the moon's minion, who slept
three score and fifteen years, and was not a hair the
worse for it.

THOMAS DEKKER

'YOU will find the tea-basket,' said Wimsey, 'behind you
in the bows.'

They had put in under the dappled shade of an over-
hanging willow a little down the left bank of the Isis.
Here there was less crowd, and what there was could

352

pass at a distance. Here, if anywhere, they might hope for comparative peace. It was, therefore, with more than ordinary irritation that Harriet, with the thermos yet in her hand, observed a heavily-laden punt approaching.

'Miss Schuster-Slatt and her party. Oh, God! and she says she knows you.'

The poles were firmly driven in at either end of the boat; escape was impossible. Ineluctably the American contingent advanced upon them. They were alongside. Miss Schuster-Slatt was crying out excitedly. It was Harriet's turn to blush for her friends. With incredible coyness Miss Schuster-Slatt apologised for her intrusion, affected introductions, was sure they were terribly in the way, reminded Lord Peter of their former encounter, recognised that he was far too pleasantly occupied to wish to be bothered with her, poured out a flood of alarming enthusiasm about the Propagation of the Fit, again drew strident attention to her own tactlessness, informed Lord Peter that Harriet was a lovely person and just too sympathetic, and favoured each of them with an advance copy of her new questionnaire. Wimsey listened and replied with imperturbable urbanity, while Harriet, wishing that the Isis would flood its banks and drown them all, envied his self-command. When at length Miss Schuster-Slatt removed herself and her party, the treacherous water wafted back her shrill voice from afar:

'Well, girls! Didn't I tell you he was just the perfect English aristocrat?'

At which point the much-tried Wimsey lay down among the tea-cups and became hysterical.

'Peter,' said Harriet, when he had finished crowing like a cock. 'your unconquerable sweetness of disposition is very shaming. I lose my temper with that harmless woman. Have some more tea.'

'I think,' said his lordship, mournfully, 'I had better stop being the perfect English aristocrat and become the great detective after all. Fate seems to be turning my one-day romance into a roaring farce. If that is the dossier, let me have it. We'll see,' he added with a faint chuckle, 'what kind of a detective you make when you're left to yourself.'

Harriet handed him the loose-leaf book and an envelope containing the various anonymous documents, all endorsed, where possible, with the date and manner of publication. He examined the documents first, separately and carefully, without manifesting surprise, disgust, or, indeed, any emotion beyond meditative interest. He then put them all back in the envelope, filled and lit a pipe, curled himself up among the cushions and devoted his attention to her manuscript. He read slowly, turning back every now and again to verify a date or detail. At the end of the first few pages he looked up to remark:

'I'll say one thing for the writing of detective fiction: you know how to put your story together; how to arrange the evidence.'

'Thank you,' said Harriet drily: 'praise from Sir Hubert is praise indeed.'

He read on.

His next observation was:

'I see you have eliminated all the servants in the Scouts' Wing on the strength of one locked door.'

'I'm not so simple-minded as that. When you come to the Chapel episode, you'll find that it eliminates them all, for another reason.'

'I beg your pardon; I was committing the fatal error of theorising ahead of my data.'

Accepting rebuke, he relapsed into silence, while she studied his half-averted face. Considered generally, as a façade, it was by this time tolerably familiar to her, but now she saw details, magnified as it were by some glass in her own mind. The flat setting and fine scroll-work of the ear, and the height of the skull above it. The glitter of close-cropped hair where the neck-muscles lifted to meet the head. A minute sickle-shaped scar on the left temple. The faint laughter-lines at the corner of the eye and the droop of the lid at its outer end. The gleam of golden down on the cheek-bone. The wide spring of the nostril. An almost imperceptible beading of sweat on the upper lip and a tiny muscle that twitched the sensitive corner of the mouth. The slight sun-reddening of the fair skin and its sudden whiteness below the base of the throat. The little hollow above the points of the collar-bone.

He looked up; and she was instantly scarlet, as though she had been dipped in boiling water. Through the confusion of her darkened eyes and drumming ears some enormous bulk seemed to stoop over her. Then the mist cleared. His eyes were riveted upon the manuscript again, but he breathed as though he had been running.

So, thought Harriet, it has happened. But it happened long ago. The only new thing that has happened is that now I have got to admit it to myself. I have known it for some time. But does he know it? He has very little excuse, after this, for not knowing it. Apparently he refuses to see it, and that may be new. If so, it ought to be easier to do what I meant to do.

She stared out resolutely across the dimpling water. But she was conscious of his every movement, of every page he turned, of every breath he drew. She seemed to be separately conscious of every bone in his body. At length he spoke, and she wondered how she could ever have mistaken another man's voice for his.

'Well, Harriet, it's not a pretty problem.'

'It's not. And it simply mustn't go on, Peter. We can't have any more people frightened into the river. Publicity or no publicity, it's got to be stopped. Otherwise, even if nobody else gets hurt, we shall all go mad.'

'That's the devil of it.'

'Tell me what we are to do, Peter.'

She had once again lost all consciousness of him except as the familiar intelligence that lived and moved so curiously behind an oddly amusing set of features.

'Well – there are two possibilities. You can plant spies all over the place and wait to pounce on this person when the next outbreak occurs.'

'But you don't know what a difficult place it is to police. And it's ghastly waiting for the outbreak. And suppose we don't catch her and something horrible happens.'

'I agree. The other, and I think the better, way is to do what we can to frighten this lunatic into keeping quiet while we dig out the motive behind the whole thing. I'm sure it's not mere blind malignity; there's a method in it.'

'Isn't the motive only too painfully obvious?'

He stared pensively at her, and then said:

'You remind me of a charming old tutor, now dead, whose particular subject of research was the relations of the Papacy to the Church in England between certain dates which I do not precisely recall. At one time, a special subject on these lines was set for the History School, and undergraduates taking that subject were naturally sent to the old boy for coaching and did very well. But it was noticed that no man from his own college ever entered for that particular special – the reason being that the tutor's honesty was such that he would earnestly dissuade his pupils from taking his own subject for fear lest his encouragement might influence their decision.'

'What a charming old gentleman! I'm flattered by the comparison, but I don't see the point.'

'Don't you? Isn't it a fact that, having more or less made up your mind to a spot of celibacy you are eagerly peopling the cloister with bogies? If you want to do without personal relationships, then do without them. Don't stampede yourself into them by imagining that you've got to have them or qualify for a Freudian case-book.'

'We're not talking about me and my feelings. We're talking about this beastly case in College.'

'But you can't keep your feelings out of the case. It's no use saying vaguely that sex is at the bottom of all these phenomena – that's about as helpful as saying that human nature is at the bottom of them. Sex isn't a separate thing functioning away all by itself. It's usually found attached to a person of some sort.'

'That's rather obvious.'

'Well, let's have a look at the obvious. The biggest crime of these blasted psychologists is to have obscured the obvious. They're like a man packing for the week-end and turning everything out of his drawers and cupboards till he can't find his pyjamas and toothbrush. Take a few obvious points to start with. You and Miss de Vine met at Shrewsbury for the first time at the Gaudy, and the first letter was put into your sleeve at that time; the people attacked are nearly all dons or scholars; a few days after your tea-party with young Pomfret, Jukes goes to prison; all the letters received by post come either on a Monday or a Thursday; all the communications are in English except the Harpy quotation; the dress found on the dummy was never seen in College: do all those facts taken together suggest nothing to you beyond a general notion of sex repression?'

'They suggest a lot of things separately, but I can't make anything of them taken together.'

'You are usually better than that at a synthesis. I wish you could clear this personal preoccupation out of your mind. My dear, what are you afraid of? The two great dangers of the celibate life are a forced choice and a vacant mind. Energies bombinating in a vacuum breed chimaeras. But *you* are in no danger. If you want to set up your everlasting rest, you are far more likely to find it in the life of the mind than the life of the heart.'

'*You* say that?'

'I say that. It is *your* needs we are considering, you know; not anybody else's. That is my opinion as an honest scholar, viewing the question academically and on its merits.'

She had the old sensation of being outwitted. She grasped again at the main theme of the discussion:

'Then you think we can solve the problem by straight detection, without calling in a mental specialist?'

'I think it can be solved by a little straight and unprejudiced reasoning.'

'Peter. I seem to be behaving very stupidly. But the reason why I want to-to get clear of people and feelings and go back to the intellectual side is that that is the only side of life I haven't betrayed and made a mess of.'

'I know that,' he said, more gently. 'And it's upsetting to think that it may betray you in its turn. But why should you think that? Even if much learning makes one person mad it need not make everybody mad. All these women are beginning to look abnormal to you because you don't know which one to suspect, but actually even you don't suspect more than one.'

'No: but I'm beginning to feel that almost any one of them might be capable of it.'

'That, I fancy, is where your fears are distorting your judgment. If every frustrate person is heading straight for the asylum I know at least one danger to Society who ought to be shut up.'

'Damn you, Peter. Will you keep to the point!'

'Meaning: what steps ought we to take? Will you give me to-night to think it over? If you will trust me to deal with it, I fancy I see one or two lines that might be followed up with profit.'

'I would rather trust you than anybody.'

'Thank you, Harriet. Shall we now resume our interrupted holiday? . . . Oh, my lost youth. Here are the ducks coming up for the remains of our sandwiches. Twenty-three years ago I fed these identical ducks with these identical sandwiches.'

'Ten years ago, I too fed them to bursting-point.'

'And ten and twenty years hence the same ducks and the same undergraduates will share the same ritual feast, and the ducks will bite the undergraduates' fingers as they had just bitten mine. How fleeting are all human passions compared with the massive continuity of ducks . . . Be off, cullies, that's the lot.'

He tossed the last crumbs of bread into the water, rolled over among the cushions and lay watching the ripples with half-shut eyes . . . A punt went past, full of silent, sun-stupefied people, with a plop and a tinkle alternately as the pole entered and left the water; then a noisy party with a gramophone bawling 'Love in Bloom'; then a young man in spectacles, by himself in a canoe, and paddling as though for dear life; then another punt, paddled at a funeral pace by a whispering man and girl; then a hot and energetic party of girls in an outrigger; then another canoe, driven swiftly by two Canadian undergraduates kneeling to their work; then a very small canoe, punted dangerously by a giggling girl in a bathing-dress, with a jeering young man crouched in the bows, costumed, and obviously prepared, for the inevitable plunge; then a very sedate and fully-clothed party in a punt – mixed undergraduates being polite to a female don; then a bunch of both sexes and all ages in an inrigger with another gramophone whining 'Love in Bloom' – the Town at play; then a succession of shrill cries which announced the arrival of a hilarious party teaching a novice to punt; then, in ludicrous contrast, a very stout man in a blue suit and linen hat, solemnly propelling himself all alone in a two-pair tub, and a slim, singleted youth shooting contemptuously past him in a pair-oar skiff; then three punts side by side, in which everybody seemed to be asleep except those actually responsible for pole and paddle. One of these passed within a paddle's length of Harriet: a tousle-headed, rather paunchy young man lay with his knees cocked up, his mouth slightly open and his face flushed with the heat; a girl sprawled against his shoulder, while the man opposite, his hat over his face and his hands clasped over his chest with the thumbs beneath his braces, had also given up all interest in the outer world. The fourth passenger, a woman, was eating chocolates. The punter had a crumpled cotton frock and bare legs, much bitten. Harriet was reminded of a third-class railway compart-ment in an excursion train on a hot day; it was fatal to sleep in public; and how tempting to throw something at the paunchy youth. At that moment, the chocolate-eater screwed her remaining lollipops tightly in the bag and did throw it at the paunchy youth. It caught him in the midriff, and he woke with a loud snort. Harriet took a cigarette from her case and turned to ask her companion for a match. He was asleep.

It was a neat and noiseless kind of sleep; the posture might be described as the half-hedgehog, and offered neither mouth nor stomach as a target for missiles. But asleep he undoubtedly was. And here was Miss Harriet Vane, gone suddenly sympathetic, afraid to move for fear of waking him and savagely resenting the approach of a boatload of idiots whose gramophone was playing (for a change) 'Love in Bloom.'

'How wonderful,' says the poet, 'is Death, Death and his brother Sleep!' And, having asked whether Ianthe will wake again and being assured that she will, he proceeds to weave many beautiful thoughts about Ianthe's sleep. From this we may fairly deduce that he (like Henry who kneeled in silence by her couch) felt tenderly towards Ianthe. For another person's sleep is the acid test of our own sentiments. Unless we are savages, we react kindly to death, whether of friend or enemy. It does not exasperate us; it does not tempt us to throw things at it; we do not find it funny. Death is the ultimate weakness, and we dare not insult it. But sleep is only an illusion of weakness and, unless it appeals to our protective instincts, is likely to arouse in us a nasty, bullying spirit. From a height of conscious superiority we look down on the sleeper, thus exposing himself in all his frailty, and indulge in derisive comment upon his appearance, his manners and (if the occasion is a public one) the absurdity of the position in which he has placed his companion, if he has one, and particularly if we are that companion.

Harriet, thus cozened into playing Phœbe to the sleeping Endymion, had plenty of opportunity to examine herself. After careful consideration, she decided that what she most needed was a box of matches. Peter had used matches to light his pipe: where were they? He had gone to sleep on the whole outfit, confound him!

But his blazer was beside him on the cushions; had anybody ever known a man to carry only *one* box of matches in his pockets?

To take possession of the blazer was ticklish work, for the punt rocked at every movement and she had to lift the garment over his knees; but his sleep was the deep sleep of physical fatigue, and she crawled back in triumph without having wakened him. With a curious sense of guilt she ransacked his pockets, finding three boxes of matches, a book and a corkscrew. With tobacco and literature one could face out any situation, provided, of course, that the book was not written in an unknown tongue. The spine was untitled, and as she turned back the worn calf cover the first thing she saw was the engraved book-plate with its achievement of arms: the three silver mice on a field sable and the 'domestick Catt' couched menacingly on the helmet-wreath. Two armed Saracens supported the shield, beneath which ran the mocking and arrogant motto: 'As my Wimsey takes me,' She turned on to the title-page. *Religio Medici*. Well! . . . Well? Was that so very unexpected?

Why did he travel about with that? Did he fill in the spare moments of detection and diplomacy with musing upon the 'strange and mystical' transmigrations of silk-worms and the 'legerdemain of changelings'? or with considering how 'we vainly accuse the fury of guns and the new inventions of death'? 'Certainly there is no happiness within this circle of flesh; nor is it in the opticks of these eyes to behold felicity. The first day of our jubilee is death.' She had no wish to suppose that he could find any personal application for that; she would rather have him secure and happy in order that she might resent his happy security. She flicked the pages over hurriedly. 'When I am from him, I am dead till I be with him. United souls are not satisfied with embraces, but desire to be truly each other; which being impossible, these desires are infinite, and must proceed without a possibility of satisfaction.' That was a most uncomfortable passage, whichever way you looked at it. She turned back to the first page and began to read steadily, with critical attention to grammar and style, so as to occupy the upper current of her mind without prying too closely into what might be going on beneath the surface.

The sun moved down the sky and the shadows lengthened upon the water. There were fewer craft on the river now; the tea-parties were hurrying home to dinner and the supper-parties had not yet put out. Endymion had the air of being settled for the night; it was really time to harden her heart and pull up the poles. She put off decision from moment to moment, till a loud shriek and a bump at her end of the punt came to spare her the trouble. The incompetent novice had returned with her crew and, having left her pole in the middle of the river, had let her craft adrift across their stern. Harriet pushed the intruders off with more vigour than sympathy and turned to find her host sitting up and grinning rather sheepishly.

'Have I been asleep?'

'Getting on for two hours,' said Harriet, with a pleased chuckle.

'Good lord, what disgusting behaviour! I am frightfully sorry. Why didn't you give me a shout? What time is it? My poor girl, you'll get no dinner to-night if we don't hurry up. Look here, I do apologise most abjectly.'

'It doesn't matter a bit. You were awfully tired.'

'That's no excuse.' He was on his feet now, extricating the punt-poles from the mud. 'We might make it by double-punting – if you'll forgive the infernal cheek of asking you to work to make up for my soul-destroying sloth.'

'I'd love to punt. But, Peter!' She suddenly liked him enormously. 'What's the hurry? I mean, is the Master expecting you, or anything?'

'No; I've removed myself to the Mitre. I can't use the Master's lodgings as a hotel; besides, they've got people coming in.'

'Then couldn't we get something to eat somewhere along the river and make a day of it? I mean, if you feel like it. Or must you have a proper dinner?'

'My dear, I would gladly eat husks for having behaved like a hog. Or thistles. Preferably thistles. You are a most forgiving woman.'

'Well, give me the pole. I'll stay up in the bows and you can do the steering.'

'And watch you bring the pole up in three.'

'I promise to do that.'

She was conscious, nevertheless, of Wimsey of Balliol's critical eye upon her handling of the heavy pole. For either you look graceful or you look ghastly; there is no middle way in punting. They set their course towards Iffley.

'On the whole,' said Harriet, as they took boat again some little time later, 'thistles would have been preferable.'

'That kind of food is provided for very young people whose minds are elsewhere. Men of passions but not parts. I am glad to have dined on apricot flan and synthetic lemonade; it enlarges one's experience. Shall I, you or we pole? Or shall we abandon aloofness and superiority and paddle in beauty side by side?' His eyes mocked her. 'I am tame; pronounce.'

'Whichever you prefer.'

He handed her gravely to the stem seat and coiled himself down beside her.

'What the devil am I sitting on?'

'Sir Thomas Browne, I expect. I'm afraid I rifled your pockets.'

'Since I was such a bad companion, I'm glad I provided you with a good substitute.'

'Is he a constant companion of yours?'

'My tastes are fairly catholic. It might easily have been *Kai Lung* or *Alice in Wonderland* or Machiavelli—'

'Or Boccaccio or the Bible?'

'Just as likely as not. Or Apuleius.'

'Or John Donne?'

He was silent for a moment, and then said in a changed voice:

'Was that a bow drawn at a venture?'

'A good shot?'

'Whang in the gold. Between the joints of the harness . . . If you would paddle a little on your side it would make it handier to steer.'

'Sorry . . . Do you find it easy to get drunk on words?'

'So easy that, to tell you the truth, I am seldom perfectly sober. Which accounts for my talking so much.'

'And yet, if anybody had asked me, I should have said you had a passion for balance and order – no beauty without measure.'

'One may have a passion for the unattainable.'

'But you do attain it. At least, you appear to attain it.'

'The perfect Augustan? No! I'm afraid it's at most a balance of opposing forces . . . The river's filling up again.'

'Lots of people come out after supper.'

'Yes – well, bless their hearts, why shouldn't they? You're not feeling cold?'

'Not the least bit.'

That was the second time within five minutes that he had warned her off his private ground. His mood had changed since the early hours of the afternoon and all his defences were up once more. She could not again disregard the 'No Thoroughfare' sign; so she left it to him to start a fresh subject.

He did so, courteously enough, by asking how the new novel was getting on.

'It's gone sticky.'

'What happened to it?'

This involved a full rehearsal of the plot of *Death 'twixt Wind and Water*. It was a complicated story, and the punt had covered a good deal of water before she reached the solution.

'There's nothing fundamentally wrong with that,' said he; and proceeded to offer a few suggestions about detail.

'How intelligent you are, Peter. You're quite right. Of course that would be much the best way to get over the clock difficulty. But why does the whole story sound so dead and alive?'

'If you ask me,' said Wimney, 'it's Wilfrid. I know he marries the girl – but must he be such a mutt? Why does he go and pocket the evidence and tell all those unnecessary lies?'

'Because he thinks the girl's done it.'

'Yes – but why should he? He's dotingly in love with her – he thinks she's absolutely the cat's pyjamas – and yet, merely because he finds her handkerchief in the bedroom he is instantly convinced, on evidence that wouldn't hang a dog, that she not only is Winchester's mistress but has also murdered him in a peculiarly diabolical way. That may be one way of love, but—'

'But, you would like to point out, it isn't yours – and in fact, it wasn't yours.'

There it was again – the old resentment, and the impulse to hit back savagely for the pleasure of seeing him wince.

'No,' he said, 'I was considering the question impersonally.'

'Academically, in fact.'

'Yes – please. . . . From a purely constructional point of view, I don't feel that Wilfrid's behaviour is sufficiently accounted for.'

'Well,' said Harriet, recovering her poise, 'academically speaking I admit that Wilfrid is the world's worst goop. But if he doesn't conceal the handkerchief where's my plot?'

'Couldn't you make Wilfrid one of those morbidly conscientious people, who have been brought up to think that anything pleasant must be wrong – so that, if he *wants* to believe the girl an angel of light she is, for that very reason, all the more likely to be guilty. Give him a puritanical father and a hell-fire religion.'

'Peter, that's an idea.'

'He has, you see, a gloomy conviction that love is sinful in itself, and that he can only purge himself by taking the young woman's sins upon him and wallowing in vicarious suffering. . . . He'd still be a goop, and a pathological goop, but he would be a bit more consistent.'

'Yes – he'd be interesting. But if I give Wilfrid all those violent and lifelike feelings, he'll throw the whole book out of balance.'

'You would have to abandon the jig-saw kind of story and write a book about human beings for a change.'

'I'm afraid to try that, Peter. It might go too near the bone.'

'It might be the wisest thing you could do.'

'Write it out and get rid of it?'

'Yes.'

'I'll think about that. It would hurt like hell.'

'What would that matter, if it made a good book?'

She was taken aback, not by what he said, but by his saying it. She had never imagined that he regarded her work very seriously, and she had certainly not expected him to take this ruthless attitude about it. The protective male? He was being about as protective as a can-opener.

'You haven't yet,' he went on, 'written the book you could write if you tried. Probably you couldn't write it when you were too close to things. But you could do it now, if you had the-the—'

'The guts?'

'Exactly.'

'I don't think I could face it.'

'Yes, you could. And you'll get no peace till you do. I've been running away from myself for twenty years, and it doesn't work. What's the good of making mistakes if you don't use them? Have a shot. Start on Wilfrid.'

'Damn Wilfrid! . . . All right. I'll try. I'll knock the sawdust out of Wilfrid, anyhow.'

He took his right hand from the paddle and held it out to her, deprecatingly.

'"Always laying down the law with exquisite insolence to somebody." I'm sorry.'

She accepted the hand and the apology and they paddled on in amity. But it was true, she thought, that she had had to accept a good deal more than that. She was quite surprised by her own lack of resentment.

They parted at the postern.

'Good night, Harriet. I'll bring back your manuscript tomorrow. Would some time in the afternoon suit you? I must lunch with young Gerald, I suppose, and play the heavy uncle.'

'Come round about six, then. Good night – and thank you very much.'

'I am in your debt.'

He waited politely while she shut and locked the heavy grille against him.

'And so-o-o' (in saccharine accents), 'the co-onvent gates closed behind So-o-onia!'

He smote his forehead with a theatrical gesture and an anguished cry and reeled away almost into the arms of the Dean, who was coming up the road at her usual brisk trot.

'Serve him right,' said Harriet, and fled up the path without waiting to see what happened.

As she got into bed she recalled the extempore prayer of a well-meaning but incoherent curate, heard once and never forgotten:

'Lord, teach us to take our hearts and look them in the face however difficult it may be.'

16

From noise of Scare-fires rest ye free,
From Murders *Benedicite*.
From all mischances, they may fright
Your pleasing slumbers in the night:
Mercie secure ye all, and keep
The Goblin from ye, while ye sleep.

ROBERT HERRICK

'Oh, miss!'

'We are so sorry to disturb you, madam.'

'Good gracious, Carrie, what is it?'

When you have been lying awake for an hour or so wondering how to reconstruct a Wilfrid without inflicting savage mayhem upon your plot, and have just tumbled into an uneasy slumber haunted by the embalmed bodies of dukes, it is annoying to be jerked into consciousness again by two excited and partly hysterical maid-servants in dressing-gowns.

'Oh, miss, the Dean said to come and tell you. Annie and me have been so frightened. We nearly caught it.'

'Caught what?'

'Whatever it is, miss. In the Science lecture-room, miss. We saw it there. It was awful.'

Harriet sat up, dazed.

'And it's gone off, miss, rampaging something horrible, and nobody knows what it mayn't be up to, so we thought we ought to tell somebody.'

'For goodness' sake, Carrie, *do* tell me. Sit down, both of you, and begin from the beginning.'

'But, miss, didn't we ought to see what's gone with it? Out through the dark-room window, that's where it went, and it may be murdering people at this very minute. And the room locked and the key inside – there might be a dead body lying there, all blood.'

'Don't be ridiculous,' said Harriet. But she got out of bed, none the less, and began to hunt for her slippers. 'If somebody's playing another practical joke, we must try and stop it. But don't let's have any nonsense about blood and bodies. Where did it go to?'

'We don't know, miss.'

Harriet looked at the stout and agitated Carrie, whose face was puckered and twitching and her eyes bolting with imminent hysteria. She had never thought the present head scout any too dependable, and was inclined to put down her abundant energy to an excess of thyroid.

'Where is the Dean, then?'

'Waiting by the lecture-room door, miss. She said to fetch you—'

'All right.'

Harriet put her torch into her dressing-gown pocket and hustled her visitors out.

'Now tell me quickly what's the matter, and don't make a noise.'

'Well, miss, Annie comes to me and says—'

'When was this?'

'About a quarter of an hour ago, miss, or it might be more or less.'

'About that, madam.'

'I was in bed and asleep, never dreaming of nothing, and Annie says, "Have you got the keys, Carrie? There's something funny going on in the lecture-room." So I says to Annie—'

'Just a minute. Let Annie tell her part first.'

'Well, madam, you know the Science lecture-room at the back of the New Quad, and how you can see it from our wing. I woke up about half-past one and happened to look out of my window and I saw a light in the lecture-room. So I thought, that's funny, as late as this. And I saw a shadow on the curtain, like somebody moving about.'

'The curtains were drawn, then?'

'Yes, madam; but they're only buff casement-cloth, you know, so I could see the shadow as plain as plain. So I watched a bit, and the shadow went away but the light stayed on and I thought it was funny. So I went and woke Carrie and said to her to give me the keys so as I could go and look in case it was something that wasn't quite right. And she saw the light, too. And I said, "Oh, Carrie, come with me; I don't like to go alone." So Carrie came down with me.'

'Did you go through the Hall or across the yard?'

'Across the yard, madam. We thought it would be quicker. Through the yard and the iron gate. And we tried to look through the window, but it was tight shut and the curtains pulled close.'

They were out of Tudor Building now; its corridors as they passed through had seemed quiet enough. Nor did there seem to be any disturbance in the Old Quad. The Library Wing was dark, except for a lamp burning in Miss de Vine's window and the dim illumination of the passage lights.

'When we came to the lecture-room door, it was locked and the key in it, because I stooped down to look through the hole, but I couldn't see anything. And then I saw that the curtain wasn't quite drawn across the door – it has glass panels, you know, madam. So I looked through the crack and saw something all in black, madam. And I said, "Oh, there it is!" And Carrie said, "Let me see," and she gave me a bit of a push and my elbow bumped against the door and that must have frightened it, because the light went out.'

'Yes, miss,' said Carrie, eagerly. 'And I said, "There now!" and then there was a most awful crash inside – dreadful, it was, and something bumping, and I calls out, "Oh, it's coming out after us!"'

'And I said to Carrie, "Run and fetch the Dean! We've got it in here." So Carrie went for the Dean and I heard whoever it was moving about a bit, and then I didn't bear anything more.'

'And the Dean came along and we waited a bit, and I said, "Ooh! do you think it's lying in there with its throat cut?" and the Dean said, "There, now! How silly we've been. It'll have gone out through the window." And I says, "But all them windows are barred," I says. And the Dean says, "The dark-room window, that's where it's gone." The dark-room door was locked too, so we run round outside and sure enough, there's the window wide open. So the Dean says, "Fetch Miss Vane." So we comes for you, miss.'

By this time they had reached the east angle of the New Quad, where Miss Martin stood waiting.

'Our friend's vanished, I'm afraid,' said the Dean. 'We ought to have been quick enough to think of that window. I've been round this quad, but I can't find anything wrong there. Let's hope the creature's gone back to bed.'

Harriet examined the door. It was certainly locked from the inside, and the curtain over the glass panel did not fit quite closely. But everything within was dark and silent.

'What does Sherlock Holmes do now?' inquired the Dean.

'I think we go in,' said Harriet. 'I suppose you haven't such a thing as a pair of long-nosed pliers? No. Well, it's probably just as good to break the glass.'

'Don't cut yourself.'

How many times, thought Harriet, had her detective Robert Templeton broken through doors to discover the dead body of the murdered financier! With a ludicrous feeling that she was acting a part, she laid a fold of her dressing-gown across the panel and delivered a sharp blow upon it with her closed fist. Rather to her astonishment, the panel broke inwards exactly as it should have done, to the accompaniment of a modest tinkle of glass. Now – a scarf or handkerchief wrapped round to protect the hand and wrist, and prevent leaving extra finger-prints on the key and handle. The Dean obligingly fetched this needful accessory; and the door was opened.

Harriet's first glance by torch-light was for the switch. It stood in the 'Off' position, and she struck it down with the handle of the torch. The room stood revealed.

It was a rather bare, uncomfortable place, furnished with a couple of long tables, a quantity of hard chairs and a blackboard. It was called the Science lecture-room partly because Miss Edwards occasionally used it for coachings that needed little in the way of apparatus, but chiefly because some dead-and-damned benefactor had left to the College a sum of money, together with a quantity of scientific books, anatomical casts, portraits of deceased scientists and glass cases filled with geological specimens; saddling this already sufficiently embarrassing bequest with the condition that all the bric-à-brac should be housed in one room together. Otherwise there was nothing that particularly fitted the room for scientific study, except that it communicated on one side with a closet containing a sink. The closet was occasionally used by photographic enthusiasts as a dark-room, and was so called.

The cause of the crash and bumping heard by the two scouts was plain enough as soon as the light was turned on. The blackboard had been flung to the ground and a few chairs displaced, as though somebody, hurriedly making her way from the room in the dark, had become entangled among the furniture. The most interesting thing about the room was the collection of things that lay on one of the tables. There was a spread sheet of newspaper, on which stood a paste-pot with a brush in it, part of a cheap scribbling block and the lid of a cardboard box, filled with cut-out letters. Also, laid out upon the table were several messages, couched in the Poison-Pen's now familiar style, and pasted together in the usual way; while a half-finished work in the same style of art had fluttered to the floor, showing that the Pen had been interrupted in the middle of her work.

'So here's where she does it!' cried the Dean.

'Yes,' said Harriet. 'I wonder why. It seems unnecessarily public. Why not her own room? . . . I say, Dean – don't pick that up, if you don't mind. Better leave everything as it is.'

The door in the dark-room was open. Harriet went in and examined the sink, and the open window above it. Marks in the dust showed clearly where something had scrambled over the sill.

'What's underneath this window outside?'

'It's a flagged path. I'm afraid you won't find much there.'

'No; and it happens to be a spot that's overlooked by absolutely nothing except those bathroom windows in the corridor. It's very unlikely that the person should have been seen getting out. If the letters *had* to be concocted in a lecture-room, this is as good a place as any. Well! I don't see that we can do much here at the moment.' Harriet turned sharply on the two scouts. 'You say you saw the person, Annie.'

'Not exactly saw her, madam, not to recognise. She had on something black and was sitting at the far table with her back to the door. I thought she was writing.'

'Didn't you see her face when she got up and came across to turn off the light?'

'No, madam. I told Carrie what I saw and Carrie asked to look and bumped the door, and while I was telling her not to make a noise the light went out.'

'Didn't you see anything, Carrie?'

'Well, I don't hardly know, miss, I was in such a fluster. I saw the light, and then I didn't see nothing.'

'Perhaps she crept round the wall to get to the light,' said the Dean.

'Must have, Dean. Will you go in and sit at the table on the chair that's pulled out a bit, while I see what I can see from the door. Then, when I knock on the glass, will you get up and out of sight as quickly as you can and work round to the switch and turn it off? Is the curtain much as it was, Annie, or did I disarrange it when I broke the glass?'

'I think it's much the same, madam.'

The Dean went in and sat down. Harriet shut the door and put her eye to the chink in the curtain. This was at the hinge-side of the door, and gave her a sight of the window, the ends of the two tables and the place where the blackboard had stood beneath the window.

'Have a look, Annie; was it like that?'

'Yes, madam. Only the blackboard was standing up then, of course.'

'Now – do as you did then. Say to Carrie whatever it was you said, and Carrie, you knock on the door and then look in as you did the first time.'

'Yes, madam. I said "There she is! we've got her." And I jumped back like this.'

'Yes, and I said, "Oh, dear! Let's have a look!" – and then I sort of caught against Annie and knocked – like that.'

'And I said, "Look out – now you've done it."'

'And I says, "Coo!" or something like that, and I looked in and I didn't see nobody—'

'Can you see anybody now?'

'No, miss. And I was trying to see when the light went out all of a sudden.'

The light went out.

'How did that go off?' asked the Dean, cautiously, with her mouth at the hole in the panel.

'First-rate performance,' said Harriet. 'Dead on time.'

'The second I heard the knock. I just nipped away to the right and crept round the wall. Did you hear me?'

'Not a sound. You've got soft slippers on, haven't you?'

'We didn't hear the other one either, miss.'

'She'd be wearing soft slippers, too. Well, I suppose that settles that. We'd better have a look round College to see that all's well and get back to bed. You two can be off now, Carrie – Miss Martin and I can see to things.'

'Very good, miss. Come along, Annie. Though I'm sure I don't know how anybody's to get to sleep—'

'*Will* you stop making that filthy row!'

An exasperated voice heralded the appearance of an exceedingly angry student in pyjamas.

'Do remember some people want to get a bit of rest at night. This corridor's a— Oh, I'm sorry, Miss Martin. Is anything wrong?'

'Nothing at all, Miss Perry. I'm sorry we disturbed you. Somebody left the lights on in the lecture-room and we came to see if it was all right.'

The student vanished, with a jerk of a tousled head that showed what she thought of the matter. The two servants went their way. The Dean turned to Harriet.

'Why all that business of reconstructing the crime?'

'I want to find out whether Annie could really have seen what she said she saw. These people sometimes let their imagination run away with them. If you don't mind, I'm going to lock these doors and remove the keys. I'd rather like a second opinion.'

'Aha!' said the Dean. 'The exquisite gentleman who kissed my feet in St. Cross Road, crying, *Vera incessu patuit dean*?'

'That sounds characteristic. Well, Dean, you have got pretty feet. I've noticed them.'

'They have been admired,' said the Dean, complacently, 'but seldom in so public a place or after five minutes' acquaintance. I said to his lordship, "You are a foolish young man." He said, "A man, certainly; and sometimes foolish enough to be young." "Well," I said, "please get up; you can't be young here." So then he said, very nicely, "I beg your pardon for behaving like a mountebank; I have no excuse to offer, so will you forgive me?" So I asked him to dinner.'

Harriet shook her head.

'I'm afraid you're susceptible to fair hair and a slim figure. That in the slender's but a humorous word which in the stout is flat impertinence.'

'It might have been extremely impertinent, but actually

378

it was not. I shall be interested to know what he makes of to-night's affair. We'd better go and see if there's been any more funny business.'

Nothing unusual was, however, to be observed.

Harriet rang up the Mitre before breakfast.

'Peter, could you possibly come round this morning instead of at six o'clock?'

'Within five minutes, when and where you will. "If she bid them, they will go barefoot to Jerusalem, to the great Cham's court, to the East Indies, to fetch her a bird to wear in her hat." Has anything happened?'

'Nothing alarming; a little evidence *in situ*. But you may finish the bacon and eggs.'

'I will be at the Jowett Walk Lodge in half an hour.'

He came accompanied by Bunter and a camera. Harriet took them into the Dean's room and told them the story, with some assistance from Miss Martin, who asked whether he would like to interview the two scouts,

'Not for the moment. You seem to have asked all the necessary questions. We'll go and look at the room. There's no way to it, I take it, except along this passage. Two doors on the left – students' rooms, I suppose. And one on the right. And the rest bathrooms and things. Which is the door of the dark-room? This? In full view of the other door – so there was no escape except by the window. I see. The key of the lecture-room was inside and the curtain left exactly like that? You're sure? All right. May I have the key?'

He threw the door open and glanced in.

'Get a photograph of this, Bunter. You have very nice, well-fitting doors in this building. Oak. No paint, no polish.'

He took a lens from his pocket and ran it, rather perfunctorily, over the light-switch and the door-handle.

'Am I really going to see finger-prints discovered?' asked the Dean.

'Why, of course,' said Wimsey. 'It won't tell us anything, but it impresses the spectator and inspires confidence. Bunter, the insufflator. You will now see,' he pumped the white powder rapidly over the frame and handle of the door, 'how inveterate is the habit of catching hold of doors when you open them.' An astonishing number of superimposed prints sprang into view above the lock as he blew the superfluous powder away. 'Hence the excellent old-fashioned institution of the finger-plate. May I borrow a chair from the bathroom? . . . Oh, thank you, Miss Vane; I didn't mean *you* to fetch it.'

He extended the blowing operations right up to the top of the door and the upper edge of the frame.

'You surely don't expect to find finger-prints up there,' said the Dean.

'Nothing would surprise me more. This is merely a shop window display of thoroughness and efficiency. All a matter of routine, as the policeman says. Your college is kept very well dusted; I congratulate you. Well, that's that. We will now direct our straining eyes to the dark-room door and do the same thing there, The key? Thank you. Fewer prints here, you see. I deduce that the room is usually approached by way of the lecture-room. That probably also accounts for the presence of dust along the top of the door. Something always gets overlooked, doesn't it? The linoleum, however, has been honourably swept and polished. Must I go down on my knees and do the floor-walk for foot-prints? It is shockingly bad for one's trousers and seldom useful. Let us rather examine the window. Yes – somebody certainly seems to have got out here. But we knew that already. She climbed over the sink and knocked that beaker off the draining-board.'.

'She trod in the sink,' said Harriet, 'and left a damp smear on the sill. It's dried up now, of course.'

'Yes; but that proves she really did get out this way and at that time. Though it scarcely needed proving. There *is* no other way out. This isn't the old problem of a hermetically sealed chamber and a body. Have you finished in there, Bunter?'

'Yes, my lord; I have made three exposures.'

'That ought to do. You might clean those doors, would you.' He turned, smiling, on the Dean. 'You see, even if we did identify all those finger-prints, they would all belong to people who had a perfect right to be here. And in any case, our culprit, like everybody else these days, probably knows enough to wear gloves.'

He surveyed the lecture-room critically.

'Miss Vane!'

'Yes?'

'Something worried you about this room. What was it?'

'You don't need to be told.'

'No; I am convinced that our two hearts beat as one. But tell Miss Martin.'

'When the Poison-Pen turned off the light, she must have been close to the door. Then she went out by way of the dark-room. Why did she knock over the blackboard, which is right out of the line between the two doors?'

'Exactly.'

'Oh!' cried the Dean, 'but that's nothing. One often loses one's way in a dark room. My reading-lamp fused one night, and I got up to try and find the wall-switch and brought up with my nose against the wardrobe.'

'There!' said Wimsey. 'The chill voice of common sense falls on our conjectures like cold water on hot glass, and shatters them to bits. But I don't believe it. She had only to feel her way along the wall. She must have had some reason for going back into the middle of the room.'

'She'd left something on one of the tables.'

'That's more likely. But what? Something identifiable.'

'A handkerchief or something that she'd been using to press down the letters as she pasted them on.'

'We'll say it was that. These papers are just as you found them, I imagine. Did you test them to see if the paste was still wet?'

'I just felt this unfinished one on the floor. You see how it's done. She drew a line of paste right across the paper and then dabbed the letters on. The unfinished line was just tacky, but not wet. But then, you see, we didn't get in till after she'd been gone for five or ten minutes.'

'You didn't test any of the others?'

'I'm afraid not.'

'I wondered how long she'd been working here. She's managed to get through a good bit. But we may be able to find out another way.' He took up the box-lid containing the odd letters.

'Rough brown cardboard; I don't think we'll bother to look for finger-prints on this. Or to trace it; it might have come from anywhere. She'd nearly finished her job; there are only a couple of dozen letters left, and a lot of them are Q's and K's and Z's and such-like unhandy consonants. I wonder how this last message was meant to end.'

He picked the paper from the floor and turned it over.

'Addressed to you, Miss Vane. Is this the first time you have been honoured?'

'The first time – since the first time.'

'Ah! "You needn't think you'll get me, you make me laugh, you . . ." Well, the epithet remains to be supplied – from the letters in the box. If your vocabulary is large enough you may discover what it was going to be,'

'But . . . Lord Peter—'

It was so long since she had addressed him by his title that she felt self-conscious about it. But she appreciated his formality.

'What I want to know is, why she came to this room at all.'

'That is the mystery, isn't it?'

There was a shaded reading-lamp on the table, and he stood idly clicking the light on and off. 'Yes. Why couldn't she do it in her own room? Why invite discovery?'

'Excuse me, my lord.'

'Yes, Bunter?'

'Would this be any contribution to the inquiry?'

Bunter dived beneath the table and came up, holding a long black hairpin.

'Good heavens, Bunter! This is like a leaf out of a forgotten story. How many people use these things?'

'Oh, quite a number, nowadays,' said the Dean. 'Little buns in the neck have come back. I use them myself, but mine are bronze ones. And some of the students. And Miss Lydgate – but I think hers are bronze, too.'

'I know who uses black ones this shape,' said Harriet. 'I once had the pleasure of sticking them in for her.'

'Miss de Vine, of course. Always the White Queen. And she *would* drop them all over the place. But I should think she was about the only person in College who would never, by any chance, come into this room. She gives no lectures or classes and never uses the dark-room or consults scientific works.'

'She was working in her room when I came across last night,' said Harriet.

'Did you see her?' said Wimsey, quickly.

'I'm sorry. I'm an idiot. I only meant that her reading-lamp was on, close to her window.'

'You can't establish an alibi on the strength of a reading-lamp,' said Wimsey. 'I'm afraid I shall have to do the floor-walk after all.'

It was the Dean who picked up a second hairpin – in the place where one might most reasonably expect to find it – in a corner near the sink in the dark-room. She was so pleased with herself as a detective that she almost forgot the implications of the discovery, till Harriet's distressed exclamation forced them upon her.

'We haven't identified the hairpins for certain,' said Peter, comfortingly. 'That will be a little task for Miss Vane.' He gathered up the papers. 'I'll take these and add them to the dossier. I suppose there's no message for us on the blackboard?'

He picked up the board, which contained only a few chemical formulæ, scribbled in chalk, in Miss Edwards's handwriting, and restored the easel to an upright position, on the far side of the window.

'Look!' said Harriet, suddenly. 'I know why she went round that way. She meant to get out by the lecture-room window, and had forgotten the bars. It was only when she pulled the curtain aside and saw them that she remembered the dark-room and plunged away in a hurry, knocking over the blackboard and tumbling into the chairs on the way. She must have been between the window and the easel, because the board *and* the easel fell forward into the room, and not backwards towards the wall.'

Peter looked at her thoughtfully. Then he went back into the dark-room and lowered and raised the window-sash. It moved easily and almost in silence.

'If this place wasn't so well built,' he said, almost accusingly, to the Dean, 'somebody would have heard this window go up and run round in time to catch the lady. As it is, I wonder that Annie didn't notice the noise of the beaker falling into the sink . . . But if she did, she probably thought it was something in the lecture-room – one of those glass cases or what not. You didn't hear anything after you arrived, did you?'

'Not a thing.'

'Then she must have got out while Carrie was fetching you out of bed. I suppose nobody saw her go.'

'I've asked the only three students whose windows overlook that wall, and they saw nothing,' said Harriet.

'Well, you might ask Annie about the beaker. And ask both of them whether they noticed, as they came past, if the dark-room window was open or shut, I don't suppose they noticed anything, but you never can tell.'

'What does it matter?' asked the Dean.

'Not very much. But if it was shut, it rather supports Miss Vane's idea about the blackboard. If it was open, it would suggest that a retreat had been planned in that direction. It's a question of whether we're dealing with a short-sighted or a long-sighted person – mentally, I mean. And you might inquire at the same time whether any of the other women in the Scouts' Wing saw the light in the lecture-room, and if so, how early.'

Harriet laughed.

'I can tell you that at once. None of them. If they had, there would have been an eager rush to tell us all about it. You may be perfectly certain that Annie's and Carrie's adventure formed the staple of conversation in the servants' hall this morning.'

'That,' said his lordship, 'is very true indeed.'

There was a pause. The lecture-room seemed to offer no further field for research. Harriet suggested that Wimsey might like to look round the College.

'I was about to suggest it,' said he, 'if you can spare the time.'

'Miss Lydgate is expecting me in half an hour for a fresh attack on the *Prosody*,' said Harriet. 'I mustn't cut that, because her time is so precious, poor dear, and she's suddenly thought of a new appendix.'

'Oh, *no*!' cried the Dean.

'Alas, yes! But we could just go round and view the more important battlefields.'

'I should like particularly to see the Hall and Library and the connection between them, the entrance to Tudor Building, with Miss Barton's former room, the lay-out of the Chapel with reference to the postern and the place where, with the help of God, one leaps over the wall, and the way from Queen Elizabeth into the New Quad.'

'Great Heavens!' said Harriet. 'Did you sit up all night with the dossier?'

'Hush! no, I woke rather early. But don't let Bunter hear, or he will start being solicitous. Men have died and the worms have eaten them, but not for early rising. In fact, it is said that it's the early worm that gets the bird.'

'You remind me,' said the Dean, 'that there are half a dozen worms waiting in my room to get the bird this minute. Three late-without leaves, two gramophones-out-of-doors, and an irregular motor-vehicle. We shall meet again at dinner, Lord Peter.'

She ran briskly away to deal with the malefactors, leaving Peter and Harriet to make their tour. From

Peter's comments, Harriet could make out little of his mind; she fancied, indeed, that he was somewhat abstracted from the matter in hand.

'I fancy,' he said at last, as they came to the Jowett Walk Lodge, where he had left the car, 'that you will have very little more trouble at night.'

'Why?'

'Well, for one thing, the nights are getting very short, and the risks very great . . . All the same – shall you be offended if I ask you – if I suggest that you should take some personal precautions?'

'What sort of precautions?'

'I won't offer you a revolver to take to bed with you. But I have an idea that from now on you and at least one other person may be in some danger of attack. That may be imagination. But if this joker is alarmed and bottled up for a bit – and I think she has been alarmed – the next outrage may be a serious one – when it comes.'

'Well,' said Harriet, 'we have her word for it that she finds me merely funny.'

His attention seemed to be attracted by something among the dash-board fittings, and he said, looking not at her but at the car:

'Yes. But without any vanity, I wish I were your husband or your brother or your lover, or anything but what I am.'

'You mean, your being here is a danger – to me?'

'I dare say I'm flattering myself.'

'But it wouldn't stop *you* to damage *me*.'

'She may not think very clearly about that.'

'Well, I don't mind the risk, if it is one. And I don't see why it would be any less if you were a relation of mine.'

'There'd be an innocent excuse for my presence, wouldn't there? . . . Don't think I'm trying to make capital out of this on my own account. I'm being careful to observe the formalities, as you may have noticed. I'm only warning you that I'm sometimes a dangerous person to know.'

'Let's have this clear, Peter. You think that your being here may make this person desperate and that she may try to take it out of me. And you are trying to tell me, very delicately, that it might be safer if we camouflaged your interest.'

'Safer for you.'

'Yes – though I can't see why you think so. But you're sure I'd rather die than make such an embarrassing pretence.'

'Well, wouldn't you?'

'And on the whole you'd rather see me dead than embarrassed.'

'That is probably another form of egotism. But I am entirely at your service.'

'Of course, if you're such a perilous ally, I could tell you to go away.'

'I can see you urging me to go away and leave a job undone.'

'Well, Peter, I'd certainly rather die than make any sort of pretence to you or about you. But I think you're exaggerating the whole thing. You don't usually get the wind up like this.'

'I do, though; quite often. But if it's only my own risk, I can afford to let it blow. When it comes to other people—'

'Your instinct is to clap the women and children under hatches.'

'Well,' he admitted, deprecatingly, 'one can't suppress one's natural instincts altogether; even if one's reason and self-interest are all the other way.'

'Peter, it's a shame. Let me introduce you to some nice little woman who adores being protected.'

'I should be wasted on her. Besides, she would always be deceiving me, in the kindest manner, for my own good; and that I could not stand. I object to being tactfully managed by somebody who ought to be my equal. If I want tactful dependents, I can hire them. And fire them if they get too tactful. I don't mean Bunter. He braces me by a continual cold shower of silent criticism. I don't protect him; he protects me, and preserves an independent judgment . . . However; without presuming to be protective, may I yet suggest that you should use a reasonable caution? I tell you frankly I don't like your friend's pre-occupation with knives and strangling.'

'Are you serious?'

'For once.'

Harriet was about to tell him not to be ridiculous; then she remembered Miss Barton's story about the strong hands that had seized her from behind. It might have been quite true. The thought of perambulating the long corridors by night was suddenly disagreeable.

'Very well; I'll be careful.'

'I think it would be wise. I'd better push off now. I'll be round in time to face the High Table at dinner. Seven o'clock?'

She nodded. He had interpreted strictly her injunction to come 'this morning instead of at six.' She went, feeling a little blank, to cope with Miss Lydgate's proofs.

17

He that questioneth much shall learn much, and content much; but especially if he apply his questions to the skill of the persons whom he asketh; for he shall give them occasion to please themselves in speaking, and himself shall continually gather knowledge. But let his questions not be troublesome, for that is fit for a poser; and let him be sure to leave other men their turns to speak.

FRANCIS BACON

'You look,' said the Dean, 'like a nervous parent whose little boy is about to recite *The Wreck of the Hesperus* at a School Concert.'

'I feel,' said Harriet, 'more like the mother of Daniel.

> King Darius said to the lions:—
> Bite Daniel. Bite Daniel.
> Bite him. Bite him. Bite him.'

'G'rrrrr!' said the Dean.

They were standing at the door of the Senior Common Room, which conveniently overlooked the Jowett Walk Lodge. The Old Quad was animated. Late-comers were hurrying over to change for dinner; others, having changed, were strolling about in groups, waiting for the bell; some were still playing tennis; Miss de Vine emerged from the Library Building, still vaguely pushing in hairpins (Harriet had checked up on those hairpins and identified them); an elegant figure paraded towards them from the direction of the New Quadrangle.

'Miss Shaw's got a new frock,' said Harriet.

'So she has! How posh of her!

> And she was as fine as a melon in the corn-field,
> Gliding and lovely as a ship upon the sea.

That, my dear, is meant for Daniel,'

'Dean, darling, you're being a cat.'

'Well, aren't we all? This early arrival of everybody is exceedingly sinister. Even Miss Hillyard is arrayed in her best black gown with a train to it. We all feel there's safety in numbers.'

It was not out of the way for the Senior Common Room to collect outside their own door before dinner for a fine summer's day, but Harriet, glancing round, had to admit that there were more of them there that evening than was usual before 7 o'clock. She thought they all seemed apprehensive and some even hostile. They tended to avoid one another's eyes; yet they gathered together as though for protection against a common menace. She suddenly found it absurd that anybody should be alarmed by Peter Wimsey; she saw them as a harmless collection of nervous patients in a dentist's waiting-room.

'We seem,' said Miss Pyke's harsh voice in her ear, 'to be preparing a somewhat formidable reception for our guest. Is he of a timid disposition?'

'I should say he was completely hard-boiled,' said Harriet.

'That reminds me,' said the Dean. 'In the matter of shirt-fronts—'

'Hard, of course,' said Harriet, indignantly. 'And if he pops or bulges, I will pay you five pounds.'

'I have been meaning to ask you,' said Miss Pyke. 'How is the popping sound occasioned? I did not like to ask Dr. Threep so personal a question, but my curiosity was very much aroused.'

'You'd better ask Lord Peter,' said Harriet.

'If you think he will not be offended,' replied Miss Pyke, with perfect seriousness, 'I will do so.'

The chimes of New College, rather out of tune, played the four quarters and struck the hour.

'Punctuality,' said the Dean, her eyes turned towards the Lodge, 'seems to be one of the gentleman's virtues. You'd better go and meet him and settle his nerves before the ordeal.'

'Do you think so?' Harriet shook her head. 'Ye'll no fickle Tammas Yownie.'

It may, perhaps, be embarrassing for a solitary man to walk across a wide quadrangle under a fire of glances from a collection of collegiate females; but it is child's play compared, for example, with the long trek from the pavilion at Lord's to the far end of the pitch, with five wickets down and ninety needed to save the follow-on. Thousands of people then alive might have recognised that easy and unhurried stride and confident carriage of the head. Harriet let him do three-quarters of the journey alone, and then advanced to meet him.

'Have you cleaned your teeth and said your prayers?'

'Yes, mamma; and cut my nails and washed behind the ears and got a clean handkerchief.'

Looking at a bunch of students who happened to pass at the moment, Harriet wished she could have said the same of them. They were grubby and dishevelled and she felt unexpectedly obliged to Miss Shaw for having made an effort in the matter of dress. As for her convoy, from his sleek yellow head to his pumps she distrusted him; his mood of the morning was gone, and he was ready for mischief as a wilderness of monkeys.

'Come along then, and behave prettily. Have you seen your nephew?'

'I have seen him. My bankruptcy will probably be announced to-morrow. He asked me to give you his love, no doubt thinking I can still be lavish in that commodity. It all returned from him to you though it was mine before. That colour is very becoming to you.'

His tone was pleasantly detached and she hoped he was referring to her dress; but she was not sure. She was glad to relinquish him to the Dean, who came forward to claim him and to relieve her of the introductions. Harriet watched in some amusement. Miss Lydgate, far too unselfconscious to have any attitude at all, greeted him exactly as she would have greeted anybody else, and asked eagerly about the situation in Central Europe; Miss Shaw smiled with a graciousness that emphasised Miss Stevens's brusque 'How-d'ye-do' and immediate retreat into animated discussion of college affairs with Miss Allison; Miss Pyke pounced on him with an intelligent question about the latest murder; Miss Barton, advancing with an evident determination to put him right about capital punishment, was disarmed by the blank amiability of the countenance offered for her inspection and observed instead that it had been a remarkably fine day.

'Comedian!' thought Harriet, as Miss Barton, finding she could make nothing of him, passed him on to Miss Hillyard.

'Ah!' said Wimsey instantly, smiling into the History Tutor's sulky eyes, 'this is delightful. Your paper in the *Historical Review* on the diplomatic aspects of the Divorce. . .'

(Heavens! thought Harriet, I hope he knows his stuff.)

'. . . really masterly. Indeed, I felt that, if anything, you had slightly underestimated the pressure brought to bear upon Clement by. . . .'

'. . . consulted the unedited dispatches in the possession of . . .'

'. . . you might have carried the argument a trifle farther, You very rightly point out that the Emperor . . .'

(Yes; he had read the article all right.)

'. . . disfigured by prejudice, but a considerable authority on the Canon Law . . .'

'. . . needing to be thoroughly overhauled and re-edited. Innumerable mistranscriptions and at least one upscrupulous omission. . . .'

'. . . if at any time you require access, I could probably put you in touch with . . . official channels . . . personal introduction . . . raise no difficulties . . .'

'Miss Hillyard,' said the Dean to Harriet, 'looks as though she has been given a birthday present.'

'I think he's offering her access to some out-of-the-way source of information.' (After all, she thought, he is Somebody, though one never seems able to remember it.)

'. . . not so much political as economic.'

'Ah!' said Miss Hillyard, 'when it comes to a question of national finance, Miss de Vine is the real authority.'

She effected the introduction herself, and the discussion continued.

'Well,' said the Dean, 'he has made a complete conquest of Miss Hillyard.'

'And Miss de Vine is making a complete conquest of him.'

'It's mutual, I fancy. At any rate, her back hair's coming down, which is a sure sign of pleasure and excitement.'

'Yes,' said Harriet. Wimsey was arguing with intelligence about the appropriation of monastic funds, but she had little doubt that the back of his mind was full of hairpins.

'Here comes the Warden. We shall have to separate them forcibly. He's *got* to face Dr. Baring and take her in to dinner. . . . All's well. She has collared him. That firm assertion of the Royal Prerogative! . . . Do you want to sit next him and hold his hand?'

'I don't think he needs any assistance from me. You're the person for him. Not a suspect, but full of lively information.'

'All right; I'll go and prattle to him. You'd better sit opposite to us and kick me if I say anything indiscreet.'

By this arrangement, Harriet found herself placed a little uncomfortably between Miss Hillyard (in whom she always felt an antagonism to herself) and Miss Barton (who was obviously still worried about Wimsey's detective hobbies), and face to face with the two people whose glances were most likely to disturb her gravity. On the other side of the Dean sat Miss Pyke; on the other side of Miss Hillyard was Miss de Vine, well under Wimsey's eye. Miss Lydgate, that secure fortress, was situated at the far end of the table, offering no kind of refuge.

Neither Miss Hillyard nor Miss Barton had much to say to Harriet, who was thus able to follow, without too much difficulty, the Warden's straightforward determination to size up Wimsey and Wimsey's diplomatically veiled but equally obstinate determination to size up the Warden; a contest carried on with unwavering courtesy on either side.

Dr. Baring began by inquiring whether Lord Peter had been conducted over the College and what he thought of it, adding, with due modesty that architecturally, of course, it could scarcely hope to compete with the more ancient foundations.

'Considering,' said his lordship plaintively, 'that the architecture of my own ancient foundation is mathematically compounded of ambition, distraction, uglification and derision, that remark sounds like sarcasm.'

The Warden, almost seduced into believing herself guilty of a breach of manners, earnestly assured him that she had intended no personal allusion.

'An occasional reminder is good for us,' said he. 'We are mortified in nineteenth-century Gothic, lest in our overweening Balliolity we forget God. We pulled down the good to make way for the bad; you, on the contrary, have made the world out of nothing – a more divine procedure.'

The Warden, manoeuvring uneasily on this slippery ground between jest and earnest, found foothold:

'It is quite true that we have had to make what we can out of very little – and that, you know, is typical of our whole position here.'

'Yes; you are practically without endowments?'

The question was so offered as to include the Dean, who said cheerfully:

'Quite right. All done by cheeseparing.'

'That being so,' he said seriously, 'even to admire seems to be a kind of impertinence. This is a very fine hall – who is the architect?'

The Warden supplied him with a little local history, breaking off to say:

'But probably you are not specially interested in all this question of women's education.'

'Is it still a question? It ought not to be. I hope you are not going to ask me whether I approve of women's doing this and that.'

'Why not?'

'You should not imply that I have any right either to approve or disapprove.'

'I assure you,' said the Warden, 'that even in Oxford we still encounter a certain number of people who maintain their right to disapprove.'

'And I had hoped I was returning to civilisation.'

The removal of fish-plates caused a slight diversion, and the Warden took the opportunity to turn her inquiries upon the situation in Europe. Here the guest was on his own ground. Harriet caught the Dean's eye and smiled. But the more formidable challenge was coming. International politics led to history, and history – in Dr. Baring's mind – to philosophy. The ominous name of Plato suddenly emerged from a tangle of words, and Dr. Baring moved out a philosophical speculation, like a pawn, and planted it temptingly *en prise*.

Many persons had plunged to irretrievable disaster over the Warden's philosophic pawn. There were two ways of taking it: both disastrous. One was to pretend to knowledge; the other, to profess an insincere eagerness for instruction. His lordship smiled gently and refused the gambit:

'That is out of my stars. I have not the philosophic mind.'

'And how would you define the philosophic mind, Lord Peter?'

'I wouldn't; definitions are dangerous. But I know that philosophy is a closed book to me, as music is to the tone-deaf.'

The Warden looked at him quickly; he presented her with an innocent profile, drooping and contemplative over his plate, like a heron brooding by a pond.

'A very apt illustration,' said the Warden; 'as it happens, I am tone-deaf myself.'

'Are you? I thought you might be,' he said, equably.

'That is very interesting. How can you tell?'

'There is something in the quality of the voice.' He offered candid grey eyes for examination. 'But it's not a very safe conclusion to draw, and, as you may have noticed, I didn't draw it. That is the art of the charlatan – to induce a confession and present it as the result of deduction.'

'I see,' said Dr. Baring. 'You expose your technique very frankly.'

'You would have seen through it in any case, so it is better to expose one's self and acquire an unmerited reputation for candour. The great advantage about telling the truth is that nobody ever believes it – that is at the bottom of the ψευδη λέγειν ὡς δει.'

'So there is one philosopher whose books are not closed to you? Next time, I will start by way of Aristotle.'

She turned to her left-hand neighbour and released him.

'I am sorry,' said the Dean, 'we have no strong drink to offer you.'

His face was eloquent of mingled apprehension and mischief.

'The toad beneath the harrow knows where every separate tooth point goes. Do you always prove your guests with hard questions?'

'Till they show themselves to be Solomons. You have passed the test with great credit.'

'Hush! there is only one kind of wisdom that has any social value, and that is the knowledge of one's own limitations.'

'Nervous young dons and students have before now been carried out in convulsions through being afraid to say boldly that they did not know.'

'Showing themselves,' said Miss Pyke across the Dean, 'less wise than Socrates, who made the admission fairly frequently.'

'For Heaven's sake,' said Wimsey, 'don't mention Socrates. It might start all over again.'

'Not now,' said the Dean. 'She will ask no questions now except for instruction.'

'There is a question on which I am anxious to be instructed,' said Miss Pyke, 'if you will not take it amiss.'

Miss Pyke, of course, was still worried about Dr. Threep's shirt-front, and determined on getting enlightenment. Harriet hoped that Wimsey would recognise her curiosity for what it was: not skittishness, but the embarrassing appetite for exact information which characterises the scholarly mind.

'That phenomenon,' he said, readily, 'comes within my own sphere of knowledge. It occurs because the human torso possesses a higher factor of variability than the ready-made shirt. The explosive sound you mention is produced when the shirt-front is slightly too long for the wearer. The stiff edges, being forced slightly apart by the inclination of the body come back into contact with a sharp click, similiar to that emitted by the elytra of certain beetles. It is not to be confused, however, with the ticking of the Death-watch, which is made by tapping with the jaws and is held to be a love-call. The clicking of the shirt-front has no amatory significance, and is, indeed, an embarrassment to the insect. It may be obviated by an increased care in selection or, in extreme cases, by having the garment made to measure.'

'Thank you so much,' said Miss Pyke. 'That is a most satisfactory explanation. At this time of day, it is perhaps not improper to adduce the parallel instance of the old-fashioned corset, which was subject to a similar inconvenience.'

'The inconvenience,' added Wimsey, 'was even greater in the case of plate armour, which had to be very well tailored to allow of movement at all.'

At this point, Miss Barton captured Harriet's attention with some remark or other, and she lost track of the conversation on the other side of the table. When she picked up the threads again, Miss Pyke was giving her neighbours some curious details about Ancient Minoan civilisation, and the Warden was apparently waiting till she had finished to pounce on Peter again. Turning to her right, Harriet saw that Miss Hillyard was watching the group with a curiously concentrated expression. Harriet asked her to pass the sugar, and she came back to earth with a slight start.

'They seem to be getting on very well over there,' said Harriet.

'Miss Pyke likes an audience,' said Miss Hillyard, with so much venom that Harriet was quite astonished.

'It's good for a man to have to do the listening sometimes,' she suggested.

Miss Hillyard agreed absently. After a slight pause, during which dinner proceeded without incident, she said:

'Your friend tells me he can obtain access for me to some private collections of historical documents in Florence. Do you suppose he means what he says?'

'If he says so, you may be sure he can and will.'

'That is a testimonial,' said Miss Hillyard. 'I am very glad to hear it.'

Meanwhile, the Warden had affected her capture, and was talking to Peter in a low tone and with some earnestness. He listened attentively, while he peeled an apple, the narrow coils of the rind sliding slowly over his fingers. She concluded with some question; and he shook his head.

'It is very unlikely. I should say there was no hope of it at all.'

Harriet wondered whether the subject of the Poison-Pen had risen at last to the surface; but presently he said:

'Three hundred years ago it mattered comparatively little. But now that you have the age of national self-realisation, the age of colonial expansion, the age of the barbarian invasions and the age of the decline and fall, all jammed cheek by jowl in time and space, all armed alike with poison-gas and going through the outward motions of an advanced civilisation,, principles have become more dangerous than passions. It's getting uncommonly easy to kill people in large numbers, and the first thing a principle does – if it really is a principle – is to kill somebody.'

' "The real tragedy is not the conflict of good with evil but of good with good"; that means a problem with no solution.'

'Yes. Afflicting, of course, to the tidy mind. One may either hulloo on the inevitable, and be called a blood-thirsty progressive; or one may try to gain time and be called a blood-thirsty reactionary. But when blood is their argument, all argument is apt to be – merely bloody.'

The Warden passed the adjective at its face-value.

'I sometimes wonder whether we gain anything by gaining time.'

'Well – if one leaves letters unanswered long enough, some of them answer themselves. Nobody can prevent the Fall of Troy, but a dull, careful person may manage to smuggle out the Lares and Penates – even at the risk of having the epithet *pius* tacked to his name.'

'The Universities are always being urged to march in the van of progress.'

'But epic actions are all fought by the rearguard – at Roncevaux and Thermopylæ.'

'Very well,' said the Warden, laughing, 'let us die in our tracks, having accomplished nothing but an epic.'

She collected the High Table with her eye, rose, and made a stately exit. Peter effaced himself politely against the panelling while the dons filed past him, arriving at the edge of the dais inn time to pick up Miss Shaw's scarf as it slipped from her shoulders. Harriet found herself descending the staircase between Miss Martin and Miss de Vine, who remarked:

'You are a courageous woman.'

'Why?' said Harriet lightly. 'To bring my friends here and have them put to the question?'

'Nonsense,' interrupted the Dean. 'We all behaved beautifully. Daniel is still uneaten – in fact; at one point he bit the lion. Was that genuine, by the way?'

'About tone-deafness? Probably just a little more genuine than he made out.'

'Will he lay traps all evening for us to walk into?'

Harriet realised for a moment how queer the whole situation was. Once again, she felt Wimsey as a dangerous alien and herself on the side of the women who, with so strange a generosity, were welcoming the inquisitor among them. She said, however:

'If he does, he will display all the mechanism in the most obliging manner.'

'After one is inside. That's very comforting.'

'That,' said Miss de Vine, brushing aside these surface commentaries, 'is a man able to subdue himself to his own ends. I should be sorry for anyone who came up against *his* principles – whatever they are, and if he has any.'

She detached herself from the other two, and went on into the Senior Common Room with a sombre face.

'Curious,' said Harriet. 'She is saying about Peter Wimsey exactly what I have always thought about herself.'

'Perhaps she recognises a kindred spirit.'

'Or a foe worthy of – I ought not to say that.'

Here Peter and his companion caught them up, and the Dean, joining Miss Shaw, went on in with her. Wimsey smiled at Harriet, an odd, interrogative smile.

'What's worrying you.'

'Peter – I feel exactly like Judas.'

'Feeling like Judas is part of the job. No job for a gentleman, I'm afraid. Shall we wash our hands like Pilate and be thoroughly respectable?'

She slid her hand under his arm.

'No; we're in for it now. We'll be degraded together.'

'That will be nice. Like the lovers in that Stroheim film, we'll go and sit on the sewer.' She could feel his bone and muscle, reassuringly human, under the fine broadcloth. She thought: 'He and I belong to the same world, and all these others are the aliens.' And then: 'Damn it all! this is our private fight – why should they have to join in?' But that was absurd.

'What do you want me to do, Peter?'

'Chuck the ball back to me if it runs out of the circle. Not obviously. Just exercise your devastating talent for keeping to the point and speaking the truth.'

'That sounds easy.'

'It is – for you. That's what I love you for. Didn't you know? Well, we can't stop to argue about it now; they'll think we're conspiring about something.'

She released his arm and went into the room ahead of him, feeling suddenly embarrassed and looking, in consequence, defiant. The coffee was already on the table, and the S.C.R. were gathered about it, helping themselves. She saw Miss Barton advance upon Peter, with a courteous offer of refreshment on her lips but the light of determination in her eye. Harriet did not for the moment care what happened to Peter. He had given her a new bone to worry. She provided herself with coffee and a cigarette, and retired with them and the bone into a corner. She had often wondered, in a detached kind of way, what it was that Peter valued in her and had apparently valued from that first day when she had stood in the dock and spoken for her own life. Now that she knew, she thought that a more unattractive pair of qualities could seldom have been put forward as an excuse for devotion.

'But do you really feel comfortable about it, Lord Peter?'

'No – I shouldn't recommend it as a comfortable occupation. But is your or my or anybody's comfort of very great importance?'

Miss Barton probably took that for flippancy; Harriet recognised the ruthless voice that had said, 'What does it matter if it hurts . . .' Let them fight it out . . . Unattractive; but if he meant what he said, it explained a great many things. Those were qualities that could be recognised under the most sordid conditions. . . . 'Detachment . . . if you ever find a person who likes you because of it, that liking is sincere.' That was Miss de Vine; and Miss de Vine was sitting not very far away, her eyes, behind their thick glasses, fixed on Peter with a curious, calculating look.

Conversations, carried on in groups, were beginning to falter and fall into silence. People were sitting down. The voices of Miss Allison and Miss Stevens rose into prominence. They were discussing some collegiate question, and they were doing it intently and desperately. They called upon Miss Burrows to give an opinion. Miss Shaw turned to Miss Chilperic and made a remark about the bathing at 'Spinsters' Splash.' Miss Chilperic replied elaborately – too elaborately; her answer took too long and attracted attention; she hesitated, became confused, and stopped speaking. Miss Lydgate, with a troubled face, was listening to an anecdote that Mrs. Goodwin was telling about her little boy; in the middle of it, Miss Hillyard, who was within earshot, rose pointedly, stabbed out her cigarette on a distant ash-tray, and moved slowly, and as though despite herself, to a window-seat close to where Miss Barton was still standing. Harriet could see her angry, smouldering glance fix itself on Peter's bent head and then jerk away across the quad, only to return again. Miss Edwards, close to Harriet and a little in front of her on a low chair, had her hands set squarely and rather mannishly on her knees, and was leaning forward; she had the air of waiting for something. Miss Pyke, on her feet, lighting a cigarette, was apparently looking for an opportunity to engage Peter's attention; she appeared eager and interested, and more at her ease than most of the others. The Dean, curled on a humpty, was frankly listening to what Peter and Miss Barton were saying. They were all listening, really, and at the same time most of them were trying to pretend that he was there as an ordinary guest – that he was not an enemy, not a spy. They were trying to prevent him from becoming openly the centre of attention as he was already the centre of consciousness.

The Warden, seated in a deep chair near the fireplace, gave nobody any help. One by one, the spurts of talk failed and died, leaving the one tenor floating, like a solo instrument executing a cadenza when the orchestra has fallen silent:

'The execution of the guilty is unpleasant – but not nearly so disturbing as the slaughter of the innocents. If you are out for my blood, won't you allow me to hand you a more serviceable weapon?'

He glanced round and, finding that everybody but Miss Pyke and themselves was sitting down silent, made a brief, interrogative pause, which looked like politeness, but which Harriet mentally classed as 'good theatre.'

Miss Pyke led the way to a large sofa near Miss Hillyard's window-seat and said, as she settled herself in the corner of it:

'Do you mean the murderer's victims?'

'No,' said Peter, 'I meant my own victims.'

He sat down between Miss Pyke and Miss Barton, and went on in a pleasantly conversational tone:

'For example; I happened to find out that a young woman had murdered an old one for her money. It didn't matter much: the old woman was dying in any case, and the girl (though she didn't know that) would have inherited the money in any case. As soon as I started to meddle, the girl set to work again, killed two innocent people to cover her tracks and murderously attacked three others. Finally she killed herself. If I'd left her alone, there might have been only one death instead of four.'

'Good gracious!' said Miss Pyke. 'But the woman would have been at large.'

'Oh, yes. She wasn't a nice woman, and she had a nasty influence on certain people. But who killed those other two innocents – she or society?'

'They were killed,' said Miss Barton, 'by her fear of the death-penalty. If the unfortunate woman had been medically treated, they and she would still be alive to-day.'

'I told you it was a good weapon. But it isn't as simple as all that. If she hadn't killed those others, we should probably never have caught her, and so far from being medically treated she would be living in prosperity – and incidentally corrupting one or two people's minds, if you think that of any importance.'

'You are suggesting, I think,' said the Warden, while Miss Barton rebelliously grappled with this problem, 'that those innocent victims died for the people; sacrificed to a social principle.'

'At any rate, to *your* social principles,' said Miss Barton

'Thank you. I thought you were going to say, to my inquisitiveness.'

'I might have done so,' said Miss Barton, frankly. 'But you lay claim to a principle, so we'll stick to that.'

'Who were the other three people attacked?' asked Harriet. (She had no fancy to let Miss Barton get away with it too easily.)

'A lawyer, a colleague of mine and myself. But that doesn't prove that I have any principles. I'm quite capable of getting killed for the fun of the thing. Who isn't?'

'I know,' said the Dean. 'It's funny that we get so solemn about murders and executions and mind so little about taking risks in motoring and swimming and climbing mountains and so on. I suppose we *do* prefer to die for the fun of the thing.'

'The social principle seems to be,' suggested Miss Pyke, 'that we should die for our fun and not other people's.'

'Of course I admit,' said Miss Barton, rather angrily, 'that murder must be prevented and murderers kept from doing further harm. But they ought not to be punished and they certainly ought not to be killed.'

'I suppose they ought to be kept in hospitals at vast expense, along with other unfit specimens,' said Miss Edwards. 'Speaking as a biologist, I must say I think public money might be better employed. What with the number of imbeciles and physical wrecks we allow to go about and propagate their species, we shall end by devitalising whole nations.'

'Miss Schuster-Slatt would advocate sterilisation,' said the Dean.

'They're trying it in Germany, I believe,' said Miss Edwards.

'Together,' said Miss Hillyard, 'with the relegation of woman to her proper place in the home.'

'But they execute people there quite a lot,' said Wimsey, 'so Miss Barton can't take over their organisation lock, stock and barrel.'

Miss Barton uttered a loud protest against any such suggestion, and returned to her contention that *her* social principles were opposed to violence of every description.

'Bosh!' said Miss Edwards. 'You can't carry through any principle without doing violence to somebody. Either directly or indirectly. Every time you disturb the balance of nature you let in violence. And if you leave nature alone you get violence in any case. I quite agree that murderers shouldn't be hanged – it's wasteful and unkind. But I don't agree that they should be comfortably fed and housed while decent people go short. Economically speaking, they should be used for laboratory experiments.'

'To assist the further preservation of the unfit?' asked Wimsey, drily.

'To assist in establishing scientific facts,' replied Miss Edwards, more drily still.

'Shake hands,' said Wimsey. 'Now we have found

common ground to stand on. Establish the facts, no matter what comes of it.'

'On that ground, Lord Peter,' said the Warden, 'your inquisitiveness becomes a principle. And a very dangerous one.'

'But the fact that A killed B isn't necessarily the whole of the truth,' persisted Miss Barton. 'A's provocation and state of health are facts, too.'

'Nobody surely disputes that,' said Miss Pyke. 'But one can scarcely ask the investigator to go beyond his job. If we mayn't establish any conclusion for fear somebody should make an injudicious use of it, we are back in the days of Galileo. There would be an end to discovery.'

'Well,' said the Dean. 'I wish we could stop discovering things like poison-gas.'

'There can be no objection to the making of discoveries,' said Miss Hillyard; 'but is it always expedient to publish them? In the case of Galileo, the Church—'

'You'll never get any scientist to agree there,' broke in Miss Edwards. 'To suppress a fact is to publish a falsehood.'

For a few minutes Harriet lost the thread of the discussion, which now became general. That it had been deliberately pushed to this point, she could see; but what Peter wanted to make of it, she had no idea. Yet he was obviously interested. His eyes, under their half-closed lids, were alert. He was like a cat waiting at a mousehole. Or was she half-consciously connecting him with his own blazon? 'Sable: three mice courant argent; a crescent for difference. The crest, a domestick catt. . . .'

'Of course,' said Miss Hillyard, in a hard, sarcastic voice, 'if you think private loyalties should come before loyalty to one's job. . . .'

('Couched as to spring, proper.') That was what he

409

had been waiting for, then. One could almost see the silken fur ripple.

'Of course, I don't say that one should be disloyal to one's job for private reasons,' said Miss Lydgate. 'But surely, if one takes on personal responsibilities, one owes a duty in that direction. If one's job interferes with them perhaps one should give up the job.'

'I quite agree,' said Miss Hillyard. 'But then, my private responsibilities are few, and possibly I have no right to speak. What is your opinion, Mrs. Goodwin?'

There was a most unpleasant pause.

'If you mean that personally,' said the Secretary, getting up and facing the Tutor, 'I am so far of your opinion that I have asked Dr. Baring to accept my resignation. Not because of any of the monstrous allegations that have been made about me, but because I realise that under the circumstances I can't do my work as well as I ought. But you are all very much mistaken if you think *I* am at the bottom of the trouble in this college. I'm going now, and you can say what you like about me – but may I say that anybody with a passion for facts will do better to collect them from unprejudiced sources. Miss Barton at least will admit that mental health is a fact like another.'

Into the horrified silence that followed, Peter dropped three words like lumps of ice.

'Please don't go.'

Mrs. Goodwin stopped short with her hand on the door.

'It would be a great pity,' said the Warden, 'to take anything personally that is said in a general discussion. I feel sure Miss Hillyard meant nothing of that kind. Naturally, some people have better opportunities than others for seeing both sides of a question. In your own line of work, Lord Peter, such conflicts of loyalty must frequently occur.'

'Oh, yes. I once thought I had the agreeable choice between hanging my brother or my sister. Fortunately, it came to nothing.'

'But supposing it had come to something?' demanded Miss Barton, pinning the *argumentum ad hominem* with a kind of relish.

'Oh, well— What does the ideal detective do then, Miss Vane?'

'Profesional etiquette,' said Harriet, 'would suggest an extorted confession, followed by poison for two in the library.'

'You see how easy it is, when you stick to the rules,' said Wimsey. 'Miss Vane feels no compunction. She wipes me out with a firm hand, rather than damage my reputation. But the question isn't always so simple. How about the artist of genius who has to choose between letting his family starve and painting pot-boilers to keep them?'

'He's no business to have a wife and family,' said Miss Hillyard.

'Poor devil! Then he has the further interesting choice between repressions and immorality. Mrs. Goodwin, I gather, would object to the repressions and some people might object to the immorality.'

'That doesn't matter,' said Miss Pyke. 'You have hypothesised a wife and family. Well – he could stop painting. That, if he really is a genius, would be a loss to the world. But he mustn't paint bad pictures – that would be really immoral.'

'Why?' asked Miss Edwards. 'What do a few bad pictures matter, more or less?'

'Of course they matter,' said Miss Shaw. She knew a

good deal about painting. 'A bad picture by a good painter is a betrayal of truth – his own truth.'

'That's only a relative kind of truth,' objected Miss Edwards.

The Dean and Miss Burrows fell headlong upon this remark, and Harriet, seeing the argument in danger of getting out of hand, thought it time to retrieve the ball and send it back. She knew now what was wanted, though not why it was wanted.

'If you can't agree about painters, make it someone else. Make it a scientist.'

'I've no objection to scientific pot-boilers,' said Miss Edwards. 'I mean, a popular book isn't necessarily unscientific.'

'So long,' said Wimsey, 'as it doesn't falsify the facts. But it might be a different kind of thing. To take a concrete instance – somebody wrote a novel called *The Search*—'

'C. P. Snow,' said Miss Burrows. 'It's funny you should mention that. It was the book that the—'

'I know,' said Peter. 'That's possibly why it was in my mind.'

'I never read the book,' said the Warden.

'Oh, I did,' said the Dean. 'It's about a man who starts out to be a scientist and gets on very well till, just as he's going to be appointed to an important executive post, he finds he's made a careless error in a scientific paper. He didn't check his assistant's results, or something. Somebody finds out, and he doesn't get the job. So he decides he doesn't really care about science after all.'

'Obviously not,' said Miss Edwards. 'He only cared about the post.'

'But,' said Miss Chilperic, 'if it was only a mistake—'

'The point about it,' said Wimsey, 'is what an elderly

scientist says to him. He tells him: "The only ethical principle which has made science possible is that the truth shall be told all the time. If we do not penalise false statements made in error, we open up the way for false statements by intention. And a false statement of fact, made deliberately, is the most serious crime a scientist can commit." Words to that effect. I may not be quoting quite correctly.'

'Well, that's true, of course. Nothing could possibly excuse deliberate falsification.'

'There's no sense in deliberate falsification, anyhow,' said the Bursar. 'What could anybody gain by it?'

'It has been done,' said Miss Hillyard, 'frequently. To get the better of an argument. Or out of ambition.'

'Ambition to be what?' cried Miss Lydgate. 'What satisfaction could one possibly get out of a reputation one knew one didn't deserve? It would be horrible.'

Her innocent indignation upset everybody's gravity.

'How about the Forged Decretals . . . Chatterton . . . Ossian . . . Henry Ireland . . . those Nineteenth-Century Pamphlets the other day . . .'

'I know,' said Miss Lydgate, perplexed. 'I know people do it. But *why*? They must be mad.'

'In the same novel,' said the Dean, 'somebody deliberately falsifies a result – later on, I mean – in order to get a job. And the man who made the original mistake finds it out. But he says nothing, because the other man is very badly off and has a wife and family to keep.'

'These wives and families!' said Peter.

'Does the author approve?' inquired the Warden.

'Well,' said the Dean, 'the book ends there, so I suppose he does.'

'But does anybody here approve? A false statement is published and the man who could correct it lets it go, out of charitable considerations. Would anybody here do that? There's your test case, Miss Barton, with no personalities attached.'

'Of course one couldn't do that,' said Miss Barton. 'Not for ten wives and fifty children.'

'Not for Solomon and all his wives and concubines? I congratulate you, Miss Barton, on striking such a fine, unfeminine note. Will nobody say a word for the women and children?'

('I knew he was going to be mischievous,' thought Harriet.)

'You'd like to hear it, wouldn't you?' said Miss Hillyard.

'You've got us in a cleft stick,' said the Dean. 'If we say it, you can point out that womanlinesss unfits us for learning; and if we don't, you can point out that learning makes us unwomanly.'

'Since I can make myself offensive either way,' said Wimsey, 'you have nothing to gain by not telling the truth.'

'The truth is,' said Mrs. Goodwin, 'that nobody could possibly defend the indefensible.'

'It sounds, anyway, like a manufactured case,' said Miss Allison, briskly. 'It could seldom happen; and if it did—'

'Oh, it happens,' said Miss de Vine. 'It has happened. It happened to me. I don't mind telling you – without names, of course. When I was at Flamborough College, examining for the professorial theses in York University, there was a man who sent in a very interesting paper on a historical subject. It was a most persuasive piece of argument; only I happened to know that the whole contention was quite untrue, because a letter that absolutely contradicted it was actually in existence in a

414

certain very obscure library in a foreign town. I'd come across it when I was reading up something else. That wouldn't have mattered, of course. But the internal evidence showed that the man must have had access to that library. So I had to make an inquiry, and I found that he really had been there and must have seen the letter and deliberately suppressed it.'

'But how could you be so sure he had seen the letter?' asked Miss Lydgate anxiously. 'He might carelessly have overlooked it. That would be a very different matter.'

'He not only had seen it,' replied Miss de Vine; 'he stole it. We made him admit as much. He had come upon that letter when his thesis was nearly complete, and he had no time to rewrite it. And it was a great blow to him apart from that, because he had grown enamoured of his own theory and couldn't bear to give it up.'

'That's the mark of an unsound scholar, I'm afraid,' said Miss Lydgate in a mournful tone, as one speaks of an incurable cancer.

'But here is the curious thing,' went on Miss de Vine. 'He was unscrupulous enough to let the false conclusion stand; but he was too good a historian to destroy the letter. He kept it.'

'You'd think,' said Miss Pyke, 'it would be as painful as biting on a sore tooth.'

'Perhaps he had some idea of rediscovering it some-day,' said Miss de Vine, 'and setting himself right with his conscience. I don't know, and I don't think he knew very well himself.'

'What happened to him?' asked Harriet.

'Well, that was the end of him, of course. He lost the professorship, naturally, and they took away his M.A. degree as well. A pity, because he was brilliant in his own way – and very good-looking, if that has anything to do with it.'

'Poor man!' said Miss Lydgate. 'He must have needed the post very badly.'

'It meant a good deal to him financially. He was married and not well off. I don't know what became of him. That was about six years ago. He dropped out completely. One was sorry about it, but there it was.'

'You couldn't possibly have done anything else,' said Miss Edwards.

'Of course not. A man as undependable as that is not only useless, but dangerous. He might do anything.'

'You'd think it would be a lesson to him,' said Miss Hillyard. 'It didn't pay, did it? Say he sacrificed his professional honour for the women and children we hear so much about – but in the end it left him worse off.'

'But that,' said Peter, 'was only because he committed the extra sin of being found out.'

'It seems to me,' began Miss Chilperic, timidly – and then stopped.

'Yes?' said Peter.

'Well,' said Miss Chilperic, 'oughtn't the women and children to have a point of view? I mean – suppose the wife knew that her husband had done a thing like that for her, what would she feel about it?'

'That's a very important point,' said Harriet. 'You'd think she'd feel too ghastly for words.'

'It depends,' said the Dean. 'I don't believe nine women out of ten would care a dash.'

'That's a monstrous thing to say,' cried Miss Hillyard.

'You think a wife might feel sensitive about her husband's honour – even if it was sacrificed on her account?' said Miss Stevens. 'Well – I don't know.'

'I should think,' said Miss Chilperic, stammering a

little in her earnestness, 'she would feel like a man who – I mean, wouldn't it be like living on somebody's immoral earnings?'

'There,' said Peter, 'if I may say so, I think you are exaggerating. The man who does that – if he isn't too far gone to have any feelings at all – is hit by other considerations, some of which have nothing whatever to do with ethics. But it is extremely interesting that you should make the comparison.' He looked at Miss Chilperic so intently that she blushed.

'Perhaps that was rather a stupid thing to say.'

'No. But if it ever occurs to people to value the honour of the mind equally with the honour of the body, we shall get a social revolution of a quite unparalleled sort – and very different from the kind that is being made at the moment.'

Miss Chilperic looked so much alarmed at the idea of fostering social revolution that only the opportune entry of two Common-Room scouts to remove the coffee-cups and relieve her of the necessity of replying seemed to have saved her from sinking through the floor.

'Well,' said Harriet, 'I agree absolutely with Miss Chilperic. If anybody did a dishonourable thing and then said he did it for one's own sake, it would be the last insult. How could one ever feel the same to him again?'

'Indeed,' said Miss Pyke, 'it must surely vitiate the whole relationship.'

'Oh, nonsense!' cried the Dean. 'How many women care two hoots about anybody's intellectual integrity? Only over-educated women like us. So long as the man didn't forge a cheque or rob the till or do something socially degrading, most women would think he was perfectly justified. Ask Mrs. Bones the Butcher's Wife or

Miss Tape the Tailor's Daughter how much they would worry about suppressing a fact in a mouldy old historical thesis.'

'They'd back up their husbands in any case,' said Miss Allison. 'My man, right or wrong, they'd say. Even if he *did* rob the till.'

'Of course they would,' said Miss Hillyard. 'That's what the man wants. *He* wouldn't say thank you for a critic on the hearth.'

'He must have the womanly woman, you think?' said Harriet. 'What is it, Annie? My coffee-cup? Here you are . . . Somebody who will say, "The greater the sin the greater the sacrifice – and consequently the greater devotion." Poor Miss Schuster-Slatt! . . . I suppose it is comforting to be told that one is loved whatever one does.'

'Ah, yes,' said Peter, in his reediest, wood-wind voice:

'And these say: "No more now my knight
Or God's knight any longer" – you,
Being than they so much more white,
So much more pure and good and true,

'Will cling to me for ever—

William Morris had his moments of being a hundred-per-cent manly man.'

'Poor Morris!' said the Dean.

'He was young at the time,' said Peter, indulgently. 'It's odd, when you come to think of it, that the expressions "manly" and "womanly" should be almost more offensive than their opposites. One is tempted to believe that there may be something indelicate about sex after all.'

'It all comes of this here eddication,' pronounced the Dean, as the door shut behind the last of the coffee-service. 'Here we sit round in a ring, dissociating ourselves from kind Mrs. Bones and that sweet girl, Miss Tape—'

'Not to mention,' put in Harriet, 'those fine, manly fellows, the masculine Tapes and Boneses—'

'And clacking on in the *most* unwomanly manner about intellectual integrity.'

'While I,' said Peter, 'sit desolate in the midst, like a lodge in a garden of cucumbers.'

'You look it,' said Harriet, laughing. 'The sole relic of humanity in a cold, bitter and indigestible wilderness.'

There was a laugh, and a momentary silence. Harriet could feel a nervous tension in the room – little threads of anxiety and expectation strung out, meeting, crossing, quivering. Now, they were all saying to themselves, now something is going to be said about IT. The ground has been surveyed, the coffee has been cleared out of the road, the combatants are stripped for action – now, this amiable gentleman with the well-filed tongue will come out in his true colours as an inquisitor, and it is all going to be very uncomfortable.

Lord Peter took out his handkerchief, polished his monocle carefully, readjusted it, looked rather severely at the Warden, and lifted up his voice in emphatic, pained and querulous complaint about the Corporation dump.

The Warden had gone, expressing courteous thanks to Miss Lydgate for the hospitality of the Senior Common Room, and graciously inviting his lordship to call upon her in her own house at any convenient time during his stay in Oxford. Various dons rose up and drifted away, murmuring that they had essays to look through before they went to bed. The talk had ranged pleasantly over a variety of topics. Peter had let the reins drop from his hands and let it go whither it would, and Harriet, realising this, had scarcely troubled to follow it. In the end, there remained only herself and Peter, the Dean, Miss Edwards (who seemed to have taken a strong fancy to Peter's conversation), Miss Chilperic, silent and half-hidden in an obscure position and, rather to Harriet's surprise, Miss Hillyard.

The clocks struck eleven. Wimsey roused himself and said he thought he had better be getting along. Everybody rose. The Old Quad was dark, except for the gleam of lighted windows; the sky had clouded, and a rising wind stirred the boughs of the beech trees.

'Well, good night,' said Miss Edwards. 'I'll see that you get a copy of that paper about blood-groups. I think you'll find it of interest.'

'I shall, indeed,' said Wimsey. 'Thank you very much.'

Miss Edwards strode briskly away.

'Good night, Lord Peter.'

'Good night, Miss Chilperic. Let me know when the social revolution is about to begin and I'll come to die upon the barricades.'

'I think you would,' said Miss Chilperic, astonishingly, and, in defiance of tradition, gave him her hand.

'Good night,' said Miss Hillyard, to the world in general, and whisked quickly past them with her head high.

Miss Chilperic flitted off into the darkness like a pale moth, and the Dean said, 'Well!' And then, interrogatively, 'Well?'

'Pass, and all's well,' said Peter, placidly.

'There were one or two moments, weren't there?' said the Dean. 'But on the whole – as well as could be expected.'

'I enjoyed myself very much,' said Peter, with the mischievous note back in his voice.

'I bet you did,' said the Dean. 'I wouldn't trust you a yard. Not a yard.'

'Oh, yes, you would,' said he. 'Don't worry.'

The Dean, too, was gone.

'You left your gown in my room yesterday,' said Harriet. 'You'd better come and fetch it.'

'I brought yours back with me and left it at the Jowett Walk Lodge. Also your dossier. I expect they've been taken up.'

'You didn't leave the dossier lying about!'

'What do you take me for? It's wrapped up and sealed.'

They crossed the quad slowly.

'There are a lot of questions I want to ask, Peter.'

'Oh, yes. And there's one I want to ask you. What is your second name? The one that begins with a D?'

'Deborah, I'm sorry to say. Why?'

'Deborah? Well, I'm damned. All right. I won't call you by it. There's Miss de Vine, I see, still working.'

The curtains of the Fellow's window were drawn back this time, and they could see her dark untidy head, bent over a book.

'She interests me very much,' said Peter.

'I like her, you know.'

'So do I.'

'But I'm afraid those are her kind of hairpins.'

'I know they are,' said he. He took his hand from his pocket and held it out. They were close under Tudor, and the light from an adjacent window showed a melancholy, spraddle-legged hairpin lying across his palm. 'She shed this on the dais after dinner. You saw me pick it up.'

'I saw you pick up Miss Shaw's scarf.'

'Always the gentleman. May I come up with you, or is that against the regulations!'

'You can come up.'

There were a number of students scurrying about the corridors in undress, who looked at Peter with more curiosity than annoyance. In Harriet's room, they found her gown lying on the table, together with the dossier. Peter picked up the book, examined the paper and string and the seals which secured them, each one stamped with the crouching cat and arrogant Wimsey motto.

'If that's been opened, I'll make a meal of hot sealing-wax.'

He went to the window and looked out into the quad.

'Not a bad observation post – in its way. Thanks. That's all I wanted to look at.'

He showed no further curiosity, but took the gown she handed to him and followed her downstairs again.

They were half-way across the quad when he said suddenly:

'Harriet. Do you really prize honesty above every other thing?'

'I think I do. I hope so. Why?'

'If you don't, I am the most blazing fool in Christendom. I am busily engaged in sawing off my own branch. If I am honest, I shall probably lose you altogether. If I am not—'

His voice was curiously rough, as though he were trying to control something; not, she thought, bodily pain or passion, but something more fundamental.

'If you are not,' said Harriet, 'then *I* shall lose *you*, because you wouldn't be the same person, would you?'

'I don't know. I have a reputation for flippant insincerity. You think I'm honest?'

'I know you are. I couldn't imagine your being anything else.'

'And yet at this moment I'm trying to insure myself against the effects of my own honesty. "I have tried if I could reach that great resolution, to be honest without a thought of heaven or hell." It looks as though I should get hell either way, though; so I need scarcely bother about the resolution. I believe you mean what you say – and I hope I should do the same thing if I didn't believe a word of it.'

'Peter, I haven't an idea what you're talking about.'

'All the better. Don't worry. I won't behave like this another time. "The Duke drained a dipper of brandy-and-water and became again the perfect English gentleman." Give me your hand.'

She gave it to him, and he held it for a moment in a firm clasp, and then drew her arm through his. They moved on into the New Quad, arm in arm, in silence. As they passed the archway at the foot of the Hall stairs, Harriet fancied she heard somebody stir in the darkness and saw the faint glimmer of a watching face; but it was gone before she could draw Peter's attention to it.

Padgett unlocked the gate for them; Wimsey, stepping pre-occupied over the threshold, tossed him a heedless good night.

'Good night, Major Wimsey, sir!'

'Hullo!' Peter brought back the foot that was already in St. Cross Road, and looked closely into the porter's smiling face.

'My god, yes! Stop a minute. Don't tell me. Caudry – 1918 – I've got it! Padgett's the name. Corporal Padgett.'

'Quite right, sir.'

'Well, well, well. I'm damned glad to see you. Looking dashed fit, too. How are you keeping?'

'Fine, thank you, sir.' Padgett's large and hairy paw closed warmly over Peter's long fingers. 'I says to my wife, when I 'eard you was 'ere, "I'll lay you anything you like," I says, "the Major won't have forgotten."'

'By jove, no. Fancy finding you here! Last time. I saw you, I was being carried away on a stretcher.'

'That's right, sir. I 'ad the pleasure of 'elping to dig you out.'

'I know you did. I'm glad to see you now, but I was a dashed sight gladder to see you then.'

'Yes, sir. Gorblimey, sir – well, there! We thought you was gone that time. I says to Hackett – remember little Hackett, sir?'

'The little red-headed blighter? Yes, of course. What's become of him?'

'Driving a lorry over at Reading, sir, married and three kids. I says to Hackett, "Lor' lumme!" I says, "there's old Winderpane gawn – excuse me, sir – and he says, "'Ell! wot ruddy luck!" So I says, "Don't stand there grizzlin' – maybe 'e ain't gawn after all." So we—'

'No,' said Wimsey. 'I fancy I was more frightened than hurt. Unpleasant sensation, being buried alive.'

'Well, sir! W'en we finds yer there at the bottom o' that there old Boche dug-out with a big beam acrost yer, I says to Hackett, "Well," I says, "'e's all 'ere, anyhow." And he says, "Thank gawd for Jerry!" 'e says – meanin', if it 'adn't been for that there dug-out—'

'Yes,' said Wimsey. 'I had a bit of luck there. We lost poor Mr. Danbury, though.'

'Yes, sir. Bad thing, that was. A nice young gentleman. Ever see anything of Captain Sidgwick nowadays, sir?'

'Oh, yes. I saw him only the other day at the Bellona Club. He's not very fit these days, I'm sorry to say. Got a dose of gas, you know. Lungs groggy.'

'Sorry to hear that, sir. Remember how put about 'e was over that there pig—'

'Hush, Padgett. The less said about that pig, the better.'

'Yes, sir. Nice bit o' crackling that pig 'ad on 'im. Coo!' Padgett smacked reminiscent lips. 'You 'eard wot 'appened to Sergeant-major Toop?'

'Toop? No – I've quite lost sight of him. Nothing unpleasant, I hope. Best sergeant-major I ever had.'

'Ah! he was a one.' Padgett's grin widened. 'Well, sir, 'e found 'is match all right. Little bit of a thing – no 'igher than that, but lummy!'

'Go on, Padgett. You don't say so.'

'Yes, sir. When I was workin' in the camel 'ouse at the Zoo—'

'Good God, Padgett!'

'Yes, sir – I see them there and we passed the time o' day. Went round to look 'em up afterwards. Well, there! She give 'im sergeant-major all right. Put 'im through the 'oop proper. You know the old song: Naggin' at a feller as is six foot three—'

'And her only four foot two! Well, well! How are the mighty fallen! By the bye, I'll tell you who I ran into the other day – now, this will surprise you—'

The stream of reminiscence ran remorselessly on, till Wimsey, suddenly reminded of his manners, apologised to Harriet and plunged hastily out, with a promise to return for another chat over old times, Padgett, still beaming, swung the heavy gate to, and locked it.

'Ah!' said Padgett, 'he ain't changed much, the major 'asn't. He was a lot younger then, o' course – only just gazetted – but he was a regular good officer for all that – and a terror for eye-wash, *And* shavin' – lumme!'

425

Padgett, supporting himself with one hand against the brickwork of the lodge, appeared lost in the long ago.

' "Now, men," 'e'd say, when we was expectin' a bit of a strafe, "if you gotter face your Maker, fer Gawd's sake, face 'Im with a clean chin." Ah! Winderpane, we called 'im, along of the eyeglass, but meanin' no disrespect. None on us wouldn't 'ear a word agin 'im. Now, there was a chap came to us from another unit – 'ulkin' foul-mouthed fellow, wot nobody took to much – 'Uggins, that was the name, 'Uggins. Well, this bloke thinks 'e's goin' to be funny, see – and 'e starts callin' the major Little Percy, and usin' opprobrious epithets—'

Here Padgett paused, to select an epithet fit for a lady's ear, but, failing, repeated,

'Opprobrious epithets, miss. And I says to 'im – mind you, this was afore I got my stripes; I was jes a private then, same as 'Uggins – I says to 'im. "Now, that's quite enough o' that." And 'e says to me— Well, anyway, the end of it was, we 'ad a lovely scrap, all round the 'ouses.'

'Dear me,' said Harriet.

'Yes, miss. We was in rest at the time, and next morning, when the sergeant-major falls us in for parade – coo, lummy! we was a pair o' family portraits. The sergeant-major – Sergeant-major Toop, that was, 'im wot got married like I was sayin' – 'e didn't say nothin' – 'e knew. And the adjutant, 'e knew too, and 'e didn't say nothin' neither. And blest if, in the middle of it all, we don't see the Major comin' strollin' out. So the adjutant forms us up into line, and I stands there at attention, 'oping as 'Uggins's face looked worse nor what mine did. "Morning," says the Major; and the adjutant and Sergeant-major Toop says, "Morning, sir." So 'e starts to chat casual-like to the sergeant-major, and I see 'is eye goin' up and down the line. "Sergeant-major!" says he, all of a sudden. "Sir!" says the sergeant-major. "What's the man there been doin' to 'imself?" says 'e, meanin' me. "Sir?" says the sergeant-major, starin' at me like 'e was surprised to see me. "Looks as if he'd had a nasty accident," says the Major. "And what about that other fellow? Don't like to see that sort of thing. Not smart. Fall 'em out." So the sergeant-major falls us both out. "H'm" says the Major. "I see. What's this man's name?" "Padgett, sir," says the sergeant-major. "Oh," says he. "Well, Padgett, what have you been doing to get yourself into a mess like that?" "Fell over a bucket, sir," says I, starin' 'ard over 'is shoulder with the only eye I could see out of. "Bucket?" says 'e, "very awkward things, buckets. And this other man – I suppose he trod on the mop, eh, sergeant-major?" "Major wants to know if you trod on the mop," says Sergeant-major Toop,. "Yessir," says 'Uggins, talkin' like 'is mouth 'urt 'im. "Well," says the Major, "when you've got this lot dismissed, give these two men a bucket and a mop a-piece and put 'em on fatigue. That'll learn 'em to 'andle these dangerous implements." "Yessir," says Sergeant-major Toop. "Carry on," says the Major. So we carries on. 'Uggins says to me arterwards. "D'you think 'e knew!" "Knew?" says I, "course 'e knew. Ain't much 'e don't know." Arter that, 'Uggins kep'' 'is epithets to 'isself.'

Harriet expressed due appreciation of this anecdote, which was delivered with a great deal of gusto, and took leave of Padgett. For some reason, this affair of a mop and a bucket seemed to have made Padgett Peter's slave for life. Men were very odd.

There was nobody under the Hall arches as she returned, but as she passed the West end of the Chapel, she thought she saw something dark pass like a shadow into the Fellows' Garden. She followed it. Her eyes were growing accustomed to the dimness of the summer night and she could see the figure walking swiftly up and down, up and down, and hear the rustle of its long skirt upon the grass.

There was only one person in College who had worn a trailing frock that evening, and that was Miss Hillyard. She walked in the Fellows' Garden for an hour and a half.

18

Go tell that witty fellow, my godson, to get home. It is no season to fool it here!

QUEEN ELIZABETH

'Lor'!' said the Dean.

She gazed with interest from the Senior Common Room window, teacup in hand.

'What's the matter?' inquired Miss Allison.

'*Who* is this incredibly beautiful young man?'

'Flaxman's fiancé, I expect, isn't it?'

'A beautiful young man?' said Miss Pyke. 'I should like to see him.' She moved to the window.

'Don't be ridiculous,' said the Dean. 'I know Flaxman's Byron by heart. This is an ash-blond in a House blazer,'

'Oh, dear me!' said Miss Pyke. 'Apollo Belvedere in spotless flannels. He appears to be unattached. Remarkable.'

Harriet put down her cup and rose from the depths of the largest armchair.

'Perhaps he belongs to that bunch playing tennis,' hazarded Miss Allison.

'Little Cooke's scrubby friends? My *dear*!'

'Why all the excitement, anyway?' asked Miss Hillyard.

'Beautiful young men are always exciting,' said the Dean.

'That,' said Harriet, at length getting a glimpse of the wonder-youth over Miss Pyke's shoulder, 'is Viscount Saint-George.'

'Another of your aristocratic friends?' asked Miss Barton.

'His nephew,' replied Harriet; not very coherently.

'Oh!' said Miss Barton. 'Well, I don't see why you need all gape at him like a lot of school-girls.'

She crossed over to the table, cut herself a slice of cake and glanced casually out of the farther window.

Lord Saint-George stood, with a careless air of owning the place, at the corner of the Library Wing, watching a game of tennis being played between two bare-backed students and two young men whose shirts kept on escaping from their belts. Growing tired of this, he sauntered past the windows towards Queen Elizabeth, his eye roving over a group of Shrewsburians a-sprawl under the beeches, like that of a young Sultan inspecting a rather unpromising consignment of Circassian slaves.

'Supercilious little beast!' thought Harriet; and wondered if he was looking for her. If he was, he could wait, or ask properly at the Lodge.

'Oho!' said the Dean. 'So *that's* how the milk got into the coconut!'

From the door of the Library Wing there issued slowly Miss de Vine, and behind her, grave and deferential, Lord Peter Wimsey. They skirted the tennis court in earnest conversation. Lord Saint-George, viewing them from afar, advanced to meet them. They joined forces on the path. They stood for a little time talking. They moved away towards the Lodge.

'Dear me!' said the Dean. 'Abduction of Helen de Vine by Paris and Hector.'

'No, no,' said Miss Pyke. 'Paris was the brother of

Hector, not his nephew. I do not think he had any uncles.'

'Talking of uncles,' said the Dean, 'is it true, Miss Hillyard, that Richard III – I thought she was here.'

'She *was* here,' said Harriet.

'Helen is being returned to us,' said the Dean. 'The siege of Troy is postponed.'

The trio were returning again up the path. Half-way along Miss de Vine took leave of the two men and returned towards her own room.

At that moment, the watchers in the S.C.R. were petrified to behold a portent. Miss Hillyard emerged from the foot of the Hall stair, bore down upon the uncle and nephew, addressed them, cut Lord Peter neatly off from his convoy and towed him firmly away towards the New Quad.

'Glory *alleluia!*' said the Dean. 'Hadn't you better go out and rescue your young friend? He's been deserted again.'

'You could offer him a cup of tea,' suggested Miss Pyke. 'It would be an agreeable diversion for us.'

'I'm surprised at you, Miss Pyke,' said Miss Barton. 'No man is safe from women like you.'

'Now, where have I heard that sentiment before?' said the Dean.

'In one of the Poison-letters,' said Harriet.

'If you're suggesting—' began Miss Barton.

'I'm only suggesting,' said the Dean, 'that it's a bit of a cliché.'

'I meant it for a joke,' retorted Miss Barton, angrily. 'Some people have no sense of humour.'

She went out, and slammed the door. Lord Saint-George had wandered back and was sitting in the loggia leading up to the Library. He rose politely as Miss Barton stalked past him on the way to her room, and made some remark, to which the Fellow replied briefly, but with a smile.

'Insinuating men, these Wimseys,' said the Dean. 'Vamping the S.C.R. right and left.'

Harriet laughed, but in Saint-George's quick, appraising glance at Miss Barton she had again seen his uncle look for a moment out of his eyes. These family resemblances were unnerving. She curled herself into the window-seat and watched for nearly ten minutes, The viscount sat still, smoking a cigarette, and looking entirely at his ease. Miss Lydgate, Miss Burrows and Miss Shaw came in and began to pour out tea. The tennis-party finished the set and moved away. Then, from the left, came a quick, light step along the gravel walk.

'Hullo!' said Harriet to the owner of the step.

'Hullo!' said Peter. 'Fancy seeing you here!' He grinned. 'Come and talk to Gerald. He's in the loggia.'

'I see him quite plainly,' said Harriet. 'His profile has been much admired.'

'As a good adopted aunt, why didn't you go and be kind to the poor lad?'

'I never was one to interfere. I keep myself *to* myself.'

'Well, come now.'

Harriet got down from the window-seat and joined Wimsey outside.

'I brought him here,' said Peter, 'to see if he could make any identifications. But he doesn't seem able to.'

Lord Saint-George greeted Harriet enthusiastically.

'There was another female went past me,' he said, turning to Peter. 'Grey hair badly bobbed. Earnest manner. Dressed in sackcloth. Institutional touch about her. I got speech of her.'

'Miss Barton,' said Harriet.

'Right sort of eyes; wrong sort of voice. I don't think it's her. It might be the one that collared you, Uncle. She had a kind of a lean and hungry look.'

'H'm!' said Peter. 'How about the first one?'

'I'd like to see her without her glasses.'

'If you mean Miss de Vine,' said Harriet, 'I doubt whether she could see very far without them.'

'That's a point,' said Peter, thoughtfully.

'I'm sorry to be so vague and all that,' said Lord Saint-George. 'But it's not easy to identify a hoarse whisper and a pair of eyes seen once by moonlight.'

'No,' said Peter, 'it needs a good deal of practice.'

'Practice be blowed,' retorted his nephew. 'I'm not going to make a practice of it.'

'It's not a bad sport,' said Peter, 'You might take it up till you can start games again.'

'How's the shoulder getting on?' inquired Harriet.

'Oh, not too bad, thanks. The massage bloke is working wonders with it. I can lift the old arm shoulder-high now. It's quite serviceable – for some things.'

By the way of demonstration he threw the damaged arm around Harriet's shoulders, and kissed her rapidly and expertly before she could dodge him.

'Children, children!' cried his uncle, plaintively, 'remember where you are.'

'It's all right for *me*,' said Lord Saint-George. '*I'm* an adopted nephew. Isn't that right, Aunt Harriet?'

'Not bang underneath the windows of the S.C.R.,' said Harriet.

'Come round the corner, then,' said the viscount, impenitently, 'and I'll do it again. As Uncle Peter says, these things need a good deal of practice.'

He was impudently set upon tormenting his uncle, and Harriet felt extremely angry with him. However, to show

433

annoyance was to play into his hands. She smiled upon him pityingly and uttered the Brasenose porter's classic rebuke:

'It's no good you making a noise, gentlemen. The Dean ain't a-coming down to-night.'

This actually silenced him for the moment. She turned to Peter, who said:

'Have you any commissions in Town?'

'Why, are you going back?'

'I'm running up to-night and on to York in the morning. I expect to get back on Thursday.'

'York?'

'Yes; I want to see a man there – about a dog, and all that.'

'Oh, I see. Well – if you wouldn't be out of your way to call at my flat, you might take up a few chapters of manuscript to my secretary. I'd rather trust you than the post. Could you manage it?'

'With very great pleasure,' said Wimsey, formally.

She ran up to her room to get the papers, and from the window observed that the Wimsey family was having the matter out with itself. When she came down with the parcel she found the nephew waiting at the door of Tudor, rather red in the face.

'Please, I am to apologise.'

'I should think so,' said Harriet, severely. 'I can't be disgraced like this in my own quad. Frankly, I can't afford it.'

'I'm most frightfully sorry,' said Lord Saint-George. 'It was rotten of me. Honestly, I wasn't thinking of anything except getting Uncle Peter's goat. And if it's any satisfaction to you,' he added, ruefully, 'I got it'

'Well, be decent to him; he's very decent to you.'

'I will be good,' said Peter's nephew, taking the parcel

from her, and they proceeded amicably together till Peter rejoined them at the Lodge.

'Damn that boy!' said Wimsey, when he had sent Saint-George ahead to start up the car.

'Oh, Peter, don't worry about every little thing so dreadfully. What does it matter? He only wanted to tease you.'

'It's a pity he can't find some other way to do it. I seem to be a perfect mill-stone tied round your neck, and the sooner I clear out the better.'

'Oh, for goodness' sake!' said Harriet, irritated. 'If you're going to be morbid about it, it certainly would be better for *you* if you *did* clear out. I've told you so before.'

Lord Saint-George, finding his elders dilatory, blew a cheerful 'hi-tiddley-hi-ti, pom, pom' on the horn.

'Damn and blast!' said Peter. He took gate and path at a bound, pushed his nephew angrily out of the driving-seat, jerked the door of the Daimler to noisily and shot off up the road with a bellowing roar. Harriet, finding herself unexpectedly possessed of a magnificent fit of bad temper, went back, determined to extract the last ounce of enjoyment out of it; an exercise in which she was greatly helped by the discovery that the little episode on the loggia had greatly intrigued the Senior Common Room, and by learning from Miss Allison, after Hall, that Miss Hillyard, when she heard of it, had made some very unpleasant observations, which it was only right that Miss Vane should know about.

Oh, God! thought Harriet, alone in her room, what have I done, more than thousands of other people, except have the rotten luck to be tried for my life and have the whole miserable business dragged out into daylight? . . .

Anybody would think I'd been punished enough. . . . But nobody can forget it for a moment. . . . I can't forget it. . . . Peter can't forget it. . . . If Peter wasn't a fool he'd chuck it. . . . He must see how hopeless it all is. . . . Does he think I like to see him suffering vicarious agonies? . . . Does he really suppose I could ever marry him for the pleasure of seeing him suffer agonies? . . . Can't he see that the only thing for me to do is to keep out of it all? . . . What the devil possessed me to bring him to Oxford? . . . Yes – and I thought it would be so nice to retire to Oxford . . . to have 'unpleasant observations' made about me by Miss Hillyard, who's half potty, if you ask me. . . . Somebody's potty, anyhow . . . that seems to be what happens to one if one keeps out of the way of love and marriage and all the rest of the muddle. . . . Well if Peter fancies I'm going to 'accept the protection of his name' and be grateful, he's damn well mistaken. . . . A nice, miserable business that'd be for him. . . . It's a nice, miserable business for him, too, if he really wants me – if he does – and can't have what he wants because I had the rotten luck to be tried for a murder I didn't do. . . . It looks as if he was going to get hell either way. . . . Well, let him get hell, it's his look-out. . . . It's a pity he saved me from being hanged – he probably wishes by now he'd left me alone. . . . I suppose any decently grateful person would give him what he wants. . . . But it wouldn't be much gratitude to make him miserable. . . . We should both be perfectly miserable, because neither of us could ever forget. . . . I very nearly did forget the other day on the river. . . . And I had forgotten this afternoon, only he remembered it first. . . . Damn that impudent little beast! how horribly cruel the young can be to the middle-aged! . . . I wasn't frightfully kind myself. . . . And I did know what I was doing. . . . It's a good thing Peter's gone . . . but I wish he hadn't gone and left me in this ghastly place where people go off their heads and write horrible letters. . . .. 'When I am from him I am dead till I be with him.' . . . No, it won't do to feel like that. . . . I won't get mixed up with that kind of thing again. . . . I'll stay out of it. . . . I'll stay here . . . where people go queer in their heads. . . . Oh, God, what have I done, that I should be such a misery to myself and other people? Nothing more than thousands of women . . .

Round and round, like a squirrel in a cage, till at last Harriet had to say firmly too herself: This won't do, or I shall go potty myself. I'd better keep my mind on the job. What's taken Peter to York? Miss de Vine? If I hadn't lost my temper I might have found out, instead of wasting time in quarrelling. I wonder if he's made any notes on the dossier.

She took up the loose-leaf book, which was still wrapped in its paper and string and sealed all over with the Wimsey crest. 'As my Whimsy takes me' – Peter's whimsies had taken him into a certain amount of trouble. She broke the seals impatiently; but the result was disappointing. He had marked nothing – presumably he had copied out anything he wanted. She turned the pages, trying to piece some sort of solution together, but too tired to think coherently. And then – yes; here was his writing, sure enough, but not on a page of the dossier. This was the unfinished sonnet – and of all the idiotic things to do, to leave half-finished sonnets mixed up with one's detective work for other people to see! A school-girl trick, enough to make anybody blush. Particularly since, from what she remembered of the sonnet, its sentiments had become remarkably inappropriate to the state of her feelings.

But here it was: and in the interval it had taken to itself a sestet and stood, looking a little unbalanced, with her own sprawling hand above and Peter's deceptively neat script below, like a large top on a small spindle.

Here then at home, by no more storms distrest,
  Folding laborious hands we sit, wings furled;
  Here in close perfume lies the rose-leaf curled,
Here the sun stands and knows not east nor west,
Here no tide runs; we have come, last and best,
  From the wide zone in dizzying circles hurled
  To that still centre where the spinning world
Sleeps on its axis, to the heart of rest.

Lay on thy whips, O Love, that me upright,
  Poised on the perilous point, in no lax bed
    May sleep, as tension at the verberant core
Of music sleeps; for, if thou spare to smite,
  Staggering, we stoop, stooping, fall dumb and dead,
    And, dying so, sleep our sweet sleep no more.

Having achieved this, the poet appeared to have lost countenance for he had added the comment:

'A very conceited, metaphysical conclusion!'

So. So there was the turn she had vainly sought for the sestet! Her beautiful, big, peaceful humming-top turned to a whip-top, and sleeping, as it were, upon compulsion. (And, damn him! how *dared* he picked up her word 'sleep' and use it four times in as many lines, and each time in a different foot, as though juggling with the accent-shift were child's play? And drag out the last half-line with those great, heavy, drugged, drowsy mono-syllables, contradicting the sense so as to deny their own contradiction? It was not one of the world's great sestets, but it was considerably better than her own octave: which was monstrous of it.)

But if she wanted an answer to her questions about Peter, there it was, quite appallingly plain. He did not want to forget, or to be quiet, or to be spared things, or to stay put. All he wanted was some kind of central stability, and he was apparently ready to take anything that came along, so long as it stimulated him to keep that precarious balance. And of course, if he really felt like that, everything he had ever said or done, as far as she was concerned, was perfectly consistent. 'Mine is only a balance of opposing forces.' . . . 'What does it matter if it hurts like hell, so long as it makes a good book?'. . . 'What is the use of making mistakes if you don't make use of them?' . . . 'Feeling like Judas is part of the job.' . . . 'The first thing a principle does is to kill somebody.' . . . If that was his attitude, it was clearly ridiculous to urge him, in kindly tones, to stand aside for fear he might get a rap over the shins.

He had tried standing aside. 'I have been running away from myself for twenty years, and it doesn't work.' He no longer believed that the Ethiopian could change his skin to rhinoceros hide. Even in the five years or so that she had known him, Harriet had seen him strip off his protections, layer by layer, till there was uncommonly little left but the naked truth.

That, then, was what he wanted her for. For some reason, obscure to herself and probably also to him, she had the power to force him outside his defences. Perhaps, seeing her struggling in a trap of circumstances, he had walked out deliberately to her assistance. Or perhaps the sight of her struggles had warned him what might happen to him, if he remained in a trap of his own making.

Yet with all this, he seemed willing to let her run back behind the barriers of the mind, provided – yes, he was consistent after all – provided she would make her own way of escape through her work. He was, in fact, offering her the choice between himself and Wilfrid. He did recognise that she had an outlet which he had not.

And that, she supposed, was why he was so morbidly sensitive about his own part in the comedy. His own needs were (as he saw the matter) getting between her and her legitimate way of escape. They involved her in difficulties which he could not share, because she had consistently refused him the right to share them. He had nothing of his nephew's cheerful readiness to take and have. Careless, selfish little beast, thought Harriet (meaning the viscount), can't he leave his uncle alone?

. . . It was just conceivable, by the way, that Peter was quite plainly and simply and humanly jealous of his nephew – not, of course, of his relations with Harriet (which would be disgusting and ridiculous), but of the careless young egotism which made those relations possible.

And, after all, Peter had been right. It was difficult to account for Lord Saint-George's impertinence without allowing people to assume that she was on terms with Peter which would explain that kind of thing. It had undoubtedly made an awkwardness. It was easy to say, 'Oh, yes. I knew him slightly and went to see him when he was laid up after a motor accident.' She did not really very much mind if Miss Hillyard supposed that with a person of her dubious reputation all and any liberties might be taken. But she did mind the corollary that might be drawn about Peter. That after five years' patient friendship he should have acquired only the right to look on while his nephew romped in public went near to making him look a fool. But anything else would not be true. She had placed him in exactly that imbecile position, and she admitted that that was not very pretty conduct.

She went to bed thinking more about another person than about herself. This goes to prove that even minor poetry may have its practical uses.

On the following night, a strange and sinister thing happened.

Harriet had gone, by appointment, to dine with her Somerville friend, and to meet a distinguished writer on the mid-Victorian period, from whom she expected to gain some useful information about Lefanu. She was sitting in the friend's room, where about half a dozen people were gathering to do honour to the distinguished writer, when the telephone rang.

'Oh, Miss Vane,' said her hostess. 'Somebody wants you from Shrewsbury.'

Harriet excused herself to the distinguished guest, and went out into the small lobby in which the telephone was placed. A voice which she could not quite recognise answered her 'Hullo!'

'Is that Miss Vane?'

'Yes – who's that speaking?'

'This is Shrewsbury College. Could you please come round quickly. There's been another disturbance.'

'Good heavens! What's happened? Who is speaking, please?'

'I'm speaking for the Warden. Could you please—?'

'Is that Miss Parsons?'

'No, miss. This is Dr. Baring's maid.'

'But what has happened?'

'I don't know, miss. The Warden said I was to ask you to come at once.'

'Very well. I'll be there in about ten or fifteen minutes. I haven't got the car. I'll be there about eleven.'

'Very good, miss. Thank you.'

The connection was severed. Harriet hurriedly got hold of her friend, explained that she had been called away suddenly, said her good-byes and hurried out.

She had crossed the Garden Quad and was just passing between the Old Hall and the Maitland Buildings, when she was visited with an absurd recollection. She remembered Peter's saying to her one day:

'The heroines of thrillers deserve all they get. When a mysterious voice rings them up and says it is Scotland Yard, they never think of ringing back to verify the call. Hence the prevalence of kidnapping.'

She knew where Somerville kept its public call-box; presumably she could get a call from there. She went in; tried it; found that it was through to the Exchange; dialled the Shrewsbury number, and on getting it asked to be put through to the Warden's Lodgings.

A voice answered her; not the same person's that had rung her up before.

'Is that Dr. Baring's maid?'

'Yes, madam. Who is speaking, please?'

('Madam' – the other voice had said 'miss.' Harriet knew now why she had felt vaguely uneasy about the call. She had subconsciously remembered that the Warden's maid said 'Madam.')

'This is Miss Harriet Vane, speaking from Somerville. Was it you who rang me up just now?'

'No, madam.'

'Somebody rang me up, speaking for the Warden. Was it Cook, or anybody else in the house?'

'I don't think anybody has telephoned from here, madam.'

442

(Some mistake. Perhaps the Warden had sent her message from somewhere in College and she had misunderstood the speaker or the speaker her.)

'Could I speak to the Warden?'

'The Warden isn't in College, madam. She went out to the theatre with Miss Martin. I'm expecting them back any minute.'

'Oh, thank you. Never mind. There must have been some mistake. Would you please put me back to the Lodge?'

When she heard Padgett's voice again she asked for Miss Edwards, and while the connection was being made, she thought fast.

It was beginning to look very much like a bogus call. But why, in Heaven's name? What would have happened if she had gone back to Shrewsbury straight away? Since she had not the car with her, she would have gone in by the private gate, past the thick bushes by the Fellows' Garden – the Fellows' Garden, where people walked by night—

'Miss Edwards isn't in her room, Miss Vane.'

'Oh! The scouts are all in bed, I suppose.'

'Yes, miss. Shall I ask Mrs. Padgett to see if she can find her?'

'No – see if you can get Miss Lydgate.'

Another pause. Was Miss Lydgate also out of her room? Was every reliable don in College out, or out of her room? Yes – Miss Lydgate was out, too; and then it occurred to Harriet that, of course, they were dutifully patrolling the College before turning in to bed. However, there was Padgett. She explained matters as well as she could to him.

'Very good, miss,' said Padgett, comfortingly. 'Yes, miss – I can leave Mrs. Padgett on the Lodge. I'll get down to the private gate and have a look round. Don't you worry, miss. If there's anybody a-laying in wait for you, miss, I'm sorry for 'em, that's all. No, miss, there ain't been no disturbance to-night as I knows on; but if I catches anybody a-laying in wait, miss, then the disturbance will proceed according to schedule, miss, trust me.'

'Yes, Padgett; but don't make a row about it. Slip down quietly and see if there's anybody hanging round – but don't let them see you. If anybody attacks me when I come in, you can come to the rescue; but if not, keep out of sight.'

'Very good, miss.'

Harriet hung up again and stepped out of the call-box. A centre light burned dimly in the entrance-hall. She looked at the clock. Seven minutes to eleven. She would be late. However, the assailant, if there was one, would wait for her. She knew where the trap would be – must be. Nobody would start a riot just outside the Infirmary or the Warden's Lodgings, where people might overhear and come out. Nor would anyone hide under or behind the walls on that side of the path. The only reasonable lurking-place was the bushes in the Fellows' Garden, near the gate, on the right side of the path as you went up.

One would be prepared, and that was an advantage; and Padgett would be somewhere at hand; but there would be a nasty moment when one had to turn one's back and lock the private gate from the inside. Harriet thought of the breadknife in the dummy, and shuddered.

If she bungled it and got killed – melodramtic, but possible, when people weren't quite sane – Peter would have something to say about it. Perhaps it would be only decent to apologise beforehand, in case. She found somebody's notebook astray on a window-seat, borrowed a sheet of it, scribbled half a dozen words with the pencil from her bag, folded the note addressed it and put it away with the pencil. If anything happened, it would be found.

The Somerville porter let her out into the Woodstock Road. She took the quickest way: by St. Giles' Church, Blackhall Road, Museum Road, South Parks Road, Mansfield Road, walking briskly, almost running. When she turned into Jowett Walk, she slowed down. She wanted her breath and her wits.

She turned the corner into St. Cross Road, reached the gate and took out the key. Her heart was thumping.

And then, the whole melodrama dissipated itself into polite comedy. A car drew up behind her; the Dean deposited the Warden and drove on round to the tradesmen's entrance to garage her Austin, and Dr. Baring said pleasantly:

'Ah! it's you, Miss Vane? Now I shan't have to look for my key. Did you have an interesting evening? The Dean and I have been indulging in a little dissipation. We suddenly made up our minds after dinner . . .'

She walked on up the path with Harriet, chatting with great amiability about the play she had seen. Harriet left her at her own gate, refusing an invitation to come in and have coffee and sandwiches. Had she, or had she not, heard something stir behind the bushes? At any rate, the opportunity was by now lost. She had offered herself as the cheese, but, owing to the slight delay in setting the trap, the Warden had innocently sprung it.

Harriet stepped into the Fellows' Garden, switched on her torch and looked round. The garden was empty. She suddenly felt a complete fool. Yet, when all was said and done, there must have been some reason for that telephone call.

She made her way towards the St. Cross Lodge. In the New Quad she met Padgett.

'Ah!' said Padgett, cautiously. 'She was there right enough, miss.' His right hand moved at his side, and Harriet fancied it held something suspiciously like a cosh. 'Sittin' on the bench be'ind them laurels near the gate. I crep' along careful, like it was a night reconnaissance, miss, and 'id be'ind them centre shrubs. She didn't tumble to me, miss, But when you an' Dr. Baring come through the gate a-talking, she was up and orf like a shot.'

'Who was it, Padgett?'

'Well, miss, not to put too fine a point upon it, miss, it was Miss 'Illyard. She come out at the top end of the Garden, miss, and away to her own rooms. I follored 'er and see 'er go up. Going very quick she was. I stepped out o' the gate, and I see the light go up in her window.'

'Oh!' said Harriet. 'Look here, Padgett, I don't want anything said about this. I know Miss Hillyard does sometimes take a stroll in the Fellows' Garden at night. Perhaps the person who sent the telephone call saw her there and went away again.'

'Yes, miss. It's a funny thing about that there telephone call. It didn't come through the Lodge, miss.'

'Perhaps one of the other instruments was through to the Exchange.'

'No, they wasn't miss. I 'ad a look to see. Afore I goes to bed at 11 o'clock, I puts the Warden, the Dean, and the Infirmary and the public box through, miss, for the night. But they wasn't through at 10.40, miss, that I'll swear.'

'Then the call must have come from outside.'

'Yes, miss. Miss 'Illyard come in at 10.50, miss, jest afore you rang up.'

'Did she? Are you sure?'

'I remember quite well, miss, because of Annie passing a remark about her. There's no love lost between her and Annie,' added Padgett, with a chuckle. 'Faults o' both sides, that's what I say, miss, and a 'asty temper—'

'What was Annie doing in the Lodge at that hour?'

'Jest come in from her half-day out, miss. She set in the Lodge a bit with Mrs. Padgett.'

'Did she? You didn't say anything about this business to her, did you, Padgett? She doesn't like Miss Hillyard, and if you ask me, I think she's a mischief-maker.'

'I didn't say one word, miss, not even to Mrs. Padgett, and nobody could 'ave 'eard me on the 'phone, because after I couldn't find Miss Lydgate and Miss Edwards and you begins to tell me, I shuts the door between me an' the settin'-room. Then I jest puts me 'ead in afterwards and says to Mrs. Padgett, "Look after the gate, would you?" I says. "I jest got to step over and give Mullins a message." So this here remains wot I might call confidential between you an' me, miss.'

'Well, see that it stays confidential, Padgett. I may have been imagining something quite absurd. The 'phone call was certainly a hoax, but there's no proof that anybody meant mischief. Did anybody else come in between 10.40 and 11?'

'Mrs. Padgett will know, miss. I'll send you up a list of the names. Or if you like to step into Lodge now—'

'Better not. No – give me the list in the morning.'

Harriet went away and found Miss Edwards, of whose discretion and common sense she had a high opinion, and told her the story of the 'phone call.

'You see,' said Harriet, 'if there *had* been any disturbance, the call might have been intended to prove an alibi, though I don't quite see how. Otherwise, why try to get me back at eleven? I mean, if the disturbance was due to start then, and I was brought there as a witness, the person might have wangled something so as to appear to be elsewhere at the time. But why was it necessary to have me as a witness?'

'Yes – and why say the disturbance had already happened, when it hadn't? And why wouldn't you do as a witness when you had the Warden with you?'

'Of course,' said Harriet, 'the idea might have been to make a disturbance and bring me on to the scene in time to be suspected of having done it myself.'

'That would be silly; everybody knows *you* can't be the Poltergeist.'

'Well, then, we come back to my first idea. I was to be attacked. But why couldn't I be attacked at midnight or any other time? Why bring me back at eleven?'

'It couldn't have been something timed to go off at eleven, while the alibi was being established?'

'Nobody could know to a moment the exact time I should take coming from Somerville to Shrewsbury. Unless you are thinking of a bomb or something that would go off when the gate was opened. But that would work equally well at any time.'

'But if the alibi was fixed for eleven—'

'Then why didn't the bomb go off? As a matter of fact, I simply can't believe in a bomb at all.'

'Nor can I – not really,' said Miss Edwards. 'We're just being theoretical. I suppose Padgett saw nothing suspicious?'

'Only Miss Hillyard,' replied Harriet, lightly, 'sitting in the Fellows' Garden.'

'Oh!'

'She does go there sometimes at night; I've seen her. Perhaps she frightened away – whatever it was.'

'Perhaps,' said Miss Edwards. 'By the way, your noble friend seems to have overcome her prejudices in a re-markable manner. I don't mean the one who saluted you in the quad – the one who came to dinner.'

'Are you trying to make a mystery out of yesterday afternoon?' asked Harriet, smiling. 'I think it was only a matter of introductions to some man in Italy who owns a library.'

'So she informed us,' said Miss Edwards. Harriet realised that, when her own back was turned, a good deal of chaff must have been flying about the History Tutor's ears. 'Well,' Miss Edwards went on, 'I promised him a paper on blood-groups, but he hasn't started to badger me for it yet. He's an interesting man, isn't he?'

'To the biologist?'

Miss Edwards laughed. 'Well, yes – as a specimen of the pedigree animal. Shockingly overbred, but full of nervous intelligence. But I didn't mean that.'

'To the woman, then?'

Miss Edwards turned a candid eye on Harriet.

'To many women, I should imagine.'

Harriet met the eye with a level gaze.

'I have no information on that point.'

'Ah!' said Miss Edwards. 'In your novels, you deal more in material facts than in psychology, don't you?'

Harriet readily admitted that this was so.

'Well, never mind,' said Miss Edwards; and said good night rather brusquely.

Harriet asked herself what all this was about. Oddly enough, it had never yet occurred to her to wonder what other women made of Peter, or he of them. This must argue either very great confidence or very great indiffer-ence on her own part; for, when one came to think of it, eligibility was his middle name.

On reaching her room, she took the scribbled note from her bag and destroyed it without re-reading it. Even the thought of it made her blush. Heroics that don't come off are the very essence of burlesque.

Thursday was chiefly remarkable for a violent, prolonged and wholly inexplicable row between Miss Hillyard and Miss Chilperic, in the Fellows' Garden after Hall. How it started or what it was about, nobody could afterwards remember. Somebody had disarranged a pile of books and papers on one of the Library tables, with the result that a History Schools candidate had arrived for a coaching with a tale of a set of notes mislaid or missing, Miss Hillyard, whose temper had been exceedingly short all day, was moved to take the matter personally and, after glowering all through dinner, burst out – as soon as the Warden had gone – into a storm of indignation against the world in general.

'Why *my* pupils should always be the ones to suffer from other people's carelessness, I don't know,' said Miss Hillyard.

Miss Burrows said she didn't see that they suffered more than anybody else. Miss Hillyard angrily adduced instances extending over the past three terms of History students whose work had been interfered with by what looked like deliberate persecution.

'Considering,' she went on, 'that the History School is the largest in the College and certainly not the least important—'

Miss Chilperic pointed out, quite correctly, that in that particular year there happened to be more candidates for the English School than any other.

'Of course you would say that,' said Miss Hillyard. 'There may be a couple more this year – I dare say there may – though why we should need an extra English tutor to cope with them, when I have to grapple single-handed—'

It was at that point that the origin of the quarrel became lost in a fog of personalities, in the course of which Miss Chilperic was accused of insolence, arrogance, inattention to her work, general incompetence and a desire to attract notice to herself. The extreme wildness of these charges left poor Miss Chilperic quite bewildered. Indeed, nobody seemed to be able to make anything of it, except, perhaps, Miss Edwards, who sat with a grim smile knitting herself a silk jumper. At length the attack extended itself from Miss Chilperic to Miss Chilperic's fiancé, whose scholarship was submitted to scathing criticism.

Miss Chilperic rose up, trembling.

'I think, Miss Hillyard,' she said, 'you must be beside yourself. I do not mind what you say about me, but I cannot sit here while you insult Jacob Peppercorn.' She stumbled a little over the syllables of this unfortunate name, and Miss Hillyard laughed unkindly. 'Mr. Peppercorn is a very fine scholar,' pursued Miss Chilperic, with rising anger as of an exasperated lamb, 'and I insist that—'

'I'm glad to hear you say so,' said Miss Hillyard, 'If I were you, I should make do with him.'

'I don't know what you mean,' cried Miss Chilperic.

'Perhaps Miss Vane could tell you,' retorted Miss Hillyard, and walked away without another word.

'Good gracious!' cried Miss Chilperic, turning to Harriet. 'Whatever is she talking about?'

'I haven't the least idea,' said Harriet.

'I don't know, but I can guess,' said Miss Edwards. 'If people will bring dynamite into a powder factory, they must expect explosions.' While Harriet was rooting about in the back of her mind for some association that these words called up, Miss Edwards went on:

'If somebody doesn't get to the bottom of these disturbances within the next few days, there'll be murder done. If we're like this now, what's going to happen to us at the end of term? You ought to have had the police in from the start, and if I'd been here, I'd have said so. I'd like to deal with a good, stupid sergeant of police for a change.'

Then she, too, got up and stalked away, leaving the rest of the dons to stare at one another.

19

O well-knit Samson! strong-jointed Samson! I do excel
thee in my rapier, as much as thou didst excel me in
carrying gates. I am in love, too.

WILLIAM SHAKESPEARE

HARRIET had been only too right about Wilfrid. She had
spent portions of four days in altering and humanising
Wilfrid, and to-day, after a distressful morning with him,
had reached the dismal conclusion that she would have
to rewrite the whole thing from the beginning. Wilfrid's
tormented humanity stood out now against the competent vacuity of the other characters like a wound. Moreover, with the reduction of Wilfrid's motives to what was
psychologically credible, a large lump of the plot had
fallen out, leaving a gap through which one could catch
glimpses of new and exciting jungles of intrigue. She
stood aimlessly staring in the window of the antique
shop. Wilfrid was becoming like one of those coveted
ivory chessmen. You probed into his interior and discovered an intricate and delicate carved sphere of sen-
sibilities, and, as you turned it in your fingers, you found
another inside that, and within that, another again.

Behind the table where the chessmen stood was a
Jacobean dresser in black oak, and, as she stood at gaze,
a set of features limned themselves pallidly against the
dark background, like Pepper's ghost.

'What is it?' asked Peter over her shoulder; 'Toby jugs

or pewter pots or the dubious chest with Brummagem handles?'

'The chessmen,' said Harriet. 'I have fallen a victim too them. I don't know why. I have no possible use for them. It's just one of those bewitchments.'

' "The reason no man knows, let it suffice. What we behold is censured by our eyes." To be possessed is an admirable reason for possessing.'

'What would they want for them, I wonder?'

'If they're complete and genuine, anything from forty to eighty pounds.'

'Too much. When did you get back?'

'Just before lunch. I was on my way to see you. Were you going anywhere in particular?'

'No – just wandering. Have you found out anything useful?'

'I have been scouring England for a man called Arthur Robinson. Does the name mean anything to you?'

'Nothing whatever.'

'Nor to me. I approached it with a refreshing absence of prejudice. Have there been any developments in College?'

'Well, yes. Something rather queer happened the other night. Only I don't quite understand it.'

'Will you come for a run and tell me about it? I've got the car, and it's a fine afternoon.'

Harriet looked round, and saw the Daimler parked by the kerb.

'I'd love to.'

'We'll dawdle along the lanes and have tea some-where,' he added, conventionally, as he handed her in.

'How original of you, Peter!'

'Isn't it?' They moved decorously down the crowded High Street. 'There's something hypnotic about the word tea. I am asking you to enjoy the beauties of the English countryside, to tell me your adventures and hear mine, to plan a campaign involving the comfort and reputation of two hundred people, to honour me with your sole presence and bestow upon me the illusion of Paradise – and I speak as though the pre-eminent object of all desire were a pot of boiled water and a plateful of synthetic pastries in Ye Olde Worlde Tudor Tea-Shoppe.'

'If we dawdle till after opening-time,' said Harriet, practically, 'we can get bread-and-cheese and beer in the village pub.'

'Now you have said something.

> The crystal springs, whose taste illuminates
> Refinéd eyes with an eternal sight,
> Like triéd silver, run through Paradise
> To entertain divine Zenocrate.'

Harriet could find no adequate reply to this, but sat watching his hands as they lay lightly on the driving-wheel. The car passed on through Long Marston and Elsfield. Presently he turned it into a side-road and thence into a lane and there drew up.

'There comes a moment when one must cease voyaging through strange seas of thought alone. Will you speak first, or shall I?'

'Who is Arthur Robinson?'

'Arthur Robinson is the gentleman who behaved so strangely in the matter of a thesis. He was an M.A. of York University, held various tutorships from time to time in various seats of learning, applied for the Chair of Modern History at York, and there came up against the formidable memory and detective ability of your Miss de Vine, who was then Head of Flamborough College and on the examining body. He was a fair, handsome man, aged about thirty-five at the time, very agreeable and popular, though hampered a little in his social career by having in a weak moment married his landlady's daughter. After the unfortunate episode of the thesis, he disappeared from academic circles, and was no more heard of. At the time of his disappearance he had one female child of two years of age and another expected. I managed to hunt up a former friend of his, who said that he had heard nothing of Robinson since the disaster, but fancied that he had gone abroad and changed his name. He referred me to a man called Simpson, living in Nottingham. I pursued Simpson, and found that he had, in the most inconvenient way, died last year. I returned to London and dispatched sundry members of Miss Climpson's Bureau in search of other friends and colleagues of Mr. Arthur Robinson, and also to Somerset House to hunt through the Marriage and Birth Registers. That is all I have to show for two days of intensive activity – except that I honourably delivered your manuscript to your secretary.'

'Thank you very much. Arthur Robinson. Do you think he can possibly have anything to do with it?'

'Well, it's rather a far cry. But it's a fact that until Miss de Vine came here there were no disturbances, and the only thing she has ever mentioned that might suggest a personal enmity is the story of Arthur Robinson. It seemed just worth while following up.'

'Yes, I see. . . . I hope you're not going to suggest that Miss Hillyard is Arthur Robinson in disguise, because I've known her for ten years.'

'Why Miss Hillyard? What's she been doing?'

'Nothing susceptible of proof.'

'Tell me.'

Harriet told him the story of the telephone call, to which he listened with a grave face.

'Was I making a mountain out of a mole-hill?'

'I think not. I think our friend has realised that you are a danger and is minded to tackle you first. Unless it is a quite separate feud – which is just possible. On the whole it's as well that you thought of ringing back.'

'You may take the credit for that. I hadn't forgotten your scathing remarks about the thriller-heroine and the bogus message from Scotland Yard.'

'Hadn't you? . . . Harriet, will you let me show you how to meet an attack if it ever does come?'

'Meet a—? Yes, I should like to know. Though I'm fairly strong, you know. I think I could cope with most things, except a stab in the back. That was what I rather expected.'

'I doubt if it will be that,' said he, coolly. 'It makes a mess and leaves a messy weapon to be disposed of. Strangling is cleaner and quicker and makes no noise to speak of.'

'Yeough!'

'You have a nice throat for it,' pursued his lordship, thoughtfully. 'It has a kind of arum-lily quality that is in itself an invitation to violence. I do not want to be run in by the local bobby for assault; but if you will kindly step aside with me into this convenient field, it will give me great pleasure to strangle you scientifically in several positions.'

'You're a gruesome companion for a day's outing.'

'I'm quite serious.' He had got out of the car and was holding the door open for her. 'Come, Harriet. I am very civilly pretending that I don't care what dangers you run. You don't want me to howl at your feet, do you?'

'You're going to make me feel ignorant and helpless,'

said Harriet, following him nevertheless to the nearest gate. 'I don't like it.'

'This field will do charmingly. It is not laid down for hay, it is reasonably free from thistles and cow-pats, and there is a high hedge to screen us from the road.'

'And it is soft to fall on and has a pond to throw the corpse into if you get carried away by your enthusiasm. Very well. I have said my prayers.'

'Then kindly imagine me to be an unpleasant-faced thug with designs on your purse, your virtue and your life.'

The next few minutes were rather breathless.

'Don't thrash about,' said Peter, mildly. 'You'll only exhaust yourself. Use *my* weight to upset me with. I'm putting it entirely at your disposal, and I can't throw it about in two directions at once. If you let my vaulting ambition overleap itself, I shall fall on the other side with the beautiful precision of Newton's apple.'

'I don't get that.'

'Try throttling me for a change, and I'll show you.'

'Did I say this field was soft?' said Harriet, when her feet had been ignominiously hooked from under her. She rubbed herself resentfully. 'Just let me do it to you, that's all.'

And this time, whether by skill or favour, she did contrive to bring him off his balance, so that he only saved himself from sprawling by a complicated twist suggestive of an eel on a hook.

'We'd better stop now,' said Peter, when he had instructed her in the removal of the thug who leaps from in front, the thug who dives in from behind, and the more sophisticated thug who starts operations with a silk scarf. 'You'll feel tomorrow as if you'd been playing football.'

'I think I shall have a sore throat.'

'I'm sorry. Did I let my animal nature get the better of me? That's the worst of these rough sports.'

'It would be a good bit rougher if it was done in earnest. I shouldn't care to meet *you* in a narrow lane on a dark night, and I only hope the Poison-Pen hasn't been making a study of the subject. Peter, you don't seriously think—'

'I avoid serious thought like the plague. But I assure you I haven't been knocking you about for the fun of it.'

'I believe you. No gentleman could throttle a lady more impersonally.'

'Thank you for the testimonial. Cigarette?'

Harriet took the cigarette, which she felt she had deserved, and sat with her hands about her knees, mentally turning the incidents of the last hour into a scene in a book (as is the novelist's unpleasant habit) and thinking how, with a little vulgarity on both sides, it could be worked up into a nice piece of exhibitionism for the male and provocation for the female concerned. With a little manipulation it might come in for the chapter where the wart Everard was due to seduce the glamorous but neglected wife, Sheila. He could lock her to him, knee to knee and breast to breast in an unbreakable grip and smile challengingly into her flushed face; and Sheila could go all limp – at which point Everard could either rain fierce kisses on her mouth, or say, 'My God! don't tempt me!' which would come to exactly the same thing in the end. 'It would suit them very well,' thought Harriet, 'the cheap skates!' and passed an exploring finger under the angle of her jaw, where the pressure of a relentless thumb had left its memory.

'Cheer up,' said Peter. 'It'll wear off.'

'Do you propose to give Miss de Vine lessons in self-defence?'

'I'm rather bothered about her. She's got a groggy heart, hasn't she?'

'She's supposed to have. She wouldn't climb Magdalen Tower.'

'And presumably she wouldn't rush round College and steal fuses or climb in and out of windows. In which case the hairpins would be a plant. Which brings us back to the Robinson theory. But it's easy to pretend your heart is worse than it is. Ever seen her have a heart-attack?'

'Now you mention it, I have not.'

'You see,' said Peter, 'she put me on to Robinson. I gave her the opportunity to tell a story, and she told it. Next day, I went to see her and asked for the name. She made a good show of reluctance, but she gave it. It's easy to throw suspicion on people who owe you a grudge, and that without telling any lies. If I wanted you to believe that somebody was having a smack at me, I could give you a list of enemies as long as my arm.'

'I suppose so. Do they ever try to do you in?'

'Not very often. Occasionally they send silly things by post. Shaving-cream full of nasty bugs and so on. And there was a gentleman with a pill calculated to cure lassitude and debility. I had a long correspondence with him, all in plain envelopes. The beauty of his system was that he made you pay for the pill, which still seems to me a very fine touch. In fact, he took me in completely; he only made the one trifling miscalculation of supposing that I wanted the pill – and I can't really blame him for that, because the list of symptoms I produced for him would have led anybody to suppose I needed the whole pharmacopœia. However, he sent me a week's supply – seven pills – at shocking expense; so I virtuously toddled round with them to my friend at the Home Office who deals with charlatans and immoral advertisements and so on, and he was inquisitive enough to analyse them. "H'm," said he, "six of 'em would neither make nor mar you; but the other would cure lassitude all right." So I naturally asked what was in it. "Strychnine," said he. "Full lethal dose. If you want to go rolling round the room like a hoop with your head touching your heels, I'll guarantee the result." So we went out to look for the gentleman.'

'Did you find him?'

'Oh, yes. Dear old friend of mine. Had him in the dock before on a cocaine charge. We put him in jug – and I'm dashed if, when he came out, he didn't try to blackmail me on the strength of the pill correspondence. I never met a scoundrel I liked better. . . . Would you care for a little more healthy exercise, or shall we take the road again?'

It was when they were passing through a small town that Peter caught sight of a leather-and-harness shop, and pulled up suddenly.

'I know what you want,' he said. 'You want a dog-collar. I'm going to get you one. The kind with brass knobs.'

'A dog-collar? Whatever for? As a badge of owner-ship?'

'God forbid. To guard against the bites of sharks. Excellent also against thugs and throat-slitters.'

'My dear man!'

'Honestly. It's too stiff to squeeze and it'll turn the edge of a blade – and even if anybody hangs you by it, it won't choke you as a rope would.'

'I can't go about in a dog-collar.'

'Well, not in the day-time. But it would give confidence when patrolling at night. And you could sleep in it with a little practice. You needn't bother to come in – I've had my hands round your neck often enough to guess the size.'

He vanished into the shop and was seen through the window conferring with the proprietor. Presently he came out with a parcel and took the wheel again.

'The man was very much interested,' he observed, 'in my bull-terrier bitch. Extremely plucky animal, but reckless and obstinate fighter. Personally, he said, he preferred greyhounds. He told me where I could get my name and address put on the collar, but I said that could wait. Now we're out of the town, you can try it on.'

He drew in to the side of the road for this purpose, and assisted her (with, Harriet fancied, a touch of self-satisfaction), to buckle the heavy strap. It was a massive kind of necklace and quite surprisingly uncomfortable. Harriet fished in her bag for a hand-mirror and surveyed the effect.

'Rather becoming, don't you think?' said Peter. 'I don't see why it shouldn't set a new fashion.'

'I do,' said Harriet. 'Do you mind taking it off again.'

'Will you wear it?'

'Suppose somebody grabs at it from behind.'

'Let go and fall back on them – heavily. You'll fall soft, and with luck they'll crack their skull open.'

'Bloodthirsty monster. Very well. I'll do anything you like if you'll take it off now.'

'That's a promise,' said he, and released her. 'That collar,' he added, wrapping it up again and laying it on her knee, 'deserves to be put in a glass case.'

'Why?'

'It's the only thing you've ever let me give you.'

'Except my life – except my life – except my life.'

'Damn!' said Peter, and stared out angrily over the wind-screen. 'It must have been a pretty bitter gift, if you can't let either of us forget it.'

'I'm sorry, Peter. That was ungenerous and beastly of me. You *shall* give me something if you want to.'

'May I? What shall I give you? Roc's eggs are cheap today.'

For a moment her mind was a blank. Whatever she asked him for, it must be something adequate. The trivial, the commonplace or the merely expensive would all be equally insulting. And he would know in a moment if she was inventing a want to please him. . . .

'Peter – give me the ivory chessmen.'

He looked so delighted that she felt sure he had expected to be snubbed with a request for something costing seven-and-sixpence.

'My dear – of course! Would you like them now?'

'This instant! Some miserable undergraduate may be snapping them up. Every day I go out I expect to find them gone. Be quick.'

'All right. I'll engage not to drop below seventy, except in the thirty-mile limit.'

'Oh, God!' said Harriet, as the car started. Fast driving terrified her, as he very well knew. After five breath-taking miles, he shot a glance sideways at her, to see how she was standing it, and slacked his foot from the accelerator.

'That was my triumph song. Was it a bad four minutes?'

'I asked for it,' said Harriet, with set teeth. 'Go on.'

'I'm damned if I will. We will go at a reasonable pace and risk the undergraduate, damn his bones!'

The ivory chessmen were, however, still in the window when they arrived. Peter subjected them to a hard and monocled stare, and said:

'They *look* all right.'

'They're lovely. Admit that when I do do a thing, I do it

463

handsomely. I've asked you now for thirty-two presents at once.'

'It sounds like *Through the Looking-Glass*. Are you coming in, or will you leave me to fight it out by myself?'

'Of course I'm coming in. Why? – Oh! Am I looking too keen?'

'Much too keen.'

'Well, I don't care. I'm coming in.'

The shop was dark, and crowded with a strange assortment of first-class stuff, junk, and traps for the unwary. The proprietor, however, had all his wits about him and, recognising after a preliminary skirmish of superlatives that he had to do with an obstinate, experienced and well-informed customer, settled down with something like enthusiasm to a prolonged siege of the position. It had not previously occurred to Harriet that anybody could spend an hour and forty minutes in buying a set of chessmen. Every separate carved ball in every one of thirty-two pieces had to be separately and minutely examined with finger-tips and the naked eye and a watchmaker's lens for signs of damage, repair, substitution or faulty workmanship; and only after a sharp catechism directed to the 'provenance' of the set, and a long discussion about trade conditions in China, the state of the antique market generally and the effect on the American slump on prices, was any figure mentioned at all; and when it was mentioned, it was instantly challenged, and a further discussion followed, during which all the pieces were scrutinised again. This ended at length in Peter's agreeing to purchase the set at the price named (which was considerably above his minimum, though within his maximum estimate) provided the board was included. The unusual size of the pieces made it necessary that they should have their own board; and the dealer rather reluctantly agreed, after having it firmly pointed out to him that the board was sixteenth-century Spanish – clean out of the period – and that it was therefore almost a condescension on the purchaser's part to accept it as a gift.

The combat being now brought to an honourable conclusion, the dealer beamed pleasantly and asked where the parcel should be sent.

'We'll take it with us,' said Peter, firmly. 'If you'd rather have notes than a cheque—'

The dealer protested that the cheque would be quite all right but that the parcel would be a large one and take some time to make up, since the pieces ought all to be wrapped separately.

'We're in no hurry,' said Peter. 'We'll take it with us;' thus conforming to the first rule of good nursery behaviour, that presents must always be taken and never delivered by the shop.

The dealer vanished upstairs to look for a suitable box, and Peter turned apologetically to Harriet.

'Sorry to be so long about it. You've chosen better than you knew. I'm no expert, but I'm very much mistaken if that isn't a very fine and ancient set, and worth a good bit more than he wants for it. That's why I haggled so much. When a thing looks like a bargain, there's usually a snag about it somewhere. If one of those dashed pawns wasn't the original, it would make the whole lot worthless.'

'I suppose so.' A disquieting thought struck Harriet. 'If the set hadn't been perfect, should you have bought it?'

'Not at any price.'

'Not if I still wanted it?'

'No. That's the snag about *me*. Besides, you wouldn't want it. You have the scholarly mind and you'd always feel uncomfortable knowing it was wrong, even if nobody else knew.'

'That's true. Whenever anybody admired it I should feel obliged to say, "Yes, but one of the pawns is modern" – and that would get so tedious. Well, I'm glad they're all right, because I love them with a perfectly idiotic passion. They have been haunting my slumbers for weeks. And even now I haven't said thank you.'

'Yes, you have – and anyway, the pleasure is all mine . . . I wondered whether that spinet's in order.'

He threaded his way through the dark backward and abysm of the antique shop, clearing away a spinning-wheel, a Georgian wine-cooler, a brass lamp and a small forest of Burmese idols that stood between him and the instrument. 'Variations on a musical-box,' he said, as he ran his fingers over the keys, and, disentangling a coffin-stool from his surroundings, sat down and played, first a minuet from a Bach suite and then a gigue, before striking into the air of *Greensleeves*.

> 'Alas my love, you do me wrong
> To cast me off discourteously,
> And I have lovèd you so long,
> Delighting in your company.'

He shall see that I don't mind that, thought Harriet, and raised her voice cheerfully in the refrain:

> 'For O Greensleeves was all my joy,
> And O Greensleeves was my delight—'

He stopped playing instantly.

'Wrong key for you. God meant you for a contralto.' He transposed the air into E minor, in a tinkling cascade of modulations. 'You never told me you could sing. . . . No, I can hear you're not trained . . . chorus-singer?

Bach Choir? . . . of course – I might have guessed it. . . .
"And O Greensleeves was my heart of gold And who put
my Lady Greensleeves" . . . Do you know any of Mor-
ley's *Canzonets for Two Voices*? . . . Come on, then,
"When lo! by Break of Morning" . . . Whichever part
you like – they're exactly the same. . . . "My love herself
adorning." . . . G natural my dear, G natural. . . .'

The dealer, descending with his arms full of packing
materials, paid no attention to them. He was well
accustomed to the eccentricities of customers; and,
moreover, probably cherished hopes of selling them
the spinet.

'This kind of thing,' said Peter, as tenor and alto
twined themselves in a last companionable cadence, 'is
the body and bones of music. Anybody can have the
harmony, if they will leave us the counterpoint. What
next? . . . "Go to Bed, sweet Muse"? Come, come! Is it
true? is it kind? is it necessary? . . . "Love is a fancy, love
is a frenzy." . . . Very well, I owe you one for that,' and
with a mischievous eye he played the opening bars of
'Sweet Cupid, Ripen her Desire.'

'No,' said Harriet, reddening.

'No. Not in the best of taste. Try again.'

He hesitated; ran from one tune to another; then
settled down to that best-known of all Elizabethan
love-songs.

> 'Fain would I change that note
> To which fond love hath charmed me . . . .'

Harriet, with her elbows on the lid of the spinet and
her chin propped on her hands, let him sing alone. Two
young gentlemen, who had strayed in and were talking
rather loudly in the front part of the shop, abandoned a
half-hearted quest for brass candlesticks and came stum-

bling through the gloom to see who was making the noise.

> 'True house of joy and bliss
> Where sweetest pleasure is
> I do adore thee;
> I see thee what thou art,
> I love thee in my heart
> And fall before thee.'

Tobias Hume's excellent air rises to a high-pitched and triumphant challenge in the penultimate line, before tumbling with a clatter to the key-note. Too late, Harriet signed to the singer to moderate his voice.

'Here, you!' said the larger of the two young gentlemen, belligerently. 'You're making a filthy row. Shut up!'

Peter swung round on the stool.

'Sir?' He polished his monocle with exaggerated care, adjusted it and let his eye travel up the immense tweedy form lowering over his. 'I beg your pardon. Was that obligin' observation addressed to me?'

Harriet started to speak, but the young man turned to her.

'Who,' he demanded loudly, 'is this effeminate bounder?'

'I have been accused of many things,' said Wimsey, interested; 'but the charge of effeminacy is new to me. Do you mind explaining yourself?'

'I don't like your song,' said the young man, rocking slightly on his feet, 'and I don't like your voice, and I don't like your tom-fool eye-glass.'

'Steady on, Reggie,' said his friend.

'You're annoying this lady,' persisted the young man. 'You're making her conspicuous. Get out!'

'Good God!' said Wimsey, turning to Harriet. 'Is this by any chance Mr. Jones of Jesus?'

'Who are you calling a bloody Welshman?' snarled the young man, much exasperated. 'My name's Pomfret.'

'Mine's Wimsey,' said Peter. 'Quite as ancient though less euphonious. Come on, son, don't be an ass. You mustn't behave like this to senior members and before ladies.'

'Senior member be damned!' cried Mr. Pomfret, to whom this unfortunate phrase conveyed only too much. 'Do you think I'm going to be sneered at by you? Stand up, blast you! Why can't you stand up for yourself?'

'First,' replied Peter, mildly, 'because I'm twenty years older than you are. Secondly, because you're six inches taller than I am. And thirdly, because I don't want to hurt you.'

'Then,' said Mr. Pomfret, 'take that, you sitting rabbit!'

He launched an impetuous blow at Peter's head, and found himself held by the wrist in an iron grip.

'If you don't keep quiet,' said his lordship, 'you'll break something. Here, you, sir. Take your effervescent friend home, can't you? How the devil does he come to be drunk at this time of the day?'

The friend offered a confused explanation about a lunch-party and subsequent cocktail binge. Peter shook his head.

'One damn gin after another,' he said, sadly. 'Now, sir. You had better apologise to the lady and beetle off.'

Mr. Pomfret, much subdued and tending to become lachrymose, muttered that he was sorry to have made a row. 'But why did you make fun of me with that?' he asked Harriet, reproachfully.

'I didn't, Mr. Pomfret. You're quite mistaken.'

'Damn your senior members!' said Mr. Pomfret.

'Now, don't begin all over again,' urged Peter, kindly.

He got up, his eyes about on a level with Mr. Pomfret's chin. 'If you want to continue the discussion, you'll find me at the Mitre in the morning. This way out.'

'Come on, Reggie,' said the friend.

The dealer, who had returned to his packing after assuring himself that it would not be necessary to send for the police or the proctors, leapt helpfully to open the door, and said '*Good* afternoon, gentlemen,' as though nothing out of the way had happened.

'I'm damned if I'll be sneered at,' said Mr. Pomfret, endeavouring to stage a come-back on the doorstep.

'Of course not, old boy,' said his friend. 'Nobody's sneering at you. *Come* on! You've had quite enough fun for one afternoon.'

The door shut them out.

'Well, well!' said Peter.

'Young gentlemen will be lively,' said the dealer. 'I'm afraid it's a bit bulky, sir. I've put the board up separate.'

'Stick 'em in the car,' said Peter. 'They'll be all right'

This was done; and the dealer, glad enough to get his shop cleared, began to put up his shutters, as it was now long past closing-time.

'I apologise for my young friend,' said Harriet.

'He seems to have taken it hard. What on earth was there so infuriating about my being a senior?'

'Oh, poor lamb! He thought I'd been telling you about him and me and the proctor. I suppose I *had* better tell you now.'

Peter listened and laughed a little ruefully.

'I'm sorry,' he said. 'That kind of thing hurts like hell when you're his age. I'd better send him a note and set that right. I say!'

'What?'

'We never had that beer. Come round and have one

with me at the Mitre, and we'll concoct a salve for wounded feelings.'

With two half-pint tankards on the table before them, Peter produced his epistle.

The Mitre Hotel,
Oxford.

To Reginald Pomfret, Esq.

Sir,

I am given to understand by Miss Vane that in the course of our conversation this afternoon I unhappily made use of an expression which might have been misconstrued as a reference to your private affairs. Permit me to assure you that the words were uttered in complete ignorance, and that nothing could have been farther from my intentions than to make any such offensive allusion. While deprecating very strongly the behaviour you thought fit to use, I desire to express my sincere regret for any pain I may have inadvertently caused you, and beg to remain,

Your obedient servant,
PETER DEATH BREDON WIMSEY.

'Is that pompous enough?'

'Beautiful,' said Harriet. 'Scarcely a word under three syllables and all the names you've got. What your nephew calls "Uncle Peter at his stuffiest" All it wants is the crest and sealing-wax. Why not write the child a nice, friendly note?'

'He doesn't want friendliness,' said his lordship, grinning. 'He wants satisfaction.' He rang the bell and sent the waiter for Bunter and the sealing-wax. 'You're right about the beneficial effects of a red seal – he'll think it's a challenge. Bunter, bring me my seal ring. Come to think of it, that's an idea. Shall I offer him the choice of swords or pistols on Port Meadow at daybreak?'

'I think it's time you grew up,' said Harriet.

'Is it?' said Peter, addressing the envelope. 'I've never challenged anybody. It would be fun. I've been challenged three times and fought twice; the third time the police butted in. I'm afraid that was because my opponent didn't fancy my choice of weapon. . . . Thanks, Bunter. . . . A bullet, you see, may go anywhere, but steel's almost bound to go somewhere.'

'Peter,' said Harriet, looking gravely at him, 'I believe you're showing off.'

'I believe I am,' said he, setting the heavy ring accurately down upon the wax. 'Every cock will crow upon his own dung-hill.' His grin was half petulant, half deprecating. 'I hate being loomed over by gigantic undergraduates and made to feel my age.'

20

For, to speak in a word, envy is naught else but *tristitia de bonis alienis*, sorrow for other men's good, be it present past, or to come: and *gaudium de adversis*, and joy at their harms. . . . 'Tis a common disease, and almost natural to us, as *Tacitus* holds, to envy another man's prosperity.

ROBERT BURTON

IT is said that love and a cough cannot be hid. Nor is it easy to hide two-and-thirty outside ivory chessmen; unless one is so inhuman as to leave them swaddled in their mummy-clothes of wadding and entombed within the six sides of a wooden sarcophagus. What is the use of acquiring one's heart's desire if one cannot handle and gloat over it, show it to one's friends and gather an anthology of envy and admiration? Whatever awkward deductions might be drawn about the giver – and, after all, was that anybody's business? – Harriet knew that she must needs display the gift or burst in solitary ecstasy.

Accordingly, she put a bold face on it, marched her forces openly into the Senior Common Room after Hall, and deployed them upon the table, with the eager assistance of the dons.

'But where are you going to keep them?' asked the Dean, when everybody had sufficiently exclaimed over the fineness of the carving, and had taken her turn at twisting and examining the nests of concentric globes.

'You can't just leave them in the box. Look at those fragile little spears and things and the royal head-dresses. They ought to be put in a glass case.'

'I know,' said Harriet. 'It's just like me to want something completely impracticable. I shall have to wrap them all up again.'

'Only then,' said Miss Chilperic, 'you won't be able to look at them. I know, if they were mine, I shouldn't be able to take my eyes off them for a moment.'

'You can have a glass case if you like,' said Miss Edwards. 'Out of the Science lecture-room.'

'The very thing,' said Miss Lydgate. 'But how about the terms of the bequest? I mean, the glass cases—'

'Oh, blow the bequest,' cried the Dean. 'Surely one can *borrow* a thing for a week or two. We can lump some of those hideous geological specimens together and have one of the small cases taken up to your room.'

'By all means,' said Miss Edwards, 'I'll see to it.'

'Thank you,' said Harriet; 'that will be lovely.'

'Aren't you simply aching to play with the new toy?' asked Miss Allison. 'Does Lord Peter play chess?'

'I don't know,' said Harriet. 'I'm not much of a player. I just fell in love with the pieces.'

'Well,' said Miss de Vine, kindly, 'let us have a game. They are so beautiful, it would be a pity not to use them.'

'But I expect you could play my head off.'

'Oh, do play with them!' cried Miss Shaw, sentimentally. 'Think how they must be longing for a little life and movement after sitting all that time in a shop window.'

'I will give you a pawn,' suggested Miss de Vine.

Even with this advantage, Harriet suffered three humiliating defeats in quick successon: first, because she was but a poor player; secondly, because she found it difficult to remember which piece was which; thirdly, because the anguish of parting at one fell swoop with a fully-armed warrior, a prancing steed and a complete nest of ivory balls was such that she could scarcely bear to place so much as a pawn in jeopardy. Miss de Vine, viewing with perfect equanimity the disappearance even of a robed counsellor with long moustaches or an elephant carrying a castleful of combatants, soon had Harriet's king penned helplessly among his own defenders. Nor was the game made any easier for the weaker party by being played under the derisive eye of Miss Hillyard, who, pronouncing chess to be the world's most wearisome amusement, yet would not go away and get on with her work, but sat staring at the board as though fascinated and (what was worse) fiddling with the captured pieces and putting Harriet into an agony for fear she would drop one.

Moreover, when the games were finished, and Miss Edwards had announced that a glass case had been dusted and taken up to Harriet's room by a scout, Miss Hillyard insisted on helping to carry the pieces over, grasping for the purpose the white king and queen, whose headgear bore delicate waving ornaments like antennæ, extremely liable to damage. Even when the Dean had discovered that the pieces could be more safely transported standing upright in their box, Miss Hillyard attached herself to the party that escorted them across the quad, and was officious in helping to set the glass case in a convenient position opposite the bed, 'so that,' as she observed, 'you can see them if you wake up in the night.'

The following day happened to be the Dean's birthday. Harriet, going shortly after breakfast to purchase a tribute of roses in the Market, and coming out into the High Street with the intention of making an appointment at the hair-dresser's, was rewarded by the rather unexpected sight of two male backs, issuing from the Mitre and proceeding, apparently in perfect amity, in an easterly direction. The shorter and slighter of the two she could have singled out from a million backs anywhere; nor was it easy to mistake the towering bulk and breadth of Mr. Reginald Pomfret. Both parties were smoking pipes, and she concluded from this that the object of their excursion could scarcely be swords or pistols on Port Meadow. They were strolling in a leisurely after-breakfast manner, and she took care not to catch them up. She hoped that what Lord Saint-George called the 'famous family charm' was being exerted to good purpose; she was too old to enjoy the sensation of being squabbled over – it made all three of them ridiculous. Ten years ago, she might have felt flattered; but it seemed that the lust to power was a thing one grew out of. What one wanted, she thought, standing amid the stuffy per-fumes of the hairdresser's establishment, was peace, and freedom from the pressure of angry and agitated person-alities. She booked an appointment for the afternoon and resumed her way. As she passed Queen's, Peter came down the steps alone.

'Hullo!' said he. 'Why the floral emblems?'

Harriet explained.

'Good egg!' said his lordship. 'I like your Dean.' He relieved her of the roses. 'Let me also be there with a gift.

Make her a goodly chapilet of azur'd Colombine,
And wreathe about her coronet with sweetest Eglan-tine,
With roses damask, white, and red, and fairest flower delice,
With Cowslips of Jerusalem, and cloves of Paradise.

Though what Cowslips of Jerusalem may be I do not know, and they are probably not in season.'

Harriet turned with him marketwards.

'Your young friend came to see me,' pursued Peter.

'So I observed. Did you "fix a vacant stare and slay him with your noble birth"?'

'And he my own kin in the sixteenth degree on the father's mother's side? No; he's a nice lad, and the way to his heart is through the playing-fields of Eton. He told me all his griefs and I sympathised very kindly, mentioning that there were better ways of killing care than drowning it in a butt of malmsey. But, O God, turn back the universe and give me yesterday! He was beautifully sozzled last night, and had one breakfast before he came out and another with me at the Mitre. I do not envy the heart of youth, but only its head and stomach.'

'Have you heard anything fresh about Arthur Robinson?'

'Only that he married a young woman called Charlotte Ann Clarke, and had by her a daughter, Beatrice Maud. That was easy, because we know where he was living eight years ago, and could consult the local registers. But they're still hunting the registers to find either his death – supposing him to be dead, which is rather less likely than otherwise – or the birth of the second child, which – if it ever occurred – might tell us where he went to after the trouble at York. Unfortunately, Robinsons are as plentiful as blackberries, and Arthur Robinsons not uncommon. And if he really did change his name, there may not be any Robinson entries at all. Another of my searchers has gone to his old lodgings – where, you may remember, he very imprudently married the landlady's daughter; but the Clarkes have moved, and it's going to be a bit of a job finding them. Another line is to inquire among the scholastic agencies and the small and inferior private schools, because it seems probable— You're not attending.'

'Yes, I am,' said Harriet, vaguely. 'He had a wife called Charlotte and you're looking for him in a private school.' A rich, damp fragrance gushed out upon them as they turned into the Market, and she was overcome by a sense of extravagant well-being. 'I love this smell – it's like the cactus-house in the Botanical Gardens.'

Her companion opened his mouth to speak, looked at her, and then, as one that will interfere with fortune, let the name of Robinson die upon his lips.

'*Madragoræ dederunt odorem.*'

'What do you say, Peter?'

'Nothing. The words of Mercury are harsh after the songs of Apollo.' He laid his hand gently upon her arm. 'Let us interview the merchant with the sops-in-wine.'

And when both roses and carnations had been despatched – this time by a messenger – to their destination, it seemed natural, since the Botanical Gardens had been mentioned, to go there. For a garden, as Bacon observes, is the purest of human pleasures and the greatest refreshment to the spirit of man; and even idle and ignorant people who cannot distinguish *Leptosiphon hybridus* from *Kauljussia amelloides* and would rather languish away in a wilderness than break their backs with dibbling and weeding may get a good deal of pleasant conversation out of it, especially if they know the old-fashioned names of the commoner sorts of flowers and are both tolerably well acquainted with the minor Elizabethan lyrists.

It was only when they had made the round of the Gardens and were sitting idly on the bank of the river that Peter, wrenching his attention back to the sordid present, remarked suddenly:

'I think I shall have to pay a visit to a friend of yours. Do you know how Jukes came to be caught with the stuff on him?'

'I've no idea.'

'The police got an anonymous letter.'

'No—?'

'Yes. One of them there. By the way, did you ever try and find out what was to have been the last word of that message to you? The one we found in the Science Lecture-Room?'

'No – she couldn't have finished it, anyhow. There wasn't a single vowel left in the box. Not even a B and a dash!'

'That was an oversight. I thought so. Well, Harriet, it's easy to put a name to the person we want, isn't it? But proof's a different matter. We've tied the thing up so tight. That lecture-room episode was meant to be the last of the nocturnal prowls, and it probably will be. And the best bit of evidence will be at the bottom of the river by this time. It's too late to seal the doors and set a watch.'

'On whom?'

'Surely you know by this time? You *must* know, Harriet, if you're giving your mind to the thing at all. Opportunity, means, motive – doesn't it stand out a mile? For God's sake, put your prejudices aside and think it out. What's happened to you that you can't put two and two together?'

'I don't know.'

'Well,' said he drily, 'if you really don't know, it's not for me to tell you. But if you will turn your attention for one moment to the matter in hand and go through your own dossier of the case carefully—'

'Undeterred by any casual sonnets I may find by the way?'

'Undeterred by any personal consideration whatever,' he burst out, almost angrily. 'No; you're quite right. That was a stupidity. My talent for standing in my own light amounts to genius, doesn't it? But when you have come to a conclusion about all this, will you remember that it was *I* who asked *you* to take a dispassionate view and I who told *you* that of all devils let loose in the world there was no devil like devoted love. . . . I don't mean passion. Passion's a good, stupid horse that will pull the plough six days a week if you give him the run of his heels on Sundays. But love's a nervous, awkward, over-mastering brute; if you can't rein him, it's best to have no truck with him.'

'That sounds very topsy-turvy,' said Harriet, mildly. But his unwonted excitement had already flickered out.

'I'm only walking on my head, after the manner of clowns. If we went along to Shrewsbury now, do you think the Warden would see me?'

Later in the day, Dr. Baring sent for Harriet.

'Lord Peter Wimsey has been to see me,' she said, 'with a rather curious proposition which, after a little consideration, I refused. He told me that he was almost certain in his own mind of the identity of the – the offender, but that he was not in a position at the moment to offer a complete proof. He also said that the person had, he thought, taken the alarm, and would be doubly careful from now on to escape detection. The alarm might, in fact, be sufficient to prevent further outbreaks until the end of the term at any rate; but as soon as our vigilance was relaxed, the trouble would probably break out again in a more violent form. I said that that would be very unsatisfactory, and he agreed. He asked whether he should name the person to me, in order that a careful watch might be kept upon her movements. I said I saw two objections to that: first, that the person might discover that she was being spied upon and merely increase her caution, and secondly, that if he happened to be mistaken as to the offender's identity, the person spied upon would be subjected to the most intolerable suspicions. Supposing, I said, the persecutions merely ceased, and we were left suspecting this person – who might be quite innocent – without proof either way. He replied that those were precisely the objections that had occurred to him. Do you know the name of the person to whom he alludes, Miss Vane?'

'No,' said Harriet, who had been exercising her wits in the interval. 'I am beginning to have an idea; but I can't make it fit. In fact, I simply can't believe it.'

'Very well. Lord Peter then made a very remarkable proposition. He asked whether I would allow him to interrogate this person privately, in the hope of surprising her into some admission. He said that if this bluff, as he called it, came off, the culprit could then make her confession to me and be suffered to depart quietly, or be dealt with medically, as we might decide was advisable. If, however, it did not come off and the person denied everything, we might be placed in a very disagreeable position. I replied that I quite saw that, and could not possibly consent to have such methods used upon anybody in this College. To which he replied that that was exactly what he had expected me to say.

'I then asked him what evidence, if any, he had against this person. He said that all his evidence was circumstantial; that he hoped to have more of it in the course of the next few days, but that in default of a fresh outbreak and the capture of the culprit red-handed, he doubted whether any direct evidence could be produced at this stage. I inquired whether there was any reason why we should not at least wait for the production of the additional evidence.'

Dr. Baring paused and looked keenly at Harriet.

'He replied that there was only one reason, and that was the culprit, instead of becoming more cautious, might throw caution to the winds and proceed to direct violence. "In which case," he said, "we should very likely catch her, but only at the cost of somebody's death or serious injury." I asked what persons were threatened with death or injury. He had said the most probable victims were – yourself, Miss de Vine and another person whom he could not name, but whose existence, he said, he deduced. He also surprised me by saying that an abortive attack had already been made upon you. Is that true?'

'I shouldn't have put it as strongly as that,' said Harriet. She briefly outlined the story of the telephone call. At the name of Miss Hillyard, the Warden looked up:

'Do I understand that you entertain a definite suspicion of Miss Hillyard?'

'If I did,' said Harriet, cautiously. 'I shouldn't be the only person to do so. But I'm bound to say that she doesn't seem to fit in at all with the line of Lord Peter's inquiries, so far as I am acquainted with them.'

'I am glad to hear you say that,' replied Dr. Baring. 'Representations have been made to me which – in default of evidence – I have been very unwilling to listen to.'

So Dr. Baring had kept abreast of the feeling of the S.C.R. Miss Allison and Mrs. Goodwin had probably been talking. Well!

'In the end,' pursued the Warden, 'I informed Lord Peter that I thought it would be better to wait for the further evidence. But that decision must, of course, be subject to the willingness of yourself and Miss de Vine to face the risks involved. The willingness of the unknown third party cannot, naturally, be ascertained.'

'I don't in the least mind what risks *I* take,' said Harriet. 'But Miss de Vine ought to be warned, I suppose.'

'That is what I said. Lord Peter agreed.'

So, thought Harriet, something has decided him to acquit Miss de Vine. I'm glad. Unless this is a Machiavellian ruse to throw her off her guard.

'Have you said anything to Miss de Vine, Warden?'

'Miss de Vine is in Town, and will not return till tomorrow evening. I propose to speak to her then.'

So there was nothing to do but to wait. And in the meantime, Harriet became aware of a curious change in the atmosphere of the Senior Common Room. It was as though they had lost sight of their mutual distrust and their general apprehensions and had drawn together like spectators at the ring-side to watch another kind of conflict, in which she was one of the principals. The curious tension thus produced was scarcely relieved by the Dean's announcement to a few select spirits that in *her* opinion, Flaxman's young man had given her the chuck and serve her right; to which Miss Flaxman's tutor sourly replied that she wished people wouldn't have these upheavals in the Summer Term, but that, fortunately, Miss Flaxman didn't take her final Schools till next year. This prompted Harriet to ask Miss Shaw how Miss Newland was getting on. It appeared that Miss Newland was doing well, having completely got over the shock of her immersion in the Cherwell, so that her chances for a First looked pretty good.

'Splendid!' said Harriet. 'I've ear-marked my winnings already. By the way, Miss Hillyard, how is our young friend Cattermole?'

It seemed to her that the room waited breathlessly for the answer. Miss Hillyard replied, rather shortly, that Miss Cattermole seemed to have recovered such form as she had ever possessed, thanks, as she understood from the young woman herself, to Miss Vane's good advice. She added that it was very kind of Harriet, amid her many preoccupations, to interest herself in the History students. Harriet made some vague reply and the room, as it seemed to her, breathed again.

Later in the day, Harriet took an outrigger on the river with the Dean, and, rather to her surprise, observed Miss Cattermole and Mr. Pomfret sharing a punt. She had received a penitent letter from Mr. Pomfret, and waved a cheerful hand as the boats passed, in token of peace restored. If she had known that Mr. Pomfret and Miss Cattermole had found a bond of sympathy in devotion to herself, she might have speculated on what may happen to rejected lovers who confide their troubles to willing ears; but this did not occur to her, because she was wondering what, exactly, had happened that morning at the Mitre; and her thoughts had strayed away into the Botanical Gardens before the Dean pointed out, rather sharply, that she was setting a very irregular and leisurely stroke.

It was Miss Shaw who innocently precipitated a flare-up.

'That's a very handsome scarf,' she said to Miss Hillyard. The dons were assembling, as usual, for Hall,

484

outside the S.C.R.; but the evening was dull and chilly and a thick silk scarf was a grateful addition to evening dress.

'Yes,' said Miss Hillyard. 'Unfortunately it isn't mine. Some careless person left it in the Fellows Garden last night and I rescued it. I brought it along to be identified – but I'm ready to admit that I can do with it this evening.'

'I don't know whose it can be,' said Miss Lydgate. She fingered it admiringly. 'It looks more like a man's scarf.' she added.

Harriet, who had hot been paying much attention, turned round, conscience-stricken.

'Good lord!' she said, 'that's mine. At least, it's Peter's. I couldn't think where I'd left it.'

It was, in fact, the very scarf that had been used for a strangling demonstration on the Friday, and been brought back to Shrewsbury by accident together with the chess-men and the dog-collar. Miss Hillyard turned brick-red and snatched it off as though it were choking her.

'I *beg* your pardon, Miss Vane,' she said, holding it out.

'It's all right. I don't want it now. But I'm glad to know where it is. I'd have got into trouble if I'd lost it.'

'Will you kindly take your property,' said Miss Hill-yard.

Harriet, who was already wearing a scarf of her own, said:

'Thank you. But are you sure you won't—'

'I will *not*,' said Miss Hillyard, dropping the scarf angrily on the steps.

'Dear me!' said the Dean, picking it up. 'Nobody seems to want this nice scarf. I shall borrow it. I call it a nasty, chilly evening, and I don't know why we can't all go inside.'

She twisted the scarf comfortably round her neck, and the Warden mercifully arriving at that moment, they went in to dinner.

At a quarter to ten, Harriet, after an hour or so spent with Miss Lydgate on her proofs – now actually nearing the stage when they might really be sent to the printer – crossed the Old Quad to Tudor Building. On the steps, just coming out, she met Miss Hillyard.

'Were you looking for me?' asked Harriet, a little aggressively.

'No,' said Miss Hillyard, 'I wasn't. Certainly not.' She spoke hurriedly, and Harriet fancied that there was something in her eyes both furtive and malicious; but the evening was dark for the middle of May, and she could not be sure.

'Oh!' said Harriet. 'I thought you might be.'

'Well, I wasn't,' said Miss Hillyard again. And as Harriet passed her she turned back and said, almost as though the words were forced out of her:

'Going to work – under the inspiration of your beautiful chessmen?'

'More or less,' said Harriet, laughing.

'I hope you will have a pleasant evening,' said Miss Hillyard.

Harriet went on upstairs and opened the door of her room.

The glass case had been shattered, and the floor was strewn with broken glass and with smashed and trampled fragments of red and white ivory.

For about five minutes, Harriet was the prey of that kind of speechless rage which is beyond expression or control. If she had thought of it, she was at that moment in a mood to sympathise with the Poltergeist and all her works. If she could have beaten or strangled anybody, she would have done it and felt the better for it. Happily, after the first devastating fury, she found the relief of bad language. When she found she could keep her voice steady, she locked her bedroom door behind her and went down to the telephone.

Even so, she was at first so incoherent that Peter could hardly understand what she said. When he did understand, he was maddeningly cool about it, merely asking whether she had touched anything or told anybody. When assured that she had not he replied cheerfully that he would be along in a few minutes.

Harriet went out and raged distractedly about the New Quad till she heard him ring – for the gates were now shut – and only a last lingering vestige of self-restraint prevented her from rushing at him and pouring out her indignation in the presence of Padgett. But she waited for him in the middle of the quad.

'Peter – oh, Peter!'

'Well,' said he, 'this is rather encouraging. I was afraid we might have choked off these demonstrations for good and all.'

'But my chessmen! I could kill her for that.'

'My dear, it's sickening that it should be your chessmen. But don't let's lose all sense of proportion. It might have been you.'

'I wish it had been. I could have hit back.'

'Termagant. Let's go and look at the damage.'

'It's horrible, Peter. It's like a massacre. It's – it's rather frightening, somehow – they've been hit so hard.'

When he saw the room, Wimsey looked grave enough.

'Yes,' he said, kneeling amid the wreckage. 'Blind, bestial malignity. Not only broken but ground to powder. There's been a heel at work here, as well as the poker; you can see the marks on the carpet. She hates you, Harriet. I didn't realise that. I thought she was only afraid of you . . . Is there yet any that is left of the house of Saul? . . . Look! one poor warrior hiding behind the coal-scuttle – remnant of a mighty army.'

He held up the solitary red pawn, smiling; and then scrambled hurriedly to his feet.

'My dear girl, don't cry about it. What the hell does it matter?'

'I loved them,' said Harriet, 'and you gave them to me.'

He shook his head.

'It's a pity it's that way round. "You gave them to me, and I loved them" is all right, but, "I loved them and you gave them to me" is irreparable. Fifty thousand rocs' eggs won't supply their place. "The virgin's gone and I am gone; she's gone, she's gone and what shall I do?" But you needn't weep over the chest of drawers while I have a shoulder at your disposal, need you?'

'I'm sorry. I'm being a perfect idiot.'

'I told you love was the devil and all. Two-and-thirty chessmen, baked in a pie. "And all the powerful kings and all the beautiful queens of this world were but as a bed of flowers" . . .'

'I might have had the decency to take care of them.'

'That's foolish,' said he, with his mouth muffled in her hair. 'Don't talk so soft, or I shall get foolish too. Listen. When did all this happen?'

'Between Hall and a quarter to ten.'

'Was anybody absent from Hall? Because this must have made a bit of a noise. After Hall, there'd be students about, who might hear the glass smash or notice if anybody unusual was wandering about.'

'There might be students here all through Hall – they

often have eggs in their rooms. And – good God! there was somebody unusual— She said something about the chessmen, too. And she was queer about them last night.'

'Who was that?'

'Miss Hillyard.'

'Again!'

While Harriet told her story he fidgeted restlessly about the room, avoiding the broken glass and ivory on the floor with the automatic precision of a cat, and stood at length in the window with his back to her. She had drawn the curtains together when she had brought him up, and his gaze at them seemed purely preoccupied.

'Hell!' he said, presently. 'That's a devil of a complication.' He still had the red pawn in his hand, and he now came back, and set it with great precision in the centre of the mantelpiece. 'Yes. Well, I suppose you'll have to find out—'

Somebody knocked at the door, and Harriet went to open it.

'Excuse me, madam, but Padgett sent over to the Senior Common Room to see if Lord Peter Wimsey was there, and seeing he thought you might know—'

'He's here, Annie. It's for you, Peter.'

'Yes?' said Peter, coming to the door.

'If you please, sir, they've rung up from the Mitre to say there's a message come from the Foreign Office and would you kindly ring up at once.'

'What? Oh, lord, that *would* happen! Very well, thank you, Annie. Oh, one moment. Was it you who saw the – er – the person who was playing tricks in the lecture-room?'

'Yes, sir. Not to know her again, sir.'

'No; but you did see her, and she may not know you couldn't recognise her. I think if I were you I'd be rather careful how you go about the College after dark. I don't want to frighten you, but you see what's happened to Miss Vane's chessmen?'

'Yes, I see, sir. What a pity, isn't it?'

'It would be more than a pity if anything unpleasant happened to you personally. Now, don't get the wind up – but if I were you, I'd take somebody with me when I went out after sunset. And I should give the same advice to the scout who was with you.'

'To Carrie? Very well, I'll tell her.'

'It's only a precaution, you know. Good night, Annie.'

'Good night, sir. Thank you.'

'I shall have to make quite an issue of dog-collars,' said Peter. 'You never know whether to warn people or not. Some of them get hysterics, but she looks fairly level-headed. Look here, my dear, this is all very tiresome. If it's another summons to Rome, I shall have to go. (I should lock that door.) Needs must when duty calls, and all that. If it *is* Rome, I'll tell Bunter to bring round all the notes I've got at the Mitre and instruct Miss Climpson's sleuths to report direct to you. In any case, I'll ring you up this evening as soon as I know what it's all about. If it isn't Rome, I'll come round again in the morning. And in the meantime, don't let anybody into your room. I think I'd lock it up and sleep elsewhere to-night.'

'I thought you didn't expect any more night disturbances.'

'I don't; but I don't want people walking over that floor.' He stopped on the staircase to examine the sole of his shoes. 'I haven't carried away any bits. Do you think you have?'

Harriet stood first on one leg and then another.

'Not this time. And the first time I didn't walk into the mess at all. I stood in the doorway and swore.'

'Good girl. The paths in the quad are a bit damp, you know, and something might have stuck. As a matter of fact, it's raining a little now. You'll get wet.'

'It doesn't matter. Oh, Peter! I've got that white scarf of yours.'

'Keep it till I come again – which will be to-morrow, with luck, and otherwise, God knows when. Damn it! I knew there was trouble coming.' He stood still under the beech-trees. 'Harriet, don't choose the moment my back's turned to get wiped out or anything – not if you can help it; I mean, you're not very good at looking after valuables.'

'I might have the decency to take care? All right, Peter. I'll do my best this time. Word of honour.'

She gave him her hand and he kissed it. Once again Harriet thought she saw somebody move in the darkness, as on the last occasion they had walked through the shadowy quads. But she dared not delay him and so again said nothing. Padgett let him out through the gate and Harriet, turning away, found herself face to face with Miss Hillyard.

'Miss Vane, I should like to speak to you.'

'Certainly,' said Harriet. 'I should rather like to speak to *you*.'

Miss Hillyard, without another word, led the way to her own rooms. Harriet followed her up the stairs and into the sitting-room. The tutor's face was very white as she shut the door after them and said, without asking Harriet to sit down:

'Miss Vane. What are the relations between that man and you?'

'What do you mean by that?'

'You know perfectly well what I mean. If nobody else will speak to you about your behaviour, I must. You

491

bring the man here, knowing perfectly well what his reputation is—'

'I know what his reputation as a detective is.'

'I mean his moral reputation. You know as well as I do that he is notorious all over Europe. He keeps women by the score—'

'All at once or in succession?'

'It's no use being impertinent. I suppose that to a person with your past history, that kind of thing is merely amusing. But you must try to conduct yourself with a little more decency. The way you look at him is a disgrace. You pretend to be the merest acquaintance of his and call him by his title in public and his Christian name in private. You take him up to your room at night—'

'Really, Miss Hillyard, I can't allow—'

'I've seen you. Twice. He was there to-night. You let him kiss your hands and make love to you—'

'So that was you, spying about under the beeches.'

'How dare you use such a word?'

'How dare you say such a thing?'

'It's no affair of mine how you behave in Bloomsbury. But if you bring your lovers here—'

'You know very well that he is not my lover. And you know very well why he came to my room to-night.'

'I can guess.'

'And I know very well why you came there.'

'I came there? I don't know what you mean.'

'You do. And you know that he came to see the damage you did in my room.'

'I never went into your room.'

'You didn't go into my room and smash up my chess-men?'

Miss Hillyard's dark eyes flickered.

'Certainly I did not. I told you I hadn't been anywhere near your room to-night.'

'Then,' said Harriet, 'you told a lie.'

She was too angry to be frightened, though it did cross her mind that if the furious white-faced woman attacked her, it might be difficult to summon assistance on this isolated staircase, and she thought of the dog-collar.

'I know it's a lie,' said Harriet, 'because there's a piece of broken ivory on the carpet under your writing-table and another stuck on the heel of your right shoe. I saw it, coming upstairs.'

She was prepared for anything after that, but to her surprise, Miss Hillyard staggered a little, sat down suddenly, and said, 'Oh, My God!'

'If you had nothing to do with smashing those chessmen,' went on Harriet, 'or with the other pranks that have been played in this College, you'd better explain those pieces of ivory.'

(Am I a fool, she thought, showing my hand like this? But, if I didn't, what would become of the evidence?)

Miss Hillyard, in a bewildered way, pulled off her slipper and looked at the sliver of white that clung to the heel, embedded in a little patch of damp gravel.

'Give it to me,' said Harriet, and took slipper and all.

She had expected an outburst of denial, but Miss Hlllyard said, faintly:

'That's evidence . . . incontrovertible. . . .'

Harriet thanked Heaven, with grim amusement, for the scholarly habit; at least, one did not have to argue about what was or was not evidence.

'I did go into your room. I went there to say to you what I said just now. But you weren't there. And when I saw the mess on the floor I thought – I was afraid you'd think—'

'I did think.'

'What did he think?'

'Lord Peter? I don't know what he thought. But he'll probably think something now.'

'You've no evidence that I did it,' said Miss Hillyard, with sudden spirit. 'Only that I was in the room. It was done when I got there. I saw it, I went to look at it. You can tell your lover that I saw it and was glad to see it. But he'll tell you that's no proof that I did it.'

'Look here, Miss Hillyard,' said Harriet, divided between anger, suspicion and a dreadful kind of pity, 'you must understand, once and for all, that he is not my lover. Do you really imagine that if he were, we should—' here her sense of the ludicrous overcame her and made it difficult to control her voice – 'we should come and misbehave ourselves in the greatest possible discomfort at Shrewsbury? Even if I had no respect for the College – where would be the point of it? With all the world and all the time there is at our disposal, why on earth should we come and play the fool down here? It would be silly. And if you really were down there in the quad just now, you must know that people who are lovers don't treat each other like that. At least,' she added rather unkindly, 'if you knew anything about it at all, you'd know that. We're very old friends, and I owe him a great deal—'

'Don't talk nonsense,' said the tutor roughly. 'You know you're in love with the man.'

'By God!' said Harriet, suddenly enlightened, 'if I'm not, I know who is.'

'You've no right to say that!'

'It's true, all the same,' said Harriet. 'Oh, damn! I suppose it's no good my saying I'm frightfully sorry.' (Dynamite in a powder factory? Yes, indeed, Miss Edwards, you saw it before anybody else. Biologically

494

interesting!) 'This kind of thing is the devil and all.' ('That's the devil of a complication,' Peter had said. He'd seen it, of course. Must have. Too much experience not to. Probably happened scores of times – scores of women – all over Europe. Oh, dear! Oh, dear! And was that a random accusation, or had Miss Hillyard been delving into the past and digging up Viennese singers?)

'For Heaven's sake,' said Miss Hillyard, 'go away!'

'I think I'd better,' said Harriet.

She did not know how to deal with the situation at all. She could no longer feel outraged or angry. She was not alarmed. She was not jealous. She was only sorry, and quite incapable of expressing any sympathy which would not be an insult. She realised that she was still clutching Miss Hillyard's slipper. Had she better give it back? It was evidence – of something. But of what? The whole business of the Poltergeist seemed to have retreated over the horizon, leaving behind it the tormented shell of a woman staring blindly into vacancy under the cruel harshness of the electric light. Harriet picked up the other fragment of ivory from under the writing-table – the little spearhead from a red pawn.

'Well, whatever one's personal feelings, evidence was evidence. Peter – she remembered that Peter had said he would ring up from the Mitre. She went downstairs with the slipper in her hand, and in the New Quad ran into Mrs. Padgett, who was just coming to look for her.

The call was switched through to the box in Queen Elizabeth.

'It's not so bad after all,' said Peter's voice, 'It's only the Grand Panjandrum wanting a conference at his private house. Sort of Pleasant Sunday Afternoon in Wild Warwickshire. It may mean London or Rome after that, but we'll hope not. At any rate, it'll do if I'm there by half-past eleven, so I'll pop round and see you about nine.'

'Please do. Something's happened. Not alarming, but upsetting. I can't tell you on the phone.'

He again promised to come, and said good night. Harriet, after locking the slipper and the piece of ivory carefully away, went to the Bursar, and was accommodated with a bed in the Infirmary.

21

Thus she there wayted until eventyde.
Yet living creature none she saw appeare.
And now sad shadows gan the world to hyde
From mortall vew, and wrap in darkness dreare;
Yet nould she d'off her weary armes, for feare
Of secret daunger, ne let sleepe oppresse
Her heavy eyes with nature's burdein deare,
But drew her self aside in sickernesse,
And her wel-pointed wepons did about her dresse.

EDMUND SPENCER

HARRIET left word at the Lodge that she would wait for Lord Peter Wimsey in the Fellows' Garden. She had breakfasted early, thus avoiding Miss Hillyard, who passed through the New Quad like an angry shadow while she was talking to Padgett.

She had first met Peter at a moment when every physical feeling had been battered out of her by the brutality of circumstance; by this accident she had been aware of him from the beginning as a mind and spirit localised in a body. Never – not even in those later dizzying moments on the river – had she considered him primarily as a male animal or calculated the promise implicit in the veiled eyes, the long, flexible mouth, the curiously vital hands. Nor, since of her he had always asked and never demanded, had she felt in him any domination but that of intellect. But now, as he advanced towards her along the flower-bordered path, she saw him with new eyes – the eyes of women who had seen him before they knew him – saw him, as they saw him, dynamically. Miss Hillyard, Miss Edwards, Miss de Vine, the Dean even, each in her own way had recognised the same thing: six centuries of possessiveness, fastened under the yoke of urbanity. She herself, seeing it impudent and uncontrolled in the nephew, had known it instantly for what it was; it astonished her that in the older man she should have been blind to it so long and should still retain so strong a defence against it. And she wondered whether it was only accident that had sealed her eyes till it was too late for realisation to bring disaster.

She sat still where she was till he stood looking down at her.

'Well?' he said, lightly, 'how doth my lady? What, sweeting, all amort? . . . Yes, something has happened; I see it has What is it, domina?'

Though the tone was half-jesting, nothing could have reassured her like that grave, academic title. She said, as though she were reciting a lesson.

'When you left last night, Miss Hillyard met me in the New Quad. She asked me to come up to her room because she wanted to speak to me. On the way up, I saw there was a little piece of white ivory stuck on the heel of her slipper. She – made some rather unpleasant accusations; she had misunderstood the position—'

'That can and shall be put right. Did you say anything about the slipper?'

'I'm afraid I did. There was another bit of ivory on the floor. I accused her of having gone into my room, and she denied it till I showed her the evidence. Then she admitted it; but she said the, damage was already done when she got there.'

'Did you believe her?'

'I might have done . . . if . . . if she hadn't shown me a motive.'

'I see. All right. You needn't tell me.'

She looked up for the first time into a face as bleak as winter, and faltered.

'I brought the slipper away with me. I wish I hadn't.'

'Are you going to be afraid of the facts?' he said. 'And you a scholar?'

'I don't think I did it in malice. I hope not. But I was bitterly unkind to her.'

'Happily,' said he, 'a fact is a fact, and your state of mind won't alter it by a hair's breadth. Let's go now and have the truth at all hazards.'

She led him up to her room, where the morning sun cast a long rectangle of brilliance across the ruin on the floor. From the chest near the door she took out the slipper and handed it to him. He lay down flat, squinting sideways along the carpet in the place where neither he nor she had trodden the night before. His hand went to his pocket and he smiled up sideways into her troubled face.

'If all the pens that ever poets held had had the feeling of their masters' thoughts, they could not write as much solid fact as you can hold in a pair of callipers.' He measured the heel of the slipper in both directions, and then turned his attention to the pile of the carpet. 'She stood here, heels together, looking.' The callipers twinkled over the sunlit rectangle. 'And here is the heel that stamped and trampled and ground beauty to dust. One was a French heel and one was a Cuban heel – isn't that what the footwear specialists call them?' He sat up and tapped the sole of the slipper lightly with the callipers. 'Who goes there? France – Pass, France, and all's well.'

'Oh, I'm glad,' said Harriet, fervently. 'I'm glad.'

'Yes. Meanness isn't one of your accomplishment, is it?' He turned his eyes to the carpet again, this time to a place near the edge.

'Look! now that the sun's out you can see it. Here's where Cuban Heel wiped her soles before she left. There are very few flies on Cuban Heel. Well, that saves us a back-breaking search all over the College for the dust of kings and queens.' He picked the sliver of ivory from the French heel, put the slipper in his pocket and stood up. 'This had better go back to its owner, furnished with a certificate of innocence.'

'Give it to me. I must take it.'

'No, you will not. If anybody has to face unpleasantness, it shan't be you this time.'

'But Peter – you won't—'

'No,' he said, 'I wont. Trust me for that.'

Harriet was left staring at the broken chessmen. Presently she went out into the corridor, found a dustpan and brush in a scout's pantry and returned with them to sweep up the debris. As she was replacing the brush and pan in the pantry, she ran into one of the students from the annexe.

'By the way, Miss Swift,' said Harriet, 'you didn't happen to hear any noise in my room like glass being smashed last night did you? Some time during or after Hall?'

'No, I didn't, Miss Vane. I was in my own room all evening. But wait a moment. Miss Ward came along about half-past nine to do some Morphology with me and' – the girl's mouth dimpled into laughter – 'she asked if you were a secret toffee-eater, because it sounded as though you were smashing up toffee with the poker. Has the College Ghost been visiting you?'

'I'm afraid so,' said Harriet. 'Thank you; that's very helpful. I must see Miss Ward.'

Miss Ward, however, could help no further than by fixing the time a little more definitely as 'certainly not later than half-past nine.'

Harriet thanked her, and went out. Her very bones seemed to ache with restlessness – or perhaps it was with having slept badly in an unfamiliar bed and with a disturbed mind. The sun had scattered diamonds among the wet grass of the quadrangle, and the breeze was shaking the rain in a heavy spatter of drops from the beeches. Students came and went. Somebody had left a scarlet cushion out all night in the rain; it was sodden and mournful-looking; its owner came and picked it up, with an air between laughter and disgust; she threw it on a bench to dry in the sunshine.

To do nothing was intolerable. To be spoken to by any member of the Senior Common Room would be still more intolerable. She was penned in the Old Quad, for she was sensitive to the mere neighbourhood of the New Quad as a person that has been vaccinated is sensitive to everything that lies on the sore side of his body. Without particular aim or intention, she skirted the tennis-court and turned in at the Library entrance. She had intended to go upstairs but, seeing the door of Miss de Vine's set stand open, she altered her mind; she could borrow a book from there. The little lobby was empty, but in the sitting-room a scout was giving the writing-table a Sunday-morning flick with the duster. Harriet remembered that Miss de Vine was in Town, and that she was to be warned when she returned.

'What time does Miss de Vine get back to-night? Do you know, Nellie?'

'I think she gets in by the 9.39, miss.'

Harriet nodded, took a book from the shelves at random, and went to sit on the steps of the loggia, where there was a deck-chair. The morning, she told herself, was getting on. If Peter had to get to his destination by 11.30, it was time he went. She vividly remembered waiting in a nursing-home while a friend underwent an operation; there had been a smell of ether, and, in the waiting-room, a large black Wedgwood jar, filled with delphiniums.

She read a page without knowing what was in it, and looked up at an approaching footstep into the face of Miss Hillyard.

'Lord Peter,' said Miss Hillyard, without preface, 'asked me to give you this address. He was obliged to leave quickly to keep his appointment.'

Harriet took the paper and said, 'Thank you.'

Miss Hillyard went on resolutely. 'When I spoke to you last night I was under a misapprehension. I had not fully realised the difficulty of your position. I am afraid I have unwittingly made it harder for you, and I apologise.'

'That's all right,' said Harriet, taking refuge in formula. 'I am sorry too. I was rather upset last night and said a great deal more than I should. This wretched business has made everything so uncomfortable.'

'Indeed it has,' said Miss Hillyard, in a more natural voice. 'We are all feeling rather overwrought. I wish we could get at the truth of it. I understand that you now accept my account of my movements last night.'

'Absolutely. It was inexcusable of me not to have verified my data.'

'Appearances can be very misleading,' said Miss Hillyard.

There was a pause.

'Well,' said Harriet at last, 'I hope we may forget all this.' She knew as she spoke that one thing at least had been said which could never be forgotten: she would have given a great deal to recall it.

'I shall do my best,' replied Miss Hillyard. 'Perhaps I am too much inclined to judge harshly of matters outside my experience.'

'It is very kind of you to say that,' said Harriet. 'Please believe that I don't take a very self-satisfied view of myself either.'

'Very likely not. I have noticed that the people who get opportunities always seem to choose the wrong ones. But it's no affair of mine. Good morning.'

She went as abruptly as she had come. Harriet glanced at the book on her knee and discovered that she was reading *The Anatomy of Melancholy*.

'*Fleat Heraclitus an rideat Democritus?* In attempting to speak of these Symptoms, shall I laugh with *Democritus* or weep with *Heraclitus*? they are so ridiculous and absurd on the one side, so lamentable and tragical on the other.'

Harriet got the car out in the afternoon and took Miss Lydgate and the Dean for a picnic in the neighbourhood of Hinksey. When she got back, in time for supper, she found an urgent message at the Lodge, asking her to ring up Lord Saint-George at the House as soon as she got back. His voice, when he answered the call, sounded agitated.

'Oh, look here! I can't get hold of Uncle Peter – he's vanished again, curse him! I say, I saw your ghost this afternoon, and I do think you ought to be careful.'

'Where did you see her? When?'

'About half-past two – walking over Magdalen Bridge

in broad daylight. I'd been lunching with some chaps out Iffley way, and we were just pulling over to put one of 'em down at Magdalen, when I spotted her. She was walking along, muttering to herself, and looking awfully queer. Sort of clutching with her hands and rolling her eyes about. She spotted me, too. Couldn't mistake her. A friend of mine was driving and I tried to catch his attention, but he was pulling round behind a bus and I couldn't make him understand. Anyhow, when we stopped at Magdalen gate, I hopped out and ran back, but I couldn't find her anywhere. Seemed to have faded out. I bet she knew I was on to her and made tracks. I was scared. Thought she looked up to anything. So I rang up your place and found you were out and then I rang up the Mitre and that wasn't any good either, so I've been sitting here all evening in a devil of a stew. First I thought I'd leave a note, and then I thought I'd better tell you myself. Rather devoted of me, don't you think? I cut a supper-party so as not to miss you.'

'That was frightfully kind of you,' said Harriet. 'What was the ghost dressed in?'

'Oh – one of those sort of dark-blue frocks with spriggy bits on it and a hat with a brim. Sort of thing most of your dons wear in the afternoon. Neat, not gaudy. Not smart. Just ordinary. It was the eyes I recognised. Made me feel all goose-flesh. Honest. That woman's not safe, I'll swear she isn't.'

'It's very good of you to warn me,' said Harriet again. 'I'll try and find out who it could have been. And I'll take precautions.'

'Please do,' said Lord Staint-George. 'I mean, Uncle Peter's getting the wind up horribly. Gone clean off his oats. Of course I know he's a fidgety old ass and I've been doing my best to soothe the troubled breast and all that, but I'm beginning to think he's got some excuse. For goodness' sake, Aunt Harriet, do something about it. I can't afford to have a valuable uncle destroyed under my eyes. He's getting like the Lord of Burleigh, you know – walking up and pacing down and so on – and the responsibility is very wearing.'

'I'll tell you what,' said Harriet. 'You'd better come and dine in College to-morrow and see if you can spot the lady. It's no good this evening, because so many people don't turn up to Sunday supper.'

'Right-ho!' said the viscount. 'That's a dashed good idea. I'd get a dashed good birthday-present out of Uncle Peter if I solved his problem for him. So long and take care of yourself.'

'I ought to have thought of that before,' said Harriet, retailing this piece of news to the Dean; 'but I never imagined he'd recognise the woman like that after only seeing her once.'

The Dean, to whom the whole story of Lord Saint-George's ghostly encounter had come as a novelty, was inclined to be sceptical. 'Personally, I wouldn't undertake to identify anybody after one glimpse in the dark – and I certainly wouldn't trust a young harum-scarum like that. The only person here I know of with a navy sprigged foulard is Miss Lydgate, and I absolutely refuse to believe *that*! But ask the young man to dinner by all means. I'm all for excitement, and he's even more ornamental than the other one.'

It was borne in upon Harriet that things were coming to a crisis. 'Take precautions.' A nice fool she would look, going about with a dog-collar round her neck. Nor would it be any defence against pokers and such things. . . . The wind must be in the south-west, for the heavy boom of Tom tolling his hundred-and-one came clearly to her ears as she crossed the Old Quad.

'Not later than half-past nine,' Miss Ward had said. If the peril had ceased to walk by night, it was still abroad of an evening.

She went upstairs and locked the door of her room before opening a drawer and taking out the heavy strap of brass and leather. There was something about the description of that woman walking wide-eyed over Magdalen Bridge and 'clutching with her hands' that was very unpleasant to think of. She could feel Peter's grip on her throat now like: a band of iron, and could hear him saying serenely, like a textbook:

'*That* is the dangerous spot. Compression of the big blood-vessels *there* will cause almost instant unconsciousness. And then, you see, you're done for.'

And at the, momentary pressure of his thumbs the fire had swum in her eyes.

She turned with a start as something rattled the doorhandle. Probably the passage window was open and the wind blowing in. She was getting ridiculously nervous.

The buckle was stiff to her fingers. (Is thy servant a dog that she should do this thing?) When she saw herself in the glass, she laughed. 'An arum-lily quality that is in itself an invitation to violence.' Her own face, in the drowned evening light, surprised her – softened and startled and drained of colour, with eyes that looked unnaturally large under the heavy black brows, and lips a little parted. It was like the head of someone who had been guillotined; the dark band cut it off from the body like the stroke of the headsman's steel.

She wondered whether her lover had seen it like that, through that hot unhappy year when she had tried to believe that there was happiness in surrender. Poor Philip

– tormented by his own vanities, never loving her till he had killed her feelings for him, and yet perilously clutching her as he went down into the slough of death. It was not to Philip she had submitted, so much as to a theory of living. The young were always theoretical; only the middle-aged could realise the deadlines of principles. To subdue one's self to one's own end might be dangerous, but to subdue one's self to other people's ends was dust and ashes. Yet there were those, still more unhappy, who envied even the ashy saltness of those dead sea apples.

Could there ever be any alliance between the intellect and the flesh? It was this business of asking questions and analysing everything that sterilised and stultified all one's passions. Experience, perhaps, had a formula to get over this difficulty; one kept the bitter, tormenting brain on one side of the wall and the languorous sweet body on the other, and never let them meet. So that if you were made that way you could argue about loyalties in an Oxford common-room and refresh yourself elsewhere with – say – Viennese singers, presenting an unruffled surface on both sides of yourself. Easy for a man, and possible even for a woman, if one avoided foolish accidents like being tried for murder. But to seek to force incompatibles into a compromise was madness; one should neither do it nor be a party to it. If Peter wanted to make the experiment, he must do it without Harriet's connivance. Six centuries of possessive blood would not be dictated to by a bare forty-five years of over-sensitised intellect. Let the male animal take the female and be content; the busy brain could very well be 'left talking' like the hero of *Man and Superman*. In a long monologue, of course; for the female animal could only listen without contributing. Otherwise one would get the sort of couple one had in *Private Lives*, who rolled on the floor and hammered one another when they weren't making love, because they (obviously) had no conventional resources. A vista of crashing boredom, either way.

The door rattled again, as a reminder that even a little boredom might be welcome by way of change from alarms. On the mantelpiece, a solitary red pawn mocked all security ... How quietly Annie had taken Peter's warning. Did she take it seriously? Was she looking after herself? She had been her usual refined and self-contained self when she brought in the Common-room coffee that night – perhaps a little brighter looking than usual. Of course, she had had her afternoon off with Beatie and Carola. ... Curious, thought Harriet, this desire to possess children and dictate their tastes, as though they were escaping fragments of one's self, and not separate individuals. Even if the taste ran ran to motor bikes. ... Annie was all right. How about Miss de Vine, travelling down from Town in happy ignorance? – With a start, Harriet saw that it was nearly a quarter to ten. The train must be in. Had the Warden remembered about warning Miss de Vine? She ought not to be left to sleep in that ground-floor room without being forearmed. But the Warden never forgot anything.

Nevertheless, Harriet was uneasy. From her window she could not see whether any lights were on in the Library Wing. She unlocked the door and stepped out (yes – the passage window was open; nobody but the wind had rattled the handle). A few dim figures were still moving at the far end of the quad as she passed along beside the tennis court. In the Library Wing, all the ground-floor windows were dark except for the dim glow of the passage-light. Miss Barton, at any rate,

was not in her room; nor was Miss de Vine back yet. Or –
yes, she must be; for the window-curtains were drawn in
her sitting-room, though no light shone as yet behind
them.

Harriet went into the building. The door of Miss
Burrows' set stood open, and the lobby was dark. Miss
de Vine's door was shut. She knocked, but there was no
answer – and it suddenly struck her as odd that the
curtains should be drawn and no light on. She opened the
door and pressed down the wall switch in the lobby.
Nothing happened. With a growing sense of disquiet, she
went on to the sitting-room door and opened that. And
then, as her fingers went out to the switch, the fierce
clutch took her by the throat.

She had two advantages; she was partly prepared, and
the assailant had not expected the dog-collar. She felt and
heard the quick gasp in her face as the strong, cruel
fingers fumbled on the stiff leather. As they shifted their
hold, she had time to remember what she had been
taught – to catch and jerk the wrists apart. But as her
feet felt for the other's feet, her high heels slipped on the
parquet – and she was falling – they were falling together
and she was undermost; they seemed to take years to fall;
and all the time a stream of hoarse, filthy abuse was
running into her ears. Then the world went black in fire
and thunder.

Faces – swimming confusedly through crackling waves
of pain – swelling and diminishing anxiously – then
resolving themselves into one – Miss Hillyard's face,
enormous and close to her own. Then a voice, agonis-
ingly loud, blaring unintelligibly like a fog-horn. Then,
suddenly and quite clearly, like the lighted stage of a
theatre, the room, with Miss de Vine, white as marble, on

the couch and the Warden bending over her, and in between, on the floor, a white bowl filled with scarlet and the Dean kneeling beside it. Then the fog-horn boomed again, and she heard her own voice, incredibly far-off and thin: 'Tell Peter—' Then nothing.

Somebody had a headache – a quite unbearably awful headache. The white bright light in the Infirmary would have been very pleasant, if it hadn't been for the oppressive neighbourhood of the person with the headache, who was, moreover, groaning very disagreeably. It was an effort to pull one's self together and find out what the tiresome person wanted. With an effort like that of a hippopotamus climbing out of a swamp, Harriet pulled herself together and discovered that the headache and the groans were her own, and that the Infirmarian had realised what she was about and was coming to lend a hand.

'What in the world—?' said Harriet.

'Ah,' said the Infirmarian, 'that's better, No – don't try to sit up. You've had a nasty knock on the head, and the quieter you keep the better.'

'Oh, I see,' said Harriet. 'I've got a beast of a headache.' A little thought located the worst part of the headache somewhere behind the right ear. She put up an exploratory hand and encountered a bandage. 'What happened?'

'That's what we'd all like to know,' said the Infirmarian.

'Well, I can't remember a thing,' said Harriet.

'It doesn't matter. Drink this.'

Like a book, thought Harriet. They always said, 'Drink this.' The room wasn't really so bright after all; the Venetian shutters were closed. It was her own eyes

510

that were extraordinarily sensitive to light. Better shut them.

'Drink this' must have had something helpfully potent about it, because when she woke up again, the headache was better and she felt ravenously hungry. Also, she was beginning to remember things – the dog-collar and the lights that wouldn't go on – and the hands that had come clutching out of the darkness. There, memory obstinately stopped short. How the headache had come into existence she had no idea. Then she saw again the picture of Miss de Vine stretched on the couch. She asked after her.

'She's in the next room,' said the Infirmarian. 'She's had rather a nasty heart-attack, but she's better now. She would try to do too much, and, of course, finding you like that was a shock to her.'

It was not till the evening, when the Dean came in and found the patient fretting herself into a fever of curiosity, that Harriet got a complete story of the night's adventures.

'Now, if you'll keep quiet,' said the Dean, 'I'll tell you. If not, not. And your beautiful young man has sent you a young gardenful of flowers and will call again in the morning. Well, now! Poor Miss de Vine got here about 10 o'clock – her train was a bit late – and Mullins met her with a message to go and see the Warden *at once*. However, she thought she'd better take her hat off first, so she went along to her rooms – all in a hurry, so as not to keep Dr. Baring waiting. Well, of course, the first thing was that the lights wouldn't go on; and then to her horror she heard *you*, my dear, snorting on the floor in the dark. So then she tried the table-lamp and that worked – and there you were, a nasty bluggy sight for a respectable female don to find in her sitting-room. You've got two beautiful stitches in you, by the way; it was the corner of the bookcase did that. . . . So Miss de Vine rushed out calling for help, but there wasn't a soul in the building, and then, my dear, she ran like fury over to Burleigh and some students tore out to see what was happening and then somebody fetched the Warden and somebody else fetched the Infirmarian and somebody else fetched Miss Stevens and Miss Hillyard and me who were having a quiet cup of tea in my room, and we rang up the doctor, and Miss de Vine's groggy heart went back on her, what with shock and running about, and she went all blue on us – we had a lovely time.'

'You must have. One other gaudy night! I suppose you haven't found who did it?'

'For quite a long time we hadn't a moment to think about that part of it. And then, just as we were settling down, all the fuss started again about Annie.'

'Annie? What's happened to her?'

'Oh, didn't you know? We found her in the coal-hole, my dear, in such a state, what with coal-dust and hammering her fists on the door; and I wonder she wasn't clean off her head, poor thing, locked up there all that time. And if it hadn't been for Lord Peter we mightn't even have begun to look for her till next morning, what with everything being in such an uproar.'

'Yes – he warned her she might be attacked. . . . How did he—? Did you get him on the 'phone, or what?'

'Oh, yes. Well, after we'd got you and Miss de Vine to bed and had made up our minds you wouldn't either of you peg out yet awhile, somebody brightly remembered that the first thing you said when we picked you up was "Tell Peter." So we rang up the Mitre and he wasn't there; and then Miss Hillyard said she knew where he was and 'phoned through. That was after midnight. Fortunately, he hadn't gone to bed. He said he'd come over at once, and then he asked what had happened to Annie Wilson. Miss Hillyard thought the shock had affected his wits, I think. However, he insisted that she ought to be kept an eye on, so we all started to look for her. Well, you know what a job it is tracking anybody down in this place, and we hunted and hunted and nobody had seen anything of her. And then, just before two, Lord Peter arrived, looking like death, and said we were to turn the place upside down if we didn't want a corpse on our hands. Nice and reassuring *that* was!'

'I wish I hadn't missed it all,' said Harriet. 'He must have thought I was an awful ass to let myself be knocked out like that.'

'He didn't say so,' said the Dean, drily. 'He came in to see you, but of course you were under the weather. And of course he explained about the dog-collar, which had puzzled us all dreadfully.'

'Yes. She went for my throat. I do remember that. I suppose she really meant to get Miss de Vine.'

'Obviously. And with her weak heart – and no dog-collar – she wouldn't have had much chance, or so the doctor said. It was very lucky for her you happened to go in there. Or did you know?'

'I think,' said Harriet, her memory still rather confused, 'I went to tell her about Peter's warning and – oh, yes! there was something funny about the window-curtains. And the lights were all off.'

'The bulbs had been taken out. Well, anyway, somewhere about four o'clock, Padgett found Annie. She was locked up in the coal-cellar under the Hall Building, at the far end of the boiler-house. The key'd been taken away and Padgett had to break in the door. She was pounding and shouting – but of course, if we hadn't been searching for her she might have yelled till Doomsday, especially as the radiators are off, and we're not using the furnace. She was in what they call a state of collapse and couldn't give us a coherent story for ever so long. But there's nothing really the matter with her except shock and bruises where she was flung down on the coal-heap. And of course her hands and arms were pretty well skinned with battering on the door and trying to climb out of the ventilator.'

'What did she say happened?'

'Why, she was putting away the deck-chairs in the loggia about half-past nine, when somebody seized her round the neck from behind and frog's-marched her off to the cellar. She said it was a woman, and very strong—'

'She was,' said Harriet. 'I can bear witness to that. Grip like steel. And a most unfeminine vocabulary.'

'Annie says she never saw who it was, but she thought that the arm that was round her face had a dark sleeve on. Annie's own impression was that it was Miss Hillyard; but she was with the Bursar and me. But a good many of our strongest specimens haven't got alibis – particularly Miss Pyke, who says she was in her room, and Miss Barton, who claims to have been in the Fiction Library, looking for a "nice book to read." And Mrs. Goodwin, and Miss Burrows aren't very well accounted for, either. According to their own story, they were each seized at the same moment with an unaccountable desire to wander. Miss Burrows went to commune with Nature in the Fellows' Garden and Mrs Goodwin to commune with a higher Authority in the Chapel. We are all looking rather askance at one another to-day.'

'I wish to goodness,' said Harriet, 'I'd been a trifle

more efficient,' she pondered a moment. 'I wonder why she didn't stay to finish me off.'

'Lord Peter wondered that, too. He said he thought she must either have thought you were dead, or been alarmed by the blood and finding she'd got the wrong person. When you went limp, she'd probably feel about and she'd know you were not Miss de Vine – short hair and no spectacles, you see – and she'd hurry off to get rid of any blood-stains before somebody came along. At least, that was his theory. He looked pretty queer about it.'

'Is he here now?'

'No; he had to go back. . . . Something about getting an early 'plane from Croydon. He rang up and made a great to-do, but apparently it was all settled and he had to go. If any of his prayers are heard, I shouldn't think anybody in the Government would have a whole place in his body this morning. So I comforted him with hot coffee and he went off leaving orders that neither you nor Miss de Vine nor Annie was to be left alone for a single moment. And he's rung up once from London and three times from Paris.'

'Poor old Peter!' said Harriet. 'He never seems to get a night's rest.'

'Meanwhile the Warden is valiantly issuing an un-convincing statement to the effect that somebody played a foolish practical joke on Annie, that you accidentally slipped and cut your head and that Miss de Vine was upset by the sight of blood. And the College gates are shut to all comers, for fear they should be reporters in disguise. But you can't keep the scouts quiet – goodness knows what reports are going out by the tradesmen's entrance. However, the great thing is that nobody's killed. And now I must be off, or the Infirmarian will have my blood and there really *will* be an inquest.'

The next day brought Lord Saint-George. 'My turn to visit the sick,' he said. 'You're a nice, restful aunt for a fellow to adopt, I don't think. Do you realise that you've done me out of a dinner?'

'Yes,' said Harriet. 'It's a pity— Perhaps I'd better tell the Dean. You might be able to identify—'

'Now don't you start laying plots,' said he, 'or your temperature will go up. You leave it to Uncle. He says he'll be back to-morrow, by the way, and the evidence is rolling in nicely and you're to keep quiet and not worry. Honour bright. Had him on the 'phone this morning. He's all of a doodah. Says anybody could have done his business in Paris, only they've got it into their heads he's the only person who can get on the right side of some tedious old mule or other who has to be placated or conciliated or something. As far as I can make out, some obscure journalist has been assassinated and somebody's trying to make an international incident of it. Hence the pyramids. I told you Uncle Peter had a strong sense of public duty; now you see it in action.'

'Well, he's quite right.'

'What an unnatural woman you are! He ought to be here, weeping into the sheets and letting the international situation blow itself to blazes.' Lord Saint-George chuckled. 'I wish I'd been on the road with him on Monday morning. He collected five summonses in the round trip between Warwickshire and Oxford and London. My mother will be delighted. How's your head?'

'Doing fine. It was more the cut than the bump, I think.'

'Scalp-wounds do bleed, don't they? Completely pig-like. Still, it's as well you're not a "corpse in the case with a sad, swelled face." You'll be all right when they get the stitches out. Only a bit convict-like that side of the head. You'll have to be cropped all round to even matters up and Uncle Peter can wear your discarded tresses next his heart.'

'Come, come,' said Harriet. 'He doesn't date back to the seventies.'

'He's ageing rapidly. I should think he's nearly got to the sixties by now. With beautiful, golden side-whiskers. I really think you ought to rescue him before his bones start to creak and the spiders spin webs over his eyes.'

'You and your uncle,' said Harriet, 'should be set to turn phrases for a living.'

22

O no, there is no end: the end is death and madness! As I
am never better than when I am mad: then methinks I am
a brave fellow; then I do wonders: but reason abuseth me,
and there's the torment, there's the hell. At the last, sir,
bring me to one of the murderers: were he as strong as
Hector, thus would I tear and drag him up and down.

BEN JONSON

THURSDAY. A heavy, gloomy and depressing Thursday,
pouring down uninteresting rain from a sky like a grey
box-lid. The Warden had called a meeting of the Senior
Common Room for half-past two – an unconsoling hour.
All three invalids were up and about again. Harriet had
exchanged her bandages for some very unbecoming and
unromantic strappings, and had not exactly a headache,
but the sensation that a headache might begin at any
moment. Miss de Vine looked like a ghost. Annie, though
she had suffered less than the others physically, seemed
to be still haunted by nervous terrors, and crept unhappily about her duties with the other Common-Room
maid always closely in attendance.

It was understood that Lord Peter Wimsey would
attend the S.C.R. meeting in order to lay certain information before the staff. Harriet had received from him a
brief and characteristic note, which said:

'Congratulations on not being dead yet. I have taken
your collar away to have my name put on.'

She had already missed the collar. And she had had, from Miss Hillyard, a strangely vivid little picture of Peter, standing at her bedside between night and dawn, quite silent, and twisting the thick strap over and over in his hands.

All morning she had expected to see him; but he arrived only at the last moment, so that their meeting took place in the Common-Room, under the eyes of all the dons. He had driven straight from Town without changing his suit, and above the dark cloth his head had the bleached look of a faint water-colour. He paid his respects politely to the Warden and the Senior dons before coming over and taking her hand.

'Well, and how are you?'

'Not too bad, considering.'

'That's good.'

He smiled, and went to sit by the Warden. Harriet, at the opposite side of the table, slipped into a place beside the Dean. Everything that was alive in him lay in the palm of her hand, like a ripe apple. Dr. Baring was asking him to begin, and he was doing so, in the flat voice of a secretary reading the minutes of a company meeting. He had a sheaf of papers before him, including (Harriet noticed) her dossier, which he must have taken away on the Monday morning. But he went on without referring to so much as a note, addressing himself to a bowl filled with marigolds that stood on the table before him.

'I need not take up your time by going over all the details of this rather confusing case. I will first set out the salient points as they presented themselves to me when I came to Oxford last Sunday week, so as to show you the basis upon which I founded my working theory. I will then formulate that theory, and adduce the supporting evidence which I hope and think you will consider conclusive. I may say that practically all the data necessary to the formation of the theory are contained in the very valuable digest of the events prepared for me by Miss Vane and handed to me on my arrival. The rest of the proof was merely what the police call routine work.'

(This, thought Harriet, is suiting your style to your company with a vengeance. She looked round. The Common-Room had the hushed air of a congregation settling down to a sermon, but she could feel the nervous tension everywhere. They did not know what they might be going to hear.)

'The first point to strike an outsider,' went on Peter, 'is the fact that these demonstrations began at the Gaudy. I may say that that was the first bad mistake the perpetrator made. By the way, it will save time and trouble if I refer to the perpetrator in the time-honoured way as X. If X had waited till term began, we should have had a much wider field for suspicion. I therefore asked myself what it was that so greatly excited X at the Gaudy that she could not wait for a more suitable time to begin.

'It seemed unlikely that any of the Old Students present could have roused X's animosity, because the demonstrations continued in the following term. But they did not continue during the Long Vacation, So my attention was immediately directed to any person who entered the College for the first time at Gaudy and was in residence the following term. Only one person answered these requirements, and that was Miss de Vine.'

The first stir went round the table, like the wind running over a cornfield.

'The first two communications came into the hand of Miss Vane. One of them, which amounted to an accusation of murder, was slipped into the sleeve of her gown and might, by a misleading coincidence, have been held to apply to her. But Miss Martin may remember that she placed Miss Vane's gown in the Senior Common Room side by side with that of Miss de Vine. I believe that X, mis-reading "H. D. Vane" as "H. de Vine" put the note in the wrong gown. This belief is, of course, not susceptible of proof; but the possibility is suggestive. The error, if it was one, distracted attention at the start from the central object of the campaign.'

Nothing altered in the level voice as he lifted the old infamy into view only to cast it in the next breath into oblivion, but the hand that had held hers tightened for a moment and relaxed. She found herself watching the hand as it moved now among the sheaf of papers.

'The second communication, picked up accidentally by Miss Vane in the quad, was destroyed like the other; but from the description I gather that it was a drawing similar to this.' He slipped out a paper from under the clip and passed it to the Warden. 'It represents a punishment inflicted by a naked, female figure upon another, which is clothed in academical dress and epicene. This appears to be the symbolical key to the situation. In the Michaelmas Term, other drawings of a similar kind appear, together with the motif of the hanging of some academical character – a motif which is repeated in the incident of the dummy found later on suspended in the Chapel. There were also communications of a vaguely obscene and threatening sort which need not be particularly considered. The most interesting and important one, perhaps, is the message addressed to (I think) Miss Hillyard. "No man is safe from women like you"; and the other, sent to Miss Flaxman, demanding that she should leave another student's fiancé alone. These suggested that the basis of X's grievance was sexual jealousy of the ordinary kind – a suggestion which, again, I believe to be entirely erroneous and to have obscured the issue in a quite fantastic manner.

'We next come (passing over the episode of the bonfire of gowns in the quad) to the more serious matter of Miss Lydgate's manuscript. I do not think it is a coincidence that the portions most heavily disfigured and obliterated were those in which Miss Lydgate attacked the conclusions of other scholars, and those scholars, men. If I am right, we see that X is a person capable of reading, and to some extent understanding, a work of scholarship. Together with this outrage we may take the mutilation of the novel called *The Search* at the exact point where the author upholds, or appears for the moment to uphold, the doctrine that loyalty to the abstract truth must override all personal considerations; and also the burning of Miss Barton's book in which she attacks the Nazi doctrine that woman's place in the State should be confined to the "womanly" occupations of *Kinder, Kirche, Kuche*.

'In addition to these personal attacks upon individuals, we get the affair of the bonfire and the sporadic outbursts of obscenity upon the walls. When we come to the disfigurement of the Library, we get the generalised attack in a more spectacular form. The object of the campaign begins to show itself clearly. The grievance felt by X, starting from a single person, has extended itself to the entire College, and the intention is to provoke a scandal, which may bring the whole body into disrepute.'

Here for the first time the speaker lifted his gaze from the bowl of marigolds, let it travel slowly round the table, and brought it to rest upon the Warden's intent face.

'Will you let me say, here and now, that the one thing which frustrated the whole attack from the first to last was the remarkable solidarity and public spirit displayed by your college as a body. I think that was the last obstacle that X expected to encounter in a community of women. Nothing but the very great loyalty of the Senior Common Room to the College and the respect of the students for the Senior Common Room stood between you and a most unpleasant publicity. It is the merest presumption in me to tell you what you already know far better than I do; but I say it, not only for my own satisfaction, but because this particular kind of loyalty forms at once the psychological excuse for the attack and the only possible defence against it.'

'Thank you,' said the Warden. 'I feel sure that everybody here will know how to appreciate that.'

'We come next,' resumed Wimsey, his eyes once more on the marigolds, 'to the incident of the dummy in the Chapel. This merely repeats the theme of the early drawings, but with a greater eye to dramatic effect. Its evidential importance lies in the "Harpy" quotation pinned to the dummy; the mysterious appearance of a black figured frock which nobody could identify; the subsequent conviction of the ex-porter Jukes for theft; and the finding of the mutilated newspaper in Miss de Vine's room, which closed that sequence of events. I will take up those points later.

'It was about this time that Miss Vane made the acquaintance of my nephew Saint-George, and he mentioned to her that, under circumstances into which we need not, perhaps, inquire, he had met a mysterious woman one night in your Fellows' Garden, and that she had told him two things. One: that Shrewsbury College was a place where they murdered beautiful boys like him and ate their hearts out; secondly: that "the other had fair hair, too."'

This piece of information was new to most of the Senior Common Room, and caused a mild sensation.

'Here we have the "murder-motif" emphasised, with a little detail about the victim. He is a man, fair, handsome and comparatively young. My nephew then said he would not undertake to recognise the woman again; but on a subsequent occasion he saw and did recognise her.'

Once again the tremor passed round the table.

'The next important disturbance was the affair of the missing fuses.'

Here the Dean could contain herself no longer and burst out: 'What a lovely title for a thriller!'

The veiled eyes lifted instantly, and the laughter-lines gathered at the corners.

'Perfect. And that was all it was. X retired, having accomplished nothing but a thriller with good publicity value.'

'And it was after *that*,' said Miss de Vine, 'that the newspaper was found in my room.'

'Yes,' said Wimsey; 'mine was a rational, not a chronological grouping. . . . That brings us to the end of the Hilary Term. The Vacation passed without incident. In the Summer Term, we are faced with the cumulative effect of long and insidious persecution upon a scholar of sensitive temperament. That was the most dangerous phase of X's activities. We know that other students besides Miss Newland had received letters wishing them bad luck in their Schools; happily, Miss Layton and the rest were of tougher fibre. But I should like particularly to draw your attention to the fact that, with a few unimportant exceptions, the animus was all directed against dons and scholars.'

Here the Bursar, who had been manifesting irritation for some time, broke in:

'I cannot imagine why they are making all that noise

underneath this building. Do you mind, Warden, if I send out and stop it?'

'I am sorry,' said Wimsey. 'I am afraid I am responsible for that. I suggested to Padgett that a search in the coal-cellar might be profitable.'

'Then,' pronounced the Warden, 'I fear we must put up with it, Bursar.' She inclined her head towards Wimsey, who went on:

'This is a brief summary of the events as presented to me by Miss Vane, when with your consent, Warden, she laid the case before me. I rather gathered' – here the right hand became restless and began to beat out a silent tattoo upon the table-top – 'that she and some others among you were inclined to look upon the outrages as the outcome of repressions sometimes accompanying the celibate life and issuing in an obscene and unreasoning malice directed partly against the conditions of that life and partly against persons who enjoyed or had enjoyed or might be supposed to enjoy a wider experience. There is no doubt that malice of that kind exists. But the history of the case seemed to me to offer a psychological picture of an entirely different kind. One member of this Common-Room has been married, and another is engaged to be married; and neither of these, who ought to have been the first victims, were (so far as I know) persecuted at all. The dominance of the naked female figure in the early drawing is also highly significant. So is the destruction of Miss Barton's book. Also, the bias displayed by X seemed to be strongly anti-scholastic, and to have a more or less rational motive, based on some injury amounting in X's mind to murder, inflicted upon a male person by a female scholar. The grievance seemed, to my mind, to be felt principally against Miss de Vine, and to be extended, from her, to the whole College and possibly to educated

525

women in general. I therefore felt we should look for a woman either married or with sexual experience, of limited education but some acquaintance with scholars and scholarship, whose past was in some way linked with that of Miss de Vine, and (though this was an assumption) who had probably come into residence later than last December.'

Harriet twisted her glance away from Peter's hand, which had ceased its soft drumming and now lay flat on the table, to estimate the effect of this on his hearers. Miss de Vine was frowning as though her mind, running back over the years, were dispassionately considering her claim to have done murder; Miss Chilperic's face wore a troubled blush, and Mrs. Goodwin's an air of protest; in Miss Hillyard's eyes was an extra-ordinary mixture off triumph and embarrassment; Miss Barton was nodding quiet assent, Miss Allison smiling, Miss Shaw faintly affronted; Miss Edwards was looking at Peter with eyes that said frankly, 'You are the sort of person I can deal with.' The Warden's grave countenance, was expressionless. The Dean's profile gave no clue to her feelings, but she uttered a little, quick sigh that sounded like relief.

'I will now come,' said Peter, 'to the material clues. First, the printed messages. It seemed to me extremely unlikely that these could have been produced, in such quantity, within the College walls, without leaving some trace of their origin. I was inclined to look for an outside source. Similarly with the figured dress found on the dummy; it seemed very strange that nobody should ever set eyes on it before, though it was several seasons old. Thirdly, there was the odd circumstances that the letters which came by post were always received either on a Monday or a Thursday, as though Sunday and Wednesday were the only days on which letters could conveniently be posted from a distant post-office or box. These three considerations might have suggested someone living at a distance, who visited Oxford only twice a week. But the nightly disturbances made it plain that the person actually lived within the walls, with fixed days for going outside them and a place somewhere outside, where clothes could be kept and letters prepared. The person who would fulfil these conditions best would be one of the scouts.'

Miss Stevens and Miss Barton both stirred.

'The majority of the scouts, however, seemed to be ruled out. Those who were not confined within the Scouts' Wing at night were trusted women of long service here – most unlikely to fulfil any of the other conditions. Most of those in the Scouts' Wing slept two in a room, and therefore (unless two of them were in collusion) could not possibly escape into the College night after night without being suspected. This left only those who had separate bedrooms: Carrie, the head scout; Annie, the scout attached first to Miss Lydgate's staircase and subsequently to the Senior Common Room, and a third scout, Ethel, an elderly and highly reputable woman. Of these three, Annie corresponded most closely to the psychological picture of X; for she had been married and had the afternoon of Sunday and the afternoon and evening of Wednesday free; she also had her children domiciled in the town and therefore a place where she could keep clothes and prepare letters.'

'But—' began the Bursar, indignantly.

'This is only the case as I saw it last Sunday week,' said Wimsey. 'Certain powerful objections at once presented themselves. The Scouts' Wing was shut off by locked doors and gates. But it was made clear at the time of the Library episode that the buttery hatch was occasionally left open for the convenience of students wishing to obtain supplies late at night. Miss Hudson had, in fact, expected to find it open that very night. When Miss Vane tried it, it was, in fact, locked. But that was *after* X had left the Library, and you will remember that X was shown to have been trapped in the Hall Building by Miss Vane and Miss Hudson at one end and Miss Barton at the other. The assumption made at the time was that she had been hiding in the Hall.

'After that episode, greater care was taken to see that the buttery hatch was kept locked, and I learn that the key, which was previously left on the inner side of the batch, was removed and placed on Carrie's key-ring. But a key can very readily be cut in a single day. Actually, it was a week before the next nocturnal episode occurred, which carries us over the following Wednesday, when a key abstracted from Carrie's bunch might readily have been copied and returned. (I know for a fact that such a key was cut on that Wednesday by an ironmonger in the lower part of the town, though I have not been able to identify the purchaser. But that is merely a routine detail.) There was one consideration which inclined Miss Vane to exonerate all the scouts, and that was, that no woman in that position would be likely to express her resentment in the Latin quotation from the *Æneid* found attached to the dummy.

'This objection had some weight with me, but not a great deal. It was the only message that was not in English, and it was one to which any school child might easily have access. On the other hand, the fact that it was unique among the other scripts made me sure that had some particular significance. I mean, it wasn't that X's feelings habitually expressed themselves in Latin hexameters. There must be something special about that passage besides its general applicability to unnatural females who snatch the meat from men's mouths. *Neo saevior ulla pestis.*'

'When I first heard of that,' broke in Miss Hillyard, 'I felt sure that a man was behind all this.'

'That was probably a sound instinct,' said Wimsey. 'I feel sure that a man did write that. . . . Well, I need not take up time with pointing out how easy it was for anybody to wander about the College at night and play tricks on people. In a community of two hundred people, some of whom scarcely know one another by sight, it is harder to find a person than to lose her. But the intrusion of Jukes upon the situation at that moment was rather awkward for X. Miss Vane showed, and announced, a disposition to inquire rather too closely into Jukes's home-life. As a result somebody who knew a good deal about Jukes's little habits laid an information and Jukes was removed to gaol. Mrs. Jukes took refuge with her relations and Annie's children were sent away to Headington. And in order that we should feel quite sure that the Jukes household had nothing to do with the matter, a mutilated newspaper appeared shortly afterwards in Miss de Vine's room.'

Harriet looked up.

'I did work that out – eventually. But what happened last week seemed to make it quite impossible.'.

'I don't think,' said Peter, 'you approached the problem – forgive me for saying so – with an unprejudiced mind and undivided attention. Something got between you and the facts.'

'Miss Vane has been helping me so generously with my books,' murmured Miss Lydgate, contritely; 'and she has had her own work to do as well. We really ought not to have asked her to spare any time for our problems.'

'I had plenty of time,' said Harriet. 'I was only stupid.'

'At any rate,' said Wimsey, 'Miss Vane did enough to make X feel she was dangerous. At the beginning of this term, we find X becoming more desperate and more deadly in intention. With the lighter evenings, it becomes more difficult to play tricks at night. There is the psychological attempt on Miss Newland's life and reason and, when that fails, an effort is made to create a stink in the University by sending letters to the Vice-Chancellor. However, the University proved to be as solid as the College; having let the women in, it was not prepared to let them down. This was no doubt exasperating to the feelings of X. Dr. Threep acted as intermediary between the Vice-Chancellor and yourselves, and the matter was presumably dealt with.'

'I informed the Vice-Chancellor,' said the Warden, 'that steps were being taken.'

'Quite so; and you complimented me by asking me to take those steps. I had very little doubt from the start as to the identity of X; but suspicion is not proof, and I was anxious not to cast any suspicion that could not be justified. My first task was obviously to find out whether Miss de Vine had actually ever murdered or injured anybody. In the course of a very interesting after-dinner conversation in this room, she informed me that, six years ago, she had been instrumental in depriving a man of his reputation and livelihood – and we decided, if you remember, that this was an action which any manly man or womanly woman might be disposed to resent.'

'Do you mean to say,' cried the Dean, 'that all that discussion was intended merely to bring out that story?'

'I offered an opportunity for the story's appearance, certainly; but if it hadn't come out then, I should have asked for it. Incidentally, I established for a certainty, what I was sure of in my own mind from the start, that there was not a woman in this Common Room, married or single, who would be ready to place personal loyalties above professional honour. That was a point which it seemed necessary to make clear – not so much to me, as to yourselves.'

The Warden looked from Miss Hillyard to Mrs. Goodwin and back to Peter.

'Yes,' she said., 'I think it was wise to establish that.'

'The next day,' said Peter, 'I asked Miss de Vine for the name of the man in question, whom we already knew to be handsome and married. The name was Arthur Robinson; and with this information I set out to find what had become of him. My working theory was that X was either the wife or some relation of Robinson: that she had come here when Miss de Vine's appointment was announced, with the intention of revenging his misfortunes upon Miss de Vine, the College and academic women in general; and that in all probability X was a person who stood in some close relation to the Jukes family. This theory was strengthened by the discovery that information was laid against Jukes by an anonymous letter similar to those circulated here.

'Now, the first thing that happened after my arrival was the appearance of X in the Science lecture-room. The idea that X was courting discovery by preparing letters in that public and dangerous manner was patently absurd. The whole thing was a clear fake, intended to mislead, and probably to establish an alibi. The communications had been prepared elsewhere and deliberately planted – in fact, there were not enough letters left in the box to finish the message that had been begun to Miss Vane. The room chosen was in full view of the Scouts' Wing, and the big ceiling light was conspicuously turned on, though there was a reading-lamp in the room, in good working order; it was Annie who drew Carrie's attention to the light in the window; Annie was the only person who claimed to have actually seen X; and while the alibi was established for both scouts, Annie was the one who most closely corresponded to the conditions required for X.'

'But Carrie heard X in the room,' said the Dean.

'Oh, yes,' said Wimsey, smiling. 'And Carrie was sent to fetch you while Annie removed the strings that had switched out the light and overturned the blackboard from the other side of the door. I pointed out to you, you know, that the top of the door had been thoroughly dusted, so that the mark of the string shouldn't show.'

'But the marks on the dark-room window-sill—' said the Dean.

'Quite genuine. She got out there the first time, leaving the doors locked on the inside and strewing a few of Miss de Vine's hairpins about to produce conviction. Then she let herself into the Scouts' Wing through the Buttery, called up Carrie and brought her along to see the fun. . . . I think, by the way, that someone of the scouts must have had her suspicions. Perhaps she had found Annie's bedroom door mysteriously locked on various occasions, or had met her in the passage at inconvenient times. Anyhow, the time had obviously arrived for establishing an alibi. I hazarded the suggestion that nocturnal ramblings would cease from that time on; and so they did. And I don't suppose we shall ever find the extra key to the Buttery.'

'All very well,' said Miss Edwards. 'But you still have no proof.'

'No. I went away to get it. In the meantime, X – if you don't like my identification – decided that Miss Vane was dangerous, and laid a trap to catch her, This didn't come off, because Miss Vane very sensibly telephoned back to College to confirm the mysterious message she had received at Somerville. The message was sent from an outside call-box on the Wednesday night at 10.40. Just before eleven, Annie came in from her day off and heard Padgett speak to Miss Vane on the 'phone. She didn't bear the conversation, but she probably heard the name.

'Although the attempt had not come off, I felt sure that another would be made, on either Miss Vane, Miss de Vine or the suspicious scout – or on all three. I issued a warning to that effect. The next thing that happened was that Miss Vane's chessmen were destroyed. That was rather unexpected. It looked less like alarm than personal hatred. Up till that time, Miss Vane had been treated with almost as much tenderness as though she had been a womanly woman. Can you think of anything that can have given X that impression, Miss Vane?'

'I don't know,' said Harriet, confused. 'I asked kindly after the children and spoke to Beatie – good Heavens, yes, Beatie! – when I met them. And I remember once agreeing politely with Annie that marriage might be a good thing if one could find the right person.'

'That was politic if unprincipled. And how about the attentive Mr. Jones of Jesus? If you will bring young men into the College at night and hide them in the Chapel—'

'Good gracious!' exclaimed Miss Pyke.

'—you must be expected to be thought a womanly woman. However; that is of no great importance. I fear the illusion was destroyed when you publicly informed me that personal attachments must come second to public duties.'

'But,' said Miss Edwards, impatiently, 'what happened to Arthur Robinson?'

'He was married to a woman called Charlotte Ann Clarke, who had been his landlady's daughter. His first child, born eight years ago, was called Beatrice. After the trouble at York, he changed his name to Wilson and took a post as junior master in a small preparatory school, where they didn't mind taking a man who had been deprived of his M.A., so long as he was cheap. His second daughter, born shortly afterwards, was named Carola. I'm afraid the Wilsons didn't find life too easy. He lost his first job – drink was the reason, I'm afraid – took another – got into trouble again and three years ago blew his brains out. There were photographs in the local paper. Here they are, you see. A fair, handsome man of about thirty-eight – irresolute, attractive, something of my nephew's type. And here is the photograph of the widow.'

'You are right,' said the Warden. 'That is Annie Wilson.'

'Yes. If you read the report of the inquest, you will see that he left a letter, saying that he had been hounded to death – rather a rambling letter, containing a Latin quotation, which the coroner translated.'

'Good gracious!' said Miss Pyke. '*Tristius haud illis monstrum*—'

'*Ita*. A man wrote that after all; you see; so Miss Hillyard was so far right. Annie Wilson, being obliged to do something to support her children and herself, went into service.'

'I had very good references with her,' said the Bursar.

'No doubt; why not? She must somehow have kept track of Miss de Vine's movements; and when the appointment was announced last Christmas, she applied for a job here. She probably knew that, as an unfortunate widow with two small children, she would receive kindly consideration—'

'What did I tell you?' cried Miss Hillyard. 'I always said that this ridiculous sentimentality about married women would be the ruin of all discipline in this College. Their minds are not, and cannot be, on their work.'

'Oh, dear!' said Miss Lydgate. 'Poor soul! brooding over that grievance in this really unbalanced way! If only we had known, we could surely have done something to make her see the thing in a more rational light. Did it never occur to you, Miss de Vine, to inquire what happened to this unhappy man Robinson?'

'I am afraid it did not.'

'Why should you?' demanded Miss Hillyard.

The noise in the coal-cellar had ceased within the last few minutes. As though the silence had roused a train of association in her mind, Miss Chilperic turned to Peter and said, hesitatingly:

'If poor Annie really did all these dreadful things, how did she get shut up in the coal-hole?'

'Ah!' said Peter. 'That coal-hole very nearly shook my faith in my theory; especially as I didn't get the report from my research-staff till yesterday. But when you come to think of it, what else could she do? She laid a plot to attack Miss de Vine on her return from Town – the scouts probably knew which train she was coming by.'

'Nellie knew,' said Harriet.

'Then she could have told Annie. By an extraordinary piece of good fortune, the attack was delivered – not against Miss de Vine, who would have been taken unawares and whose heart is not strong, but against a younger and stronger woman, who was, up to a certain point, prepared to meet it. Even so, it was serious enough, and might easily have proved fatal. I find it difficult to forgive myself for not having spoken earlier –

with or without proof – and put the suspect under observation.'

'Oh, nonsense!' said Harriet, quickly. 'If you had, she might have chucked the whole thing for the rest of the term, and we should still not know anything definite. I wasn't much hurt.'

'No. But it might not have been you. I knew you were ready to take the risk; but I had no right to expose Miss de Vine.'

'It seems to me,' said Miss de Vine, 'that the risk was rightly and properly mine.'

'The worst responsibility rests on me,' said the Warden. 'I should have telephoned the warning to you before you left Town.'

'Whose-ever fault it was,' said Peter, 'it was Miss Vane who was attacked. Instead of a nice, quiet throttling, there was a nasty fall and a lot of blood, some of which, no doubt, got on to the assailant's hands and dress. She was in an awkward position. She had got the wrong person, she was bloodstained and dishevelled, and Miss de Vine or somebody else might arrive at any moment. Even if she ran quickly back to her own room, she might be seen – her uniform was stained – and when the body was found (alive or dead) she would be a marked woman. Her only possible chance was to stage an attack on herself. She went out through the back of the loggia, threw herself into the coal-cellar, locked the door on herself and proceeded to cover up Miss Vane's bloodstains with her own. By the way, Miss Vane, if you remembered anything of your lesson, you must have marked her wrists for her.'

'I'll swear I did,' said Harriet.

'But any amount of bruising may be caused by trying to scramble through a ventilator. Well. The evidence, you see, is still circumstantial – even though my nephew is prepared to identify the woman he saw crossing Magdalen Bridge on Wednesday with the woman he met in the garden. One can catch a Headington bus from the other side of Magdalen Bridge. Meanwhile, you heard this fellow in the cellarage? If I am not mistaken, somebody is arriving with something like direct proof?'

A heavy step in the passage was followed by a knock on the door; and Padgett followed the knock almost before he was told to come in. His clothes bore traces of coal-dust, though some hasty washing had evidently been done to his hands and face.

'Excuse me, madam Warden, miss,' said Padgett. 'Here you are, Major. Right down at the bottom of the 'eap. 'Ad to shift the whole lot, I had.'

He laid a large key on the table.

'Have you tried it in the cellar-door?'

'Yes, sir. But there wasn't no need. "Ere's my label on it, "Coal-cellar" – see?'

'Easy to lock yourself in and hide the key. Thank you, Padgett.'

'One moment, Padgett,' said the Warden. 'I want to see Annie Wilson. Will you please find her and bring her here.'

'Better not,' said Wimsey, in a low tone.

'I certainly shall,' said the Warden, sharply. 'You have made a public accusation against this unfortunate woman, and it is only right that she should be given an opportunity to answer it. Bring her here at once, Padgett.'

Peter's hands made a last eloquent gesture of resignation as Padgett went out.

'I think it is *very* necessary,' said the Bursar, 'that this matter should be cleared up completely and at once.'

'Do you really think it wise, Warden?' asked the Dean.

'Nobody shall be accused in this College,' said the Warden, 'without a hearing. Your arguments, Lord Peter, appear to be most convincing; but the evidence may bear some other interpretation. Annie Wilson is, no doubt, Charlotte Ann Robinson; but it does not follow that she is the author of the disturbances. I admit that appearances are against her, but there may be falsification or coincidence. The key, for example, may have been put into the coal-cellar at any time within the last three days.'

'I have been down to see Jukes,' began Peter; when the entrance of Annie interrupted him. Neat and subdued as usual, she approached the Warden:

'Padgett said you wished to see me, madam.' Then her eye fell on the newspaper spread out upon the table, and she drew in her breath with a long, sharp hiss, while her eyes went round the room like the eyes of a hunted animal.

'Mrs. Robinson,' said Peter, quickly and quietly. 'We can quite understand how you came to feel a grievance – perhaps a justifiable grievance – against the person responsible for the sad death of your husband. But how could you bring yourself to let your children help you to prepare those horrible messages? Didn't you realise that if anything had happened they might have been called upon to bear witness in court?'

'No, they wouldn't,' she said quickly. 'They knew nothing about it. They only helped to cut out the letters. Do you think I'd let them suffer? . . . My God! You can't do that. . . . I say you can't do it. . . . You beasts, I'd kill myself first.'

'Annie,' said Dr. Baring, 'are we to understand that you admit being responsible for all these abominable

538

disturbances? I sent for you in order that you might clear yourself of certain suspicions which—'

'Clear myself! I wouldn't trouble to clear myself. You smug hypocrites – I'd like to see you bring me into court. I'd laugh in your faces. How would you look, sitting there while I told the judge how that woman there killed my husband?'

'I am exceedingly disturbed,' said Miss de Vine, 'to hear about all this. I knew nothing of it till just now. But indeed I had no choice in the matter. I could not foresee the consequences – and even if I had—'

'You wouldn't have cared. You killed him and you didn't care. I say you murdered him. What had he done to you? What harm had he done to anybody? He only wanted to live and be happy. You took the bread out of his mouth and flung his children and me out to starve. What did it matter to you? You had no children. You hadn't a man to care about. I know all about you. You had a man once and you threw him over because it was too much bother to look after him. But couldn't you leave my man alone? He told a lie about somebody else who was dead and dust hundreds of years ago. Nobody was the worse for that. Was a dirty bit of paper more important than all our lives and happiness? You broke him and killed him – all for nothing. Do you think that's a woman's job.'

'Most unhappily,' said Miss de Vine, 'it was my job.'

'What business had you with a job like that? A woman's job is to look after a husband and children. I wish I had killed you. I wish I could kill you all. I wish I could burn down this place and all the places like it – where you teach women to take men's jobs and rob them first and kill them afterwards.'

She turned to the Warden.

'Don't you know what you're doing? I've heard you sit round snivelling about unemployment – but it's you, it's women like you who take the work away from the men and break their hearts and lives. No wonder you can't get men for yourselves and hate the women who can. God keep the men out of your hands, that's what I say. You'd destroy your own husbands, if you had any, for an old book or bit of writing. . . . I loved my husband, and you broke his heart. If he'd been a thief or a murderer, I'd have loved him and stuck to him. He didn't mean to steal that old bit of paper – he only put it away. It made no difference to anybody. It wouldn't have helped a single man or woman or child in the world – it wouldn't have kept a cat alive; but you killed him for it.'

Peter had got up and stood behind Miss de Vine, with his hand over her wrist. She shook her head. Immovable, implacable, thought Harriet; this won't make her pulse miss a single beat. The rest of the Common-Room looked merely stunned.

'Oh, no!' said Annie, echoing Harriet's thoughts. '*She* feels nothing. None of them feel anything. You brazen devils – you all stand together. You're only frightened for your skins and your miserable reputations. I scared you all, didn't I? God! how I laughed to see you all look at one another! You didn't even trust each other. You can't agree about anything except hating decent women and their men. I wish I'd torn the throats out of the lot of you. It would have been too good for you, though. I wanted to see you thrown out to starve, like us. I wanted to see you all dragged into the gutter. I wanted to see you – you – sneered at and trampled on and degraded and despised as we were. It would do you good to learn to scrub floors for a living as I've done, and use your hands for something, and say "madam" to a lot of scum. . . . But I made you shake in your shoes, anyhow. You couldn't even fmd out who was doing it – that's all your wonderful brains come to. There's nothing in your books about life and marriage and children, is there? Nothing about desperate people – or love – or hate or anything human. You're ignorant and stupid and helpless. You're a lot of fools. You can't do anything for yourselves. Even you, you silly old hags – you had to get a man to do your work for you.

'*You* brought him here.' She leaned over Harriet with her fierce eyes, as though she would have fallen on her and torn her to pieces. 'And you're the dirtiest hypocrite of the lot. I know who you are. You had a lover once, and he died. You chucked him out because you were too proud to marry him. You were his mistress and you sucked him dry, and you didn't value him enough to let him make an honest woman of you. He died because you weren't there to look after him. I suppose you'd say you loved him. You don't know what love means. It means sticking to your man through thick and thin and putting up with everything. But you take men and use them and throw them away when you've finished with them. They come after you like wasps round a jam-jar, and then they fall in and die. What are you going to do with that one there? You send for him when you need him and do your dirty work, and when you've finished with him you'll get rid of him, you don't want to cook his meals and mend his clothes and bear his children like a decent woman. You'll use him, like any other tool, to break me. You'd like to see me in prison and my children in a home, because you haven't the guts to do your proper job in the world. The whole bunch of you together haven't flesh and blood enough to make you fit for a man. As for *you*—'

Peter had come back to his place and was sitting with

his head in his hands. She went over and shook him furiously by the shoulder, and as he looked up, spat in his face. 'You! you dirty traitor! You rotten little white-faced rat! It's men like you that make women like this. You don't know how to do anything but talk. What do you know about life with your title and your money and your clothes and motor-cars? You've never done a hand's turn of honest work. You can buy all the women you want. Wives and mothers may rot and die for all you care, while you chatter about duty and honour. Nobody would sacrifice anything for you – why should they? That woman's making a fool of you and you can't see it. If she marries you for your money she'll make a worse fool of you, and you'll deserve it. You're fit for nothing but to keep your hands white and father other men's children. . . . What are you going to do now, all of you? Run away and squeal to the magistrate because I made fools of you all? You daren't. You're afraid to come out into the light. You're afraid for your precious college and your precious selves. *I'm* not afraid. I did nothing but stand up for my own flesh and blood. Damn you! I can laugh at you all! You daren't touch me. You're afraid of me. I had a husband and I loved him – and you were jealous of me and you killed him. Oh, God! You killed him among you, and we never had a happy moment again.'

She suddenly burst out crying – half dreadful and half grotesque, with her cap crooked and her hands twisting her apron into a knot.

'For Heaven's sake,' muttered the Dean, desperately, 'can't this be stopped?'

Here Miss Barton got up.

'Come, Annie,' she said, briskly. 'We are all very sorry for you, but you mustn't behave in this foolish and hysterical way. What would the children think if they saw you now? You had better come and lie down quietly and take some aspirin. Bursar! will you please help me out with her?'

Miss Stevens, galvanised, got up and took Annie's other arm, and all three went out together. The Warden turned to Peter, who stood mechanically wiping his face with his handkerchief and looking at nobody.

'I apologise for allowing this scene to take place. I ought to have known better. You were perfectly right.'

'Of course he was right!' cried Harriet. Her head was throbbing like an engine. 'He's always right. He said it was dangerous to care for anybody. He said love was a brute and a devil. You're honest, Peter, aren't you? Damned honest – Oh, God! let me get out of here. I'm going to be sick.'

She stumbled blindly against him as he held the door open for her, and he had to steer her with a firm hand to the cloakroom door. When he came back, the Warden had risen, and the dons with her. They looked stupefied with the shock of seeing so many feelings stripped naked in public.

'Of course, Miss de Vine,' the Warden was saying, 'no sane person could possibly think of blaming you.'

'Thank you, Warden,' said Miss de Vine. 'Nobody, perhaps, but myself.'

'Lord Peter,' said the Warden, 'a little later on, when we are all feeling more ourselves, I think we should all like to say—'

'Please don't,' said he. 'It doesn't matter at all.'

The Warden went out, and the rest followed her like mutes at a funeral, leaving only Miss de Vine, sitting solitary beneath the window. Peter shut the door after them and came up to her. He was still passing his handkerchief across his mouth. Becoming aware of this, he tossed the linen into the waste-paper basket.

'I do blame myself,' said Miss de Vine less to him than to herself. 'Most bitterly. Not for my original action, which was unavoidable, but for the sequel. Nothing you can say to me could make me feel more responsible than I do already.'

'I can have nothing to say,' said he. 'Like you and every member of this Common Room, I admit the principle and the consequences must follow.'

'That won't do,' said the Fellow, bluntly. 'One ought to take some thought for other people. Miss Lydgate would have done what I did in the first place; but she would have made it her business to see what became of that unhappy man and his wife.'

'Miss Lydgate is a very great and a very rare person. But she could not prevent other people from suffering for her principles. That seems to be what principles are for, somehow. . . . I don't claim, you know,' he added, with something of his familiar diffidence, 'to be a Christian or anything of that kind. But there's one thing in the Bible that seems to me to be a mere statement of brutal fact – I mean, about bringing not peace but a sword.'

Miss de Vine looked up at him curiously.

'How much are *you* going to suffer for this?'

'God knows,' he said. 'That's my look out. Perhaps not at all. In any case, you know, I'm with you – every time.'

When Harriet emerged from the cloakroom, she found Miss de Vine alone.

'Thank Heaven, they've gone,' said Harriet. 'I'm afraid I made an exhibition of myself. It was rather – shattering, wasn't it? What's happened to Peter?'

'He's gone,' said Miss de Vine.

She hesitated, and then said:

'Miss Vane – I've no wish to pry impertinently into your affairs. Stop me if I'm saying too much. But we have talked a good deal about facing the facts. Isn't it time you faced the facts about the man?'

'I have been facing one fact for some time,' said Harriet, staring out with unseeing eyes into the quad, 'and that is, that if I once gave way to Peter, I should go up like straw.'

'That,' said Miss de Vine drily, 'is moderately obvious. How often has he used that weapon against you?'

'Never,' said Harriet, remembering the moments when he might have used it. 'Never.'

'Then what are you afraid of? Yourself?'

'Isn't this afternoon warning enough?'

'Perhaps. You have had the luck to come up against a very unselfish and a very honest man. He has done what you asked him without caring what it costs him and without shirking the issue. He hasn't tried to disguise the facts or bias your judgment. You admit that, at any rate.'

'I suppose he realised how I should feel about it?'

'Realised it?' said Miss de Vine, with a touch of irritation. 'My dear girl, give him the credit for the brains he's got. They are very good ones. He is painfully sensitive and far more intelligent than is good for him. But I really don't think you can go on like this. You won't break his patience or his control or his spirit; but you may break his health. He looks like a person pushed to the last verge of endurance.'

'He's been rushing about and working very hard,' said Harriet, defensively. 'I shouldn't be at all a comfortable person for him to live with. I've got a devilish temper.'

'Well, that's his risk, if he likes to take it. He doesn't seem to lack courage.'

'I should only make his life a misery.'

'Very well. If you are determined that you're not fit to black his boots, tell him so and send him away.'

'I've been trying to send Peter away for five years. It doesn't have that effect on him.'

'If you had really tried, you could have sent him away in five minutes. . . . Forgive me. I don't suppose you've had a very easy time with yourself. But it can't have been easy for him, either – looking on at it, and quite powerless to interfere.'

'Yes. I almost wish he had interfered, instead of being so horribly intelligent. It would be quite a relief to be ridden over rough-shod for a change.'

'He will never do that. That's *his* weakness. He'll never make up your mind for you. You'll have to make your own decisions. You needn't be afraid of losing your independence; he will always force it back on you. If you ever find any kind of repose with him, it can only be the repose of very delicate balance.'

'That's what he says himself. If you were me, should you like to marry a man like that?'

'Frankly,' said Miss de Vine, 'I should not. I would not do it for any consideration. A marriage of two independent and equally irritable intelligences seems to me reckless to the point of insanity. You can hurt one another so dreadfully.'

'I know. And I don't think I can stand being hurt any more.'

'Then,' said Miss de Vine, 'I suggest that you stop hurting other people. Face the facts and state a conclusion. Bring a scholar's mind to the problem and have done with it.'

'I believe you're quite right,' said Harriet. 'I will. And that reminds me. Miss Lydgate's *History of Prosody* was marked PRESS with her own hand this morning. I fled with it and seized on a student to take it down to the printers. I'm almost positive I heard a faint voice crying from the window about a footnote on page 97 – but I pretended not to hear.'

'Well,' said Miss de Vine, laughing, 'thank goodness, *that* piece of scholarship has achieved a result at last!'

23

The last refuge and surest remedy, to be put in practice
in the utmost place, when no other means will take
effect, is, to let them go together and enjoy one another;
potissima cura est ut heros amasia sua potiatur, saith
Guianerius. . . . *Æsculapius* himself, to this malady,
cannot invent a better remedy, *quam ut amanti cedat
amatum* . . . than that a Lover have his desire.

ROBERT BURTON

THERE was no word from Peter in the morning. The
Warden issued a brief and discreet announcement to the
College that the offender had been traced and the
trouble ended. The Senior Common Room, recovering
a little from its shock, went quietly about the business
of the term. They were all normal again. They had
never been anything else. Now that the distorting-glass
of suspicion was removed, they were kindly, intelligent
human beings – not seeing, perhaps, very much farther
beyond their own interests than the ordinary man
beyond his job or the ordinary woman beyond her
own household – but as understandable and pleasant
as daily bread.

Harriet, having got Miss Lydgate's proofs off her
mind, and feeling that she could not brace herself to
deal with Wilfrid, took her notes on Lefanu, and went
down to put in a little solid work at the Camera.

Shortly before noon, a hand touched her shoulder.

'They told me you were here,' said Peter. 'Can you spare a moment? We can go up on the roof.'

Harriet put down her pen and followed him across the circular chamber with its desks full of silent readers.

'I understand,' he said, pushing open the swing-door that leads to the winding staircase, 'that the problem is being medically dealt with.'

'Oh, yes. When the academic mind has really grasped a hypothesis – which may take a little time – it copes with great thoroughness and efficiency. Nothing will be overlooked.'

They climbed in silence, and came out at length through the little turret upon the gallery of the Camera. The previous day's rain had passed and left the sun shining upon a shining city. Stepping cautiously over the slatted flooring towards the south-east segment of the circle, they were a little surprised to come upon Miss Cattermole and Mr. Pomfret, who were seated side by side upon a stone projection and rose as they approached, in a flutter, like daws disturbed from a belfry.

'Don't move,' said Wimsey, graciously. 'Plenty of room for all of us.'

'It's quite all right, sir,' said Mr. Pomfret, 'We were just going. Really. I've got a lecture at twelve.'

'Dear me!' said Harriet, watching them disappear into the turret. But Peter had already lost interest in Mr. Pomfret and his affairs. He was leaning with his elbows on the parapet, looking down into Cat Street. Harriet joined him.

There, eastward, within a stone's throw, stood the twin towers of All Souls', fantastic, unreal as a house of cards, clear-cut in the sunshine, the drenched oval in the quad beneath brilliant as an emerald in the bezel of a ring. Behind them, black and grey, New College frowning like a fortress, with dark wings wheeling about her belfry louvres; and Queen's with her dome of green copper; and, as the eye turned southward, Magdalen, yellow and slender, the tall lily of towers; the Schools and the battlemented front of University; Merton, square-pinnacled, half-hidden behind the shadowed North side and mounting spire of St. Mary's. Westward again, Christ Church, vast between Cathedral spire and Tom Tower; Brasenose close at hand; St. Aldate's and Carfax beyond; spire and tower and quadrangle, all Oxford springing underfoot in living leaf and enduring stone, ringed far off by her bulwark of blue hills.

> Towery City, and branchy between towers,
> Cuckoo-echoing, bell-swarmèd, lack-charmèd,
>   rock-racked, river-rounded,
> The dapple-eared lily below.

'Harriet,' said Peter; 'I want to ask your forgiveness for these last five years.'

'I think,' said Harriet, 'it ought to be the other way round.'

'I think not. When I remember how we first met—'

'Peter, don't think about that ghastly time. I was sick of myself, body and soul. I didn't know what I was doing.'

'And I chose that time, when I should have thought only of you, to thrust myself upon you, to make demands of you, like a damned arrogant fool – as though I had only to ask and have. Harriet, I ask you to believe that, whatever it looked like, my blundering was nothing worse than vanity and a blind, childish impatience to get my own way.'

She shook her head, finding no words.

'I had found you,' he went on, a little more quietly, 'beyond all hope or expectation, at a time when I thought no woman could ever mean anything to me beyond a little easy sale and exchange of pleasure. And I was so terrified of losing you before I could grasp you that I babbled out all my greed and fear as though, God help me, you had nothing to think of but me and my windy self-importance. As though it mattered. As though the very word of love had been the most crashing insolence a man could offer you.'

'No, Peter. Never that.'

'My dear – you showed me what you thought of me when you said you would live with me but not marry me.'

'Don't. I am ashamed of that.'

'Not so bitterly ashamed as I have been. If you knew how I have tried to forget it. I told myself that you were only afraid of the social consequences of marriage. I comforted myself with pretending that it showed you liked me a little. I bolstered up my conceit for months, before I would admit the humiliating truth that I ought to have known from the beginning – that you were sick of my pestering, that you would have thrown yourself to me as one throws a bone to a dog, to stop the brute from yelping.'

'Peter, that isn't true. It was myself I was sick of. How could I give you base coin for a marriage-portion?'

'At least I had the decency to know that I couldn't take it in settlement of a debt. But I have never dared to tell you what that rebuke meant to me, when at last I saw it for what it was. . . . Harriet; I have nothing much in the way of religion, or even morality, but I do recognise a code of behaviour of sorts. I do know that the worst sin – perhaps the only sin – passion can commit, is to be joyless. It must lie down with laughter or make its bed in hell – there is no middle way. . . . Don't misunderstand me. I have bought it, often – but never by forced sale or at "stupendous sacrifice." . . . Don't, for God's sake, ever think you owe me anything. If I can't have the real thing, I can make do with the imitation. But I will not have surrenders or crucifixions. . . . If you have come to feel any kindness for me at all, tell me that you would never make me that offer again.'

'Not for anything in the world. Not now or at any time since. It isn't only that I have found a value for myself. But when I made you the offer, it meant nothing to me – now it would mean something.'

'If you have found your own value,' he said, 'that is immeasurably the greatest thing. . . . It has taken me a long time to learn my lesson, Harriet. I have had to pull down brick by brick, the barriers I had built up by my own selfishness and folly. If, in all these years, I have managed to get back to the point at which I ought to have started, will you tell me so and give me leave to begin again? Once or twice in the last few days I have fancied that you might feel as though this unhappy interval might be wiped out and forgotten.'

'No; not that. But as though I could be glad to remember it.'

'Thank you. That is far more than I expected or deserved.'

'Peter – it's not fair to let you talk like this. It's I who ought to apologise. If I owe you nothing else, I owe you my self-respect. And I owe you my life—'

'Ah!' said he, smiling. 'But I have given you that back by letting you risk it. That was the last kick that sent my vanity out of doors.'

'Peter, I did manage to appreciate that. Mayn't I be grateful for that?'

'I don't want gratitude—'

'But won't you take it, now that I want to give it you?'

'If you feel that way about it, then I have no right to refuse. Let that clear all scores, Harriet. You have given me already far more than you know. You are free now and for ever, as far as I am concerned. You saw yesterday what personal claims might lead to – though I didn't intend you to see it in quite that brutal way. But if circumstances made me a little more honest than I meant to be, still, I did mean to be honest up to a point.'

'Yes,' said Harriet, thoughtfully. 'I can't see you burking a fact to support a thesis.'

'What would be the good? What could I ever have gained by letting you imagine a lie? I set out in a lordly manner to offer you heaven and earth. I find that all I have to give you is Oxford – which was yours already. Look! Go round about her and tell the towers thereof. It has been my humble privilege to clean and polish your property and present her for your inspection upon a silver salver. Enter into your heritage and do not, as is said in another connection, be afraid with any amazement.'

'Peter dear,' said Harriet. She turned her back upon the shining city, leaning back against the balustrade, and looking at him. 'Oh, *damn*!'

'Don't worry,' said Peter. 'It's quite all right. By the way, it looks as though it was Rome again for me next week. But I shan't leave Oxford till Monday. On Sunday there's a Balliol Concert. Will you come to it? We'll have one other gaudy night, and comfort our souls with the Bach Concerto for two violins. If you will bear with me so far. After that, I shall be clearing off and leaving you—'

'To Wilfrid and Co.,' said Harriet, in a kind of exasperation.

'Wilfrid?' said Peter, momentarily at a loss, with his mind scampering after rabbits.

'Yes. I'm re-writing Wilfrid.'

'Good God, yes. The chap with the morbid scruples. How's he getting on?'

'He's better, I think. Almost human. I shall have to dedicate the book to you, I think. "To Peter, who made Wilfrid what he is" – that sort of thing. . . . Don't laugh like that. I'm really *working* at Wilfrid.'

For some reason, that anxious assurance shook him as nothing else had done.

'My dear – if anything I have said . . . If you have let me come as far as your work and your life . . . Here! I think I'd better remove myself before I do anything foolish. . . . I shall be honoured to go down to posterity in the turn-up of Wilfrid's trouser. . . . You will come on Sunday? I am dining with the Master, but I will meet you at the foot of the stairs. . . . Till then.'

He slipped away along the gallery and was gone. Harriet was left to survey the kingdom of the mind, glittering from Merton to Bodley, from Carfax to Magdalen Tower. But her eyes were on one slight figure that crossed the cobbled Square, walking lightly under the shadow of St. Mary's into the High. All the kingdoms of the world and the glory of them.

Masters, undergraduates, visitors; they sat huddled closely together on the backless oak benches, their elbows on the long tables, their eyes shaded with their fingers, or turned intelligently towards the platform where two famous violinists twisted together the fine, strong strands of the Concerto in D Minor. The Hall was very full; Harriet's gowned shoulder, touched her companion's, and the crescent of his long sleeve lay over her knee. He was wrapt in the motionless austerity with which all genuine musicians listen to genuine music. Harriet was musician enough to respect this aloofness; she knew well enough that the ecstatic rapture on the face of the man opposite meant only that he was hoping to be thought musical, and that the elderly lady over the way, waving her fingers to the beat, was a musical moron. She knew enough, herself, to read the sounds a little with her brains, laboriously unwinding the twined chains of melody link by link. Peter, she felt sure, could hear the whole intricate pattern, every part separately and simultaneously, each independent and equal, separate but inseparable, moving over and under and through, ravishing heart and mind together.

She waited till the last movement had ended and the packed hall was relaxing its attention in applause.

'Peter – what did you mean when you said that anybody could have the harmony if they would leave us the counterpoint?'

'Why,' said he, shaking his head, 'that I like my music polyphonic. If you think I meant anything else, you know what I meant.'

'Polyphonic music takes a lot of playing. You've got to be more than a fiddler. It needs a musician.'

'In this case, two fiddlers – both musicians.'

'I'm not much of a musician, Peter.'

'As they used to say in my youth: "All girls should learn a little music – enough to play a simple accompaniment." I admit that Bach isn't a matter of an autocratic virtuoso and a meek accompanist. But do you want to be either? Here's a gentleman coming to sing a group of ballads. Pray silence for the soloist. But let him be soon over, that we may hear the great striding fugue again.'

*   *   *

The final Chorale was sung, and the audience made their way out. Harriet's way lay through the Broad Street gate; Peter followed through the quad.

'It's a beautiful night – far too good to waste. Don't go back yet. Come down to Magdalen Bridge and send your love to London River.'

They turned along the Broad in silence, the light wind fluttering their gowns as they walked.

'There's something about this place,' said Peter presently, 'that alters one's values.' He paused, and added a little abruptly: 'I have said a good deal to you one way and another, lately; but you may have noticed that since we came to Oxford I have not asked you to marry me.'

'Yes,' said Harriet, her eyes fixed upon the severe and delicate silhouette of the Bodleian roof, just emerging between the Sheldonian and Clarendon Building. 'I had noticed it.'

'I have been afraid,' he said simply; 'because I knew that from anything you said to me here, there could be no going back. . . . But I will ask you now, and if you say No, I promise you that this time I will accept your answer. Harriet; you know that I love you: will you marry me?'

The traffic lights winked at the Holywell Corner: Yes; No; Wait. Cat Street was crossed and the shadows of New College walls had swallowed them up before she spoke:

'Tell me one thing, Peter. Will it make you desperately unhappy if I say No?'

'Desperately? . . . My dear, I will not insult either you or myself with a word like that. I can only tell you that if you will marry me it will give me very great happiness.'

They passed beneath the arch of the bridge and out into the pale light once more.

'Peter!'

She stood still; and he stopped perforce and turned towards her. She laid both hands upon the fronts of his gown, looking into his face while she searched for the word that should carry her over the last difficult breach.

It was he who found it for her. With a gesture of submission be bared his head and stood gravely, the square cap dangling in his hand.

'*Placetne, magistra?*'

'*Placet.*'

The Proctor, stumping grimly past with averted eyes, reflected that Oxford was losing all sense of dignity. But what could he do? If Senior Members of the University chose to stand – in their gowns, too! – closely and passionately embracing in New College Lane right under the Warden's windows, he was powerless to prevent it. He primly settled his white band and went upon his walk unheeded; and no hand plucked his velvet sleeve.

This re-issue of GAUDY NGHT has for postscript a short biography of Lord Peter Wimsey, brought up to date (May 1935) and communicated by his uncle, Paul Austin Delagardie.

I AM asked by Miss Sayers to fill up certain lacunae and correct a few trifling errors of fact in her account of my nephew Peter's career. I shall do so with pleasure. To appear publicly in print is every man's ambition, and by acting as a kind of running footman to my nephew's triumph I shall only be showing a modesty suitable to my advanced age.

The Wimsey family is an ancient one – too ancient, if you ask me. The only sensible thing Peter's father ever did was to ally his exhausted stock with the vigorous French-English strain of the Delagardies. Even so, my nephew Gerald (the present Duke of Denver) is nothing but a beef-witted English squire, and my niece Mary was flighty and foolish enough till she married a policeman and settled down. Peter, I am glad to say, takes after his mother and me. True, he is all nerves and nose – but that is better than being all brawn and no brain like his father and brothers, or a mere bundle of emotions, like Gerald's boy, Saint-George. He has at least inherited the Delagardie brains, by way of safeguard to the unfortunate Wimsey temperament.

Peter was born in 1890. His mother was being very much worried at the time of her husband's behaviour (Denver was always tiresome, though the big scandal did

558

not break out till the Jubilee year) and her anxieties may have affected the boy. He was a colourless shrimp of a child, very restless and mischievous, and always much too sharp for his age. He had nothing of Gerald's robust physical beauty, but he developed what I can best call a kind of bodily cleverness, more skill than strength. He had a quick eye for a ball and beautiful hands for a horse. He had the devil's own pluck, too: the intelligent sort of pluck that sees the risk before it takes it. He suffered badly from nightmares as a child. To his father's consternation he grew up with a passion for books and music.

His early school-days were not happy. He was a fastidious child, and I suppose it was natural that his schoolfellows should call him 'Flimsy' and treat him as a kind of comic turn. And he might, in sheer self-protection, have accepted the position and degenerated into a mere licensed buffoon, if some games-master at Eton had not discovered that he was a brilliant natural cricketer. After that, of course, all his eccentricities were accepted as wit, and Gerald underwent the salutary shock of seeing his despised younger brother become a bigger personality than himself. By the time he reached the Sixth Form, Peter had contrived to become the fashion – athlete, scholar, *arbiter elegantiarum – nec pluribus impar*. Cricket had a great deal to do with it – plenty of Eton men will remember the 'Great Flim' and his performance against Harrow – but I take credit to myself for introducing him to a good tailor, showing him the way about Town, and teaching him to distinguish good wine from bad. Denver bothered little about him – he had too many entanglements of his own and in addition was taken up with Gerald, who by this time was making a prize fool of himself at Oxford. As a matter of fact Peter never got on with his father, he was a ruthless young critic of the paternal misdemeanours, and his sympathy for his mother had a destructive effect upon his sense of humour.

Denver, needless to say, was the last person to tolerate his own failings in his offspring. It cost him a good deal of money to extricate Gerald from the Oxford affair, and he was willing enough to turn his other son over to me. Indeed at the age of seventeen. Peter came to see me of his own accord. He was old for his age and exceedingly reasonable, and I treated him as a man of the world. I established him in trustworthy hands in Paris, instructing him to keep his affairs upon a sound business footing and to see that they terminated with goodwill on both sides and generosity on his. He fully justified my confidence. I believe that no woman has ever found cause to complain of Peter's treatment; and two at least of them have since married royalty (rather obscure royalties, I admit, but royalty of a sort). Here again, I insist upon my due share of the credit; however good the material one has to work upon it is ridiculous to leave any young man's social education to chance.

The Peter of this period was really charming, very frank, modest and well-mannered, with a pretty, lively wit. In 1909 he went up with a scholarship to read History at Balliol, and here, I must confess, he became rather intolerable. The world was at his feet, and he began to give himself airs. He acquired affectations, an exaggerated Oxford manner and a monocle, and aired his opinions a good deal, both in and out of the Union, though I will do him the justice to say that he never attempted to patronise his mother or me. He was in his second year when Denver broke his neck out hunting and Gerald succeeded to the title. Gerald showed more sense of responsibility than I had expected in dealing with the estate; his worst mistake was to marry his cousin Helen, a scrawny, over-bred prude, all county from head to heel.

She and Peter loathed each other cordially; but he could always take refuge with his mother at the Dower House.

And then, in his last year at Oxford, Peter fell in love with a child of seventeen and instantly forgot everything he had ever been taught. He treated that girl as if she was made of gossamer, and me as a hardened old monster of depravity who had made him unfit to touch her delicate purity. I won't deny that they made an exquisite pair – all white and gold – a prince and a princess of moonlight, people said. Moonshine would have been nearer the mark. What Peter was to do in twenty years' time with a wife who had neither brains nor character nobody but his mother and myself ever troubled to ask, and he, of course, was completely besotted. Happily, Barbara's parents decided that she was too young to marry; so Peter went in for his final Schools in the temper of a Sir Eglamore achieving his first dragon; laid his First-Class Honours at his lady's feet like the dragon's head, and settled down to a period of virtuous probation.

Then came the War. Of course the young idiot was mad to get married before he went. But his own honourable scruples made him mere wax in other people's hands. It was pointed out to him that if he came back mutilated it would be very unfair to the girl. He hadn't thought of that, and rushed off in a frenzy of self-abnegation to release her from the engagement. I had no hand in that; I was glad enough of the result, but I couldn't stomach the means.

He did very well in France; he made a good officer and the men liked him. And then, if you please, he came back on leave with his captaincy in '16, to find the girl married – to a hardbitten rake of a Major. Somebody, whom she had nursed in the V.A.D. hospital, and whose motto with women was catch 'em quick and treat 'em rough. It was pretty brutal; for the girl hadn't the nerve to tell Peter beforehand. They got married in a hurry when they heard he was coming home, and all he got on landing was a letter, announcing the *fait accompli* and reminding him that he had set her free himself.

I will say for Peter that he came straight to me and admitted that he had been a fool. 'All right,' said I, 'you've had your lesson. Don't go and make a fool of yourself in the other direction.' So he went back to his job with (I am sure) the fixed intention of getting killed; but all he got was his majority and his D.S.O. for some recklessly good intelligence work behind the German front. In 1918 he was blown up and buried in a shell-hole near Caudry, and that left him with a bad nervous breakdown, lasting, on and off, for two years. After that, he set himself up in a flat in Piccadilly, with the man Bunter (who had been his sergeant and was, and is, devoted to him), and started out to put himself together again.

I don't mind saying that I was prepared for almost anything. He had lost all his beautiful frankness, he shut everybody out of his confidence, including his mother and me, adopted an impenetrable frivolity of manner and a dilettante pose, and became, in fact, the complete comedian. He was wealthy and could do as he chose, and it gave me a certain amount of sardonic entertainment to watch the efforts of post-war feminine London to capture him. 'It can't' said one solicitous matron, 'be good for poor Peter to live like a hermit.' 'Madam,' said I, 'if he did, it wouldn't be.' No; from that point of view he gave me no anxiety. But I could not but think it dangerous that a man of his ability should have no job to occupy his mind, and I told him so.

In 1921 came the business of the Attenbury Emeralds. That affair has never been written up, but it made a good deal of noise, even at that noisiest of periods. The trial of the thief was a series of red-hot sensations, and the biggest sensation of the bunch was when Lord Peter Wimsey walked into the witness-box as chief witness for the prosecution.

That was notoriety with a vengeance. Actually, to an experienced intelligence officer, I don't suppose the investigation had offered any great difficulties; but a 'noble sleuth' was something new in thrills. Denver was furious; personally, I didn't mind what Peter did, provided he did something. I thought he seemed happier for the work, and I liked the Scotland Yard man he had picked up during the run of the case. Charles Parker is a quiet, sensible, well-bred fellow, and has been a good friend and brother-in-law to Peter. He has the valuable quality of being fond of people without wanting to turn them inside out.

The only trouble about Peter's new hobby was that it had to be more than a hobby, if it was to be any hobby for a gentleman. You cannot get murderers hanged for your private entertainment. Peter's intellect pulled him one way and his nerves another, till I began to be afraid they would pull him to pieces. At the end of every case he had the old nightmares and shell-shock over again. And then Denver, of all people – Denver, the crashing great booby, in the middle of his fulminations against Peter's degrading and notorious police activities, must needs get himself indicted on a murder charge and stand his trial in the House of Lords, amid a blaze of publicity which made all Peter's efforts in that direction look like damp squibs.

Peter pulled his brother out of that mess, and, to my relief, was human enough to get drunk on the strength of it. He now admits that his 'hobby' is his legitimate work for society, and has developed sufficient interest in public affairs to undertake small diplomatic jobs from time to time under the Foreign Office. Of late he has become a little more ready to show his feelings, and a little less terrified of having any to show.

His latest eccentricity has been to fall in love with that girl whom he cleared of the charge of poisoning her lover. She refused to marry him, as any woman of character would. Gratitude and a humiliating inferiority complex are no foundation for matrimony; the position was false from the start. Peter had the sense, this time, to take my advice. 'My boy,' I said, 'what was wrong for you twenty years back is right now. It's not that innocent young things that need gentle handling – it's the ones that have been frightened and hurt. Begin again from the beginning – but I warn you that you will need all the self-discipline you have ever learnt.'

Well, he has tried. I don't think I have ever seen such patience. The girl has brains and character and honesty; but he has got to teach her how to take, which is far more difficult that learning to give. I think they will find one another, if they can keep their passions from running ahead of their wills. He does realise, I know, that in this case there can be no consent but free consent.

Peter is forty-five now, it is really time he was settled. As you will see, I have been one of the important formative influences in his career, and, on the whole, I feel he does me credit. He is a true Delagardie, with little of the Wimseys about him except (I must be fair) that underlying sense of social responsibility which prevents the English landed gentry from being a total loss, spiritually speaking. Detective or no detective, he is a scholar and a gentleman; it will amuse me to see what sort of shot he makes at being a husband and father. I am getting an old man, and have no son of my own (that I know of); I should be glad to see Peter happy. But as his mother says, 'Peter has always had everything except the things he really wanted,' and I suppose he is luckier than most.

PAUL AUSTIN DELAGARDIE.